Evil Alice and the Borzoi

by

DK Coutant

A Cleo Cooper Mystery

Evil Alice and the Borzoi

Cover Art by *Diana Carlile*

The Wild Rose Press, Inc.
PO Box 708
Adams Basin, NY 14410-0708
Visit us at www.thewildrosepress.com

Publishing History
First Edition, 2023
Trade Paperback ISBN 978-1-5092-4591-8
Digital ISBN 978-1-5092-4592-5

A Cleo Cooper Mystery
Published in the United States of America

As I was musing "what ifs," my eyes drifted to an intense mountain of a man in a red shirt so saturated with color I expected it to drip onto his jeans. The almost-to-the-elbow sleeves revealed ropey forearms the color of a dried kukui nut. The bones in his broad face made me think of a tiger, not traditionally handsome, but arresting. I couldn't take my eyes off him. Almost as if he could feel my scrutiny, he turned his head and looked directly at me. My pulse quickened, and I froze—an impala trapped in the gaze of a predator. I couldn't look away. A barely perceptible smile appeared on his face. He knew the effect he was having on me. Embarrassment gave me the strength to jerk my eyes down to my feet.

What the hell was wrong with me? Maybe low blood sugar? I didn't eat much breakfast.

I risked a glance back at him. Damn, he was still looking at me with his self-assured smile. He greeted my glance with a hint of a nod and turned his attention back to the speaker. Flustered, I too looked back at the speaker, but I couldn't make out what the guy was saying, so I went back to looking at the crowd, carefully avoiding the red-shirted predator.

There were a lot of locals who I didn't know, but I saw Rikki and Gina standing together. No sign of Kawika, Gina's cop-husband. I would have thought the police would want to come as part of an investigation now that they suspected foul play.

Dedication

To my darling husband, Stephen Worchel…
What a wild ride we have had. I loved sharing this and
all of our adventures with you, my love. And to the Big
Island community, mahalo for a great 16 years!

Acknowledgments

It took a village of wonderful people spread around the world to bring *Evil Alice and the Borzoi* to publication. I want to thank my Hawaii-born friends for their attempts to keep me authentic to the Big Island culture and language. I'm sure I made mistakes, but it was through no lack of trying on their part. William Higa, my former colleague and dear friend, and to one of my besties, Christine Makaweo, who despite her Hawaiian roots, has Cleo's love of travel.

I was fortunate to have great beta readers that could be kind as well as brutally honest. Thanks to Franziska Tschan Semmer, Roxanne Apple, Holly Logan, and especially Carolyn Meinel, who has been my loudest cheerleader, taskmaster, and mentor. Also a special thanks to Casey DenHollander, retired detective/ current bass player, who patiently educated me on police procedure. Pamela Rees, a fellow Guppy, thanks for being the best manuscript swap partner! I can't wait to read your next story.

Ally Robertson, my editor at The Wild Rose Press, thanks for shepherding this project through to publication. I will be eternally grateful for this opportunity to share Cleo Cooper with the world. To my mom, Sylvia Ferriter, thanks for giving me the love and support to pursue my dreams, and my brother Jerry Coutant, for his unwavering kindness.

Chapter 1

Alice

Two inches from Alice's hand, a white-mouth moray eel slithered halfway out of a crevice in the lava rock. Ali's heart almost burst through her chest. She tasted saltwater that had slipped in around the regulator and struggled to dominate her panic. The eel stared at her. Ali focused on taking slow even breaths like she had been taught. She *would* overcome this fear.

Another deep breath, and she heard the air rush through the regulator. She grasped for calmness. *Focus on the pretty colors, Ali.* From the surface, the muted gray-blue and aquamarines of the ocean had soothed her. They looked sinister at these depths.

Dread trickled into her brain. *I can do this...if can, can.*

The eel pulled back into its crevice, and Ali pushed off from the rock, but her breath was coming too fast. She was hemmed in by lava rocks and afraid to get too near in case another sea creature might pop out. *I stay fine.*

Ali wiped her mask with her gloved hand, forgetting that the fog blurring her vision was on the inside.

Yes, her life had been tough, but she had been tougher. She may be small, but she was Alice Bacunawa. She had defied everyone. She just had to overcome this stupid fear of scuba diving. She was so close to having it all.

I'll have one ticket off this junk island. I can live in Vegas, California, or whereva! I just gotta get over this stupid panic! But her control skittered away.

I should have never come down this deep...or in this lava tube. Ali heard her breath moving faster through the regulator. *Get it together!* She thrashed. Looking...reaching. *I just need to find...*

In a swipe of pain and bubbles, the mask was ripped off her face, scraping skin under her nose and around her eyebrows, pulling strands of black hair out with it. The marine environment became indistinguishable. She couldn't see to make out anything, much less her mask.

Ali's breath quickened still faster. A scream was building in her throat when another sudden jerk came, almost ripping her teeth out, and the regulator was gone. Her scream escaped. An orgy of precious crystal balls of air speeding upward, as she grabbed wildly over her shoulder, coughing and sucking in salty water. Coral and lava rock sliced her flailing hands. All but her last shred of coherent thought evaporated. She searched for the regulator. Her lungs burned and she coughed the briny water out, only to suck more back in. But everything was a blur of sparkling bubbles rushing away, just out of reach.

Chapter 2

Cleo

I squinted as a ray of sun broke through the clouds, skidding and dancing on the gray-green water of Hilo Bay. I was a long way from home. I pushed some stray, dirty-blonde hair out of my face and slid my Maui Jim's down from the top of my head to rest on my sunburned nose. The molded fiberglass bench on the port side of the Ka Nalu, the teaching vessel owned by the university, was warm against my thighs. I stretched my legs as far as I could reach, using them to brace myself against the slow rocking of the boat.

Three undergraduates glanced over to my partner, Ben, sitting next to me.

"Uh-oh, Looks like you've got trouble. Glad this isn't my class," I said.

"Careful, Cleo, or I won't let you ride along next time," Ben said. "It's probably the crank. It's been giving us problems for weeks now, but there's no money in the budget to get it fixed this semester." Standing up to his full, over six-foot height, he looked back at me and grinned. "At least I don't have a stack of papers to grade." He nodded at the two-inch pile of assignments my students had turned in the day before.

I scrunched my nose at him and picked up my red pen and papers resting next to me on the bench. I watched a young native Hawaiian, with a straight back, open shoulders, and honey-colored skin, move toward the worried students. When he turned, I recognized the doe-eyed young man.

"Looks like Kai's got this."

Kai, Ben's research assistant, approached the agitated students and smiled. They smiled back and gathered around him.

"Kai is my research assistant, not teaching assistant. But he's a natural with students." Ben ran his fingers through the hair on his forehead, pushing it up and out of his eyes. "But dealing with students isn't his job, I should go do mine and let him get back to his data collection."

I picked up the paper at the top of my pile and started reading, pen in hand. Despite my best intentions, my glance trailed after my lover and colleague. Ben made his way across the deck and responded to the agitation of another group of students that were not clustered around Kai. Ben's class, Methodology for Marine Science, was popular with undergraduates. Most of the labs were done on the ocean, so not surprising. The University of Hawaii at Hilo prided itself on hands-on learning in a living laboratory, and Ben's course was a striking example of that.

Today, Ben's class would learn how to catch and observe zooplankton, the tiny water critters that attracted whales to these Hawaiian waters. This was the fun part. The students deployed a plankton net, dragged it for a distance, then pulled it in without tangling or losing the plankton. By the end of the class, we would have crisscrossed the bay several times. Afterward, they would return to the lab with copepods, arrow worms, or larval fish to examine under microscopes.

Most students took this class to hang out on a boat and have fun. They had no idea how technical the class was or how much work Ben required of them. But out of this bunch of wanna-be surf rats, a handful would fall in love with research and go on to a successful career in the sciences.

Kai was one of those destined for academic greatness. I'd put money on it. The group surrounding Kai broke up and drifted toward the stern of the vessel. I studied the fifteen students on deck, wondering if I could pick out any others who might be superstars. The young Polynesian woman, with pursed lips, sucking on a thumbnail and leaning over the edge of the boat watching the tow net and its contents break the surface? Or maybe the blond, tan, young man who stood next to her? He suddenly turned as white as a ghost. It was unlikely to be him, if he was already seasick in this calm bay.

Then I caught a glimpse of Ben, who also paled. His mouth was set and his brow furrowed. I slid my papers into my waterproof bag and zipped it, stepping up to see if Ben needed my help. I was a cross-cultural psychologist by training, but I've been living with this marine scientist for two years. I have picked up some of the rudimentary knowledge of how to assist on a research boat.

Crossing the twenty-five-foot deck, I realized it wasn't nautical knowledge that was needed. My stomach dropped as a waxy-looking human hand breached the railing of the boat.

****

A scream broke my stunned trance. How long had I stood there staring at the hand, trying to decide if it was left over from last year's Halloween or was really a dead person? The scream from a young-looking sophomore in the crowd of students woke me.

My senses were on high alert. I tasted the tang of sea spray as the waves picked up, smelled the warm oily smoke of the engine wafting my way as the breeze shifted direction. I felt the rocking of the boat with its living (and now one dead) inhabitants. I heard the nervous mumbling of the screamer's classmates and one student softly crying.

I pulled out my phone, hoping a signal would reach us here in the middle of Hilo Bay, and looked at Ben. Although he appeared shaken, he spoke with a calm voice.

"Cleo, I don't think the phone is going to have a signal out here, let Capt. Jack call on the radio. Kai, can you help him note our GPS coordinates?" And then he muttered quietly, "What the hell should I do with this body?"

Kai left to help the boat captain contact the coast guard as I stepped up to the railing next to Ben. From here I could see the face of a young woman with dark hair. A face that was disturbingly familiar. I looked over my shoulder and saw Capt. Jack speaking intensely into the radio handset, Kai next to him looking at the gages.

"Is that—?" I started to ask.

But I was cut off by Ben's curt, "I think so." He licked his lips nervously but appeared to have made a decision.

"I think we have to pull her in the boat. I'm afraid a shark will damage her if we drag her behind us into shore. We can't leave her in the water. See if you can keep Kai away until I can figure out how to get her onto the boat without him, or any of these kids, having to help me."

I looked over at Kai, who was giving our GPS coordinates to the coast guard, and mouthed to Capt. Jack, "Keep Kai with you." Jack gave me a quizzical look but nodded that he would do it.

I turned to Ben and said, "I can help. Jack's got Kai." Ben gave me a look as if measuring whether I could handle what needed to be done. He nodded.

"It's not going to be pleasant, but I think we have to get her body out of the water, the waves are picking up and she's going to get torn up if we leave her out there and she bangs against the boat. Are you really up for this?"

"Sure. It's got to be done, right?"

"Do you want to climb over and stand on the transom? Then you can support the bottom part of her as I try to pull her up. Yell to me if...something...gets hung up on its way over. If you are sure you are up to this? I'd get down there, but with this awkward angle, if I climb over, I don't think you could handle pulling her dead weight..." He stopped and shook his head, embarrassed by his choice of words.

I threw one leg over the edge of the boat to get into position.

"I can do this," I said.

At least, I hope I can.

I crouched down on the transom to untangle the body from the tow net, and looked more closely at the face. I hoped Ben and I were wrong in our identification. Her jet-black hair, normally perfectly styled, hung limply over much of her face. But I could see the shining eyes of the beautiful young woman. Those eyes unnerved me as I, ever so slowly, untangled her limbs from the lines to the plankton net. A rogue wave washed over me, and the hair slid back from her face, revealing the striking features of the young Filipino woman who had commanded attention whenever she entered a room. There was no doubt whose life had ended.

I tried to focus on the lines and not the soft give of her arms and legs that were tangled in it ... stiff and oddly positioned. She appeared to be curled up. *An uncharacteristically vulnerable position for the young woman.*

I freed her body from the lines and told Ben he could pull her up, as I tried to support the body by holding her curled legs. There was some give to her stiff limbs, so her body moved with awkward jerks as the weight shifted, complicated by our boat rolling on the sea swells. I struggled to support the body and help Ben as he pulled, but I had to fight a strong compulsion to keep her body as far away from myself as possible, all the while maintaining my balance on the narrow, rocking transom. It was going fairly well, but just as it looked as if this nightmare situation would end, the dead girl's foot caught on the edge of the motor casing, causing a slice in the skin. I watched in horror as the skin, like a silk stocking, slipped away from the bone, just as Ben pulled the dead girl onto the deck.

I climbed back over the railing and quick-stepped away from the body, trying not to vomit.

As I blindly pushed away, I crashed straight into Kai. He was making his way toward Ben through the crowd of students, some cowering and others craning their necks to see what was happening. I put my hand flat on his chest to stop him. He looked down at me, concern flowing from his deep-brown eyes.

"You should have waited for me to help Ben. You didn't need to do that."

"Kai, I'm sorry. It's Ali."

Kai shuffled back a step and raised his fist to press it against his chest before a stillness settled over him. His face crumpled. Lines appeared where there had been none, and his healthy-looking tan drained to a sickly brown-gray. The intensity and vitality that had radiated just below the skin faded before my eyes. My heart twisted at the body blow grief inflicted on this gentle soul.

Chapter 3

Coconut Wireless

I couldn't sleep. Every time I closed my eyes, visions of Ali's waxy hand and Kai's vanquished face floated under my eyelids. At five a.m. I gave up to let Ben sleep in peace. I trod softly to the kitchen to feed the dog and make coffee. It was too early for the paper to arrive. I could read it online, but I craved the feel of the newsprint in my hands. Instead, I finished grading the papers I'd forgotten in all the turmoil yesterday, and drove in to the office.

It was raining. It rained a lot here. Last year it rained 275 days out of 365. I balanced my umbrella, laptop, and workbag and walked to my office. Hilo rains were usually gentle and came in the early morning and evening as the trade winds pushed rainclouds up Mauna Kea as the sun rose and down the mountain just after dark. The waterfalls and jungles were worth the price of admission. On the occasional sunny day, Hilo was the most beautiful place on the planet.

Today was not one of those glittering days.

After my first class, I was stopped by colleagues, as I entered the wing of the Psychology department.

"I heard you found the body yesterday," Jim said. He was standing with Crystal in front of her door. The expressions on their faces told me they had been discussing the death before I walked into the hall.

"I heard you were swimming in Ice Pond and bumped into her floating body. A student said she heard it from Angel who was fishing off the breaker wall yesterday…?"

I shrugged. "As usual, a little bit of truth mixed in with a whole bunch of other stuff. I was out on the boat with Ben and his class when Alice Bacunawa's body was pulled in with a plankton sample. It was awful. Her boyfriend, Kai, is Ben's lab assistant and was on the boat with us." My stomach twisted as I remembered the way grief had eviscerated him.

"What do the police think killed her?" Crystal asked.

"The police didn't say much. Information only flowed in one direction."

"She was a student here a few years ago. Everybody called her Ali instead of Alice. But I haven't seen her on campus in a while." Crystal cocked her head to the side and looked off into the distance. "She was smart, I remember, but she didn't seem to take school seriously… missed a lot of class."

Jim leaned forward. "But you were there, right? You saw her? Were there bullet holes? Bruising? A rope tied around her neck?"

"You've watched too many CSI episodes." Crystal made a face and turned to me, eyebrows raised. "Besides, we don't even know if Cleo got close enough to see the body." She leaned toward me a little more. "Did you?"

I couldn't suppress the shudder that ran through my body at the memory.

"Yeah, closer than I wanted. But there was nothing dramatic to see. She was wearing a shorty wetsuit and had dive gear on. It was probably just an accident."

"That's odd," Jim said. "I had Ali in a class, and I remember her saying she had a phobia about scuba diving."

"How did that come up?" Crystal asked.

"The class was 'Abnormal.' "

Crystal and I nodded. Teaching psychology had advantages and disadvantages. An advantage was that most of our students were interested in the topics we covered. A disadvantage was that they often tried to turn class lectures into counseling sessions, disclosing personal problems of family, friends, and themselves. And in Abnormal Psychology, students learned about psychological disorders, and inevitably all kinds of personal and family symptoms were revealed in class discussions.

"I remember because she told us she had a phobia about scuba but could surf or swim with no problems. I think somebody else in the class told her it was probably the mask that she was afraid of."

I thought back to the curled, semi-rigid figure I'd had to untangle from the net lines.

"Come to think of it, when we pulled her in, she didn't have a mask on," I said. "But who knows if it fell off after she died, or what. I could never scuba dive without a mask."

"Me neither," said Jim. "In my scuba lessons, years ago, I had no problem breathing compressed air underwater until the session where my instructor made me pull my mask off and practice buddy breathing. It's like my throat closed when that mask came off. It took a while to get ahold of myself and breathe normally again."

Crystal nodded. "Right. I swim without a mask or

goggles normally, but when I start breathing the air underwater, if the mask comes off and I can't see clearly, something in my brain clicks off. My breathing passages cut off involuntarily, and I have a really hard time overriding that."

I smiled a goodbye to my colleagues and continued on to my office to get some work done before my next class. Later, finished prepping my class, I ran to the campus cafeteria for a quick lunch. On my way back to the office, I saw my colleague Jim, walking in the opposite direction.

"You're eating lunch late today," I said.

"Actually, I ate lunch early. I'm going for coffee at the coffee cart, want to join me?"

I raised my eyebrows and rubbed my hands together. "Ooooh, coffee sounds good right now." And I turned around to walk with him.

"I've been thinking about our conversation earlier… about Ali Bacunawa scuba-diving." Jim's eyes stared ahead of us as we walked.

"Yeah?"

"I dive regularly, and you know, one of the cardinal rules of diving is you never do it alone."

"But from what I knew of Ali, she didn't seem to worry about following rules, cardinal or otherwise." I looked at him sideways.

"Maybe, but with her phobia of diving and all… it just seems strange."

Slowing, I turned to face Jim directly. "What are you saying, Jim?"

"I'm not sure, it's just weird the way you found her. Dive gear, but no mask, and alone."

"You mean, if she was diving with someone, they

should have helped her or at least reported that she drowned."

"Yeah, or maybe she was diving in a large group and wandered off before she got into trouble, but even then, someone in the group should have done a head count and realized she was missing."

"Even stranger," I said, "I don't know if you are aware of it, but her boyfriend runs a dive shop."

Jim scowled. "You mentioned earlier that he was one of Ben's students. Do you know him well? Is this going to be another case of domestic violence?"

"No. Not Kai."

"You know what the statistics are." Jim's eyes bored into mine.

"Yeah, I know." *They were bad.*

Jim reminded me anyway, raising a finger toward me as he spoke. "Reports suggest that here in Hawaii, more than 150 domestic violence victims will seek out an emergency shelter every day. I just lectured on this in class last week." He started to move that pointed finger toward my chest as if to poke me for emphasis but must have thought better of it and pulled it back to push into his pocket.

"I know, I know." I raised the palms of my hands to him. "My friend Gina's husband, Kawika, is a detective with HPD. Ben and I went to dinner with them one night, and over beer and poke, he told us that we should feel safe. Murder rates are low in Hawaii. And eighty-five percent of victims know their killer. When a young woman is murdered, the police look at the boyfriend first."

I put my hands down and shook my head. "But I know Kai. Ben knows him. He would never do such a thing."

"Yeah, but sometimes the worst abusers look respectable outside the home," Jim said.

"No, not Kai. I had him in a class and watched him interact with people for months. He's been Ben's RA for a year now, and Ben works with him almost every day. We had Kai and Ali over to our place for dinner several times. We would have seen some indication."

"Come on, you know how many people say that about abusers. They can be slick. Wonderful, upstanding citizens on the outside that never show their nasty side in public," Jim said.

"I might think you were right if it was anyone else. But Kai is one of the absolutely gentlest guys I know. And you should have seen his face when he found out it was Ali who was dead... He was completely demolished!"

"If you say so." Jim shrugged. "But he wouldn't be the first local guy on this island to get mad and kill his girlfriend in the heat of anger. And you have to admit it looks suspicious."

"I don't care what it looks like. I can't imagine Kai getting angry enough to kill anyone, much less Ali. He adored her."

I was getting angry. But was I mad at Jim or myself? Was I having doubts about Kai?

As we approached the coffee cart, we halted our conversation; me, to let myself cool down, and Jim, out of discretion to avoid being overheard by other people in the coffee line. As we walked back toward the psych department, we moved the conversation to safer topics until reaching our offices and separating. I sipped my latte. It tasted more bitter than usual.

Chapter 4

The end of a long day

After my last class I returned to my office to check email again before I left for the day. I taught one online class this semester, and for students in that course, email was their primary access to me.

One student asked to take the test early because she was going to Oahu for her grandmother's birthday. Another student wanted to turn in a late paper. I responded to those and noticed an email from a colleague in my field, Luc Bastien. I had met Luc years ago at a conference on the mainland. I opened it, curious whether it was a generic message announcing a book he was publishing or a specific email to me.

It was an invitation to give a talk at a conference on "peace and conflict" in Santa Fe, New Mexico. I was surprised as well as pleased. I loved Hawaii, but I had been itching to get off the island for a little break. The conference sounded perfect, small, with people I respected in the field. I sent off a quick acceptance and logged off my computer.

On the drive home I contemplated Luc's invitation to his conference and his reason for inviting me. It was a compliment to be an invited speaker, but honestly, I wasn't sure my career had reached that level. My last two papers, on immigration and acculturation as they related to intergroup conflict, had generated interest, but they weren't published in top journals. My doubts nudged an uncomfortable memory of another small conference several years ago.

I was standing in a room with a balcony overlooking a river, at a cocktail party the conference was hosting after a day of talks. It was a hazy evening, and the sky, glimpsed through skyscrapers surrounding me, was filled with pinks and blues. I felt a presence next to me, and there he stood, well over six feet tall, lush black hair with just enough curl to make me want to run my fingers through it, the rising star in our field, Luc Bastien. He smiled at me.

I smiled up at his infectious grin.

"I enjoyed your talk," I said. Luc was the keynote speaker at this conference.

"Thanks," Luc said. "Did you make it to the last panel of the day? That discussion was riveting." We chatted about our favorite papers until a fish jumped in the river below us. Our two sets of eyes began scanning the river and its banks, looking for wildlife. Luc pointed to a raccoon that had climbed out way too far on a branch overhanging the river. We laughed and tried to best each other with outrageous raccoon stories. It grew dark, and the hotel lights switched on, giving a warm glow to our balcony.

"You're empty, as am I," Luc said as he pointed to my wineglass and raised his. "If you are interested..." Luc tilted his head, raised his eyebrows, and the corners of his mouth turned up. "I have been the lucky recipient of a very nice bottle of wine in my suite. My uncle in France sent it to me here at the hotel to celebrate my keynote speech. I'd be delighted to share it with you. It has traveled so far, a wine like that shouldn't have to suffer through a trip back home in my suitcase." His grin turned up on one side, and one of his eyebrows raised a little higher.

My stomach flip-flopped. We'd been having a great time together, but I barely knew this guy except by reputation. I turned to stare at the raccoons a moment, collecting my thoughts.

This was not a completely alien experience for me. At thirty-two, I was five feet six inches tall and small-boned, as my mother used to say, with dirty-blonde hair that has been lightened in the saltwater and sun of Hawaii. The high cheekbones and green eyes I inherited from my mom have been attracting boys since I was in high school.

I took a deep breath and smiled and turned back to Luc. "It sounds lovely, but I have an early meeting. You should save your wine for a special occasion." Before he could respond, I hurried on. "So where are you off to next? I hear you are always traveling."

Luc gave a slight nod, smiled back, and started talking about an upcoming trip to visit family in Switzerland.

Now I was second-guessing the reason behind the invite to the conference. Maybe I shouldn't have accepted so quickly. Was this 'small intimate' conference going to be uncomfortable? The thought made me uneasy. As it often happens, one uneasy thought led to another. I remembered the implication by my colleague, Jim, about the high rates of domestic violence on the island and the unusual link between Ali's death while diving and Kai's diving mastery. If Jim could believe Kai was to blame, so could the police. I didn't believe it, at least I didn't think I believed it. I shook my head. Things were bad enough without me making them worse. For all I knew, Ali's death would be ruled a tragic accident or from natural causes.

As I entered the house, Ben, long and lanky, was leaning back on our leather couch, one foot propped up on the wooden coffee table, staring at the television. He looked the quintessential, hair-ruffled, handsome professor that female students crush on. His uncombed, sun-bleached hair was lighter than mine—and this evening, his sea-colored eyes looked tired and faraway, as if he was watching the news without actually seeing it.

It was understandable. Even without the drama of finding Kai's girlfriend dead yesterday, it was a little disconcerting watching news that was six hours old by the time we got home in the evening. Most news shows were taped on the east coast in New York or Atlanta and replayed here in Hawaii, long after the newscasters had gone home. We had adapted to the time change now. We called our east coast families before three in the afternoon, and we have trained them to not call us before they have finished their lunch.

Ben looked up at me as I walked in and smiled his always-warm smile, this evening tinged with a hint of sadness.

"Tough day?" I asked.

"Yeah, but Kai's day was worse."

"Oh God, did he go to campus today?"

"No, he called me to ask for the day off. But he sounded so broken up I went over to check on him."

"He didn't stay in his and Ali's place, did he?"

"No, his partner at the dive shop, Mason, let Kai

crash at his house, but Kai needed to pick up some clothes and stuff today and was pretty freaked out about having to go back there." Ben pushed his hair back from his eyes with one hand.

"It would be awful to go back to an apartment you'd shared with a loved one, the day after you lose them. But I think for native Hawaiians there is more to it," I said. "According to native Hawaiian beliefs, if a person dies in a house, it would need a blessing before anyone should live in it again. It's believed that the spirit will want to stay near the belongings it had when it was living."

Ben turned away from the television toward me, a wrinkle in his brow.

I paused. "I'm not sure if that belief still holds if a person dies outside of their house, though. That has never come up in any of the papers I've read. I'll have to look into that." I made a mental note. "Did you go with him to his house?" I asked.

"No, he gave me his keys, and I picked up the stuff he needed. That seemed the easiest way to handle it." The wrinkle in Ben's brow deepened. "I'm glad Kai didn't come with me. The neighbors said the police had been there asking questions about Kai and Ali."

I sighed and walked into the kitchen to pour myself a glass of wine. Ben followed me as I told him of my conversation with Jim and Crystal and Jim's implication that Ali's death was suspicious and that Kai would be a prime suspect.

"When you saw Kai, did he mention why she would be in dive gear? Was he giving her lessons?"

"He talked a lot about Ali. She had a tragic history, I didn't realize. But Kai was as confused as anybody about why she had been diving. He mentioned her phobia. It's such a big part of his life, he's been trying to talk her into letting him teach her how to dive. Kai thought he could get Ali past her fear."

After a pause, Ben continued, "The only thing Kai came up with is that she was trying to surprise him. She had been more difficult than usual lately, and he thought maybe she was trying to make it up to him."

I sipped the glass of shiraz I'd poured as I looked at Ben. I wasn't best friends with her or anything, but we've had them here at the house for our RA get-togethers several times. Kai always brought Ali with him, so we had a chance to talk, watch, and interact with them at least a half a dozen times. "When did you ever see Ali do anything especially nice for Kai? Kai clearly adored Ali, and Ali clearly felt entitled to that adoration."

"Yeah, it would be out of character for her. But it was the only explanation Kai could come up with, and believe me, he was wracking his brain. Like I said, he's been wanting to teach her to dive since they got together. He was sure that if he took it slow, she'd get over her fear and love diving as much as he did. Kai hated leaving her on shore during the best parts of his week."

The thought depressed me. I set my glass down and went to Ben. I slid my arms around his waist and nestled my face in that spot where his neck and shoulder meet and breathed him in. He enveloped me with his strong arms and held me tightly against his chest.

"I'm glad you helped Kai today. That was a nice thing you did." The words were muffled with my face pressed into his neck.

Ben squeezed me tighter and put his chin on top of my head. For a moment we were both awash in relief that we had each other tonight. Grateful that we weren't Kai, sitting in a borrowed bedroom, wondering how he was going to continue when the center of his world had been obliterated.

Chapter 5

A Talk with Gina

I struggled to wake up the next morning. Even after a full eight hours of sleep, I felt like I was just getting up from a pummeling by a team of attackers who had walked away amused.

A scent wafted from the kitchen. Sadly, Ben had beaten me to the coffee maker. He made weak coffee but was so proud of making it I couldn't really say anything. I was greeted by both my dog, Suki, and a pleased Ben holding my mug out to me. I smiled my thanks and tasted the coffee to show my appreciation. It was weak. But he had added the right amount of milk and not too much sugar, so how could a girl complain?

I thanked him and sat down on the floor to read the paper so my dog could join me in a morning cuddle. Our floors in Hawaii were cleaner than most places (it was an anathema to wear shoes inside the house), and my Suki was a big girl. She was an eighty-five-pound, black Bouvier de Flandres, who loved to curl up next to me and put her head on my lap. That wasn't possible if I sat on a stool at our kitchen counter. Hence we had our morning ritual of me sitting on the floor with my back to the kitchen cabinet, and a big furry black dog politely curled up next to me, placing her head, and only her head, on my lap. She was gentle. She never spilled my coffee, and the adoration in her eyes told me how much it meant to her. I enjoyed this time too. It was a relaxing way to start the morning, talking to Ben about what we had to do that day, or what we found in the paper, while I sipped my coffee and let my fingers play in Suki's warm soft curls and slowly eased into the day.

Once at the office, work kept me busy until it was time to go to canoe practice. I drove to Kam Ave, officially named Kamehameha Avenue, for the Hawaiian king who united all the islands into one kingdom. But everyone shortens it. Kam Ave separated the town of Hilo from Bayfront, the crescent moon-shaped black sand beach of Hilo Bay. The curved beach was dotted with canoe 'halau's.

One of the first things I did when I moved to Hawaii was join one of the outrigger canoe clubs. I started with the university club, but they closed down for the summer, so I moved to a local club for regatta season. I could immerse myself in local culture and have an excuse to touch the ocean at least four days a week. Swimming has always been my exercise of choice, but the canoe club was a unique experience. The sense of community and the ever-changing challenges of the ocean required a different mindset and awareness than the isolated lap swims in a concrete pool.

My mom called while I was driving.

"Hey, Momma!"

"Hey, sweetie pie! How's your day goin'?"

"Good. Work has been busy, but I'm heading to canoe practice now."

"That's my girl, you always knew how to balance work and fun. How is that darling Ben doing? You don't wanna let that one go, darlin'!"

24

My parents loved Ben. If there was anything they worried about for me, it's that I wouldn't find the right guy and settle down. I had a split personality when it came to relationships. I wanted what my parents had, a loving relationship where both people respected and deeply loved each other. But I also had a weakness for men on the wild side. I didn't introduce those guys to my folks, but I also never hid them. I had believed that I needed to sow some wild oats before I could settle down. Now I was settling down with Ben. My parents came on their one and only trip to Hawaii after Ben and I started dating, so they had a chance to meet him. My parents adored Ben. So did I. He was a perfect match for me and definitely did not have a wild side.

"Business has been hopping at the diner," Momma said. "It seems like all your daddy's hard work has caught up with him. We are hot with the DC commuting folks. Now your daddy complains he doesn't have enough time to fish."

At sixty years old my father has decided to learn fly fishing. "Well, he should take the time to fish, Momma. Remember he taught me how to balance work and fun." I laughed.

We kept the call short. I didn't want to worry Momma by telling her about the dead body, and she didn't like me talking on the phone while driving, even if I explained I had the phone on speaker and both hands on the wheel.

I pulled into the parking lot, which had only one other car. I was early. I was never early before I moved to Hilo, but I was always early here. Everything runs on "Hawaiian time," and while I was usually a few minutes late to most events, locals appeared fifteen to forty-five minutes after the appointed practice time. For social events it was later, but for an evening practice, we had a setting sun to contend with, so "Hawaiian time" was not quite as late. That was the thing about Hawaiian time, it meant late, but only locals understand how "late" was the correct arrival time.

But I wasn't the only person early for practice. I waved to my friend, Gina, who was doing some yoga off to the side of the halau. She smiled and continued to hold the pigeon pose until I was standing just a few feet from her.

"Rikki would be proud of you," I said. Rikki, our mutual friend, taught yoga. Rikki thought everybody should do more yoga, especially our intense, driven friend, Gina. "What are you doing here so early? You're never early. You're always getting stuck late at work."

"My four o'clock appointment didn't show, so I came down to Bayfront early to have a run and stretch before practice. And I wanted to hear all about you finding Ali Bacunawa." Gina unknotted herself and stood up. Her thick, long dark wavy hair, left unrestrained, flowed over her sweaty, light-brown shoulders.

"Did you know her?" I asked. Gina was 'local.' She was born and raised here, and thanks to her father's twelve siblings, related to half the island.

"We weren't close if that's what you mean, but I knew the family." She shrugged and then leaned toward me. "But I asked first. Spill, girlfriend, Kawika don't tell me nothin'."

Kawika was Gina's husband and a cop on the Hilo police force. He was a gentle giant but a quiet guy. I wasn't surprised he doesn't 'talk story' with his wife about a case.

I gave her the rundown. I'd repeated the event so many times, I kind of had a speech ready, and the emotion didn't hit me as hard. It was beginning to feel like it had been someone else there, hoisting Ali's body onto the boat with Ben. When Gina finished grilling me, she shook her head.

"It's sad, but I guess not surprising considering her history."

"What do you mean? I know she took classes at the university, but I only knew her because she has been going out with Ben's RA. And we never talked enough to get into stories of a wild past."

"Oh man, she had it tough growing up, and she grew up tough. A real tita if you know what I mean."

Tita was an interesting word. There wasn't an exact translation for it in English. A tita was a strong, often opinionated, tough, take-no-shit woman, who had loads of self-confidence. At least, that was what it meant when a woman used it to describe herself. And you had better not argue with her about it if you know what's good for you. If the term was being used to describe another woman, then a tita meant a bitch and a scary one. A 'might-beat-you-up' kind of scary. It was actually much more complex than that, but that's how I thought of it.

"Yeah, I could kinda see that," I said.

"But, like, she had to be. She had it tough growing up in Puna. Her family was a mess. The parents were both drug addicts. The dad got killed in a fight over drugs, the mom had the kids taken away because she was always high, and eventually, she got put in jail for dealing. And usually, there was a grandparent or an auntie who would step in and take the kids, but not in that family. Nobody stepped in when it would have made a difference. Except maybe for an uncle who was in and out of jail, and not so nice, I don't think. So she had no hanai family or nothing. That family got hit hard by the drugs."

Many families had been hit hard by drugs on the Big Island. For several years it was listed as a high-intensity drug trafficking area. Ice methamphetamine had wreaked havoc, destroying a shattering number of families on the Big Island.

Gina stared off in the distance for a minute, looking at her memories. When she started talking again, her voice was more hesitant.

"And then there was something with her brother, David, and one of his friends... Maka. I never knew the details, but it was something bad. They were all three tight, real tight, then it kind of exploded. Ali ended up in the hospital, and her brother and Maka disappeared." Gina shook her head. "I don't know the details, my parents wouldn't tell me. I was older than them, and I was off at college when it happened. That poor kid never had a chance. I don't know how she made it as long as she did."

Gina rolled her shoulders, and the muscles rippled. She shook her hands out as if they were wet and she wanted to dry them, shaking off the bad vibes.

"But let's talk about happier stuff. This is depressing me, and this is almost our last six-man paddle of the season. We need to get out on the water and leave this on the beach."

There were times Gina sounded just like her uncle, the head of the canoe club. Whenever anybody was in a bad mood he'd say, "*Leave it on da beach, no bring*

28

worries on da watta."

A good motto, I think.

****

The next afternoon, my mouth watered as Jack Johnson wafted from the speakers in Surfbreak Café. I sat at a table and waited for my order—an everything bagel with jalapeno-artichoke spread and killer coffee. I loved this place.

I'd taught my early class and collected another pile of papers. I had been a good little professor and graded half the stack in the hours following class, so now I had earned some ripped coffee at Surfbreak. And because I had brought the other half of the stack with me and fully intended to finish grading them here, I ordered the bagel too. Yay for me!

I cruised through the papers for an hour, happily satiated by my smooth and crunchy, sweet and spicy, toasted bagel. I was pulling out the next to the last paper to begin reading when I noticed someone approaching out of the corner of my eye and looked up. It was Jim from the department.

"I guess I'm not the only one who snuck out of the office to get some work done," he said, a smile on his face.

"I've almost polished off these papers, so no guilt here. What's your excuse?"

"Prepping a lecture. I'd forgotten how much work it is to teach a new course. Students gripe so much about having to do a fifteen-minute presentation in class, but they don't realize we have to work up thirty hours of presentations for a new class."

"Yeah, but they don't get paid for their presentations, and we do. Besides, didn't you want to teach this new course because you were getting bored with your other classes?"

Jim groaned. "Don't remind me. I'm trying not to burn out, but it's getting hard. I shouldn't have put off my sabbatical."

"Why did you?" I had been surprised when he decided to postpone. I couldn't wait for my sabbatical.

"My wife couldn't take off work, my son is in school, and I didn't want to travel without them. It's hard when your spouse is working outside academia." He paused, brow furrowed. "And the flights are long and expensive to anywhere from the Big Island. If I leave, I want to be gone for the duration."

That made sense. It was one of the issues Ben and I were struggling with right now.

"You're planning to take a sabbatical next year, aren't you?" Jim asked.

"Yeah, I hope so. I'm trying to put together a research plan now."

"How about Ben, when is he up for one?"

"He could go next year too." Although for some reason, Ben was reluctant. Our discussions on the topic were not getting anywhere.

The girl at the counter came around to give Jim his to-go order.

"Sweet!" He glanced at his watch. "That's great, I'm sure you guys will figure out something cool to do. I've got to run."

I waved goodbye as he left the café. I picked up my last couple of papers, but my mind kept straying to the sabbatical discussion. I'd suggested ideas to Ben, places where we both could do interesting work. But so far nothing appealed to him. We needed to get the applications in soon, or we would miss our chance for sabbaticals next year.

My thoughts were interrupted by my phone ringing. My childhood friend, Anna, was calling. We grew up in the same small town in Virginia. Daughters of best friends, we became best friends too. Anna lived on the mainland, and being so far away from her was hard. I greeted my old friend quickly and launched into the drama of finding Ali's dead body. There's nothing like pouring my heart out to Anna to make everything feel more manageable.

Chapter 6

Swim practice

Ben's phone woke me up. I'd been snuggling his back and untangled myself from him so he could answer it. He climbed out of bed and responded to the caller in a quiet voice as he walked into the living room. I tried to get back to sleep, but curiosity won out over drowsiness. I got up to start a pot of coffee. By the time the coffee was ready, I was dressed, and Ben was off the phone. As I poured us both a cup, I asked him who had called so early.

"That was Mason, Kai's partner in the dive shop. Kai is staying with him for now. He goes back to take care of Ali's dog and change clothes, but Kai hasn't wanted to sleep at their apartment."

"That's nice of Mason."

"Yeah, but he called because this morning the police showed up. Very early, wanting to talk to Kai. They asked him to go to the police station. Evidently, they don't think Ali's death was an accident. There are scrapes on her face consistent with her mask being forcibly removed before death. Since Kai is the boyfriend… and teaches scuba diving, they wanted to talk to him."

"Does Kai need a lawyer?"

"That's why Mason called. He told Kai not to talk

without a lawyer and wanted to call one for him, but Kai said no. Kai told Mason, and the police, he wanted to find who killed Ali, so he'd help any way he could and didn't need a lawyer. Mason wanted to call one anyway or for me to call a lawyer. He thinks Kai will listen to me."

"What did you say?"

"I said it was Kai's decision. I will be there for him if he needs me. But he is innocent, so I agree with Kai he doesn't have anything to hide." Ben tapped his thumb against his coffee cup, his brow furrowed.

I sipped my coffee, wondering what I would have said to Mason. "I hope Kai knows what he is doing."

"Me too," Ben said. He reached for the newspaper, and I got up to take Suki for her morning walk.

****

The day was gorgeous. Hilo got a lot of rain, but when the sun appeared, it was one of the most spectacularly beautiful places in the world. Savage lava rock and wild ocean fought against a verdant jungle, luxuriating in the rain and glowing like a jewel. Banyan and banana trees swayed in the breeze, causing water droplets to shimmer and mynah birds to celebrate atop tall mango trees. Gentle trade winds kept mosquitos at bay, the temperature balmy, and everybody smiled. The weather affected people's moods the world over, but in Hawaii that impact was dramatic. Native Hawaiians were traditionally tied to nature. Weather determined what 'locals' did for the day and not just for weekends, but every day. It was not unusual for a student to miss a test and come to me, wanting to do a makeup. When I asked the reason for the absence, I got a big smile and heard, "*Da waves was rockin', miss!*"

I, on the other hand, worked better with a routine. If I didn't make myself stick to my routine, I wouldn't get off the couch. I *never* skipped paddle practice or a swim workout, because once I looked out and decided it was a little overcast and might rain, then I'd wait until tomorrow… and the next tomorrow, and I would never get to the water. It was better for me to stick to a schedule. Which meant I swam or paddled according to my schedule, rain or shine. That was why, when it was sunny on my swim day, I was one of those smiling people. And today was a swim day. I have a two hour break in the middle of the day. During the break, I would go to the pool and swim before I picked up a sandwich at the health food store to eat in the office. Some might say my life was in a rut. But as ruts go, it was a pretty fabulous rut, especially on a sunny day.

My morning class went well, except for one student. He had turned his paper in late and argued I should accept it without a penalty. I had a strict paper policy. I accepted late papers but took off one letter grade for each day it was late. The student wasn't happy, and he stormed out of my office.

After my second class, I dumped my lecture notes on my desk and grabbed my car keys. I drove two miles to 'Sparky Kawamoto,' a county-run, Olympic-size pool with locker rooms and showers that were free to the public. Old Sparky must have been a much-beloved swim coach before I moved to the island. I've never met the man but loved the name of my pool. When anybody asked where I swim, I loved to say, "I swim at Sparky Kawamoto!"

Lifeguards removed the ropes separating deep and shallow areas at lunchtime, and we could swim laps lengthwise. I said "Hi" to Froilan, the lifeguard on duty, an always-smiling Filipino man. I paddled with his wife and met him when he subbed for someone. He's the person who had encouraged me to move from the short to the long lanes. I'm sure he has dark moments like everyone, but I've never seen any evidence of them. His sunny disposition brightened my day and was another reason I liked swimming at this pool.

I pulled my goggles on and jumped in. *Brrr*, the water was freezing and a shock to the system. This pool was known for its cold water. But the sun was strong, and the contrast between the heat of the sun's rays and the icy briskness of the water was a perfect combination for a good swim. I adjusted my goggles to fix a small leak and pushed off. I shifted into a trance-like state, stroke, stroke, stroke, breathe, stroke, stroke, stroke, breathe. Some people counted laps, but that has never been in my skill set. I zoned out. It was part of why I loved lap swimming. All kinds of cool sensations, running over every part of my body, contrasted with the warm air on my arms as I stretched up and forward, reaching for new, cool water in front of me. The heavenly expansion I felt in my entire body as I extended as far as I could on each stroke, beat any yoga stretch I've ever done. And my lungs expanding deeply and rhythmically on each fourth stroke as I breathed under the reaching arm, was hypnotic. I knew I didn't look glamorous, with my sturdy, full-coverage one-piece, silicone green swim cap, and goggles. But in my head, there was a very sensual experience going on.

After twenty minutes of swimming in my comfort zone, I got serious about training for the open water swim I wanted to do. As much as I loved my lap swims, it was a little ridiculous to live in Hawaii and not take advantage of the opportunities for ocean swimming. The open water swim season was getting started, and a paddle friend had talked me into trying one. It was at Kukio, on the Kona side of the island. It was a gentle, 1.3 mile swim with no rough passes. But I needed to work on my breath strokes. I've been lap swimming for so long that I do it without thinking. I was excellent at turning my head just enough to barely move my mouth above water to suck in a breath. A mistake that a lot of novice swimmers made was lifting their head up out of the water to take that breath, and it wasted a lot of energy. It was like lifting a ten pound weight with one's neck, every fourth stroke. As I have said before, I was inherently lazy. Hence, barely-moving-my-head lap swim breathing I have mastered. Open water swimming was a whole new ball game. In the calmest ocean, there were still waves. Depending on the direction I was swimming, I either had the back of my head to block the water from washing into my mouth, or warn me to close your mouth if I felt the wave start to wash over my head. Or if I was swimming the "wrong" way to the wave, that wave was washing into my oh-so-efficient-barely-above-the-water mouth. I had learned this firsthand in my first rough water swim last year. As I trained for this longer swim, I needed to learn to breathe under my left arm in addition to using my well-practiced-beautifully-implemented right-stroke breathing.

Sound easy? It's not.

I hated this part of my workout. I needed to revert to counting strokes, or I would accidently breathe on my right stroke. And for some reason, my head wanted to come up instead of just rotate to the side. I breathed in a mouthful of water and choked so bad I thought I was going to drown. I knew there was a lifeguard, but it was embarrassing. After fifteen minutes I was exhausted, physically as well as mentally, and I allowed myself to swim comfortably (a.k.a. right-side breathing) for the last five minutes. As I climbed out and pulled my goggles off, I sat on the edge of the pool, enjoying the sun warming my tired muscles. The lanes were thinning out, and I recognized the sequin-flowered, swim-capped head that popped up in the lane next to me. My friend, Rikki, grabbed the side of the pool and swung her body to a vertical position and pulled her goggles off before smiling at me.

"Good for you," she said. "That's smart to work on your breathing. It's going to help you when we are at the Kukio swim."

"I feel like an idiot, though. It's like my body has forgotten how to swim. I'm zig-zagging around the lane and even choking on water."

"No worries, Froilan was watching. Just because he smiles all the time doesn't mean he isn't good at his job. He won't let you drown. And anybody who does ocean swims has been in the same place as you. If you swim out of your lane, we'll just swim around you."

"Geez, did I actually swim out of my lane?"

"Just once on my side, but like I said, no worries. You will conquer this, girl!"

Rikki was nothing, if not encouraging. I gathered my cap and goggles as she climbed out of the pool next to me, and we headed to the showers. We shouted over the dividers and the sound of our two showers flowing full blast, catching up on what each of us had been up to. We moved to the locker room to dress and lowered the volume. The conversation turned to Ali and Kai.

"I knew Ali from when she dated Kevin. I ran into them at parties. Ali always had an attitude, like she could have any guy in the place. If we were female, we were beneath her notice. I never liked her."

Rikki's words surprised me. It was an unusually harsh judgment, coming from her.

Rikki paused to pull her shirt over her head and shake out her wet hair.

"But then Kevin told me some of her history and... I guess I still didn't like her, but I had respect for her. Coming from such a tough background and crawling her way out of it, I mean."

That sounds more like my softhearted friend.

"Yeah, I heard about her family being into drugs," I said.

"Yeah, but hell, lots of people have family with drug problems. In her climb out of that situation, she was under heavy pressure. Her brother and his friend forced her to sell drugs. She lost her whole family when there was a big drug bust. She didn't get arrested, but the brother she was closest to went down. A little after that, while she was still in high school and most of her family was in jail, she got beat up so bad it almost killed her."

That was news! If somebody tried to kill her once, he might have been successful a second time. Maybe the police were right, and Ali's death wasn't an accident.

"Do you know what happened?"

"Well, what Kevin told me is that growing up, she was best friends with David, her almost twin brother. They were born ten months apart. That's why she was so tough. She grew up playing with her brother and his friends. Anyway, David's best friend, Maka, became a major dealer on the island while still in high school. Or I should say when he dropped out of high school. David followed him, and they used Ali to sell the stuff to kids at school."

"Wow. I didn't realize she'd been selling drugs."

"Yeah, well, that's what Kevin told me. He went to high school with her. But that's not the worst part. I guess another one of their friends got caught selling and was sent to jail. And that scared Ali. She saw his life go down the tube in a blink of an eye and decided she wanted out before it happened to her. She always thought she was better than anyone else and was going to find a way off of this island. Back then, according to Kevin, she wanted to go to Hollywood and be a big star."

"So she got out of dealing?"

"Well, yeah, but it wasn't easy. When she told Maka she wanted out, he said no. I guess he'd just lost one of his dealers inside the high school, and he didn't want to lose the other. I mean what I heard was that Maka was kind of into Ali. And she thought she could talk him into letting her out, but his business sense won out over any emotions. He pulled the macho-boss-man thing and threatened her if she tried to quit dealing. She went to her brother for help. But he wasn't sympathetic and told her she better do what Maka told her. He was trying to work his way up the drug business ladder and didn't want Ali messing that up."

"I can't see Ali liking that," I said. We were both dressed by now and stepped over to the mirror on the wall to comb out our wet hair.

"No. She was more of a 'user' than a 'usee,' " said Rikki. "But Maka was big, like almost seven feet tall. He was one of those guys that lifts weights all the time and looks scary as hell. And Maka didn't make it to his level in the drug scene if he didn't know how to back up his threats."

"So what did she do?"

"Well, from what Kevin says, she kept working on him for a couple of weeks, thinking she could win him over. But one day, she must've pushed him too far, and he hit her. She went to school with a black eye. And that sent her over the edge. She had already been beaten up once, by a cousin or something I think. She wasn't going to let it happen again. After Maka gave her the black eye, she went to the police and promised to help them get Maka if they didn't press any charges on her. And they promised to put him in jail on another island."

"Can they promise that?"

"I don't know, but that's what she told Kevin, after it was all over anyway. While it was going on, she kept her mouth zipped, cool as a cucumber, nobody knew what was going on until it came out in the paper one day."

"What came out in the paper?"

"There was a big drug bust. They rounded up Maka, her brother David, and twenty-six other people in a drug ring on the island. Everybody wondered how she didn't get rounded up in the bust, but she just smiled that shit-eating grin of hers."

"Well, good for her. At least she got herself untangled."

"Not so fast, I haven't finished the story. After the bust she thought she was clear. But one of her uncles got to nosing around and visited her brother in jail and somehow figured out that Ali had given the police evidence so she could get off. He was so mad he beat her up, and good. She was in the hospital for two weeks."

"What happened to the uncle?"

"Nothing. She wouldn't tell the cops who did it. But when she got out of the hospital, the first thing she did was go and see him. Rumor has it she said she wouldn't turn him in to the cops for the beating. But if he ever touched her again, he better kill her, or she would kill him."

The locker room was empty. We had packed up our stuff and remained standing in the locker room as she finished the story. Rikki's voice had gotten quieter and quieter as she'd talked, but her last words echoed among the metal lockers and concrete floor.

****

Back at the office I was eating my lunch and checking emails when my phone rang. It was Ben.

"Don't forget Ali's funeral tomorrow."

"I won't. It's on my calendar."

"Of course it is," he said. I could almost hear the tired smile in Ben's voice. He thought I was a compulsive scheduler. He could be right.

"Is there a reception afterward? Should I pick up something to take?"

"Yeah, that would be great. I think Mason is hosting something at his place for Kai. I didn't know Mason very well before, but he has really supported Kai through all this."

I'd seen Mason a few times at Bayfront. He reminded me of an otter, long, lean, and energetic. He paddled for a different canoe club, but their halau was close to ours. We waved "Hello," but that was it.

"Okay, I'll swing by KTA... Any requests?"

"No, whatever you want, I'm sure some of Kai's

friends will bring fish and grill."

We kept the call short. We both had a class in a half hour. On the way home I went to KTA. I didn't find anything that looked good, but then I remembered we were overrun with fresh eggs at the house. Ben had bought a small farm when he first moved to Hawaii, and the half dozen chickens on it produced more eggs than we could handle. I knew Kai loved them, so I went home to make deviled eggs to feed Kai's soul after Ali's funeral.

Chapter 7

A Funeral

The day of Ali's funeral began clear and sunny, with the balmy breezes for which Hawaii was famous. The funeral was at ten. I had time to walk Suki and then work from home until it was time to leave. Ben had an eight o'clock class, so drove in separately and would meet me there. When I arrived, I was struck by how different customs were here in Hawaii. Instead of the simple black sleeveless, sheath dress and black flats that I was wearing, most of the attendees had on the flowered, color-riot you would find at any social gathering or business meeting. Not to mention the ubiquitous *slippahs*. I stood out like a grim reaper.

Several faculty from the university, mostly from Ben's department, were in the growing crowd. Like me, I guess, they were here to support Kai. It was harder to find Ben than I anticipated. People of all ages, ethnicities, and backgrounds swarmed the area. I'm not sure if that was because of a love for Ali or Kai. I suppose it didn't matter, people went to funerals for all kinds of reasons.

Nothing started on time in Hawaii, and a funeral was no exception. I finally spotted Ben. He was standing near Kai and Mason on the other side of the crowd. It would be hard for me to make my way there. They stood in the densest part of the gathering which surrounded Kai. I'd catch up to Ben after the funeral. I glanced behind me and saw a rise with a monkey pod tree. A glimpse of the sky urged me to make the few steps up the incline. I'd have a better view of the ceremony. And if the bowling ball clouds rolling in from the ocean decided to open up—I'd have a tree for shelter from the rain.

As the funeral started, I couldn't hear everything, so I settled for people watching. Ben, who had dressed more appropriately than me in his aloha shirt and khakis, looked solemn. Ben had a sincerity that I found appealing, no self-conscious wringing of hands, biting of lip, shuffling around. I read concern and respect on his face, for Kai and for Ali. We had talked about it last night. Even though neither of us thought she treated Kai well, or was a nice person for that matter, Ben had respected her courage at overcoming her past. The tragedy of such a beautiful, intelligent woman dying so young, and at the hands of another, was disturbing.

Ali was smart. Kai was smart too. Ben thought Kai should go on for a Ph.D. But Ali could argue rings around Kai. I had to wonder, if she'd been born in better circumstances, like my friend Gina, with a family that nurtured her, protected her from the dark paths that beckoned, could Ali have wound up more like Gina? Stable, secure, safe, with a loving husband, good job, and a life that made her happy? Or maybe she would have been the next Steve Jobs, creating new things we didn't know we needed and making money hand over fist? Yeah, that was more like Ali. She would have liked to make piles of money.

As I was musing 'what ifs,' my eyes drifted to an intense mountain of a man in a red shirt so saturated with color I expected it to drip onto his jeans. The almost-to-the-elbow sleeves revealed ropey forearms the color of a dried kukui nut. The bones in his broad face made me think of a tiger, not traditionally handsome, but arresting. I couldn't take my eyes off him. Almost as if he sensed my scrutiny, he turned his head and looked directly at me. My pulse quickened, and I froze - an impala trapped in the gaze of a predator. I couldn't look away. A barely perceptible smile appeared on his face. He knew the effect he was having on me. Embarrassment gave me the strength to jerk my eyes down to my feet.

What the hell was wrong with me? Maybe low blood sugar? I didn't eat much breakfast.

I risked a glance back at him. Damn, he was still looking at me with his self-assured smile. He greeted my glance with a hint of a nod and turned his attention back to the speaker. Flustered, I too looked back at the speaker, but I couldn't make out what the guy was saying, so I went back to looking at the crowd, careful to avoid the red-shirted predator.

There were a lot of locals who I didn't know, but I saw Rikki and Gina standing together. No sign of Kawika, Gina's cop-husband. I would have thought the police would want to come as part of an investigation now that they suspected foul play.

I also saw Kevin. He paddled at the same canoe club as me, but I knew him mostly because he used to date Rikki a couple of years ago. It was before I was with Ben, and Rikki and Kevin had double dated with the guy I was seeing at the time. Neither of those relationships lasted long, but Kevin was a great guy and had stayed friends with Rikki and me. Kevin was standing with people from the canoe club. His current girlfriend stood next to him with a possessive hand on Kevin's elbow. Kevin's open, cheerful face, usually rounded with a mischievous grin, today was drawn and tight. Tears glistened in his eyes. His girlfriend, on the other hand, stood tall and proud, wearing a proprietary smile, until she glanced at Kevin. An angry shadow passed over her face. She was large— probably some Samoan in her background. She had a strong, muscled build, not heavy nor willowy. Her thick inky-black hair was pulled back from her face in a high, tight bun. I thought her name was Mele.

As Mele and Kevin turned around to talk to nearby friends, I realized that the funeral was over. The crowd began shifting restlessly. I found Ben watching me. He waved when I caught his eye. Kai and Mason had already turned and were walking toward the parking area. I had driven my own car, so I signaled Ben to go with Kai.

Most of these people were probably headed to Mason's house for the reception, and the guys must be making their way back to prepare for this large group. I had to stop at our house to pick up the eggs. I hadn't wanted them to get hot in the car during the funeral.

I grabbed the deviled eggs and left our place to drive across town. I had never been to Mason's house before, but Ben had given me the address.

I loved our downtown neighborhood. It was populated with old houses, built back in the twenties. Most of them weren't fancy, other than a handful on Halai Hill or Reed's Island. Instead, they were modest little houses- practical, one board thick, and ceilings made out of canec, the waste from the sugar cane processing that had been turned into a press board. Because the canec was so readily available back in the heyday of the sugar cane industry, it was found in many of these small houses. The little houses, like ours, have crown molding from canec on their ceiling, wood floors that creak when you walk, and big windows, most with their original ribbon glass, that rattle with the wind or a slight earthquake. The homes weren't big, but they had character. They were grouped in what I thought of as healthy communities, a mix of old people, who have grandkids who mowed the lawn for them on Saturday, young families with small children, and every age in between. Some of the families had lived in these houses their entire lives, with their children or grandchildren expecting to move in when the parents or grandparents finished with it. But there were also newcomers, like Ben and me. A Portuguese family had owned our house for eighty-five years, the entire life of the house. But all the grandkids had moved to California, and when the old grandmother residing there died, they just wanted to sell. Fortunate timing for us.

Mason's neighborhood was completely different. The houses were new and modern with dormers, soaring ceilings, and high windows that nobody could reach. When I walked into Mason's house with the deviled eggs, I found a kitchen with a gleaming peach granite custom counter and the latest appliances. Guests were filling up the countertop with laulau, grilled fish, Kalua pork, purple sweet potato pie, lilikoi squares, and the ubiquitous poke in all its varied forms.

Several large Hawaiian women were talking and tasting as they uncovered bowls and stirred pots on the stove. They were not happy with someone's dish... complaining they had made it Filipino style... they cut the kabuchon pumpkin and taro too small. "In little-kine pieces. When I eat um, I like *know* its kabuchon. Big chunk- that's Hawaiian kine!" One woman declared authoritatively.

The other woman laughed and slapped her on the back. "Don't hold back, sista, dats no good fo' you, tell what you really tink!" And they both howled with laughter.

I smiled as I took the foil off my eggs, and since the aunties were clearly in charge of this reception, I asked, "Where should I put these?" I held my tray out in presentation.

"Wat you got deah, sista?" one woman asked as she pulled my tray closer for a better look.

"Is dat fo' snackin' now, or you wan' put on da counter deah fo' when da people cum by wid deah plate?"

"I was thinking it could be a pupu, but whatever works best."

"Dats good, den maybe take it out by Kai. See if you can get dat po' boy to eat somting. I'm his Auntie Charmaine by da way. Are you a friend of dat poor Ali?"

"Uh, I didn't really know Ali very well, I was one of Kai's professors at the university, and I came with his advisor Ben."

"Oh, he nice man. I shudda known you weren't no relation to Ali, you wen bring food and are too polite."

She leaned in so we could kiss on both cheeks. The other woman was also an auntie of Kai's.... maybe related by blood, maybe just 'hanai' family, hard to tell. 'Auntie' could mean anything, from one of your parents' sisters, to a close family friend that was older than you and had known you since you were a child, to a well-respected leader in the community who was everybody's auntie, to a stranger standing nearby when a little kid needed you to lift him to a drinking fountain… as in "Auntie, can you help me get a drink of water?" But clearly these aunties cared about Kai, and that was important today. I could see into the other room that Kai looked terrible. He had the unnatural paleness of shock and deep, dark circles under his eyes.

As I turned to head into the living area with my eggs, I heard a screen door opening behind me and turned to see who it was.

The red-shirted stranger from the funeral came in through the back door into the kitchen. The aunties looked up, looked quickly at one another, and then looked down at their pots. The warmth had fled the room, and there was a studied casualness, when Auntie Charmaine said, "Din't spec see you here, Tino. But come on in. I don't s'pose you brought one dish I guess."

With a smile that had a touch of amusement to it, he set a six-pack of Primo beer on the counter. "I guess I can come to my own niece's funeral if I want."

"Didn't say dat you couldn't. I guess showing respect now is betta than neva," Auntie Charmaine's eyes not leaving the pot she was stirring.

That answered my unasked question. He was Ali's uncle. But was he *the* uncle, the one Rikki told me beat Ali up and put her in the hospital when she was just a teenager? I wouldn't be surprised. A virility emanated from him in waves. A strange mix of aggression and sexuality that I wouldn't say attracted me but made me fidget a little. He was a difficult man to ignore. Physical allure must run in the family. Ali had it too. Even when she was at her bitchiest, it had been hard to take your eyes off of her.

The uncle caught my eye, still with the amused

smile, and said, "I saw you at the funeral, I'm Tino, Alice's uncle."

"I'm Cleo."

"You were a friend of my niece?"

"I knew Alice, but not well."

The smile still on his face, he lifted one eyebrow lazily in question. With a schoolgirl childishness, I rushed to answer. "I am better friends with Kai, that's how I got to know Alice."

"Ahh. Probably fortunate for you. Alice and her brother were my *kuleana*, my responsibility, but that girl... she carried trouble in her hand more often than not."

His gaze on me had never wavered, but now he dismissed me.

"Well, if you will excuse me, I should go pay my respects to the boyfriend." And with that he turned his back, graceful as a tiger stalking prey, and strode past me into the living room.

I turned back to the aunties who giggled good-naturedly. Auntie Charmaine caught my eye.

"He one hunk, eh? He can be one son-a-bitch, but all da same one hunk a man."

"Has he moved back from Maui?" asked the other auntie.

"Not dat I hear, I don' see him makin' one trip special fo' Ali's funeral. He nevah give dat girl da time of day when she wuz alive, don understand why he do it now."

"He must be here fo' one udder reason and decide he show up for da food. I call my cousin on Maui and ask. She sees him all da time. She paddle at da same halau as Tino."

After asking the aunties again if they needed any help and getting shooed away, I took my deviled eggs into the living area. The room, a matchy-matchy décor in shades of peach, tan, and gray, was comfortably filled with people.

The uncle was nowhere in sight, but I found Kai sitting on the couch, talking to Ben and Mason. They smiled and stood up as I approached them. Mason was Kai's friend and business partner. He'd moved over from the mainland a couple of years ago with family money and a love of the Hawaiian lifestyle. He followed Kai around like a puppy and eventually talked him into partnering in a dive shop with Mason's money and Kai's ocean knowledge. The two became good friends.

"Aloha! Good to see you, I'm glad you and Ben came," Mason said.

"Thanks. Good to see you, too."

I turned to Kai.

"Kai, I'm so sorry. I can't imagine how hard this must be for you."

He gave me a weak smile that didn't reach his eyes.

"Thanks, Cleo," he said in a low voice.

I leaned down, as he stood halfway up to meet me, and we kissed on both cheeks.

"I ran into your aunties in the kitchen, and I am under strict instructions to make sure you eat something." I held out the tray of deviled eggs as an offer. "They are fresh from the chickens at the farm." He gave me the same sad smile and picked one off the tray, but instead of eating it, he put it on the napkin that his drink was on.

"Thanks," he said. "Everyone's been great, Mason, Ben, the aunties, all my friends. It's just, every time the

DK Coutant

door opens, I look up expecting it to be Ali."

As if on cue, the doorbell rang. Mason yelled, "Come on in, the door's open." Two police officers walked in. Tall and brown-skinned, they looked serious and a little uncomfortable.

One of them was Kawika, Gina's cop-husband. Their eyes searched the room and finally landed on Kai. The laughing and talking died out as everyone began to notice the uniformed cops who were not making their way to the cooler of beer. Kawika's dark eyes were tense. I've never seen him on the job. His face looked hard. The two officers made their way to us and stopped in front of Kai.

"Kaikane Kimokea Higa, we are here to arrest you for the murder of Alice Puakenekene Bacunawa. We have to take you down to the police station." A shocked silence took hold of the room. I heard the wings of an elepaio as it flew by an open window.

I didn't think it was possible, but Kai's face filled with even more sadness, a deep bottomless pool of heartache. He stood without making a sound, with the grace of someone who has already passed halfway to the spirit world.

Mason jumped up, knocking over the plate of food that had been resting on the arm of his chair. The white plastic fork clattered on the tile floor like a mynah bird skittering on a tin roof. I heard a soft thud as his chicken leg landed next to it.

"Wait! What are you doing? Kai couldn't kill anybody! This is ridiculous!"

Ben rose and put a hand on Kai's arm, "I'll call a lawyer and meet you at the station. We'll get this sorted out."

52

Kai said nothing. But with pain written on a prematurely lined face, he followed the police instructions, holding his wrists in front of him, waiting to be handcuffed, never lifting his eyes from the ground.

Chapter 8

An Investigation Begins

Suki lifted her head and perked her ears up. I heard a car park in front of our house and the sound of someone slowly climbing the steps to our front door. I had been waiting for Ben to come home and rose to greet him at the door. When Kai was arrested, Ben had followed him to the police station. He promised me he would call after he'd located a lawyer to help him get Kai released on bail. That was hours and hours ago. Maybe he was so tired he decided just to come home. The police station was not far from our house.

But it wasn't Ben. Kai's Auntie Charmaine stood on the other side of our screen door, wringing her hands.

"Sorry to bust in like dis." A frown on her face, she shook her head. "But I'm crazy worried 'bout dat Kai-boy, and I don' know wat to do."

"Please come in," I said as I held the screen door open wide. "It's no trouble. Can I get you some tea or coffee, anything?"

"I take one beer if you got um. My hands a shakin'." And she held a hand out to demonstrate. "I so worried 'bout dat boy." And she returned to wringing her hands, her brow furrowed.

I brought her a beer and a glass of water for myself. She stopped wringing her hands to take the beer, and we both sat down at our dining room table. She took a swig of beer, and we sat in silence for a moment.

Auntie Charmaine took a deep breath. "Kai use to live wit me, befoa he went wid Ali." Another swig of beer. "He talk to me 'bout your class. Da one he took wid you. Justice somting it called I tink."

"Psychology of Social Justice, yeah. Kai did really well in that class."

"I nevah make da connection at da funeral. Not till afta wen I wuz at da police station waiting wid your man, Ben. We talk while we wait. He good one, dat man." Auntie Charmaine's shoulders curved inward as she stared at the table, eyebrows creased.

"He wid da lawyer now. He find one lawyer foa Kai. He tol' me ago home, and he take care a Kai."

"Well, that's good...that Kai has a lawyer now. We all know Kai is innocent. I'm sure we can get this cleared up now that he has a lawyer." I wanted to cheer up this woman. She had been such a happy soul, laughing and cooking in Mason's kitchen after the funeral, and now the weight of her sadness pushed against my heart.

Auntie Charmaine stared at the table. "See, I grew up plantation days. Sugar wuz king. One haole do somting, he get off. A local *not* do somting, he go jail... I not so sure Kai, wit his brown skin... I not so sure he see justice." Charmaine lifted her eyes to look at me.

"Dat's why I come see you. I 'member when Kai-boy took ur class. He talk about how you want justice, an' you unnerstand prejudice, an' he explain to me somtings. I don't unnerstand it all, but I know you can help him, cause you unnerstand it."

I remembered the class. I only taught it one time. There had been a court case that went against a local person, and the community had been outraged. I taught the course to try and help everyone understand the psychological research on what we knew about eyewitness testimony and its unreliability, and how we all unconsciously placed people in groups based on very little information and then treated them differently, often unfairly, without realizing it. I'd invited the defense attorney from that case to come to our class and discuss these issues one session. After the class he asked me if I'd be an expert witness for him on another case. I said yes, but the other case had settled out of court, so I wasn't needed. He was a good attorney, though. Too bad he had moved to the mainland earlier this year. I'd have suggested we get him for Kai.

The squeak of the screen door opening startled me. I looked up to see Ben standing there with a long-legged, squirming puppy in his arms. I hadn't even heard his car or him walk up the steps.

Auntie Charmaine pushed herself up from the table, looking at Ben, her face hopeful.

He shook his head sadly. "The lawyer thought he could get Kai out on bail, but Kai said no. He blames himself for Ali's death. Says he didn't keep her safe. I tried to convince him he should get out so we could prove his innocence and find the person who really killed her. But he wouldn't listen. I'll go back tomorrow and see if he is in a better frame of mind."

Auntie Charmaine nodded sadly. "Tanks for trying. I go home now, an' we try tomorrow." She kissed Ben on both cheeks; he continued to struggle with the puppy who was trying to lick both Ben and Auntie Charmaine, but she didn't appear to notice. I followed her to the door, and we kissed on both cheeks. As I pulled away, she grabbed my forearm in a tight grasp.

"Promise me. Promise me you help Kai," she said.

"Sure. Of course. I don't know what I can do, but I will certainly do everything that I can."

"You unnerstand justice don't always happen. Kai say. Kai say you tell his class dey should always fight for justice. Promise me you fight for justice for Kai."

I was helpless, facing all that trust staring at me. I nodded. "I promise."

Auntie Charmaine nodded back and walked down the steps into the night.

I didn't know what I had gotten myself into, but I turned to Ben. "Now, are you going to explain that puppy to me?"

****

The next day, two Paniola Pale Ales and a glass of cabernet sat on the elephant table on our back deck. The base was a statue of an elephant with a small, round, glass top, large enough for four glasses and a plate of pupus. I loved this table. But it didn't work in the dining room. The top was too small, and the elephant took up all the legroom. Ben had asked Mason to come over and talk about Kai's arrest and defense.

The guys were talking about fish they had caught and taking swigs of their beer.

We wanted to help Kai, but I didn't think any of us knew where to start. My promise to Auntie Charmaine hung over me like a cartoon anvil. Was I the only one who felt the tension? Like we were putting off a herculean, hopeless task? A memory of grad school pushed itself into my head. I sat around a different table with different people taking nervous swigs of beer, overwhelmed by how to start writing our dissertations.

This was a thousand times worse. Kai's life was at stake.

The thought of what was in jeopardy pressed me into action. How had I finally started my dissertation? By breaking it into subgoals. We should do that now.

"Okay guys, enough about fishing. Let's make a list of things we can do that might help Kai. Big things and little. We can even put things on this list we've already done, to recognize our progress." I picked up the legal pad of yellow paper and my favorite purple tornado pen that I'd brought when I'd carried the drinks out.

Two sets of skeptical eyes looked at me.

"I'll start. Kai needed a lawyer and, Ben, you found him one, check."

I wrote it down and checked it off. List-making calmed me.

"Mason, you rearranged the work schedule at the dive shop so it wouldn't go out of business while Kai's in jail. Check."

Mason's mouth twisted, and he shook his head. "I'm not sure that counts as helping Kai. I'm half owner of the business, so there was self-interest there." He stared at his beer for a minute, then looked back up at me. "What we really need to do is get Kai off the hook for Ali's death." He paused. "I know the police are calling it a murder, but I can't believe that. Maybe we can prove it was an accident?" His voice trailed off.

Ben sighed. "I was at the police station. They aren't going to buy that it was an accident. That just doesn't make sense with the evidence. The airtube running from her tank was cut with a knife. And there are scrape marks on her face that came before death. They believe the mask was forcibly removed from her face."

Ben's words depressed me. That must have been

terrifying. Why did people do such horrible things to each other?

Ali's dead body floated before my eyes. To wash it away I looked at the wall of green that ran across the length of our backyard. Unlike the manicured hedges of boxwood that I grew up with on the mainland, this was a riot of wildly different shapes and textures of green. It created a fabulous shield of privacy. The back of our house was only forty feet from the back wall of the house behind us. But with our orchid, fig, and banana trees, ferns, palms, and ti plants, the only glimpse caught of our neighbor's house was a small 'window'… a gap between our towering foxtail palm and an apple-banana tree. Last week Ben cut down a stalk of ripe bananas, and nothing has grown in to replace it yet. I gave it a couple of weeks before something new will have taken its place. I think someone once said, "Nature abhors a vacuum." I could attest to that in our backyard.

"Okay." I took a deep breath. "So, if we accept that Ali was murdered…"

"Why exactly do they think it is Kai?" Mason raked his fingers through his hair. "What evidence do they have?"

Ben shrugged. "The fact that he was her boyfriend, and neighbors told the police that Ali had been yelling at him a lot lately. More than usual. And the only prints on her scuba tank were Ali's and Kai's. And—"

"That's ridiculous! How can they possibly get fingerprints off a scuba tank that's been in saltwater for any length of time!" Mason smacked the deck railing with his elbow as he abruptly scooted his chair back from the table.

Ben took an extra-large swig of his beer. "I asked

the lawyer about that too. Evidently, controlled studies have found fingerprints can be recovered for up to ten days in calm saltwater." Ben shrugged. "The lawyer also said…" Ben took another drink and squirmed in his chair. "He mentioned some witnesses have said that Ali was messing around with someone on the side. They don't know who, or even for sure anything was happening, but it is enough to claim motive."

"That Ali could be a bitch," Mason said. "But if the cops don't know who it was, or if it was for sure, that's pretty weak."

Ben nodded. "I know, but they combine that with the fact that he gives dive lessons, and they claim that is opportunity. It's not helping that Kai doesn't want to request bail. I'm afraid that is making him look guilty. I agree it's not strong, but according to the lawyer, people have been convicted for less."

It was maddening that Kai resisted leaving jail. He claimed he felt guilty for not keeping Ali safe. But I think he was also reluctant to face his family and friends. Kai has always kept his nose clean and stayed out of trouble. Whether he committed the crime or not, there would be public derision from some of those in his circle that the golden boy Kai was in trouble with the law. It was a small world on the Big Island. He wouldn't be able to get away from that except by staying locked away.

"As much as Kai wants to curl up and die in a jail cell, if we post the bail, they have to release him, right?" Mason asked.

Ben nodded. "That's what the lawyer told me, his auntie Charmaine is looking for somewhere he can mourn in peace if we scrape the money together and push the bail through."

But if this goes to trial and they convict him, he's right back in jail.

"If we accept that Ali was murdered and that Kai didn't do it... we have to get the cops to move past this circumstantial evidence. I think the best way to do that is to figure out who killed her," I said.

Ben shook his head again. His mouth tightened. "We're not detectives, Cleo. Leave it to the police."

"Ben's right. We should leave it to the police," Mason said.

"Give me a break. The police are nice guys, but it's not like we get mysterious murders here every day. This is Hilo. The only murders we get are domestic violence related. Which is why they jumped to the conclusion it was Kai," I said. "They aren't even looking for anyone else. And I promised Kai's auntie Charmaine that I would try."

Mason looked like a little boy who has just been told his goldfish died. His eyebrows drawn together to hold back tears. A sentiment I shared. It was starting to get dark, and a moth landed in my wineglass. I fished him out with my fingers and gently flicked him to the tile patio floor. It took a few wobbly steps, then flew off toward a light under the eaves which overhung the porch.

"Oh yeah," Mason said. "Don't forget Ali's puppy on your list. I offered to find a new home for her, but Kai wants to keep her. It's a good thing you guys can watch her until Kai gets out." He reached down and absently stroked the long-legged, borzoi puppy lying at his feet.

After the police had arrested Kai and taken him in handcuffs from Mason's house, his biggest concern was that someone would take care of Ali's puppy. While Ben was calling lawyers and talking to police, Kai just wanted someone to promise to take good care of Ali's puppy. Maybe caring for her puppy was the way he coped with his sense of failure at not taking care of Ali when she needed him.

Ben had gone from the police station to Kai's apartment to get the dog. Ali had named her dog Bella. The anxious five-month-old borzoi puppy had been in Ben's arms when he had returned home. Bella was adorable, long legs, big eyes, nose, and floppy ears. She was mostly white, with honey-colored ears and a saddle patch on her back. We'd carefully introduced her to Suki, who appeared delighted with having a puppy in the house. And now Bella was sleeping, curled up next to Mason's chair.

"I just remembered something that might help Kai," Mason said. "Now that you mention it, I heard rumors that Ali was chasing after someone other than Kai. A professor at the university, I think."

"Really? Do you know who?" I looked back and forth between Ben and Mason.

Mason leaned back in his chair. "I think he had an animal name or something, like Bear or Cougar or Trotter or something."

"Trotter isn't an animal," I said. "Unless you are thinking of a horse or something? Is that it?"

"I can't remember." Mason threw his hands in the air. "I mean it's not any of those, but something like that." Mason put his hands flat on the table. "I can't actually even remember where I heard it. I kind of didn't want to know. I knew it would hurt Kai if he found out."

Ben remained silent, but he looked like a kid that knows he's going to have to swallow a big spoonful of castor oil.

"Who was it?" I looked Ben straight in the eyes.

"I don't *really* know." He actually squirmed in his seat, like he was six rather than thirty-six.

I narrowed my eyes and continued to stare him down.

"But you have an idea."

"I don't really know anything, I've just heard *rumors*." Ben's mouth puckered in distaste just saying the word. He hated gossip and rumor-mongering. His revulsion traced back to some incident in his childhood. He never told me explicitly, but I believed his sister had been a victim of some mean-spirited gossip when they were young. Ben was very protective of his sister.

But I was getting impatient. I knew Ben hated gossip and would rather bite off his tongue than spread a rumor. But Kai was in trouble and needed our help. The more suspects we could hand over to the police, the more likely they would realize Kai didn't kill Ali.

"So what rumors have you heard? Come on, Ben. We aren't going to spread gossip. We are *only* going to tell the police. If you have a potential lead, we need to follow up on it. If it's not true, then the guy can get his name cleared, just like we are trying to do for Kai. If it is true, and this guy may have had a reason to kill Ali, the police need to know!"

"Yeah, OK. I don't know if it's true or even if it involved Ali... but... do you know Walker Wolf in the Business Department?"

I nodded. "Just enough to know who he is."

"I was on a search committee with him about two years ago, I was the outside member, and he seemed okay to me, but people were talking about him."

Ben grew silent again.

I raised my eyebrows and tilted my forehead toward him, encouraging him to continue.

He got the hint.

"Well, the rumor mill has it that he likes to date undergrads. That if he has a good student who is attractive in his class, he waits until the class is over, grades are in…then he asks her out. I was told it has happened more than once."

"Hmm, the administration must not be crazy about that."

"No, but strictly speaking, it doesn't violate the ethics code."

"But if he has done this repeatedly…" I let the sentence hang. It might not be strictly speaking an ethics violation, but it sure could bias the higher-ups against giving him tenure.

Ben interrupted by shaking his head.

"I don't know if this is true, or if it happened one time and never again, or if Ali was involved at all. A person can do something one time, and the coconut wireless will paint them as a repeat offender. Even if he does do it, I don't know if Ali was in his class, or whether she was a student that caught his eye, so no, I don't *know* anything!" Ben, face flushed, lifted his palms in a sign of exasperated surrender.

I smiled. "No, we don't know anything. But we know who we need to talk to."

Chapter 9

Another Suspect

Ben and I were up early and walked the dogs together. I didn't know how puppy Bella would do on a leash, and two dogs could be a challenge to handle by one person if one of the dogs didn't want to cooperate. Suki was her typical, angelic self, but the puppy had clearly not been leash trained. I mentally added 'puppy training' to my list of things I could do to help Kai.

After the walk we went our separate directions. Ben planned to meet with Kai's lawyer today, and I headed in to the university. I got a text as I'd parked the car. It was from Gina.

—*Kawika finally spilled something—Ali was hapai—*

Ali was pregnant! Geez, I wonder if Kai knew. *That poor guy, how much more can he take.* I called Ben and told him. He sounded tired. Ben didn't think Kai knew about the pregnancy. He said he would check with the lawyer, who could check with police and verify. Ben would probably have to break the news to Kai.

"Ben, make sure you're taking care of yourself. You've been working hard at both the job and taking care of Kai. Try and find some way to relax, or you are going to burn out."

"And I guess that would make my psychologist

girlfriend look bad." I heard a hint of teasing in his voice, which made me worry a little less.

"Exactly. So do us both a favor and go fishing or to the beach or hiking, even if only for an hour this week." I glanced at my watch and saw the time. "I love you, but gotta run to class."

Research Methods was one of my favorite classes to teach even though it was also the longest. Today I talked about bias, leading questions, and the importance of avoiding them.

"The words you choose are important," I said. "For everything in life, not just questionnaires. Researchers have known this for a long time. That's why in some legal cases, judges will tell lawyers there are certain words they can't use because they are too prejudicial … they will bias the jury too much."

"Really, miss? Like what words?" a student asked.

"Well, using terms that might be ethnically or gender-biased. For example, calling someone a 'haole' or a 'jap,' which may trigger stereotypes. But in some especially emotional cases a judge might get specific about when the words 'baby' or 'fetus', 'protester' or 'looter' can be used. You've probably noticed that depending on which side of an issue someone is on they call it by different names, 'pro-choice' or 'pro-abortion.' "

Another student, Lei, jumped in. "All you have to do is switch back and forth between Fox news and MSNBC. They can be talking about the same story and not use any of the same words."

"Great example. We've known for a long time that using biased words can affect how people decide and judge other people. But now there are new techniques that are going even further. FMRI, or functional magnetic resonance imaging, puts people in tubes where they have to lay perfectly still, and the machine can see which part of the brain lights up when a person thinks or says something. Researchers used to believe there were specific areas of the brain where all language activity took place. But now they are finding that depending on the words that are used, different parts of the brain light up. I heard a talk by a neuroscientist. He put people into the FMRI tube and gave them metaphors for the same thing, just switching up a couple of words. Like, 'he had a bad day' or 'he had a rough day.'

"What he found is that when people heard a 'rough' day, parts of their brain related to texture lit up too. Even though we all know what 'a rough day' means, our brain still recognizes the touch component. Like, a'a lava rather than pahoehoe lava, even if we don't consciously think about a'a lava, with its scratchy texture."

The Big Island was not only birthed from a volcano, but currently had an active volcano that has been flowing for more than thirty years, adding a few feet to the girth of Hawaii Island every day. Occupants of the Big Island had an intimate knowledge of many types of lava. Pahoehoe lava, while rock hard, looked like cake batter that had been poured in wide tracks across jungle and yards. Pele's hair was fine glass-like threads that a volcano could produce. It would float in the wind after some eruptions. Our electrician was installing some wiring in our house and found broken threads of Pele's hair that had drifted into our attic through a vent during a past eruption. And a'a lava looked like a sea sponge but sharp and scratchy and would cut up the most calloused feet if you tried to walk on it.

One of my favorite students, Frankie, raised his hand with a big smile on his face. "So, Teach, if I say afta I go surfin', dat I got rolled by a bitch of a wave, wat part a my brain be lightin' up?"

"Oh, I *so* don't want to go there, Frankie!" I laughed.

As I walked back to my office after class, my thoughts returned to our discussion of word choice. The topic had fascinated Kai in my Social Justice class. The research on how mock juries would assign longer sentences for the same criminal depending on words used to describe the person. It also reminded me of the word choice of Ali's uncle Tino after the funeral - that Ali 'carried trouble around in her hand.' It had stuck in my head because I wasn't sure what he meant. Did she carry trouble around like a gun or a bat, to injure another person? Was he still mad at her for sending her brother to jail? But he also said that Alice and her brother were his 'kuleana,' the Hawaiian word for responsibility. Maybe he was sad about her death. A person who carried trouble in her hand couldn't hold another hand or caress. He had beaten her, yes, and I could never condone that. But he wouldn't be the first family member to not spare the rod as to not spoil the child. And maybe he regretted the beating now... or then, for all I know. I've been assuming he was a suspect, now I'm not so sure. I tried to think back to his facial expression for a clue, but I couldn't read his expression then, and anything I 'remembered' seeing now was colored by my suspicions. I shrugged my shoulders. Sometimes knowing all the ways our thoughts can be biased only makes it more difficult to be objective.

I drove to Bayfront after work for our last club paddle of the season. I have been learning to steer a six-man canoe. To cap off the end of the season, Afano, the head of our canoe club and Gina's uncle, decided that us new paddlers could go out past the breaker wall with the rest of the club. The breaker wall kept Hilo Bay relatively calm. Beyond the line of engineered rocks stretched the great Pacific Ocean with nothing to interrupt waves that started in Alaska. Past the breaker wall the size of the swells were untamed and could be profoundly larger than inside the bay.

But today it was calm, and Afano thought us newbies could manage it. I was excited as we carried our canoes to the water and pushed off. I've paddled around Hilo Bay so many times I knew it by heart. My crew and I knew our kuleana, based on our puka, our spot, in the canoe. The first seat was the stroker, who set the pace, the second seat counted off hut, hut, hou, so that everyone switched to the other side on hou. Third, fourth, and fifth seat were the power, for the strongest paddlers, and the sixth seat was my seat. My kuleana was steering. We knew our roles and were ready for a new adventure. Hamu, who was my mentor and taught me to steer, was steering a different canoe, but he stuck close to me. All the way across the bay, he shouted instructions... "Rememba... keep da amae on the downwave side." "Don't turn left into a wave." "Turn da canoe at da top a da crest." "Tell two and four to lean on the iakos if you get in trouble."

I smiled and nodded. The wind whipped the hair that had slipped out of my ponytail around my face. I was exhilarated and excited to practice what he had taught me. What was the worst thing that could happen? We knew how to swim and have done 'huli' drills, in case we ever tipped over. Embarrassing, but no big deal.

Hamu shouted reminders and my crew and I fell into our rhythm The winds began to pick up. By the time we paddled the twenty minutes across the bay, the swells had grown. As we reached the point where the great Pacific Ocean hurdles itself around the breaker wall, the swells mushroomed into monsters and came at us from all directions. Instead of rounded, four-foot watery hills, they grew to mountains with steep faces and sheer cliffs. In the trough of a wave, the other canoes disappeared. My crew and I looked around in amazement at the walls of water extended way over our heads on every side. We were surrounded by a phantasmagoria of deep iridescent, abalone blues, and light, bright, mermaid greens with a sparkling sun shining through the thin peaks of the waves edged in lacy foam. A minute later we were on the crest, and I saw, at the last second, Hamu's canoe a mere foot away, I maneuvered so that our bow wouldn't land on his amae. Hamu was rubber-necking, trying to find me, and when he did, he deftly moved his canoe the couple of extra inches away that saved us both. Seconds later we were sliding down the face of a wave with roller-coaster speed. I heard screams of surprise coming from my crew. One of the screams came from me. Then we were back in our private room between waves. We were still, long enough to catch our breaths and share looks of thrilled-terror at what we were experiencing, before we were pitched back to the top of another wave and inches away from another canoe I needed to frantically avoid. I lost track of Hamu, but everybody in the club was aware that I was a newbie steersman, so when they saw it was me in the canoe next to them, they quickly moved a little farther away. Another downward hurtle that I didn't know how to control. I lost all sense of time, every ounce of concentration focused on not landing on another canoe or flipping.

Sometime during the wash cycle that our canoe was getting, the realization came hard and fast that if we flipped, there was a good chance somebody would get seriously hurt. Whether crushed between two canoes being tossed by these colossal giants or by hitting a head on a flying amae. An unconscious person in this sea was not likely to survive. The breaker wall was not far away, but on this side it would be deadly to attempt to climb out of the ocean onto the rocks. Being swept by any of these fickle, chaotic, sledgehammers of water onto the rocks would surely crack a skull. And it would be impossible to rescue that cracked skull before the person housing it had drowned.

Back on shore, I found out we hadn't been out there long. Afano quickly realized the waves were far too large for anyone but his most experienced paddlers and turned us around. But it took time to convey that message to twenty canoes when everyone was crashing up and down waves. Eventually, we all made it back to calmer waters inside the bay, where the breaker wall disciplined waves to a manageable size and ferocity, and we finished our regular practice route.

Excited chatter commenced on the beach. I wasn't the only person who hadn't paddled in waves like that. Just the least experienced. Afano, a big Samoan guy with an expressionless face, found me as I was rinsing off paddles. He looked me in the eye, maybe seeing me for the first time.

"You did good out there," he said quietly, then turned his back and walked away. I think those may be the only words he said to me the entire paddle season.

As I walked to my car, Hamu caught up with me.

"Man, I was so scared for you. I thought for sure you were going to huli or crash into someone."

"Afano said I did good!" I couldn't help but beam a smile.

"Yeah, I'm sure he thought you were going to crash into somebody." Hamu laughed. "He was happy he didn't have to fish anybody out." Hamu sobered. "But he's right, you did just about everything right."

The adrenaline was still pumping, and my pride pushed out the words, "So 'almost' isn't everything. What did I do wrong?"

"Only thing you did wrong was scream. You can never show fear when you are steering. Part of your job as steersman is to keep your canoe calm. The crew is working and doing their job, if you want to keep them on track, and not panic, you need to make them feel like you got it all under control."

"So no screaming," I said.

Hamu nodded at me. "No screaming."

He turned and walked to his car, his steering paddle in his right hand. I had never noticed before, but he carried that paddle like a spear.

The sun was setting by the time I made it home. Ben had called to say he was working late. After a quick dinner and a cuddle with Bella, I took Suki for a long walk to Bayfront. Hilo Bay looked inky black, and the skyward-stretching coconut palms stood out as wafting silhouettes against the lighter shades of a cashmere-gray night sky. I sat on the beach and let Suki jump in the waves as I basked in the night sky with its big, fat, beautiful, full moon. As the moon rose, instead of piercing the night, the moonbeams bounced off of the clouds clustered around it, making it shine pearly-bright. A spotlight focused on a bejeweled blues singer in a smoky bar.

My phone made a croaking sound.

"Oh my God!" I heard when I answered my phone. "I thought of somebody else with a motive."

I recognized Rikki by her voice and the croaking ringtone she had programmed into my phone.

"Did you tell the police?"

"Oh, they would never listen to me. You're a professor. If you figure out a clue, they have to listen to you."

I didn't agree with that, but I knew that men tended to underestimate Rikki. I knew how smart she was, but because of her bubbly enthusiasm... not to mention tiny bikinis and barely there yoga costumes ... well, at first glance some people took her for a beach bimbo.

"So what's your clue?" I asked.

"Last summer I was at a party on Coconut Island."

Coconut Island was a tiny island connected by a bridge to Liliuokalani park and Bayfront. If it wasn't dark, I would be able to see it from where I was sitting.

"It was mostly locals," Rikki continued. "And it was just about the time that Ali started dating Kai. Ali was there, but Kai wasn't for some reason, I don't remember why. We were all drinking and having a good time, but as it got late, a fight almost broke out between Mele, Kevin's girlfriend, and Ali."

"Really?" Even though Ali was barely over five foot tall, she was tough and not afraid to fight dirty. I was surprised anybody who knew Ali would try to start something with her.

"Yeah, well, it was late, and people had been

drinking for a while and getting stupid."

"What was the fight over? Do you remember?"

"That's why I called. Mele was mad because she thought Ali was coming on to Kevin. You know how jealous Mele gets. You can't look sideways at Kevin without her going ballistic. It's a shame, he is so-o-o-o adorable. He deserves better."

I don't know Mele well, but I have been with Rikki in the past, when Mele gave her the stink eye just for talking to Kevin. Mele knew they used to go out and hated that Kevin stayed friends with Rikki.

"Was Mele right? Did Ali make a play for Kevin?"

"Who knows? Ordinarily I'd think it was just Mele being drunk and paranoid, but Ali had a smug, self-satisfied look on her face that night. And I didn't see Kevin, he must have split as soon as Mele caught them."

"But that happened a while ago. Why would she act on it now? I don't see her as the type to hold things in."

"Rumor has it, Mele had to go to California for work. She's a prison guard at the women's prison and had to escort a prisoner or something. She was gone for two nights. I also heard while she was on the mainland, Kevin was a busy boy. Nobody knows who he was with, but Mele got back and heard the coconut wireless too, I'm sure. That was about a week before Ali was killed. I can see her sending Ali a text to meet her at the beach from Kevin's phone. Then when she gets there… in the dark of the night … she drowns Ali!" Rikki finished, a note of triumph in her voice.

"And then pulls a wetsuit on her? It's not a bad theory, but it has some holes."

Rikki laughed. "Hey, I can't do all the work, you are the little professor. You figure out the rest of it!"

I didn't know if Kawika was going to listen to me any more than Rikki, but maybe it would help Kai's case. Somebody should tell Kawika there were other suspects.

"Ok, fair enough. I'll ask around and call Kawika at the police station. But I'm going to give him your name as my source, okay?"

"Sure, anything to help Kai."

We hung up after setting a date to go swimming at "4-mile," a beach four miles out on the road to Keaukaha. My routine was to swim laps at the pool. But Rikki always pushed me to get "out of the concrete box" and do ocean swimming. She was right. But it wasn't practical on workdays. And speaking of workdays, I had another one tomorrow. I called Suki away from waves and put her back on the leash before we headed home.

Chapter 10

Richardson's beach

I rolled my shoulders as I exited our raucous faculty meeting. The university had declared across the board budget cuts, and all departments were feeling the pinch. For us in psychology, it was more like a slam. The department was fed up. I walked into my office and heard the office phone ringing at three thirty on this Friday afternoon. I was tempted not to answer. The good angel on my shoulder won out, and I picked up.

"Hello, this is Cleo Cooper. How can I help you?"

"You can be in the parking lot in ten minutes, ready to go to Richardson's," Ben answered.

"Give me fifteen, and I'm there," the little devil on my other shoulder answered.

Thirty minutes later, we pulled into the parking lot at Richardson's Beach Park. It wasn't the kind of beach most people thought of when they picture Hawaiian beaches. Clouds were gathering over Hilo Town, but still-strong rays of sun warmed our bodies as we waded into the water at the tiny, black sand beach that served as one entryway into the sheltered swimming area known as Richardson's.

Behind us and to the left were the manicured areas of the park with soft mowed grass and graceful palms arced in salutes to ancient 'fishponds.' Respect for history kept anyone from entering those. A concrete area with bathrooms and cold outdoor showers could be found in between the palms. There was a small concrete stairway on the west side that could be taken down to another, even more sheltered black sand beach. But cold spring water bubbled up from the ocean floor on that side and chased most of us away.

On the east side of the park were taller lava rocks that, during high tide, would have teenagers climbing to make the ten-foot jump into the ocean. There were fewer trees near the jumping rocks, so most of the sun-loving college students spread their towels on that side.

Ben and I entered on the middle black sand beach where families hung out. The gentle sloping shoreline, with fewer rocks, made it our preferred entry spot. Ben and I dodged kids playing in the surf and then their watchful parents bobbing up and down in the waves a few feet deeper. After threading our way through, we were past the crowd and had the main swimming area to ourselves.

This is where Ben and I fell in love. Stolen kisses behind lava rocks and watery caresses that lingered underwater where they couldn't decently above water. Ben was in his element in the ocean, happy, confident, and relaxed. He taught me to notice inexplicable sea currents and creatures. His eagerness was intoxicating, and I fell hard for him. It was nice to be back in the ocean with him. It has been awhile. We leisurely half swam, half floated, looking down at yellow tangs, raccoon butterfly fish, saddleback wrasses, and humuhumunukunukuapua'a. It took me six months to learn how to pronounce that Hawaiian name for the triggerfish that was Hawaii's state fish. We dodged an occasional honu, or green sea turtle, their shells rising and falling with the swells as they munched on the short sea grasses that grew on submerged lava rock. Their four flippers managed to maneuver so that mouths could steadily munch a patch of seagrass.

My body temperature dropped to the point where I was shivering after forty-five minutes. The water felt good when I got in, but if I wasn't actively swimming, I couldn't maintain my body heat. Ben wanted to stay in the water, so I swam to shore. I found an unoccupied sunny spot, wrapped myself in a beach towel, and watched the swells floated up to meet the tops of the ring of lava rock that sheltered Richardson's. Ocean swells hypnotized me. So much power in the smooth rise and fall of tens of thousands of gallons of saltwater that have traveled with grace, halfway around the world.

Slowly warming like an iguana on a cold winter's morning, I thought back to yesterday's paddle and the elation and terror of experiencing watery mountains up close. As I sat on my rock drying, my thoughts drifted to Ali and how she must have felt scuba diving. I wondered if she felt triumph and exhilaration at conquering her fear. I hoped so. She must have felt the panic when she was drowning and couldn't get any air. Did she scream? Did she know she was pregnant? Did she scream for her baby? Is that why she didn't make it to the surface? Did she release her last strongholds of air in a scream?

Ben plopped down next to me. Wet, dripping, and grinning, he bumped his shoulder into mine. "Lighten up. You look like you have the weight of the world on your back."

I had been so lost in my thoughts I hadn't noticed his approach. I smiled back at him, glad for the interruption. "You're right. It's a beautiful day, and the ocean is fabulous. I don't know why we don't do this more often."

"Because we have jobs." He leaned over to wipe the saltwater off of his face onto my towel. "Just enjoy it when we *can* get here." Ben sat back, leaning on his arms stretched out behind him, legs extended in front, with ankles crossed, a lazy smile on his face as he looked out on the water and happy beach-goers. It was the most relaxed I had seen him in a week.

His eyes focused on something in the distance, and his smile faded. He was silent for a minute, then asked, "Do you remember that guy Mason was talking about the other day, Walker Wolf?"

I sat up straight and leaned in closer to Ben. "Yeah. The guy he heard a rumor about, the professor who Ali might have been seeing on the side?"

"He's here." Ben's jaw tightened. "And he's heading this way. I know you think this will help Kai. But please don't drag me into this conversation."

I looked in the direction Ben was looking and saw a dark-haired, Caucasian man approaching us. It didn't appear that he noticed us or intended to join us. We just happened to be sitting near the path that connected the little black sand beach and the other little cove.

"Fine," I said in a terse whisper. "But at least say hi to him and introduce me so if I go talk to him later I won't be a stranger."

Walker Wolf climbed the path that led past the rocky point where we were sitting. As he approached, he lifted his eyes, noticing us for the first time. His eyes creased in vague recognition when they focused on Ben.

"Hey, Walker," Ben said, not a drop of enthusiasm

in his voice.

"Hi. We were on a search committee together a few years ago, weren't we? Ben, right?"

"Yeah." Ben reluctantly reached up to shake the hand that Walker had leaned over and extended. "And this is Cleo Cooper. She's in the Psych department." Ben nodded in my direction.

Walker's eyes appraised me, wet, tangled hair and all. I was glad to be wrapped in my towel, or I'd be feeling seriously uncomfortable.

"Student or faculty?" he asked and shot me a dazzling smile, clearly not afraid to flirt with me in front of Ben.

"I'm on the faculty," I answered, maybe a little primly, and smiled politely back. I didn't want to encourage him, but I wanted to discuss Ali with him later, when Ben wasn't around. "So what department are you in?" I opened my eyes wide and batted my eyelashes a couple of times the way my mother had taught me, in what I hoped gave a naive impression.

"I'm in business. I specialize in tourism and how to make money while people are enjoying life. Probably not so different from what you do in Psychology." Another dazzling grin came my way before he glanced at his phone. "Excuse me, but I'm meeting someone soon, and running late. But it was good to see you again, Ben, and to meet you, Cleo." He waved and continued on the path.

Chapter 11

A conversation with Crystal

A week later, I was at the office working on my presentation for the Santa Fe conference. Every time I thought about the big names that would be there, like Luc Bastien, I got butterflies in my stomach. Luckily, my friend, Tyler, would be there, too. He had a wicked sense of humor that helped me survive six grueling years of graduate school. With him at the conference, it would be fun. *If* I got my presentation together. Progress on that would help with the butterflies. I had collected data on immigrants and acculturation practices. The analysis wasn't finished, and I needed it for the my presentation. I didn't have to teach today, so it was a perfect time to work on it. I usually left my door open so students would feel welcome to drop in, but if I was analyzing data, I needed the door shut so I wasn't distracted by conversations that walked by.

After a couple of hours, I had a general idea of what data I would present and how I wanted to lay it out. I stood up to stretch and opened my door. I found my colleagues, Crystal and Jim, standing in the hall, talking about the last department meeting. They had walked to the coffee cart for a break between classes, and an intense discussion had come up about the hiring situation. They looked at me when I opened my door, and I felt obligated to smile and join the conversation. It was fun to watch Crystal talk when she was energized on a topic. Her shoulders shrugged, hands waved, grabbed, and punched the air to emphasize her point.

I listened to the discussion until it began to wind down. Jim looked like he was backing away toward his door, as Crystal laughed and raised both her arms to wave him away.

"Before you go... do either of you know Walker Wolf in the Business Department?" I asked.

"I know he comes from Texas," Crystal said.

"And money," Jim said. "I mean he is a nice guy and all, but he comes from a rich family. I was talking to him about snowboarding, and he mentioned learning at his family's cabin at Telluride, and how as a kid he always liked going there rather than St. Moritz. Yikes, I've got to get to class, I'm teaching chi square today in my stats class." Jim turned to head down the hall to his office.

Crystal stood, unmoving, next to me as Jim walked off, then quietly asked, "Why are you asking about Walker Wolf?"

She had waited until Jim was gone to broach this. She was preternaturally still. Crystal knew something. I couldn't tell from her behavior if he was someone she liked or not. Walker was a good-looking man, and Crystal might be interested in him. I didn't want to tell her my unconfirmed suspicions if she had a thing for him.

I reached for a neutral comment.

"I don't know. I met him at Richardson's the other day. And I've kind of heard some things. I'm just trying to get a read on the guy."

Crystal crossed her arms and lifted one hand to her

chin, rubbing it slowly between her thumb and forefinger. After a minute, she nodded and said, "I've heard some things too. Do you remember a student named Sandra Choi?"

"The name is familiar, but I never had her in class. I think she was a senior my first year here. She was Psychology Student of the Year or something like that, wasn't she?"

Crystal nodded. "Yep, she was my advisee. Brilliant. Gorgeous. Popular. All-around fabulous."

I raised my eyebrows and waited.

"Well, she started out as a business major and was getting As but switched to Psychology." Crystal paused again.

Again, I waited to see if more would trickle out. It did.

"Like I said, she was 'popular,' with faculty as well as students." Another meaningful pause.

"Was she more popular with one particular faculty?"
Crystal nodded.

"I heard he liked smart and attractive students. I guess Sandra fit that description."

Crystal nodded again.

"Did Sandra tell you anything about it?" I asked.

"Yeah, they dated for a while, then he got tired of her and dropped her, and she was so hurt she transferred out of the department."

"Wow," I said. "Bad form."

"Yeah, and I don't think she is the only one he has done this with. I've heard rumors, and Sandra thought he dropped her because he was interested in another student."

"And maybe that other student was Alice

Bacunawa?"

"Maybe." Crystal shrugged her shoulders and held her hands upward in supplication. "I don't know any more than that."

"Thanks," I said. "That is actually a big help."

"Well, that Kai is a good boy. I think you are right. I just don't see him hurting anybody."

Crystal's phone rang. "How is your cold, Auntie? Are you feeling better?" Crystal smiled at me and lifted one hand in a small wave as she turned to head to her office, the other hand holding her phone to her ear. "You should just stay in bed. It's no good you being up cleaning the house for Uncle, just stay in bed."

She walked away, talking on her phone. I went back into my office. Should I call Walker Wolf or go see him in person? He was a lead I needed to follow up if I was going to help Kai. But I hated phone conversations, and when I looked at my watch, I realized I also had too much work to do this afternoon to traipse across campus looking for his office. Maybe tomorrow, never do today what you can put off until tomorrow. I grimaced. I hated it when I was a coward. But I sat down at my computer and re-opened my data file.

****

Gina, Rikki, and I met at Bayfront after work the next day for a walk-and-talk session. It gave us a chance to get a brisk walk in and catch up on what was happening in our lives. I was suffering a crisis of confidence. Doubts had been building the last couple days, that I could do anything to help Kai. And with Ben at work all the time and unavailable, I had called in my besties to help me hash it out.

"I mean, who do I think I am? I don't have police

training. I'm not a lawyer. I am probably just muddying the waters and getting in the way."

"Whoa, whoa, whoa, girlfriend." Gina stepped in front of me and put a hand on my chest, forcing me to stop. Rikki took one more step but stopped and swung around as soon as she saw what Gina had done. "You have a PhD, girlfriend. You know how to do research and make hypotheses and look for evidence. How do you think Kawika and police guys investigate? You know how to think analytically, girl. You are smart!"

"Yeah," said Rikki. "And you're a psychologist, so you know about people. You understand how their minds work. Whenever I don't understand why somebody did something crazy, I tell you, and you are able to help me understand it from their point of view."

"Right," said Gina. "Remember that big fight I got into with Kawika's sister... I never would have worked it out with her, if you hadn't talked me through what she might be feeling under all that bluster."

I smiled. How could I not, with Gina and Rikki to support me?

"You guys are the best!"

Chapter 12

A doctor's appointment

My doctor's appointment today was just a checkup, and I needed to get my birth control pill prescription renewed.

Or not. That was one of the topics I wanted to discuss with my doctor.

I was getting to the age where I needed to make a decision soon. Ben and I had been living together for a while now. Maybe it was time to start thinking about a baby.

We had a shortage of doctors on the island. Many places had that problem, but it was more of an issue on an island. Say you have allergies, the doctor flies over one day a week from Honolulu. Or at least the doctor used to come once a week when inter-island fares could be bought in packages of ten coupons for not much money. Now those docs only came once a month, or not at all. The only other option was flying to Honolulu if you needed a specialist. I was lucky and found a good doctor when I landed here. Unfortunately, she retired a year ago. I made the mistake of waiting until I needed to go to the doctor to check that list. When I finally checked the list, every single name I called- and I called all of them- was no longer taking new patients. The only place still accepting patients was the clinic that focused on

Native-Hawaiian and low income patients. They said they would take me, even though I didn't fall into either category.

I booked the earliest appointment I could get that day, eight thirty a.m. I have learned that for any medical appointment, the later in the day it is, the more likely an emergency has popped up, or someone's case was more complicated than expected, and I would have to wait. I booked doctor, or vet, appointments as early as possible in the day. It was with genuine disappointment that I walked in five minutes early to find the waiting room full of people. There was an old woman in her eighties, another woman, around thirty, a little girl about two, and a young woman in her late teens who looked to be her mother. There were also two young men, strongly built and I guess late twenties. All of them, apparently, were ahead of me. I gave the nurse my name and settled in to wait. I had the latest stack of papers that needed grading in the car, so after filling out the obligatory stack of 'new patient' forms, I went back out to the parking lot, grabbed my papers, and returned to take the last seat.

As I headed for the only empty seat, next to the two burly young men, a nurse entered from the hallway next to the reception desk and called out, "Cleo Cooper?"

I looked up, surprised.

"Yes? That's me."

"The doctor can see you now."

I looked around at all the people in the waiting room, and it occurred to me that they all looked like Pacific Islanders. Was this one of those instances where I was getting preferential treatment because I was white? Or because I had insurance? Should I say I was willing to wait my turn? Probably. But I really needed to get to the office in time to prep before class. I changed direction from the empty chair and headed toward the nurse. I snuck sheepish looks at the patients who had arrived earlier than me but were kept waiting. None of them acted disgruntled. My guilt lifted somewhat as I went in for the visit.

I did those uncomfortable things that women have to do every couple of years. And I asked the doctor about birth control and pregnancy now that I'm in my thirties. It was a sobering conversation.

"It is medically possible for woman to have babies later in life nowadays. And you are healthy," my doctor said. Her eyebrows scrunched together. "But you should know it involves more complications and risks to mothers and their babies. If you want to get pregnant, you should plan to spend a year trying, and do it sooner rather than later. A woman's ability to get pregnant starts declining at around thirty and drops rapidly around thirty-five years old. And you are what?" She lifted my chart up, her eyes searching it.

"Thirty-two," I told her.

"Thirty-two." Her eyes raised from the chart, and she looked at me, a kind smile on her face.

I always pictured children in my future, but to feel like I needed to make that decision now… I wasn't sure I was ready. I wasn't sure we were ready.

Maybe we were, though. I think I would be a good mom, and Ben, a great dad. But would we be the same kind of parents? Would we be good together as parents? I liked to travel, and Ben hated to leave the island. And speaking of raising kids on the island. It was a wonderful place for kids to grow up, at least until they got into school. While there were a few standouts, most of the schools here left a lot to be desired.

I shook my head. I was getting ahead of myself.

"I hear what you are saying, Doctor. For now let me get a new prescription for birth control. I can always go off next month."

She nodded and left the room.

I felt a pang of regret but realized it was the only decision I could make at this point. I should talk to Ben about this. I wasn't the only one involved in this decision. But that reminded me of Ali's pregnancy. *I wonder why she didn't tell Kai. Was she considering ending the pregnancy? Or maybe Kai wasn't the father?*

That was what I should focus on now, not a baby for Ben and me. We had talked around the issue before… for sometime in the future. But not now, not while Kai was in jail with a dead girlfriend who was pregnant with his baby. Ben and I could think about this when Kai was out of jail and cleared of Ali's murder.

Having talked myself down from my momentary freak out, I paid my copay and started to leave. As I left through the same reception area I'd entered, I noticed all the same people were there, but in motion. With one addition, a frail, little bird of an old man with a vacant expression on his face and claw-like hands resting indifferently on the arms of his wheelchair.

Ah, I knew what was going on. Those people in the waiting room were all family members, there to support the one grandfather. The older woman must be his wife, the younger woman was translating and getting instructions and information for the people who must be her grandparents. As she finished up with the nurse, she scooped up the little one and asked the teenager, "Was she good?"

I didn't hear the answer because the teenager had exited in front of the woman who must have been her mother, and her role must have been to babysit while her mom helped the grandparents. The only mystery left was the purpose of the two young men, because they, also, left with the family. That question was answered in the parking lot. I walked out of the clinic in time to see the two burly young men lifting the wheelchair into the back of a truck. They must have lifted the grandfather in and out of the car into the wheelchair and then put the wheelchair on and off the truck. The young men soon drove away, following the large sedan containing the rest of the family. I smiled at this classic example of collectivism. All of those people took time off work or school, because someone in the family needed their help. It was nice to see in action, and the smile stayed on my face all the way to campus.

I put in a full day at work and considered staying late to finish up a project when I realized this was one of the rare nights Ben left the office at a reasonable hour. I headed home, hoping to catch him in a good mood, I had something I wanted to talk to him about.

****

"Don't you get how lucky we are? Most people in this world don't get a paid sabbatical every six years. And of those lucky few, most of them don't have a partner who *also* gets a sabbatical. And of those extremely fortunate few, almost *never* do those sabbaticals fall at the same time. I mean it would be laughing in the face of the Universe's largesse for us *not* to take advantage of this opportunity to travel together!"

I took a deep breath to calm myself. Our talk was not going as I had hoped. I had come home, full of ideas and plans. I'd start with the sabbatical discussion and then shift to the bigger, baby issue. We never progressed past the sabbatical, though. I laid out ideas, and Ben had shot them down without considering even one.

Ben shrugged and took a slow drink from his beer. "I've told you, I can do my research here. I don't need to go anywhere else."

He took another slow drink from his beer, watching me. He wiped his mouth with the back of his hand. "And what about Kai? What if the case against him is still ongoing? What will happen with your investigation?" He lifted both hands, one holding the beer bottle and made air quotes when he said the word investigation.

My mood darkened.

Ben and I were on the back porch. We had added it onto our little house last year. It was raised, like the rest of our living space, and extended from our back door off the kitchen. It gave the dog a sheltered place to do her business underneath the porch during our rainy weeks. And when we sat in just the right place, we had an ocean view. Through two sets of telephone lines, with a tangerine tree on the left and an orchid tree on the right, I could see a patch of pink and baby-blue sky lying atop the slate-gray ocean. The breaker wall protecting Hilo Bay looked like just another electrical wire from here.

I knew Ben didn't want to travel over his sabbatical, but I have been trying to change his mind for the last six months. We had a deadline to get our applications in, and I had assumed by now we would have come up with a plan and a place where we could both do new and interesting research. In academics, after a professor received tenure, they could apply to conduct research and study somewhere else for a semester. The idea was to help us keep up to date with research that was going on around the world and stimulate our creative juices and motivation. Some of my colleagues grumbled that the salaries of professors were low. They pointed to other professions like physicians or lawyers that also required four to six years post-graduate training, and all made more money than faculty on average. But I figured a paid sabbatical every six years covered that disparity. Give me travel over a few extra dollars at the end of the month. If faculty wanted more money, they could go into industry and receive larger salaries, but they wouldn't get a sabbatical. Or have the freedom to study what interests them. I'll drive my fourteen-year-old car, and happily live in our little house, to have that freedom.

I thought Ben would come around and agree to travel with me. I'd found Marine Science research centers in California and Woods Hole in Massachusetts. Researchers were doing dolphin work in Hong Kong and Australia too. And for each place, I also found someone doing some interesting work in my area. I had laid out ten options. Ben hadn't even looked at them. He just said no. And now he was belittling my attempts to help Kai. To say I was frustrated at this moment was like saying Big Bird was sort of yellow.

I took a deep breath, and a thought occurred to me. Ali had wanted to move to the mainland. I remember her saying that at the gatherings at our house. Kai was Hawaii-born and never wanted to leave. I wondered if they had fights like Ben and I were having.

I heard shrieks of laughter. The neighbor kids who lived across the street were playing in the front of our house. They took over our narrow street as part of their kickball field, and the travelers palm in our front yard was third base. Their boisterous game was one of the reasons we had moved to the porch on the back of the house. Their cheers, jeers, and howls of excitement could still be heard back here, but at a more pleasant level.

I didn't want to draw any lines in the sand with Ben, but I was fed up. Early in our relationship Ben had traveled with me one summer to a conference. He hated it and never traveled with me again. I made the mistake of trying to show him too many places, hoping he would find something to enjoy. But we only spent a day or two in each spot. He never had a chance to get comfortable, and I think he felt off-balance the entire trip. At the time I realized how much he disliked it but couldn't change our itinerary. Ever since then I've pondered the situation. I thought if we could go somewhere for three months, then he could get settled and feel more at home. I have been looking forward to our sabbatical together. It would be a big step for us, for our relationship. Ben and I were good together, and we have had conversations about moving on to 'next levels.' But how could I bring up the baby issue when he wouldn't even discuss sabbatical options with me? I wasn't sure I wanted to permanently tie myself to a man who won't travel with me. And dammit, he could be right about Kai. How was I supposed to help him? I wasn't getting anywhere. Why should I give up my travel plans tilting at windmills?

Ben must have read my thoughts.

"I know you're disappointed. You always need someplace new, some new excitement. I feel like Hawaii is paradise. Our life here is perfect. To spend money to travel somewhere I'm not going to like just seems crazy to me. I'm not sure why you can't be happy here, with me, Suki, and our farm."

What could I say to that? I mimicked him and took a long slow drink of my wine and kept my mouth closed. How could I explain that I didn't think there was one single perfect place in the world? There were so many wonderful ways of living. Hawaii was one, yes, but there were others. I thought of the impossibly breathtaking mountain villages of Switzerland. Or Paris, with its boulangeries, fromageries, and women in elegant dresses and four-inch heels running down steps to catch a metro. I thought of eating dinner with a large group of Italian psychologists where I was stuffed after the second course, but they kept laughing and insisting I try the third and fourth and fifth course… that were all made especially for me. I thought of Tbilisi with its buildings from the single-digit centuries, lit up with colored lights and a decadently rich dish of walnuts and zucchini. And asking the young Georgian psychologist sitting next to me if it was safe to walk around alone in the evening with all of the 'displaced' young men that hung around in large groups on the street. And her look of surprise when she answered, "Of course it is safe. They are just looking for work, why would they hurt you?"

How could I explain this to Ben? The crazy wonderfulness that could unpredictably appear in the unexpected places of this cornucopia of a world. The one time we had traveled together, all he had seen, all he had noticed, was how each place was not Hawaii. Not his one version of perfection.

I took a deep breath, and reminded myself of all the traits I admired in Ben. But just as quickly would jump into my mind, 'But do I want to spend the rest of my life traveling alone? Do I want to spend my life with a man who has no sense of adventure? And what if we had kids? If I wanted to show them the world, would I have to do that alone?'

"I need to go out for a while," I said.

Ben's eyebrows shot up. I was the talker, the let's-work-this-out person in the relationship. Not this time. I have worked out as much as I could work out for the moment. I was worried about Kai, and as great a guy as Ben was, I just couldn't figure out if he was the 'one' for me.

Chapter 13

A no good, very bad day

It was a dark, blustery day, with a feeling of misfortune in the air. Or maybe there was just a black cloud suspended over me. After our confrontation last night, I drove to Liliuokalani Park and walked. Finally perching on the wall, I watched the evening light sparkle on Hilo Bay while Mauna Kea rose serenely, a dark shadow towering silently over Hilo. I don't know how long I sat there, watching the colors change and fade into grays and blacks. Some fishermen farther down the wall were drinking beer, and eventually their loud, drunken banter roused me to go back to my car. But I wasn't ready to go home and drove around the corner to Kam Avenue and Bayfront and parked in front of my canoe club's halau. I walked past the canoes and sat in the sand, hearing more than seeing the gentle waves lap the shore. The calmness of the bay eventually pacified my spirit. I didn't decide anything, but I realized the decision could wait until another day. I arrived home late, and Ben was already asleep. He left a note on the table that he had to leave early in the morning before I would be up. I didn't want us to start another day with things strained, so I decided to get up early and try to somehow bridge the gap with him. I tossed and turned all night, thinking and rethinking what I should, and should not, say to Ben in the morning. I didn't fall asleep until around three a.m.

When I woke up, Ben was gone.

I had the whole day ahead of me to 'stew in my own juices' as my mother would say. It was Saturday, so I made the usual round at the farmer's market, the blustery omen I'd awoken to held true. My favorite lettuce mix had sold out, there were no shishito peppers that Ben liked, and when I stopped at my favorite bakery, they had sold out of not only my favorite, salmon and artichoke baby quiche, but also my second, third, and fourth choices for a treat.

I gave up on errands and took the dogs up to the farm. It was actually Ben's farm. We didn't move to Hawaii together, we met after arriving. When I landed, I bought the little house downtown where we live. Ben, when he landed, rented a tiny apartment and bought this piece of property ten miles north of Hilo on the Hamakua coast. It was populated with a few cows, chickens, hardwoods, and bamboo. It was Ben's playground. He grew up in Nebraska, farming was in his roots. It was also Suki's playground and favorite place to run. This was Bella's first visit. It was the first time I've had her off-leash in such a large area. It was a joy to see her build up some of that famous borzoi speed. The wind and light rain didn't bother the dogs, and I sat on our covered deck, wrapped in my sweatshirt with a good book, and watched restless clouds meander through the sky.

It felt strange to be at the farm without Ben. But he was on the other side of the island with a group of students collecting data. Normally, Kai would have led that expedition, but, well, that wasn't an option now. And today Ben probably didn't mind an escape from the tension between us.

Suki was delighted. With her black coat, she got hot quickly when galloping around the farm and needed frequent splashes in the stream. Today it was cool enough that after her first dunking, she could explore uninterrupted in her hunt for mongoose and wild pig trails. She loved to track a mongoose. Her ears would lift with an excitement I loved to watch. The puppy bounced and frolicked behind her. Bella's white coat illustrated how deep she'd gone in the stream and that she had followed Suki through the recent 'pig digs' by the level and density of the mud on her coat. I couldn't figure out what we were going to do with the puppy. As cute as she was, Ben's allergies were getting worse the longer we had her with us. Bouviers, like Suki, had a 'hypoallergenic' coat. Borzois did not. We could manage a while longer, but if Kai was convicted...

"Stop it," I said aloud. I couldn't think like that.

Suki stopped in midstride and turned to look at me. The puppy, not so observant, kept running right into Suki's backside. I smiled.

"Good girl, Suk! I was talking to myself, but I appreciate you listening. It's okay."

And with the "okay," Suki resumed her hunt for a mongoose whose trail she was probably following. I had to quit thinking negative thoughts about Kai. I know he wouldn't kill Ali. I just couldn't figure out how to convince the police.

I promised Auntie Charmaine.

I would keep poking around and see if I could turn something up that I could pass on to Gina's husband. I was determined to follow up early next week on the business professor, Walker Wolf, who might have been having an affair with Ali. And today I could stop by and talk to Mason on my way home. I could check on how the shop was doing and see if Mason had any other ideas on how we could help Kai's case.

I fed the cows and loaded the dogs into the car to go in search of Mason. Both Suki and Bella were exhausted and curled up on the back seat. Suki took up most of the room, but the pup managed to squeeze in and snuggled next to Suki. They were both asleep before I'd closed and locked the gate behind us. I stopped first at the dive shop. It was Saturday afternoon so it should be open. As I pulled in to the empty parking lot, I saw the "closed" sign on the door. I parked and got out to see if Mason was in the back. Maybe he was working with a customer in the loading area in back where people picked up equipment. But there was no sign of him. Checking all the doors, I found them all locked. When I got back around to the front, I looked through the window with one last, fleeting hope I'd see Mason. No luck. I climbed back into the car with the dogs sleeping and drove to Mason's house.

When I arrived, I found a closed garage door and no car in the driveway. I couldn't tell from the street if he was home. The dogs were sleeping, and the light rain had stopped, so I rolled the windows two thirds of the way down to allow airflow for them, and got out. When the puppy heard the door shut, she woke up and climbed into the front seat.

"Hmm, I'm not sure I trust you unsupervised in my car if you are awake," I said to Bella.

I reopened the door, pulled a plastic bag out of the side pocket of my car where I always keep an emergency supply, snapped a leash on Bella, and let her jump out of the car. Suki raised her head and looked at me. I looked back at those intelligent eyes and told her I would be right back but I wanted to make sure the puppy didn't pee in the car. Suki put her head back down and appeared to go back to sleep. I knew she didn't understand what I was saying, but sometimes it was hard to make myself believe that.

I followed the pup around Mason's front yard for a few minutes until she found the perfect spot, squatted, and peed. It didn't look as if Mason was home. All the curtains were open to catch the breeze, and I didn't see any movement inside the house.

But, it couldn't hurt to try. I'd knock on Mason's door before returning Bella to the car, just in case he was there. I was steps from the front door when a woman in her late sixties came flying out of a neighboring house, wearing a colorful skirt and waving one of her arms, clearly unhappy about something. She was local, some mysterious mix of southeast Asian and Polynesian, about five feet nothing, with brown creased skin, black hair going gray, and a thickening around the middle.

"No, no, no! I told him dat dog no can come back," she said. "Dat dog cry and cry and keep my keikis awake when dey suppose to nap!"

The woman reached us, and the puppy backed up until she bumped into my legs, then circled around behind them, tangling herself in her leash.

"I'm sorry," I said. "I'm just checking to see if Mason is home. The puppy was just in my car with me, she isn't staying."

"I *know* she no stay. I no let you leave dat dog here like dat last girl." A broom appeared out of nowhere, she must have been carrying it with her, but I didn't see it until she started pushing it toward Bella who had ventured to take a step out from behind me. With little jabbing motions toward the puppy, she said, "Go home, you get back in dat lady's car, I tol' Mason you no can come back. You look cute, but you make lotta problems."

I scooped Bella up in my arms, hoping to keep her safe from the broom, I didn't want her terrorized. Hell, I wasn't crazy about that broom either.

"Ok, ok, ok," I said, backing up to the car. I looked over my shoulder for the door handle. Suki had woken up and had her head out of the window, watching us intently. She must not sense we were in any danger, because I didn't hear her low rumbling growl that could make our house vibrate. She looked surprised and curious as I awkwardly jerked the door open, with the puppy still in my arms, and encouraged Bella to get in. The pup jumped gratefully in the car with Suki, who looked quizzically at her, as if wondering how she could have gotten into so much trouble so quickly.

The woman had followed us to the car, but as she saw me deposit Bella inside, she stepped back and smiled.

"I no mean disrespect," she said. "You nice lady, not like dat udda one, but dat dog dug holes in my yard, tore up one pepper bush, and chase one cat. When I make Mason keep her inside, she cry and cry all day and keep my keikis up in da afternoon. And I *need* dat quiet time when da keiki sleep," she said, with just a hint of sheepishness in her voice. "I not so spry as when dea mom was little."

"Sure, I understand," I said, relieved that the broom was no longer pointing at me. "But are you sure it is the same dog? It belongs to a friend of mine, I didn't think the puppy had ever been to Mason's house."

"Same dog," she said firmly before she turned around and marched back to her house. I didn't go back and knock on Mason's door. I looked back at the curtains in the window and, for a moment, thought I saw movement there but couldn't be sure. Anyway, if he was home, he would have heard his neighbor yelling at me and come out to see what the commotion was all about. And there was no sign of him.

I drove back to the house and gave the dogs a quick rinse, to get the farm mud off them. Then brought my laptop onto the back deck so the dogs could dry while I got a little work done. The Wi-Fi reached back here, so I checked email first. I quickly answered a couple of students with questions, then with curiosity opened an email with 'Grade Challenge' in the header. My bad day continued. The student who had stormed out of my office last week because I wouldn't accept his super-late paper was going above my head and had filed an appeal with the dean.

I groaned. Now I had to produce a defense of my decision. The student didn't have any grounds for having it overturned, but I was required to collect and organize proof of my policy, as well as any evidence I could find that I have been consistent in its implementation. This was going to take hours.

I thought about moving on to what really needed doing, my presentation for the conference. But my heart wasn't in it. Frustrated by the dean's email, I dove into preparing my response.

****

I looked up and realized it was starting to get dark. Time flies when I was mad, motivated, and armed with the internet. I petted the dogs at my feet. They were dry.

I gathered up my stuff and let them follow me into the house. Ben would be heading home when it got dark in Kona, so about two hours from now, he'd be coming in the front door. Maybe I would surprise him with a nice dinner. I didn't want this sabbatical fight to destroy us. Maybe if I killed him with kindness, I could win him over. I'd gotten veggies at the market, as well as a nice piece of fresh ono. That wouldn't take long, so I had time to jump in the shower.

Right on time, Ben walked in the front door. The dogs got up to greet him. Suki slowly, but with grace, Bella, frantically, eagerly, tripping all over herself. Ben smiled as he scratched their heads. I came out of the kitchen, carrying a beer for him.

"I bet you're ready for this after a long day."

"Yeah, thanks." He gave me a smile, as he took the beer out of my hand. It was easy to read the relief on his face, thankful that he was getting a reprieve from last night's sabbatical fight.

"I made dinner for you too, ono and veggies cooked in parchment paper." I was proud of myself. I didn't get fancy with my cooking very often.

Ben's smile transformed into slight apprehension. "Oh gosh, sorry, Cleo. I didn't know you were cooking. We stopped in Waimea and got burgers on the way back."

It figured. Once a day starts off with bad juju… bad juju would follow me the rest of the day. As soon as I woke up and felt the blustery misfortune in the air, I should have turned around and crawled back into bed.

Chapter 14

Weezy

I had no luck catching Walker Wolf in his office this week. I also failed to reach Kawika at the police station to tell him about my conversation with Rikki and the possibility that Kevin's girlfriend, Mele, had a motive for killing Ali. We had been playing phone tag. I'd leave a message at the station, and he would call back when I was in class. Maybe my best option was to pass the information on to Gina and let her tell her husband.

I was caught up on grading and had an empty Sunday in front of me. Ben had gone to his lab to get caught up on all the work Kai would have done last week, so I had the day to myself. Well, me and the dogs. I looked down at them sleeping at my feet.

Baby Bella had three speeds: eating, playing, and sleeping. While I didn't seem to be making much progress on finding a plausible alternative to who, and how, someone had killed Ali, at least I could take the best possible care of the puppy Kai inherited. That way, when Kai was finally cleared, he would have a healthy, well-adjusted, partially-trained Bella to welcome him home. And maybe help him move on with his new life, without Ali.

Before I could act on that thought, my phone rang. It was Anna, my oldest friend. We not only grew up together, but we had both stayed in school and gotten our PhDs. Anna was on the faculty of a college in North Carolina, and even though we were now on opposite ends of the country, we stayed in touch.

"Hey, girl, what's up?"

"Hey, yourself. I need to catch up on grading, and it looks like I'll be spending all weekend on it. I needed a break, so I figured if I can't fly to Hawaii for a mini-vacation, the next best thing is to call my best friend who lives there." Anna said. "Tell me every non-work detail of your weekend so I can live vicariously through you."

I laughed. "Nothing exciting, I was just getting ready to take the dogs to the park."

"Oh, that's right! You told me you were taking care of that murdered girl's dog. A young borzoi, right? How is she doing?"

"Well, Bella is young, and I don't think she has been socialized at all. She jumps and tucks her tail. Cowers at every new noise or experience. I've made up my mind to work on that."

"Good. I'm sure that's all she needs. But is she old enough to take her into public?"

"Yeah, but there are two schools of thought on the age it should be started. In the US, and Hawaii, we are warned of all the diseases out there on every public sidewalk. Even with all the vaccinations, the immune systems of young puppies might not be up to the job. Most dog trainers won't allow puppies to come to a 'puppy' class until they are sixteen weeks old."

"I sense a 'but' coming…" Anna said.

"But… a friend of mine in Europe showed me notes from her vet. They believe that the critical socialization period is between eight and sixteen weeks. And if it hasn't happened by then, it will never happen. If that is correct, all of our puppies in the US are going to wind up with terribly socialized dogs."

"So what did you do with Suki?"

"I think the truth lies somewhere in the middle. I made sure Suki had all her shots, and I avoided stray animals when she was young, but I got her out and about as much as possible the first year of her life. And this little borzoi, Bella, is going to see the world as long as I've got her."

"I can't wait until I live somewhere I can have a dog," Anna said. "You have to promise to be my dog godmother when that happens."

"Promise!" We chatted a few minutes more with her catching me up on why she was behind on grading... a man, until she sighed.

"I better get back to work. You go take your dogs to the park, lucky girl, while I pay penance with my grading."

"Bye, Anna, say 'Hi' to your mom from me when you talk to her."

"Right back at you, Cleo."

I gathered up both dogs and went to Liliuokalani Park. The park faces Hilo Bay, with a view of the Hamakua coast and Mauna Kea. There was a short pier with a couple of benches in the middle of the ocean side of the park, which usually had fisherman and people in T-shirts, board shorts, and 'slippahs,' just hanging out with friends. The rest of the park was a Japanese-style garden with Hawaiian-style fishponds winding under a myriad of diverse bridges. This jewel sat between hotels and a bridge to little Coconut Island on one side, and on the other side, Suisan Fish Market where fishermen delivered and sold their catch each morning. Liliuokalani Park was a favorite place to exercise or meet up for people of all ages and backgrounds.

The first week I arrived in Hilo, a celebration of Queen Liliuokalani's birthday was commemorated. More than twenty hula clubs and people from five to 105 danced hula throughout the park while helicopters circled above, releasing thousands of orchid blossoms over their heads. The dancers honored the former queen who had so loved her people that she abdicated her throne to save their lives from an unwinnable war. The spectacle was unforgettable and one of the reasons I loved Hilo. These festivities, whether it was the annual dragon boat racing or mochi-pounding, were 'for the people and by the people' celebrations. The focus wasn't to attract tourists but to honor traditions, values, and heritages. Okay, maybe Merrie Monarch pushed that boundary a little, with hula halaus' from all over the world, and more visitors than locals in attendance. But it was Hilo's one claim to fame, so who could fault them for that?

Today, feral kittens played in the roots of an ever-spreading banyan tree. Each banyan was named for a famous visitor or local dignitary who had been honored back in the 1930s by the planting of a baby banyan. Most of the names were unknown to me, but there were a few banyan-planters, like Babe Ruth and Cecil B DeMille, that I recognized. Bridges of all shapes and sizes crawled, sprawled, and danced over the fishponds connecting tiny islands and peninsulas in the Japanese-style garden. There were small arches, tall arches, and long, flat bridges, mere inches above the brackish water during tidal changes. A Japanese-style gazebo in the middle of another bridge was well-used by the community, to shelter from rain, too-bright sunshine, or steal a kiss. My favorite crossings were the stepping stone bridges. Flat rocks were placed, disconnected, but in a line, a step's length away in the water until one reached the peninsula on the other side.

Traversing these bridges was excellent practice for the puppy to learn to negotiate different types of surfaces and experiences. Unfortunately, to hold the stepping stones in place, the water was shallow and the mud deep. Seeing the bottom so close, Bella stepped off the stone into knee-deep mud. It was a messy struggle, but I got her loose and sort of rinsed off, although there was a gray look to her fur from the bottom of her paws up to her no-longer-white belly. I looked for a bench after that escapade. It was time to take the lazy approach to puppy socialization.

We found a bench in the shade of a banyan tree, facing the ocean, with a parade of dogs, baby strollers, bikers, and a group of teenagers with a boombox loud enough to shake the bench, walking past us. Myna birds swooped in to land nearby, which stimulated the long-legged pup. A couple walked by with an excited little dog and sat at a nearby bench. Bella pulled at her leash, but Suki's only indication she had noticed was a twitch of her ears. I wished her tail wasn't docked. If it was wagging, I would get up and walk her over to introduce her and the puppy to the couple and their little dog. But without a tail to indicate her mood, I had to rely on other cues. Today, Suki didn't seem to be quite herself. Maybe she wasn't feeling good. I wouldn't press the encounter, even though it would have benefited the puppy.

I pulled out a recently published article of a

colleague that I had brought with me. But instead of reading it, I sat back and enjoyed the sun, sea breeze, and people parading along, laughing with the joy of the day. My eyelids were beginning to get heavy when I recognized one of the joggers heading toward us.

I smiled and waved as Gina jogged over to us, pulling her earbuds out of her ears as she came. We kissed both cheeks, and she crouched down to give a pet, and get a lick, from Suki and Bella. Smiling, she collapsed, sweaty and breathing hard, on the other end of my bench.

"Hey, I was going to call you today, I haven't been able to reach Kawika at the station. Can you tell him we might know of another person who could have a motive to want Ali out of the way?"

"Sure, but I've got some news too."

"What?"

"Ali's brother is back in town."

I set my journal article down hard on the bench. "What did you say?"

Gina smiled. "I knew you would find that interesting."

"I thought you told me he was in jail? That Ali put him in jail."

"I guess he got out."

"Do you know him? Can you find out if he was out before, or after, his sister was killed?"

"I know who he is, but I don't know him *that* well. I mean, geez, he's a drug dealer who just got out of prison. That's like, scary. I don't want to go try look him up."

She was right. It was scary. I had to work up the nerve whenever I called Walker Wolf, a professor. But

Gina was my connection to the local community. She grew up here and had a huge family. If she didn't know somebody, she knew somebody who knew, or was related, to that somebody. As we sat there and stared out at the ocean, I was overcome by a wave of helplessness. Who the hell did I think I was? I'm a haole digging into past conflicts and tragedies in a community that has drowned in conflicts and tragedies. Native Hawaiians had one of the lowest per-capita incomes in the islands but some of the highest rates of diabetes, cancer mortality, domestic violence, and alcoholism. For a people with a beautiful culture, they have more than their share of struggles.

The nice thing with an ocean, though, was just as it carried dead fish and garbage onto shore; if you sat with it long enough and watched those waves, the breakers would wash that mess back out to sea. So, we watched those waves, me with the dogs, and Gina next to me, intermittently squirting water from her water bottle into her mouth, staring at the same rhythmic ocean. Suddenly Gina stood up.

"I think I see somebody who might know about Ali's brother." I could tell we had both been swimming through the same wave of futility as Gina picked our conversation up at the exact place we'd dropped it. But Gina's comment raised my hopes.

"Who?"

"See that woman over there on the pier in the green shorts and white tank top. She's standing next to the guy that's fishing on the left side."

I could see who she was talking about. She had sun-darkened skin and long tangled black hair that hung down her back, half in and half out of a long braid, as thick as a young monkeypod tree trunk.

"I see her. You know her?"

"We went to high school together."

Maybe I was looking at the wrong person. This woman looked to have led a long hard life and be twenty years older than Gina. I scanned the pier for another woman that fit Gina's description. Nope. She was one of only two women out there and the only one wearing green shorts and white shirt.

I turned to look directly at my friend.

"You went to high school with her? She looks way older than you."

Gina's lips compressed.

"We were friends as kids, but she took a different path in high school. She got into drugs and ran away from home to live on the beach with some guy. You know what my parents are like. I had a curfew until I was twenty and got in *major* trouble if I didn't make the honor roll every year."

Gina shrugged, but her face was cemetery serious. "There, but for the grace of God, go I. Remind me after this to give my parents a call and say thanks." Gina watched her childhood playmate with tight lips and a knitted brow.

"I didn't really track her, but I know she was pretty heavy into crack and meth for several years. Someone told me she was doing better lately, but I think that guy she's talking to is no good." Gina sat there for another minute as if searching for some similarity between this worn-out woman and the girl she used to know.

"Come on." Gina rose and walked purposefully over to her former childhood friend. The woman cackled at something the fisherman has said, trying to play the coquette but utterly failing. I followed Gina, dragging my feet like I used to do when as a kid, my friends would pull me into a haunted house on Halloween. Both dogs in tow, behind us, as we approached the sketchy pair, Suki stepped up to my side.

The woman cackled again, this time with delight, arms flung into the air dramatically, although the right hand dropped quickly to catch the cigarette that almost fell out of her mouth with the motion. She had the jerky movements of someone with a large buzz on.

"I like your dog!" she sang out, pointing at Suki. Then looking up at Gina. "Dat you, Gina-girl? I don see you long time."

"Howzit, Weezy," Gina said. Her eyes flicked occasionally to the man fishing next to the witch-woman, Weezy.

Weezy's eyes found Suki again. And the semi-vacant look warmed. "I really like your dog," she said again, her smile faded as her voice softened. "Nobody mess wid you wid a dog like dat."

My heart broke for this train wreck of a woman. My comfortable, safe life felt like an embarrassment of riches in the face of her vulnerability. I didn't know what to say.

Luckily, Gina stepped up to the plate.

"I guess you heard about Ali Bacunawa."

Weezy nodded, her eyebrows scrunched in worry, but she remained silent.

Gina continued. "I was just wondering with my friend here"—and Gina's head jerked in my direction—"about her braddah. I heard he got outta jail."

Weezy nodded again. "Yeah, he out."

"You know if he and Ali wen make up befoa she

wen die?" Gina asked.

Weezy made a twisting shrug and ducked her head a little, glancing at the fisherman next to her out of the corner of her eye. He appeared to be engrossed in his fishing. If he was paying any attention to us, he gave no sign.

"I heah stuff." The sound of gentle waves washing against the lava rocks made Weezy's words barely audible.

Gina took a step closer. "Wat you heah?" she said in a low voice. It amazed me how easily Gina crossed back and forth like a traffic light between Hawaiian creole, with its lyrical cadence, dropped consonants, verbs, and prepositions - and sounding like a Californian, 'th's intact, but lacking melody.

"Well, I heah…" Weezy began and stepped away from the fisherman. She clearly enjoyed the attention from us, even if she didn't want the fisherman to know what she was saying.

"Wat I heah, is dat Ali felt bad, she felt real bad, about her braddah. You know, him goen jail an all. Dey wuz like two peas in one kine pod growin' up. Wen he got back to Hilo, he wuz one mad mudda-fucka, but she try make it up to him. She tol' him she got one guy who gonna marry her and take her to da mainland and live in one big house and she wuz goin' take him wid her if he want. But her braddah, cuz he mad, he no wanna go. He no even listen."

Fhwapp!

The fisherman jerked his pole up with vigor, hitting the nearby light pole, a nasty sneer on his face. "Hey bitch! You come fo' hep wid da fish- oh you come fo' fuckin' jabber wid dees bitches?"

Weezy, delighted that he wanted her attention, became all aflutter, like bamboo bouncing in a fierce wind—each stalk quivering and vibrating in a different direction. "I heah, I heah, I heah! Wat you need?"

"Grab da net, grab da mudda-fuckin' net!"

Weezy rushed toward the net, which leaned against the pier railing, but in her flapping and fluttering, she knocked the net pole, pushing it sliding to the ground, but not before it had fallen and bounced off of the fisherman's knee.

"Stupid fuckin bitch! Get da fuckin net!" Spittle flying, his face began to turn purple.

Weezy, with her buzz on, continued her happy flittering—but as she eagerly picked up the net, with its eight-foot pole attached, she knocked the fisherman's beer over, which had been sitting on the ground next to his chair.

Then his rant came in earnest. Even in her altered state, Weezy picked up on his fury. Her actions changed from happy and fluttering to clumsy, jerky, frightened motions.

Suki took a step forward, eyes intent on the fisherman, and the puppy was getting agitated by all the emotion. I backed away a few steps with the dogs. I didn't want Bella's leash getting tangled with the fishing gear and making things worse. Gina saw me step away and followed but continued without pausing to cross to the other side of the street. I looked back at Weezy and saw that she had finally gotten the pole to the fisherman and stared at him with rapt attention, a desperate eagerness to please on her face. The fisherman had calmed a bit and was focused on his fish.

I led the dogs across the street to join Gina, and we

watched them for a minute.

"You said he was a 'bad guy'… a drug dealer?"

"No, he's a user. He uses drugs and people. Not to mention he has an anger management problem. Most of the women who hang out with him wind up in the hospital."

We continued watching for a few minutes. The fisherman had stopped yelling and caught his fish. Weezy got him another beer from his cooler and sat nearby, watching his face. Waiting. For what I didn't know. Gina stretched her neck and rolled her shoulders. "Looks like he's calmed down—lets get outta here."

Chapter 15

A talk with Ben

I awoke to a seriously rainy day. Not our light, it-will-stop-in-a-few-minutes rain that we usually get, but piercing, pounding rain. It thundered on the tin roof and sent waves of cool air in the windows, not from regular wind patterns but due to a rapid displacement of air created by gallons of water drops falling from the sky. Water saturated the air. The street was empty, the neighborhood dogs were quiet, huddled under the eaves of the tin roofs. Suki lay stretched out at my feet, but Bella huddled under the dining room table as if she wanted a second layer of protection, not trusting the roof to withstand the onslaught. I had planned to work in the office this morning and force myself to track down Walker Wolf and ask him about his relationship with Ali.

There didn't appear to be any movement on Kai's case, at least no movement in the right direction. The DNA test on Ali's fetus was due to come back this week. I looked out at the waterfall coming off our eaves, battering the bird-of-paradise planted below the window, and decided I would put off the Walker Wolf confrontation for yet another day. Coward that I was.

I worked on my computer at the kitchen table but couldn't sit still during the cacophony of rain on our tin roof. I considered calling Anna, but I wouldn't be able to hear her over the roar of the downpour. I got up and looked in at Ben. He was working on his computer in the office.

I stuck my head in his door and Ben turned to me, "I figure it's a good day to make the revisions on this paper I've been meaning to do. There is nothing important enough to make me go out in this. How about you?"

"Yeah, I think I'll work from home this morning, too. I'm going to make a pot of coffee, you interested?"

"Sure." He smiled at me and then looked back at his screen and started typing again. The noise of the rain on the roof didn't seem to bother him. I made coffee and found an open box of ginger snaps in the cabinet. I put a handful on a plate and took them on a tray with two mugs of coffee to Ben's door.

"Can we chat?" I asked.

Things had been distant between us since our fight over the sabbatical. We had a lot going on, but relationships are like yards here in Hilo. If you don't work on them a little every week or so, a dark jungle would erupt and take over to the extent that chainsaws and bulldozers would be needed to recover. I'd rather not have to take a chainsaw to our relationship if I could head off problems with a bit of coffee talk.

Ben was aware of this predilection of mine and knew what was coming when he heard those words. After one last longing look at the journal lying open next to his laptop, he took a deep breath and forced a smile.

"Sure," he said and reached for the coffee. "Wow, you brought me ginger snaps, this must be serious." He grinned and crunched into one of three cookies he'd picked up in his hand.

I didn't find that funny. Was he implying I couldn't

do something nice for him? But I didn't want to fight. I narrowed my eyes and strained to smile. "I don't think it's serious yet. But I think we are getting off track."

Ben nodded. "I know, I know. I haven't done much with you." His head bobbed with each 'I know.' "But I'm short-handed, with Kai out of commission. You realize that, so I'm not in trouble, and you can't get mad. Right?"

My irritation began to uncoil. I pushed it back down.

"You aren't in trouble. I'm not *mad* at you. I just think the only time we see each other is when there is a problem to solve. All of our *fun* times are spent with other people."

Ben's mouth straightened, and his eyebrows went up on the last comment, his teasing attitude evaporated.

"Are you trying to tell me something?"

"Yes! No... not that, I mean the other people are Gina and Rikki... paddlers and swimmers... not like some guy or anything. But I think it's a problem. I know you don't like me to get all psychological, but if you are always paired with problems for me, and I'm always paired with problems for you, it's classical conditioning. We will condition ourselves to dread seeing each other. And if our fun times are always paired with someone else, well, you see where that could lead."

My voice trailed off. I didn't want to be overdramatic or threaten him, but I've seen too many good relationships split apart because people didn't pay attention to stuff like this.

Ben watched me as I spoke. After a minute he nodded his head.

"Okay, you are the psychologist. I'll trust you on this. What do we do?"

"We find the time to do something we both enjoy together."

Ben took a big slurp of his coffee. "OK. It sounds like a great idea, but are you going to be mad if I say I *really* have to get back to work now? As soon as I finish these revisions, I need to prep a lecture for that three-hour class I teach tonight, and I am nowhere close to being ready for it."

He at least had the decency to wait until I'd nodded, before he reached for the journal article he had been reading when I'd interrupted him. I picked up the tray, with the empty cookie plate and my coffee, and left. A glance over my shoulder found him reading the journal and slowly, absently, lifting the last ginger snap toward his open, waiting mouth.

Chapter 16

Walker Wolf

The rain cleared the next day, and Hilo sparkled. Mauna Kea crisply outlined against a china-blue sky, I breathed in the scent of ginger as I trekked across campus to the business department and found the office with 'William Walker Wolf, Assistant Professor, College of Business' on the door. I checked his door card with his schedule on it. As planned, my visit fell within his office hours. I knocked and waited. The smell of burned coffee drifted down the hall, and a copy machine ground out copies. I hated to think how much paper a university went through in a week. If we weren't shoving paper at students in the form of six-page syllabi, full of mandated announcements and notifications, students were shoving paper at us in the form of homework and term papers. We were moving to online and digital versions, but too slowly. How many forests have been felled in the name of higher education?

The door opened with an abrupt pull, and Walker Wolf stood there in all his glory. Dark hair falling over dazzling, deep-blue eyes, with thick dark lashes, and just a trace of crinkled lines radiating from the outside edges, like faint impressions on a notepad after the note has been torn off. Clues to a life enjoyed thus far. The blue of his eyes was set off by a tailored, cerulean shirt, tucked in to slim cut khakis, and leather shoes rather than the typical 'slippers' we all wore here in Hawaii. His high cheekbones were burnished bronze, with a small scar on the left side, an inch long. A puzzled but playful smile was on his face.

"Please come in." His smile broadened. "I know, we met at Richardson's. Cleo, right?"

"Right. Is this a good time? I wanted to talk to you about something. If you are busy, I can set up an appointment for later?"

He stepped back and waved me in. "I was just editing some proofs. You'll be a welcome break from that slog." And I was the recipient of another spectacular smile.

I stepped through the door in the direction he had gestured, to a seat. Walker Wolf's Texan heritage was on display. Like most faculty, he had floor-to-ceiling bookshelves on one wall, but in his case, a longhorn cow skull was balanced on the top shelf. An old, probably antique, Texas state map that had been personalized with arrows and faded red circles was framed and hanging on the wall next to his diplomas. An iron hat rack made from enlarged, stylized barbwire stood in one corner. Hanging on it was a pale, perfectly shaped cowboy hat banded with a leather strap, studded with silver stars and turquoise lumps. Both his office chair and the miniature easy chair he had directed me toward were covered in a patchwork of cowhide. And another small animal skin served as a rug. If I didn't know better, I'd think this office was at the University of Texas rather than Hawaii.

"To what do I owe this pleasure?" he asked, turning his desk chair to face me as he sat.

"Well..." I realized my hands were poised to start

flicking my fingernails, something I did when stressed. As soon as I became aware of it I stopped and laced my fingers together and folded them in my lap to keep them still.

"I guess you've heard about Alice Bacunawa's death. And that Kai Higa was arrested."

He nodded. The smile disappeared. His eyes focused on me like a raptor, searching my face for some hint of where I was going with this.

"Yeah, sure. Everybody has."

"Right. Well, I know Kai, I mean Ben and I know Kai pretty well, and we are convinced he didn't kill her." Walker remained silent, watching, waiting for me to continue. "So, well, I'm trying to talk to everybody who knew her to see if I can find any information that might help Kai's defense. And someone... suggested you knew her." My final sentence came out in a rush. It was remarkably stressful telling a colleague you think he might be a killer. But my words were out, and not too accusatory. I don't think. My turn to watch and wait.

Walker took a deep breath and slowly let it out, his eyes never leaving my face, assessing me. He spoke deliberately. "Yes. I knew Alice. She took a class from me. I don't know what you heard, but if someone implied that there was anything more than that, between her and I... then he or she was wrong."

I was prepared for a denial. Deciding two could play at the slow-response game, I waited a minute before I continued.

"Did she ever come to see you here in your office?" My glance strayed to the animal skin splayed on his office floor.

"Yes, but it was related to class, she wasn't doing

very well in it." He waved his hand dismissively.

"You only talked about classwork with her?"

"I just said she needed help with class, that's why she came in to see me."

Hmm, not a direct answer. "Did you ever meet her anywhere other than your office or the classroom?"

Wolf stood up, clenched his fists, then appeared to realize he had clenched his fists and unclenched them before he shoved them into his pockets. He made two large steps to stand in front of his window and look out at the campus, his back to me.

"There was one other time. I didn't initiate it. She found me at the Burger Joint, I go there sometimes after work to have a beer and unwind. One evening she come in about five minutes after me and sat down next to me at the bar." He turned around to face me. "I swear, I didn't invite her, and it wasn't arranged in advance."

"What happened? After you didn't invite her. . . at this 'un-arranged encounter.' "

"Well, small talk at first. She kind of made a play for me, but she wasn't my type."

Not his type? From what Crystal had said, the other student he had dated had the dark-haired local look, like Ali. And Ali was stunning. So I had to ask...

"What exactly is your type?"

"Smart. Smart, educated, cultured, ambitious." Walker pulled his hands out of his pockets and pointed in no general direction, for emphasis. "I'm planning on going somewhere. Hilo is a nice place to build a resume and experience a different walk of life, but no way I'm spending the rest of my life here. I'm going back to civilization in a couple of years. I'm not interested in a woman who can't maintain an intelligent conversation on a subject more complicated than surfing or bikini styles for more than five minutes -doesn't have time to read a newspaper or a book. A woman who expects to trade on her looks forever… or at least until she gets her hooks into some rich guy who will be her retirement plan."

I sat back. I don't know what I expected, but it wasn't this.

"And you thought Alice didn't fit that type."

"She was smart. I'll give you that, and ambitious." His mouth made a bitter twist. "But she had no self-discipline." Walker took a breath and swallowed. "She came to me with an idea for a new business. That was the class she took from me, 'Intro to Entrepreneurial Enterprises.' But that night at the bar, she was trying to seduce me because she wanted me to do all the research legwork, track down consumer statistics, like demographics on the potential target consumer groups, potential competitors, that kind of thing."

"And you didn't want to do that."

"No, I didn't. First of all, as I am sure you have already heard"—he looked like he had swallowed a big gulp of wine that had turned to vinegar—"I was already involved once with an undergrad. My department chair gently suggested it not happen again or I could expect to be turned down for tenure. Second of all, like I said before, I am attracted to women who can be partners, not freeloaders. She was a user, I could see that by the end of the first week of class."

I couldn't think of anything else to ask. He had described Ali exactly. Everything he said made sense.

"Thank you for talking to me. I'm sorry that I asked so many questions, I'm sure Kai didn't do it, and I'm trying to find some piece of information that will help." I stood up to go.

Walker nodded stiffly, accepting my apology, if not gracefully. But then again, maybe I wouldn't either if our positions were reversed.

As I stepped toward the door, I thought of something else and turned. "One last question while I'm here…" Walker, who had pulled out his office chair, looked at me, his mouth a straight line with both ends turned down, one eyebrow raised as his eyes bored into me. His impatience for my departure was palpable.

"What was Alice's business idea?"

His eyes, that had been drilling me with irritation, slid off me like an awkward puppy that someone sends down a playground slide. His posture changed from foreboding to defensive.

"To be honest, I don't remember," he said a little too quickly. "Do you have any idea how many business concepts my students bring to me?" He made an elaborate wave with the hand not gripping his desk chair, trying for dismissive but not quite pulling it off.

"I can't keep track of all of them, and this was months ago. I don't remember a thing about it. If you will excuse me, my publisher is waiting for these proofs." And he did everything but actually touch me, in an effort to push me out his door.

When I got back to my building, I took the back stairs that would open up near my office. As I pulled the door to the enclosed stairwell, the happy, earthy, chords of an ukulele floated and danced around me. It reminded me of street performers in Europe who set up in the subway to take advantage of the acoustics. No subways in Hilo, so our music-loving students would set up in the stairwell with their ukuleles to practice, teach a friend, or simply to escape lecture halls and computer labs with a musical interlude. I took the steps slowly, letting the sounds drift over me, hoping it would wash away the unpleasantness of the last conversation. It helped, but my steps were not quite slow enough. Traces of emotional pebbles lingered and lodged themselves somewhere between my shoulder blades as I exited the stairwell and walked into my office.

Chapter 17

Ali's brother

I finished my grading, stood up to stretch, and looked out the window. I found a baby-blue sky with a few cotton-ball clouds just waiting to be interpreted by dreamers on a beach blanket. At least that's what it looked like from my office window. But I needed to work on my presentation for Santa Fe. My old grad school friend, Tyler, would be there to support me, but there were influential power players in my field, like Luc Bastien, the organizer, who would also be there. I needed to prepare a first-class presentation. I took one last, longing look out the window before returning to my computer. My phone buzzed with an incoming text message from Ben.

—Want to do something fun with me now? I hear Richardson's calling?—

I turned off my computer, grabbed my bag, and texted back.

—I'll race you to my car!—

Ben beat me, but his office was closer. We both kept a towel and bathing suit in our cars. The back of Ben's truck had a mini clothesline they could dry on. I spread mine over my back seat. I grabbed my suit and towel and jumped in Ben's truck, which was parked nearby, and we drove to the end of Keaukaha Point, to Richardson's beach park.

After swimming with the fishes, literally, we made our way through the small crowd of kids jumping and chasing each other to the little black sand beach. We slid into the slippers we had left steps away from the water's edge and walked up the slight incline to the east of the black sand beach. We spread our towels on the point that rose about eight feet over the small waves that crashed onto lava rocks. It was our favorite spot. Very close to the water, but dry, no chance of a rogue wave catching you most days, and just off a footpath that led from one beach area to another, so most people walked right on by. Best of all, it was often empty, just waiting for us. Sun exposure was terrible for the skin, but it felt like heaven to have the sun warm my seawater-chilled skin.

I had just begun to dry off and could see Ben getting restless when a voice called out, "Dr. Harper!"

Ben turned his head and smiled. "Hey, Billy! Good job on your presentation on echinoids today. Your poster and description of collector sea urchins was great."

"Thanks Dr. H!" A big grin took over the young man's face.

"Billy-boy, where da fuck are ya?" a voice called from around the corner.

"Heah."

A second later another young man came around a naupaka bush, with a surfboard under his arm.

"Oh, deah you stay. We gon catch one wave oh what, brah?"

"Yeah, yeah, jus' one minute. Dis my professor."

"Hey, is dis da one dat foun' Ali Bacunawa?"

Billy shot a shy look Ben's way. "Yeah, I tink so. Right, Professor?"

The smile disappeared, but Ben nodded.

The newcomer to the group, a caramel-colored young man with a wooly mop of black curls hanging in disarray, looked from Ben, to Billy, to me, and back to Billy. "You know her braddah ova deah," he said.

My antennae shot up. If I could talk to Ali's brother, then I wouldn't have to put it on Gina. She had made it clear she wasn't comfortable tracking down a convicted drug dealer.

"He is?" I asked. "Here at the beach?"

The young man gave a solemn nod.

"Would you mind pointing him out to me? I'd like to pay my respects," I said.

"Sure." He pointed to a rocky area on the other side of the lifeguard tower. "Dat guy wid da short hair an da red shorts, holdin da kine."

I searched the shoreline and found a twenty-something young man in red shorts and no shirt. 'Da kine' could mean anything, but in this case meant a small cooler.

I thanked them, and the boys smiled their goodbyes and climbed down lava rocks to the water. They put their boards in and paddled out to the gap between the rocks which sheltered Richardson beach. Surfable waves came in here whenever there was a northern swell. We had a moderate-sized surf today, so as they paddled out, occasionally duck diving the larger waves. Ben and I watched them, although my attention was split between them and watching Ali's brother, out of the corner of my eye. He appeared to be just hanging and watching the surfers like us. I knew I should go ask him some questions, but I didn't know what to ask or whether he would have any interest in talking to me. When he started gathering his stuff as if to leave, I knew I better do something. I turned to tell Ben where I was going, but he had been watching me.

"Better hurry, he's leaving."

I pulled Ben's T-shirt over my head, wrapped the sarong I had been sitting on around my waist, and made my way over the rocky path so I'd intercept him before he got to the parking lot. He stopped at the showers to rinse off, which gave me a chance to station myself between him and the parking lot. I didn't want to look like I was chasing him. Now he'd have to walk past me. I watched him rinse the salt off. He was darker skinned than Ali, but had the same exotic features, large eyes, and high strong cheekbones. But whereas Ali had reminded me of a cat, her brother made me think of an anaconda. He was slim and not tall, but muscles rippled in his back as he stretched up to adjust the nozzle. He noticed me watching him as he approached me on the way to the exit and narrowed his eyes.

"Do I know you?" Standard English, no pidgin or local accent. He knew I wasn't 'local' and wasn't flirting with me.

"Are you Ali Bacunawa's brother?" I asked. I knew he was, but I didn't want him thinking I was stalking him.

His eyes shifted down and to the right, then back up to me. "Why you care?" he asked.

"I knew Ali."

He remained silent, with his eyes fixed on me.

"I'm sorry for your loss. It's tragic that she died so young. And, I think the police have arrested the wrong guy." My last words brought his shoulders up, head back, and his eyes narrowed again.

"Wat- you tink I did it?" he asked.

"That's not what I said. I don't know you, I don't even know your name. I just know Kai didn't kill her. I thought, since she was your sister, you might want the real killer in jail."

We stood there scrutinizing each other in a mini-standoff. Finally he spoke.

"David."

Confused, I scrunched my forehead and bit my lip. Before I could ask who David was, he continued.

"My name. It's David. And yeah, she was my sista, but if you know dat, you probly also know dat we din get along so well. Dat bitch sent me to prison, so why da fuck should I give a damn 'bout her?"

He walked past me with exaggerated slowness, his chest out and back ramrod straight.

I didn't try to stop him again.

Chapter 18

A drink with friends

Ben and I went up to the farm the next day. It was a beautiful piece of land with rolling hills and a stream perched a thousand feet up the side of Mauna Kea, with views forever. Ben wanted to build a house out here one day. But for now, he rode the tractor, mowing his twelve acres. Because I was up here in case he got into trouble, he worked on the steep part. Riding a tractor looked easy, but on steep slopes, it was dangerous. One of our neighbors, a guy from California, wanted to start a ginger farm. He bought a brand new seventy-three horsepower John Deere tractor. His first time out, he tipped it over and was trapped under it for five hours before another neighbor returned home and heard him hollering. The guy had a broken leg, but it could have been worse. He moved back to California the next month and sold his property.

Meanwhile, it was time for me to clean out my little patch. In our early days, I wanted to plant some stuff on Ben's farm that he thought was crazy. Ben offered me a little section where the stream made two turns before it left the property. I loved it. With the stream and twenty feet on each side, I planted chocolate trees (cacao), starfruit, cinnamon, and a few vanilla plants. I wanted a dessert farm. The bottom near the stream was flat, but it quickly sloped up to a dirt road and the edge of the property. Ben took care of everything on the farm but my little patch. I later realized why Ben was so quick to agree to hand over that section. It was dangerously steep and often too soggy for him to get his tractor in there.

To keep the grass under control, I used a weed eater on the forty-five-degree slope that made up most of my corner of the property. Clearing it was a challenge. The farm rested on the slopes of an old volcano, Mauna Kea. The soil was rich and deep, and the grass on Mauna Kea slopes grew fast and long. It could climb up, and pull down tall trees. When I left it for too long, the grass could be a good ten to twenty feet over my head, tangled into branches of the cacao and starfruit trees I'd planted. I could cut the grass low, at ankle height, but it would continue to hang in place, intertwined in branches, unless I grabbed a clump of it and walked backward fifteen feet. By then the largest part of the grass was off the tree branch and would slide down, pulled by its own weight.

It was strange sometimes. I could be in there weed-eating a section I knew I had already cut, and a dangling piece of grass would tickle me on the back of the neck. It reminded me of those Tolkien tales of Middle Earth with trees that talked and walked. Only here it was the grass. It could be spooky, especially when some twenty-foot strand I've already cut and pulled down wrapped itself around my ankle so that I fell on my butt the next time I tried to take a step. This always happened more when I was tired. And it was happening now. I tripped on grass three times in the last four steps.

I gathered my tools and dragged them back to the barn, where I swapped them out for the cooler and the water bowl I'd brought for the pups. With dogs following, I took it all up to the little deck we'd built at the highest point on the property. Ben could see me there from most places on the property and would join me whenever he finished. Until then, I'd brought a book to read, but mostly I watched the dogs playing. They loved the farm. As Suki played with Bella, I noticed a slight favoring of one of Suki's back legs. Not consistent, just every once in a while. Hmm, I should keep an eye on that.

Sitting back in my foldout chair, I must have dozed off because when I opened my eyes again, Ben was reaching into the cooler to grab himself a can of lemonade. He looked tired.

When he saw I was awake, he said, "I was thinking while I was on the tractor, if we go away for six months like you want for sabbatical, the farm will go wild while we're gone."

"We can get someone to take care of it for us."

Ben grimaced but didn't say anything else. We sat and watched the dogs romp in silence.

"Is it me, or is Suki limping a little?" I asked Ben.

"Maybe. Come here, Suk, let me see if you have something stuck in your paw."

The big black dog ran to him and plopped herself down with a resounding thump that reverberated across the deck. Ben ran his hand gently up and down her leg and paw. She kicked a little in response but was calm, letting him finish his manual exploration.

"I don't see or feel a sticker or anything. And she didn't whine or growl, so it can't be too painful for her. Probably a stone bruise or something. She runs her heart out up here herding the cows."

"Yeah, you're probably right," I said. But a knot

formed in my stomach.

We left soon after, and when we reached our house, Ben showered upstairs, and I went downstairs with the dogs and washed them and myself in the rustic, tin-sided shower just outside the back door. It had hot water but lacked privacy. I kept an old terry cloth robe there to get back into the house with modesty intact.

All clean, I checked my phone. There was a message from Mason. He wanted to get together with Ben and me and compare notes on what we'd learned about Ali's murder investigation. I asked Ben if he was up for it. He was tired but agreed. Mason had been supportive of Kai. Ben didn't think our trio's informal investigation would lead anywhere, but it seemed important to Mason. Ben wanted to reciprocate to Mason on Kai's behalf. I texted Mason, and he suggested a Mexican food place downtown on Kam Ave. We arranged to meet at seven.

We put Bella and Suki in the backyard, and Ben and I walked the ten minutes to downtown. This restaurant was cheap, with lots of long tables with plastic table clothes that could slide together for large parties of twenty, or apart for smaller groups.

I looked around but didn't see Mason, so we got a table. As soon as I sat down, Rikki approached from one of the long tables filled with people, a margarita in one hand, but arms outstretched.

"Ben! I haven't seen you in ages! That Cleo hides you all to herself."

I heard the faintest hint of a sigh from Ben, but he got up, smiled, hugged Rikki, and gave her the ritualistic kiss on each cheek. "Yeah, it's been awhile. Good to see you. Sorry I missed your last party. I guess Cleo's told you how busy I am." Ben raised his eyebrows, tilted his head in her direction, and gave a slight shrug of his shoulders.

"Of course, cutie, that's why you are forgiven," Rikki said.

I knew, Ben knew, and Rikki knew that Ben hated parties, so we were all aware that this was a weak excuse. But we all liked each other and let it go.

"I'm here for Haunani's baby shower. Do you know Haunani?"

"No," Ben and I said quickly before she could ask us to join them.

"We're here to meet Mason, Kai's partner at the dive shop," I said.

"Oooh, he is a hottie, that one!" She wiggled her eyebrows, a grin on her face. "Can I come back over after he arrives?" she asked. "I met him at a party but haven't run into him since."

"Of course," I said. Ben's mouth tightened. "But we're going to be talking about serious stuff. Probably a buzz kill for you."

"OK, OK, but don't forget … we're supposed to go walking tomorrow with Gina. She texted and said we should meet at Bayfront and walk to Liliolukalani. You can explain then how you're going to fix me up with this guy." After a laugh, she melted back to the baby shower table. Although why a pregnant woman would have a baby shower at a place famous for beer and margaritas I didn't know.

Before I could ruminate on that, Mason walked in.

"Howzit, brah," Mason said. He flashed a shaka sign with his pinkie and thumb extended and his other fingers curled down. But he raised it like a high five instead of any number of other ways a local might have thrown a shaka.

"Sorry I'm late, but a chickie came in right before I closed up shop." He waggled his phone at us. "I got her number but had to waste a lot of time before she'd fork it over."

The guys ordered beers, and I, a margarita. While we waited for the waitress to come back with the drinks, we talked about the dive shop. The business was suffering. Mason was a nice guy and did everything he could to help Kai, but he had two distinct disadvantages for running a small business in Hilo. 1) He didn't know how to pinch pennies. Mason had grown up with a wealthy family and never learned how to manage money. His parents had given him the cash to start the business, but Kai ran the day-to-day purchasing and management issues. And 2) Mason wasn't local and hasn't been here long enough to earn any local cred.

A person couldn't buy his way into being local. It wasn't that locals would be mean. Locals would smile at him. But that was the thing. They would smile *at* him, not necessarily with him. That being said, if a guy really tried to be local long enough, eventually he could be accepted. Maybe not as a local, but they would accept him as one of their own. But Mason hasn't been here long enough. Without Kai at the dive shop, I'm sure it put a dent into the business that locals directed to the shop. And most of the tour operators were local, so that was a significant chunk of business that Mason was missing out on without Kai.

When our drinks arrived, Mason shifted the discussion to Kai's defense. I guess we needed fortification to move to that subject.

"Have you guys found any leads?" Mason asked.

"Not me," said Ben taking a swig of his beer. "But I talked to the lawyer yesterday, and he said not to get our hopes up."

Ben stared at his beer bottle, picking at the label.

"The DNA test came back on Ali's baby. Kai was not the father."

My heart broke for Kai. No wonder he was depressed.

Ben continued, never lifting his eyes from his beer. "Based on that, the police have stopped investigating other suspects. They are tracking down a few things but figure they have enough to convict with Kai's prints on the tank and now a motive if Kai found out Ali had been cheating on him and killed her. But the lawyer also said if Kai gets convicted, we can always appeal, and we'll have a better chance getting a second trial because they stopped the investigation so early."

Mason pounded his fist on the table, and I grabbed my glass as all the drinks wobbled with the impact.

"But that's too long! The business will go under by then. I *need* Kai to make that business a success. My father's coming to town soon, and he would just *love* it if this business failed and I had to go work for him." Mason took a gulp of his beer and put it down again. Staring at the table, his eyes and voice turned cold and hard. "I will never work for my father again. I refuse to give him the satisfaction. I'll do whatever I have to so that doesn't happen." Mason looked up. "But I'm more worried about what the business crashing will do to Kai. Even if he gets out on appeal, he'll come out to nothing. No Ali, no business. The poor guy will be devastated. This is so wrong!" Anger and frustration leaked from every pore of Mason's face. One fist clenched, with the other he picked up his beer and chugged most of it.

Ben and I looked at each other. If Mason got drunk, one of us would need to drive him home, and we had walked to this restaurant.

I put my hand on Mason's arm, the one not holding the beer.

"Hang on there. That's just what the lawyer said. He doesn't know we are digging around for clues. I found some information that may help."

"Really?"

The childlike eagerness on his face made me worry I'd overstated my case in my effort to calm him down. "Well, I found a few interesting things that *might* lead to something that could help Kai's case," I said.

"What? Tell me." Mason's eyes were spotlights, focused on me.

"Well first, did you know Ali's brother is out of prison and back in town? And is still pretty pissed that she sent him to jail?"

"Oh," Ben interrupted. "Speaking of your possible suspects, the lawyer told me that the police checked, and the drug dealer that Ali testified against was let out of jail, but that he is on parole on Oahu. That was the first thing they followed up on."

Mason's face, which had started to perk up, fell again. "Damn, I was hoping it was him."

"Okay," I said. "But I've got more leads. In addition to the brother, I heard that Kevin's girlfriend, Mele, who is *very* jealous, thought that Ali was sneaking around with Kevin again."

"Oh, I know that chickie. Mele is a bitch when she's mad...I heard she worked at Kulani prison as a guard," said Mason.

"Yeah, and if Mele was jealous, she is known to have major anger issues. That gives us two more suspects… Kevin because he's afraid of Mele…"

"And Mele, herself. And wow, I just remembered, I think Kevin and Mele started one of our scuba classes with Kai. I'll go back and see if I can find Kai's records. So, what do we do with this information?" Mason asked.

"I've left messages for Kawika at the police station, but he hasn't gotten back to me. I finally told Gina, you know her, right? She's Kawika's wife?"

Mason nodded.

"She promised she would explain the situation to Kawika. She hasn't called back, but we are meeting up to go walking tomorrow morning."

Ben rolled his eyes as we theorized. The waitress came over, and we ordered something to eat. As we waited for the food, I remembered a couple more things that might help Kai's defense.

"And another thing, Mason, I followed up on that professor you mentioned last time. He's in the Business Department, and Ali took 'Intro to Entrepreneurial Enterprises' from him. I don't see a clear motive for him yet, but there are some weird things I need to check out there. Something about that situation felt 'off' to me."

"Entrepreneurial Enterprises? That's interesting, because Ali was talking about some hot business idea she wanted to start," Mason said. "She asked me if I knew how to set up one of those Kickstarter accounts." Mason shrugged his shoulders. "I don't, so I wasn't much help."

I guess not. Mason only had to ask his family if he wanted to finance a business idea.

I sipped my margarita. "And then there is an uncle. He beat her up in the past, because she sent her brother to jail. He was living on Maui but is back on the Big Island again. I'm not sure when he got here, but he has a history of violence against her. I still need to tell Kawika about him. Or, Ben, you could mention it to Kai's lawyer."

Mason's eyebrows raised, and he leaned forward with excitement. "And there are lots of inter-island flights that go back and forth every day to Maui. So even if *this* time he came over after her death... who's to say he hasn't been over here before... maybe the night she died. And he could have framed Kai. By killing her beforehand, then strapping the tank on her with Kai's fingerprints. Perfect!"

"I think you are getting ahead of yourself there a little, Mason." Ben glared at me. "I can't speak to the uncle's guilt, but the cops are pretty sure Ali was killed in the water. Cleo, do you remember how Ali's eyes were shining, like she was still alive?"

I nodded. I had dreamed of those eyes for several nights, and the wet hair getting washed away by the wave as we wrestled her body onto the boat.

"Evidently, that is a sign that she was killed in the water. If a person dies on land and then is dumped in the water, that doesn't happen, they get dull. Kai's being a scuba diver works against him here."

I sat with that for a minute. The memory of Ali's shining eyes reminded me we weren't just trying to get Kai off. Ali was killed, way before her time. No one had the right to end her life. We need to find the murderer and see that he... or she... doesn't get away with this. Ali deserved justice. Not just Kai.

"Yeah, well, I guess the airlines keep records, so let's see if we can get the police or the lawyer to check

141

on that." I looked toward Ben. "Will you ask the lawyer to do that?"

"Sure." He nodded. "You got a name?"

I closed my mouth abruptly. Stupid, stupid me, I had never gotten his full name. "No. But he was at the reception after Ali's funeral." I thought back to what the aunties had called him… "Tino, or something like that. I can call Auntie Charmaine and ask her." I turned toward Ben. "Or can you ask Kai next time you visit?"

Ben stared at the bottle in his hand as if all the secrets of the world were spelled out on the label that he was peeling off with his thumb. He sighed. "I'll try. But the last time I went to visit, he didn't want to see me. They told me he has been depressed."

"Yeah," said Mason. "Same thing happened the last time I went to visit."

A peal of high-pitched laughter rang out from the baby shower at the nearby table. It sawed through the morose mood which had settled at our table like a dull knife, leaving us bloody and jaggedly miserable.

Kai was a gentle spirit and that great big heart of his loved Ali. I hated watching as his world collapsed around him. And when he needed our support the most, the police threw him in jail. It was no wonder he had sunk into a bog of depression. I thought back to the times I had seen him listening to other students and their problems with his tender, serious, optimistic face. The karmic unfairness of his situation intensified my desire to help Kai.

"We have to get Kai out of jail. I'm going to ask Auntie Charmaine about that too when I call her. I don't care if Kai wants out or not; if we pay his bail, they have to let him out," I said.

I had to do something. We had to do something. I didn't know what, but something. I, mildly compulsive Cleo, had brought a pad of paper, and as we finished our meal, I made a list of action items for each of us. Ben and Mason smirked while I divided tasks, but who cares. It made me feel better, like we had a plan and might actually accomplish something that could help Kai.

Chapter 19

Walking and Talking

I dragged myself out of bed to meet Rikki and Gina for our early morning walk. I had planned to bring the dogs with me, but Suki was still limping. I called the vet to get her limp checked and got an appointment for the next day. I left Suki at home but brought Bella. The look on Suki's face wrenched my heart. Our sweet Suki seldom whines or complains, but her sadness at being left behind was written on her face. I didn't want to make her injury any worse, though. I left her with her favorite toy to chew and drove with Bella to Liliuokalani park.

Rikki and Gina were already there, doing yoga stretches while they waited for me.

"Sorry I'm late."

"No prob, where's Suki?" Rikki asked. Rikki claimed Suki was the coolest dog ever. She had made me promise to give her a puppy if we ever bred the Bouvier.

"She's got a pulled muscle or something. That's why I'm running behind, I made an appointment to get it checked."

"Can't you just give her some aspirin and put ice on it? Like I do for Kawika when he pulls a muscle."

Gina was not a dog lover. A dog tolerator, but not a dog lover.

Rikki gave a horrified frown, and I raised my

eyebrows.

"You *never* give a dog aspirin!" said Rikki. "It destroys their livers. Maybe it's a good thing you don't let Kawika have that dog he wants, you'd probably kill it by accident."

Gina shrugged. "You're probably right, but don't tell me, tell him. Now, if you have finished fawning over that puppy, can we start our power walk now? Puleeeeze."

Rikki, who had stooped to pet and kiss Bella, popped up, and we set off around the one-mile loop on the perimeter of the park. We started on the ocean side, walking into the fresh sea breeze as we headed along the coastline toward the bridge to Coconut Island. I asked Gina what Kawika thought of Kevin's girlfriend, Mele, as a possible suspect. Gina shrugged again.

"I told him what you had heard about Mele thinking Kevin had cheated on her with Ali ..."

Rikki shot me a look, realizing it was the information she had given me.

"But I got the impression he just shrugged it off. You know, he's the professional detective and my"—she made the air quotation marks with both hands—"little friends"—and then dropped her arms to go back to pumping, increased our pace—"are just annoying, amateur, wanna-be investigators. I gotta say he pissed me off, that guy."

Gina shook her head looking more peeved than pissed off I was glad to see. I didn't want to cause marital problems between Gina and Kawika.

"Thanks for trying," I said. Working to keep up with Gina's pace.

"No problem, Scooby-Doo crew or not, we gotta

help Kai," she said, not letting up.

We rounded a corner when Rikki asked, "So, did you set me up with Mason?"

Gina's paced slowed a little.

"That is one good-looking som-bitch." Gina smiled slyly. "You gotta tell me what he's like, girl."

"Right now he's so stressed about Kai and his business and his father coming to town. I don't think he's interested in anything but getting through this mess. We mostly talked about how to help Kai." I shot Rikki a look. "But if you wanted to help us investigate, I'm sure he would eventually fall for your winsome ways."

"Ha!" Gina smacked my arm, hard enough to make me step sideways and almost trip over Bella. "I helped you by passing that message to Kawika and introducing you to Weezy! And I didn't get no promise of a hookup with Mason."

"You're *married*!" Rikki and I said at the same time.

"Ummm- I'm going to tell Kawika you said that." Rikki laughed. "Besides, Cleo's saving Mason for me. So, sign me up!" Rikki punched one hand into the air as the three of us made the turn from Banyan Drive to the sidewalk that edged Hilo Bay. "I'll investigate with you and Mason. How can I help? You're right, I *do* have winsome ways!"

"Really?" I raised my eyebrows.

"Yes, of course I have winsome ways."

"No, I mean you really want to help investigate?"

"Yes! I want to be part of the Scooby-Doo crew. What can I do?"

"Well, you're friends with Kevin and his girlfriend, Mele, aren't you?"

"I'm friends with Kevin and put up with Mele. Like

everybody. Why is it that the nicest guys always go for the bitchiest girls?"

"Yeah, that's what you need, to get a little bitchier. Then you'll have Mason all over you." Gina laughed.

"I said 'nice' guys like bitchy girls. I'm not so sure 'nice' is the vibe I get from Mason."

"No?" I was surprised to hear Rikki say that. I had never paid much attention to Mason before Kai got in trouble. "I thought he was nice. He has really tried to help Kai."

"Aagh, you are such a literalist. Of course he's a nice guy, but he's also got a little bad-boy thing going on."

"Really?" I looked at Gina for confirmation. She nodded, pumping her arms as she increased the pace.

"Girl, I've been married long enough I'm allowed to notice. You and Ben are still in the pre-honeymoon stage, so you're not."

Hmm. Maybe he just wasn't my type. I had sure 'noticed' Ali's uncle. But not Mason.

"He's got that 'rich-playboy' kind of bad boy thing," Rikki said.

I shrugged. "OK, whatever. So back to Kevin and Mele."

"Right."

"Can you find out if she has an alibi for the night Ali was killed? And if she was suspicious that Kevin had cheated on Ali?"

"Sure, but I think it's a long shot. If she killed everybody she suspected of cheating with Kevin… half the island would be dead… the female half."

"Yeah, I know, but the alibi is the important thing. We need to give the lawyer other possible suspects to raise reasonable doubts. Right? We don't have to prove she did it."

"I'll start with Kevin," Rikki said. "That's the easy part."

"And try to ask him when his girlfriend isn't around," I told her.

"Sure. She hardly even lets him talk to other girls when she's around. Actually, I don't think Kevin would cross her. But Ali had that way about her. And I think Kevin had a soft spot for Ali. Besides, it doesn't matter if he messed with her or not. It only matters if Mele *thought* he did. And was angry enough to do something about it."

"You're right." I said and patted Rikki on the back. "You're going to be a great addition to the team,"

We had completed the big loop twice. And I checked my watch. "Do we have time for another loop?"

"Maybe halfway and then we can cut across the park instead of continuing around. I want to get some more walking in, but I've also got to make it to work," Gina said.

We started back on the sidewalk that edged Hilo Bay. Rikki regaled us with tales of the last time she got her hair cut. We all went to the same place, and every visit was fun. It reminded me of the old-time barber shops for men, where there was always at least one guy who just sat there with a newspaper and cracked jokes and gossiped with the barber and whoever was in the chair at the time getting the haircut. This was the same type of place, but instead of buzz cuts and trims, women were getting Brazilian blow outs and dye-jobs with the top half a white-blond, bottom half jet black. And somebody usually brought food to share. The woman who ran the shop should have been a comedienne, I always came out of there with a cramp from laughing so hard.

We were just getting close to the pier when we heard, "Gina-girl, Howzit, sista!"

Gina stopped in mid-stride and turned to look toward the pier. It was Weezy. Alone this time. Rikki, Bella, and I followed Gina over, a few steps behind.

"Hey, Weezy! Do you remember my friend Cleo? You met her last week." Gina put her hand on Rikki's shoulder. "And this is our other friend Rikki."

One at a time we exchanged kisses on both cheeks with Weezy.

Weezy looked better today. She had on a green-and-yellow, Puna Canoe Club T-shirt and jean shorts. But the big improvement was in her face. She looked freshly scrubbed, with clear eyes and a quick and easy smile. Now I could see her as a childhood friend of Gina. She still looked older by ten years, but there was an intelligence behind those eyes now that they weren't dulled by drugs. She bent over to pet Bella and said, "Where's da big dog? You had one big black dog da udder day, yeah?"

"Yeah. Her leg is hurt, so I left her at home to rest up."

Weezy nodded and straightened back up again.

"Well, looky who else heah," she said with a playful, singsong note to her voice. Those clear eyes looking over and past my right shoulder. We turned to see who she was looking at, and before I could focus on any one person, Gina punched Rikki in the arm.

"It's Mason! Now you can tell him you've joined the Scooby-Doo crew investigating Ali's death."

Rikki blushed. "Oh, grow up."

Then I recognized him, running in shorts, no shirt, glistening with sweat in the morning sun. I guess maybe they were right. I could see an appeal I hadn't noticed earlier. He wasn't my type, but I could understand why Rikki was interested in him. Earbuds stuck in his ears, he noticed us and veered our direction, pulling a T-shirt that had been tucked into his running shorts out to wipe the sweat off his face.

"Howzit," he said as he got closer.

We 'heyed' and 'howzited' back.

Gina grinned. "Hey, Mason, we were just talking strategy on finding clues to help Kai's case. I was going to see if Weezy could help us. Mason, do you know Weezy?"

Weezy let out a modified cackle, softer than the other day when she had been high. "Oh I seen dis boy. Yeah I seen um roun'."

Mason had a puzzled look on his face but extended his hand and said, "OK, yeah, I think I've seen you, but I don't think we've been introduced. Weezy is it? I'm Mason." And he shook Weezy's hand.

Weezy gave her odd witch-like cackle again. "Idn't dis boy ono-licious."

Bella was straining at her leash, attempting to jump up and lick Mason. This group was like kids on candy. Mason smiled and reached down to play with Bella. "So does Weezy know something that can help?"

Gina turned back to her old childhood friend. "The other day you told us about Ali wanting to take her brother back to California with her. But then, uh, our conversation got interrupted. Do you know what guy Ali was talking about? Was it Kai?"

Weezy got a playful grin on her face. "No, no Kai.

Dat Ali, she had one udder guy. She tole me she had one way to make um take her to da mainland."

Weezy put both her hands around Bella's head, and gave an awkward, overly affectionate scratch to the startled puppy, who tried to scramble away.

"Dat one cute doggy idn't Mason," Weezy said and winked at him. "But I gotta go now. I gotta meet one friend. We talk lattah maybe." And with a big fat, cat-ate-the-canary smile on her face and a wave over her shoulder, she headed off toward the trees next to Suisan on the other side of the parking lot. There were several fishermen already set up for the day.

Gina's face took on a sad, serious look, then she looked at her watch. "I've got to go too. I need to get to work."

After saying my goodbyes, Bella and I quickly followed Gina toward the parking lot, leaving Rikki to make her move on Mason if she so chose.

"Gina, wait up a sec." Gina stopped and let me catch up as Bella and I jogged up to her. "Are you ok?"

"Damn," she said. "Weezy looked so good this morning. I thought maybe she was back off the drugs. But the way she ran off, she's probably trying to catch up to her dealer. Or that abuser she was with the other day. I know it's her life. It's just… at one time, when we were little kids, Weezy was funny and smart, and I looked up to her. It's just sad."

"I'm sorry." I gave my friend a hug. "Let's keep our eyes out for her. If we see her when she's not high, like today, maybe we can invite her for coffee or something. Try to give her another option instead of looking for that guy."

Gina smiled. "Yeah," she said. "I gotta run now, but

thanks. That's a good idea."

As I put Bella in the car, I looked back. Mason and Rikki were still talking. I had faith in my girl, she'd get her date soon.

Chapter 20

A visit to the vet

"What a beautiful Bouvier," the vet said, smiling as he scratched Suki's head. "What seems to be her problem today?"

He was one of the vets at the clinic that loved big dogs. I was glad he was on duty. I explained Suki's limp, while he cooed to her, sneaking treats with one hand and running his other hand over the problematic leg.

"I feel some swelling at this joint," he said. Suki swung her head around, and a low rumble vibrated in the air. "Ahh, yes, and this hurts too, doesn't it, baby?" he said, getting up off the floor.

I like a vet that will get down on the floor with my dog.

"It looks like she maybe tore her ACL. Does she go zipping around a lot?"

"More like thundering, but yes, she loves to herd the cows, and she's very athletic. She does a lot of wheeling and changes of direction."

"That's probably it." He picked up Suki's chart and flipped through it. "It's so swollen I can't feel what's going on in there, and I don't want to run a bunch of expensive, invasive tests. She's young, only four, right?"

I nodded.

"And she looks healthy. But she's like a pro-basketball player who can be in peak performance but turns the wrong way one time and is out for the season."

"So this is fixable?"

"Absolutely. But I can't tell if it is torn or just strained," he said. "Let me show you what I mean." And he quickly drew it out on the back of Suki's chart. "These ligaments cross here, and it's so swollen and painful for her I don't want to move it around too much right now, so I can't be sure. It may just be stretched too far and will pull back into place, or it could have been torn. If it's torn, then we'll operate, but she'll be good as new after she heals from the operation."

I felt the knot in my stomach relax and smiled at the vet. I got Suki's meds and promised to bring her back for a follow-up visit. That would be right after I got back from my conference. I hated to leave her with an injury, but hopefully she would be healed when I returned.

****

The next day I was at the office putting the finishing touches on the presentation I'd give in a little over a week. I usually don't prepare this far in advance, but I wanted this presentation to be perfect. Ben's sister was also arriving for a week's visit tomorrow, and she doesn't leave until the day before I do. And Ben's sister required a lot of attention when she came to visit.

On the upside, we had scraped the money together to get Kai out on bail. Auntie Charmaine had arranged for him to stay at another auntie's farm on the north shore of Kauai. He could keep his head low and help her work the land and heal.

I was almost finished with my final edits, when my phone croaked.

"Hey, Rikki Tikki!" I answered. Rikki had once

confided to me that when she was a small child, her mother was a grad student at Berkeley and had written her dissertation on Rudyard Kipling. So all of Rikki's bedtime stories had come from *The Jungle Book*. Rikki, who had originally been christened Rebecca Tallulah after her two grandmothers, loved Rikki Tikki Tavi so much she insisted her parents call her that instead. The 'Rikki' part stuck, even if the 'Tikki Tavi' part was dropped after second grade. She occasionally lets me add the Tikki, or Tikki Tavi, if no one else was around if I promised never to invoke the 'Tallulah' middle name. I was born with Cleopatra for a first name, so I wouldn't dare cross her on this.

"Hi, Cleo." Something didn't sound quite right. Rikki's usually upbeat voice sounded forlorn.

"Is everything okay?"

"Yeah." A long pause followed. This was definitely not normal Rikki-speak.

"What's wrong Riks?"

"I don't know what to do with my life." The words tumbled out, and I heard a gulp that sounded suspiciously like a strangled sob.

"Rikki, you are amazing. You have a thriving massage practice. Your yoga classes are always overflowing. And you love what you do. Not many people can say that. What's going on, sweetie pie?"

Folksy southern-speak always entered my vocabulary when people I cared about were in pain. I inherited that from my mother.

A loud sniff came over the line. "I don't know. I just got off the phone with my parents."

I waited.

"I mean, they're both incredible, on the faculty at

Stanford for God's sake. I had the best upbringing a child could have, love, education, support to follow my dreams. I should be doing something important."

"And you don't think that guiding people to a healthier lifestyle is important?" I spoke quietly. I couldn't convince her of this, she had to convince herself.

"Oh, I know, but anybody could do what I'm doing. There are tons of yoga instructors in Hawaii. I feel like I should do more. *Be* more."

"More what?"

"More... I don't know. More professional or something?"

"You don't think you act professional in your classes?"

"Aargh- of course! That's not what I mean!"

I was quiet for a minute.

"What do you mean? What do you think you are doing wrong... or haven't done enough of? I'm still not getting it."

There was silence again, for a minute on the other end of the phone.

"School," she said, so softly I could barely hear it. "Mom and Dad both have PhDs. They believe in education and learning. They always expected me to go to graduate school. They still have a grad school fund for me in case I ever want to go."

Now we were getting somewhere. Rikki was afraid she was letting her parents down, or maybe herself, by not getting more education.

"Oka-a-y. So do you want to go back to school in something? Or do you think your parents will love and support you no matter what? ...Or both?" I asked.

"Well, I know they will accept whatever I want to do, and be happy for me. But I don't know whether I want to go back to school or not. It's a big commitment and lifestyle change." She paused. "I don't know, I need to think about it."

There was another long pause, and my thoughts drifted to my parents. I was also lucky to have supportive parents, but I knew they were disappointed I lived so far away. I heard it in my mom's voice every phone call.

"Thanks for talking, Cleo. I feel better. Sorry for bursting into your day like this."

"No problem, Rikki. I've always got time for one of my besties."

"Thanks. I mean, my parents are super understanding. They're great. It's just sometimes they try so hard and bend so far over backward to show me they support me, I can tell they wish I was on a different path. It's crazy. They are super sweet but drive me absolutely insane sometimes."

"Family are tough," I said, thinking of my parents so far away. They worked hard so that I could be successful and see the world. As a result of their efforts, I now lived more than 4000 miles away, and they hardly ever saw me. I wondered sometimes if they regretted their encouragement.

"No kidding." A half laugh, half snort came out of the phone.

"At least you don't have to deal with Ben's sister for a week," I said.

"Oh, that's right, when does she get here?"

"Tomorrow, I'm trying to get ahead on work so I'll have time to help Ben show her around the island. He's overwhelmed in the lab with Kai on Kauai."

"Poor thing. Both of you. I'll let you get back to work, and if you want to drop his sister off for a yoga class so you can have some free time… it's on the house!"

"Thanks, Rikki. I just might do that."

Chapter 21

Ben's sister comes to town

Ben's sister, Kerri, arrived the next evening. Flights from the mainland landed in the evenings at Hilo Airport. Kerri was a divorce attorney with a thriving practice in New York. She was smart, strong-willed, and used to getting what she wanted. Kerri represented wives, and she negotiated swollen settlements for them. I got along with Kerri for short intervals, but after too much time we tended to wear on each other's nerves.

We greeted Kerri at the airport with a puakenekene lei that I had picked up on the way home from work. The scent from the puakenekene flower was treasured here in Hawaii and was a popular flower for leis. Kerri didn't like it. She took it off immediately, and because the smell bothered her, she insisted we stop as we drove by Bayfront to put the lei on a picnic table, to get its scent out of the car. I hoped someone wandering the beach would enjoy it. With the late hour and time difference, Kerri turned down my offer for some food and took a big glass of water to her room and went to bed. Ben and I decided that her early-to-bed plan was a good idea and followed her example.

I taught three classes the next day, so Ben had tour guide duty and drove Kerri to some of the more spectacular waterfalls on our side of the island. Our tours included Rainbow Falls, Akaka Falls, and then a drive up the Hamakua Coast. We usually stopped at Laupahoehoe Point with its nice ocean side family park where we watched waves crash onto volcanic rocks, enthusiastically embracing the first land they've touched since California. Kerri was athletic, so I figured they would continue north to Waipio. Kerri would want to walk down the thigh-burning winding road to Waipio valley, past the skeletons of cars that in years past slid off the road but never reached the bottom, crashing and tangling in the dense jungle along the way. That trip should take them most of the day.

I was surprised when I walked in the front door from work and found Kerry, her laptop, files, and phone on speaker mode, spread out on our dining room table. Kerri was arguing with someone about Cayman accounts, so I crossed quietly through the living room and followed the short hallway to find Ben in his office.

"How was your day? Did Kerri enjoy the falls?"

Ben, who hadn't heard me enter his office, looked up and pushed back from his desk, where he had been working on his laptop.

"Yeah, I think she had a good time. She was a little distracted after she got a text from her assistant in New York. We made it to Akaka Falls but, after a quick look, skipped the rest of the tour and came back here so she could work. That was good for me, though, because I had work to do too. I just hope she gives herself a break and takes time to relax." Ben ran his fingers through his sandy blond hair, pushing it back out of his eyes.

I nodded. It was crazy how some people flew all this way to vacation on Hawaii and then spent all their time on their phone with work once they got here.

"What do you think she'd like for dinner?" I asked. "I can walk down to Sack and Save and pick up something."

"Thanks, that would be great. Kerri is pretty easy to please. I think a Huli-huli chicken would be fine, and maybe a salad. I don't think she's much of a sweets eater, so don't worry about dessert." Ben smiled and turned back to his laptop.

Dismissing me.

I don't know what I expected, maybe an offer to walk down to the store with me or something? But that wasn't going to happen.

I looked for the dogs to say 'Hi' and give them head scratches. They were in the backyard. Ben normally would have let them into the house when he got home, so I guess Kerri didn't like that idea. After a snuggle with both dogs, I grabbed my cloth bags and walked down to get our dinner. An hour later, I'd cooked some couscous with chicken broth and spices, made a salad, and heated up the pre-cooked, Huli-huli chicken that has been roasted and turned on a spit. I let Ben know and then stuck my head back into the living-dining area to see how Kerri was doing. She was finally off the phone.

"Are you hungry? I've got dinner ready."

"It smells great. Thanks, Cleo. Let me clear up my files here."

While she cleared off most of the table, I open a bottle of chilled pinot grigio and stuck my head back into the other room to ask if she wanted a glass.

"I'll take something stronger, if you've got it," she said without looking up from the files she was organizing as she stacked them.

I went back to review our selection of liquor. It was

mostly left over from previous guests. Ben drinks beer, and I mostly drink wine. As I went back yet again, I reported our meager offerings. Kerri wanted a scotch but only if we had a single malt and at least twelve years old. Ben had joined her by now and seconded her request.

We were in luck. The scotch we had fit Kerri's requirements. I poured two and carried a tray with drinks on it into the living room, where Kerri and Ben had turned on the television and were commenting on the news. Ben made an elegant toast, "to the pillars in my life," and after a couple of sips and a few minutes of polite chitchat, I headed back to the kitchen.

As I finished getting the food on the table, I overheard Ben explaining Ali's death and Kai's incarceration. I don't know why I didn't make the connection before. Kerri was a *lawyer*. A divorce lawyer, but a lawyer, maybe she would have some ideas on a defense. I let Ben do the explaining while I listened, slowly forking my food in without tasting it. When he was wrapping up, I realized he had left off one of the names on our list of suspects.

"Don't forget Walker Wolf," I said.

Ben shot me look and took a big slug of his scotch.

"Sounds like a movie character from an old western." Kerri's eyebrows lifted in the first facial change I'd seen from her since Ben started his explanation.

"Looks, and acts like one too." I grinned. "He's from Texas…"

Kerri held up her hand, the one not holding a fork. "Say no more. I've known enough Texans, well, I've represented enough wives of Texans, to know exactly what you are talking about. How is he a suspect?"

I gave details on his dubious past with undergrads and his explanation of his last encounters with Ali.

Kerri had eaten half the food on her plate and was just pushing the rest around with her fork. She put her fork down and held up her scotch glass that was empty except for ice and rattled it in Ben's direction. He dutifully got up and brought the scotch bottle back into the dining room, poured more in Kerri's glass, and set the bottle on the table near her.

"My money's on your Texas professor," she said, after she had taken her first sip from the fresh drink.

"Now wait a minute," Ben said. "Don't stereotype him just because you got some bad settlement from a Texas husband."

"No, no...first, I've *never* gotten a bad settlement from *any* husband." Kerri sat up straight in her chair, a smug smile on her face. "It's obvious, little brother, that business idea she had was a good one. And this Wolf guy wanted it for himself. Not to mention a little piece on the side."

As Ben opened his mouth to protest, she held her hand up again to stop him.

"You mark my words"—the upheld hand now pointed at him—"that Texas professor will be launching some new business in the next year... and don't be surprised if it sounds like the kind of idea a smart young Hawaiian woman would have. And you better hope it's him, because everything else points to a jealous Kai, especially since the lab reports came back and the baby wasn't his."

Ben looked like the dinner he had just consumed was giving him heartburn.

Kerri stood up. "I don't know about you two, but

I've put my case to bed for the night, I suggest you do the same with yours." And after refilling her scotch glass, she walked back to the couch, plopped down, and turned on the television.

Chapter 22

Hapuna

Ben and I were up early the next morning. He had classes all day, but I was going to work on the Methods section of a study I was writing up, and put the final touches on my Santa Fe presentation. As I pushed open the bedroom door, I could hear Kerri's voice coming from the kitchen.

"I mean it, Hank, he's hiding money somewhere, it is *your* job to find it!"

On east coast time, Kerri had been awake for hours and stood dressed in Lululemon cropped running pants and a flowered sports bra. She stood with Starbucks coffee cup in one hand and pointed at her speaker phone resting on the kitchen island. She had the glow of returning from a run and must have hit the Starbucks while she was out. I started a big pot of strong coffee. I needed it extra strong, and usually a second cup if I had to talk to anyone other than Ben or Suki, first thing in the morning. Kerri looked like she was firing on all pistons and might not be in a patient mood if I couldn't put two thoughts together. But then again, maybe I was just threatened by how good she looked in her Lululemon gear while I frumped past her in an old bathrobe.

Fortunately, Kerri didn't require responses from me as she spewed directives into her phone. Ben joined me just as the coffee was ready, and we laid out breakfast options. Last night I had picked up a coffee cake, papayas, and a pound of bacon. When I pulled the bacon out of the refrigerator, I saw Ben's mouth turn up in delight. It was Ben's favorite, and I almost never made it. Seeing his childlike joy, I felt a pang of guilt that I didn't do this more often. I assuaged my conscience by frying up the entire package and piled the bacon on a plate that I set out next to the rest of the food. Ben charged forward, and Kerri's hand snaked in to grab some too.

Ben and I ate in the dining room, passing sections of the newspaper back and forth, with Kerri and her speakerphone conversation going on in the kitchen, in the background. I was on my second cup of coffee, and Ben was putting his plate in the sink after eating his fill of bacon, Kerri finished her conversation and pushed the hang-up button on her phone with a flourish.

"There. I've got all of my little munchkins with assignments for the day, I'm ready to stretch out on a beach and soak up some rays! Where shall we go?"

Ben, already dressed for work, looked at me with panic on his face, and I saw my industrious plans of writing for the day follow the papaya rind and bacon crumbs down the garbage disposal drain. I smiled at him and then at Kerri.

"Do you have a favorite beach you want to stretch out on?"

I preferred the beaches near us, like Richardson's on the little stretch of coastline called Keaukaha. But West Hawaii beaches on the Kohala coast, like Hapuna and A-Bay, were ranked in the top three in the world every year by travel aficionados, and our side... well, not so much.

We had lava and shade from coconut palms and kaumani trees, which made secluded areas with an intimate feel. Underwater was more interesting too. The sand varied from mostly black, as hot lava shattered as it entered the cool water more than 150 years ago, to stripes of white that remained untouched by lava.

It was a challenge to practice for my open water swim on this side, though. Inside the protective coral outcroppings that made Richardson's such a great place for kids and families to enjoy a peaceful ocean dip were lava formations. The lava did not run in a straight line, but twisted around so I had difficulty finding areas deep enough to swim without danger of damaging coral. To get a straight shot of any distance, I had to go outside the rocks. Where the depth plummeted rapidly. I tried it once and got spooked. It was crystal clear, but I was so far out, all alone, and at times hidden from the lifeguard by the rocks. My old fear of sharks overcame me. I had a mini-panic attack and quickly swam back through the rocks to supposed safety.

I wasn't surprised when Kerri wanted to go to Hapuna, on the Kona side. The drive was long, but it would be a good opportunity to practice my open-water swimming. And the hour and forty-five-minute trip around the north slope of Mauna Kea was exquisite.

We stopped at Laupahoehoe since she had missed it yesterday when they turned back early. I pointed out the monument, which honored the twenty students and four teachers who were killed in the 1946 tsunami. The monument lent a heightened poignancy to the power and drama of the stunning landscape.

"Nature giveth and Nature taketh away," Kerri said.

We stopped for lunch at one of my favorite places,

'Tako taco' in Waimea.

"What's with the weird name?" Kerri asked. "Couldn't make up their mind how to spell taco?"

I looked around hoping no one had heard. "Tako is the Japanese word for boiled octopus, the kind they use in poke. Notice the sign with an octopus on it? They serve it here. In tacos."

Kerri shrugged.

I sighed.

After lunch we drove through the town of Waimea, with its split personality. The east side had towering trees and lush green hillsides with yards overflowing with bright flowers and tall leafy tree fern. But on the west side of town, the trees disappeared, and the greenery gave way to lava, cactus, and more rugged, drought-resistant plants. At Kawaihai, a major port for the island, we turned south toward the Kohala coast beaches where expensive resorts and high-priced celebrity hideaways could be found. Our university development officers called this area the millionaire ghetto. But Hawaii, true to its spirit of protecting its people, had laws that allowed public access to state parks and beaches. And locals knew the little hidey-holes, with narrow walkways that allowed a person in the know to hike between these multimillion-dollar holiday homes. With little or no parking, but perfectly legal access, a person could find herself in an amazing, unspoiled idyllic coastline spot.

"Are you up for an adventure, Kerri? We can hike out to a deserted beach we would only have to share with turtles."

"Let's keep going to Hapuna Beach. It was written up in Conde Nast."

I kept driving. Hapuna was world-famous-gorgeous.

The park service had repaved the parking lot and sidewalks, which led past 'The Three Frogs' fast food stand. The path sloped down a hill to a long, wide swath of sandy beach. The upscale Hapuna Beach Prince Hotel perched on one end, and a wild, natural cliff on the other. The wild side had a tempting cave, halfway way up the face of the cliff that cried out for exploration. In between the resort and cliff was just one heck of a long, deep, lovely, white sand beach.

While Kerri baked in the sun, I wanted to practice my alternate-breathing stroke in real open ocean. I could swim a straight shot the length of the beach and back, and not feel like I was shark bait.

My swim went well, a couple of sinus washes, but that was probably good for them. I joined Kerri, who was cooling off in the water, and we both walked onto the beach together. We chatted for a while about her client until Kerri picked up her book.

"I'm going to read, if you don't mind. I'm on vacation," Kerri said, then stretched out on her back and held the hardback book directly over her face to shade it from sun.

I'd brought a journal article I needed to read, but after thirty minutes I was itching to move around. I told Kerri I was going for a walk and invited her to join me. She declined.

As I was turning back from the cliff to head to the other end of the beach, I heard someone call out.

"Hey, Professor Cooper!"

I looked around and found one of my students sitting up, book in hand, on a nearby blanket with a friend stretched out next to her, belly down, with bikini top straps untied and face turned away. I smiled and walked over.

"Howzit," she said. And held up her Cross-Cultural Psychology book. "I'm studying, Professor, see!"

"Good for you, Lei. I brought work too, so I'm not completely playing hooky today." I pointed in the general direction of Kerri and our stuff. "I'm just taking a break from it. I promise."

"Yeah, sure, I saw you swimming earlier too." She giggled. "But I won't tell."

I laughed. "You don't tell and I won't."

Her friend rolled over, one hand holding her top on, to see who Lei was talking to. Kevin's girlfriend, Mele, looked up at me.

"Hey, Mele, I didn't realize that was you."

She looked at me blankly.

"I paddled with Kevin at the University Canoe Club, and I've met you at a few of the potlucks."

The blank stare morphed into the beginning of a glare.

Lei ignored her friend's hostile mood and elbowed her.

"Hey, Mele, I heard that the professor is trying to find out who killed Ali Bacunawa. She's trying to get Kai outta trouble. That's right, isn't it, Professor?" Lei turned from Mele to me.

The naissance of a glare blossomed into a full-blown glower. But despite the waves of antipathy emanating from her, Mele remained silent.

"Yea, I guess. I'm not a private eye or anything, but Kai's auntie asked if I would help him. I'm asking around to see if I can hear anything that might help Kai's lawyer." I bolstered my courage and looked back at Mele's angry stare, to include her as well as Lei in my next question.

"Have either of you heard anything that might help Kai?"

Lei looked at Mele. A slight crease began to grow in her brow as she looked at her friend. Her mouth opened, as if to speak, but she abruptly closed it again, her eyes on Mele.

Mele, slowly, with exaggerated casualness, turned herself over, one hand still holding her top up. Her gaze shifted from a glower to an icy boredom. After she was sure that she had both of our attention by her movements, she casually released the only words she would contribute to this discussion. "Ali was a grade-A bitch, and the world is a better place since Kai killed her."

My jaw dropped as she languorously lay back down and closed her eyes. I looked at Lei who avoided returning my gaze. We exchanged uncomfortable goodbye-see-you-tomorrows.

When I got back to Kerri, she was sitting up and had obviously been looking for me.

"Is there somewhere around here we can get a drink?" she asked.

"Well, the Three Frogs is fast food, so I'm sure we can get a bottled water or soda there."

Kerri shot me a look of exasperation. "I'm on vacation. And not twelve."

"O-o-or there is the Hapuna Beach Prince Hotel, they've got a beach bar and a reef lounge, where you can get something stronger."

"Now, you're talking."

Several fruity cocktails later, at least for Kerri, we started the drive home. I had stuck to seltzer water with a wedge of lime, since I was driving and hoped to get some work in after we got home. Kerri could be a bit bossy, and this only got stronger after a few drinks. I had to listen to her give me directions home, even though I was the one who lived here. I somehow managed to not snap at her.

"Well, if you *insist* on going home the same way we came, at *least* stop at some of the places Ben showed me yesterday- the waterfall places. I was so distracted by my client I forgot to take any pictures," Kerri said.

"It will put us back pretty late. Can it wait until tomorrow? Ben won't mind bringing you back."

"Nope, I need the pictures tonight, I want to post something on Instagram that will make my assistant jealous." Kerri laughed and pulled her book out to read until we got to the waterfall.

I sighed.

By the time we made it back to the house, it was getting dark, and Ben had beaten us home. Of course, he hadn't started dinner.

He offered to take us all out, but Kerri wanted to stay in. She was tired after the day's outing. I opened a jar of spaghetti sauce and started water boiling for some pasta. Kerri followed me into the kitchen. Oh joy.

As I chopped onions and pulled some mushrooms out of the fridge, Kerri looked over my shoulder and pointed to some capers on the door.

"Ooo, I love capers, put some of those in. And have you ever tried adding some of the squash to spaghetti sauce? I see you have some. It's great." Kerri walked to the cabinet where we kept the glasses and pulled one out before filling it with ice.

"Ben doesn't like squash, I bought it for my lunch tomorrow, but capers sound good, I'll add those," I said.

"Don't tell him the squash is in there. What he doesn't know won't hurt him." And she laughed as she walked to the liquor cabinet to add scotch to her glass.

I ignored her and added the capers without squash. Ben had picked up a fresh baguette, I guess hoping I'd make my signature garlic bread. I sliced it, dipped each piece in olive oil, then sprinkled with some oregano, fresh chopped garlic, and pepper. Kerri, who had been watching me, reached across and sprinkled some old pre-grated parmesan from a cardboard cylinder that she had found in the back of the refrigerator, onto the garlic bread.

"There. That will perk it up," Kerri said.

I gritted my teeth and restrained myself from throwing the pan of bread at her and placed it into the oven.

As I stirred the pot of sauce, she followed me and shook some crushed red pepper into the sauce without asking. I held up a hand. "Not too much."

Kerri rolled her eyes. "You are such a lightweight."

Kerri was in a good mood during dinner and kept up a constant stream of stories about difficult cases that she had won, decorating ideas I should do around the house, "if you really want to make this place something special," and recipes I should make for Ben. I escaped the room as soon as dinner was over, took the dogs for a walk, and pleading fatigue, went to bed early.

The next morning I saw Lei, my student that I'd seen at the beach. She acknowledged my greeting when she was leaving class and looked like she thought about stopping to talk. But after a moment's hesitation moved on wordlessly, looking at the ground. I didn't want to press her, and I let her go.

Over the next couple of days I worked in the office, leaving early and getting home late. It felt good to push through and finalize my presentation and get caught up before my trip. I survived our dinners with Kerri without losing my temper or offending her. She loved her little brother, but she didn't think he knew how to run his life or choose his life partner. She didn't think I was the right woman for him. Oh, she didn't say it in so many words, but she alluded to it in a thousand and one comments. And the more time I spent in my office to avoid her, the more convinced she was that I wasn't there for Ben.

Fortunately, Ben picked up on some if not all of her snarky comments. During Kerri's last evening, after several scotches she began elaborating more than usual about what Ben and I should be doing with our lives. I could tell by the look in Ben's eyes that he knew how much I resented her comments. I didn't expect him to intervene or try to curb Kerri. She was his sister, and Ben wouldn't or couldn't say anything. Other men might be able to, but not Ben. For him, confrontation with a loved one was difficult. I guess because of his alcoholic, psychologically abusive father. After years of watching his father ridicule and pick fights with his sister and mother, he could only protect and cushion them. It didn't matter how pushy or unreasonable Kerri was … he was not capable of any feelings other than those to protect his sister.

Ben, as the only son, had been favored by his father and held up as untouchable to his mother and sister. One might have expected Ben to develop into an egotistical megalomaniac with similar misogynistic leanings. He did not. Somehow his mother's parenting prevailed, and Ben grew to become the kind and loving man I knew today.

I wish I could have met his mother. She died before Ben and I encountered each other. In one of those early, falling-in-love-tell-all conversations that take place in the wee hours of the morning, Ben revealed to me a treasured conversation with his mother. As tragic as her early death was, from breast cancer at the age of fifty-one, in one of her last bedside talks with him, she confided that she believed her greatest accomplishment in life was that Ben had turned out so different from his father.

No matter how many smart-ass, critical comments his sister made, Ben couldn't allow himself to get angry. He would spend the rest of his life making reparations for the abuse his father had heaped on his sister. So, I appreciated, and settled for, the apology I saw in his eyes.

I smiled back at him. I was still irritated by the audacity of Kerri, but Ben had enough guilt on his shoulders without him feeling he had to make reparations to me. I knew he would try anyway. The next time he ran to the store, he would pick up a dark chocolate candy bar for me. Or tonight he would offer to take the puppy on her last, late-night pee walk. And that would be nice. Maybe a little extra guilt on his shoulders wasn't such a bad thing. And his sister really was a handful.

I managed to get through Kerri's last day without any conflicts by spending most of it at work and encouraging Ben to take his sister for a last dinner on the way to the airport without me. I spent a quiet evening at home packing for my trip to the conference in Santa Fe.

****

On my day of departure, the air was thick with vog.

We don't have enough traffic here in Hilo to get smog. But we had Kilauea, an active volcano. And sometimes Madame Pele was a little gassy. Vog was the term scientists gave to volcanic smog. When our normal trade winds blew, Hilo had crystal clear air, super-washed in its trip across the car-less Pacific Ocean, while the Kona side, and islands north and west of us, got the hazy gray vog from the Pu'u 'O'o vent of Kilauea. But when the trade winds stalled, and today there was not a breath of a breeze, then the vog rolled down into Hilo from the Pu`u `O`o vent like pea soup.

This afternoon at the farm, a smoky gray haze blocked my view of the ocean. It gave the world an eerie, surreal feel to the day. Vog gave me a scratchy throat, itchy skin, and made me tired. The dogs seemed more irritable with each other too, more growls and harmless snarls than usual coming from Suki, directed at the ever-playful puppy. Suki was also licking the swollen place on her leg. I couldn't blame that on the vog, though.

It was my last chance to bring the dogs to the farm before my conference trip, and Suki, despite the occasional snarls, seemed to be enjoying herself despite the leg injury. I kept her on a leash so she wouldn't aggravate her injury. But she sniffed and smelled as we walked the farm, and Bella ran and played until the puppy collapsed on the deck in exhaustion. Ben would make sure they got food and water, but he was so busy I wasn't sure how much attention or exercise they would get while I was gone. I hoped this outing would last them for a couple of days. I flew out tonight and would be back in five days.

Chapter 23

A Trip to Santa Fe

The trip from Hilo to Santa Fe was more than a couple of plane rides. It was a transition from 'slippahs' and sarongs to a land of moneyed homes and ostrich boots that cost more than my car. Exhausted from my overnight flight, I crashed in my hotel. After the nap, I worked in my room until it was time for dinner.

As I finished up, a text came in from my old friend from graduate school, Tyler. He had arrived for the conference and wanted to know if I was in yet. A couple of texts later and we had agreed to meet in the lobby in an hour. That gave me time to jump in the shower, and Tyler time to research restaurants on his iPhone. In the lobby of La Posada, I found Tyler at the bar, chatting with a dark-eyed beauty of a bartender. He waved to me as I entered the room.

"My friend here says there is fabulous Spanish food nearby." He winked at the bartender who gave him a warm smile. "In the mood for tapas?" Tyler asked me.

"If you like Spanish food, there is a good one nearby," the pretty little bartender said. "I gave your friend the name." With a regretful look, the bartender excused herself to go check on another customer. Tyler was gay, but he turned women's heads and could flirt with the best of them.

Tyler swallowed the last of his drink, and we walked to the restaurant. We discussed the conference. I presented the first day. But Tyler got stuck with the next-to-the-last presentation time. Tyler was explaining the political intrigue in his department when our food arrived just as my phone rang. I checked to see that it wasn't Ben or my parents, and when I saw it was Gina, I turned the ringer off. I would call her back later.

The food was amazing, artichoke hearts stuffed with herbed goat cheese flash-fried drizzled with a romensco sauce, jamon Serrano, and baby calamari, this time in a roast garlic-caper aioli sauce. The delicacies held our attention until, to our delight, jazz music started on a small stage in the corner of the room. We were so engrossed in our conversation and the food I hadn't noticed the musicians setting up. After the hectic preparations for leaving and a sleepless night on a plane, I was starving and ate an embarrassing amount of food. Between being satiated with delectable tapas and sharing a bottle of wine with my old friend, I could feel all the tension ease out of neck and shoulder muscles. Tyler and I sat companionably quiet but perfectly content, listening to the music sparkle.

When the band took a break, Tyler got up to use the restroom, and I checked the phone call from earlier to see if Gina left a message. She had, so I listened to it while Tyler was away from the table and the band was on break.

"Cleo- are you still in town? Doesn't matter— Kawika just called me... Weezy is dead. Some surfers just found her body down at Pohoiki. Call me back."

Oh my God! Weezy dead? I immediately hit the 'call back' button. I got her voicemail. "Gina, this is

Cleo. I'm so sorry. What happened? How did Weezy die? Was it that guy- the fisherman? You probably don't know yet. I'm so sorry. I know you were close with her when you were kids. I'm not in Hilo, I got to Santa Fe this afternoon, but call me if you want to—" I was cut off by her voicemail. I set the phone down. My hands were shaking when Tyler returned to the table.

"Cleo, what's wrong? Are you okay?" The edges of his mouth turned down, and his forehead wrinkled.

"I don't know. I just checked my voicemail, and it was a friend telling me that someone we just talked to last week is dead." I reached for my glass of wine and took a shaky drink.

"Aw hell, I'm sorry. Is it someone close to you? Do you need to go back to Hilo?" He gave my forearm a gentle squeeze.

I took a deep breath. "No, we weren't close, I just met her. And she was…" Damn, how to describe Weezy? I thought back to when I met her at Liliuokalani park, her fluttering nervously around that fishing jerk while he screamed at her.

"She was a lost soul, following an unlucky star."

"What happened? How did she die?"

I thought for a minute. "I don't know how she died, but she was living with an abuser. I guess… I don't know what to think. If I should get mad because the asshole killed her, or sad. Or if she was high and did something stupid, that got her killed? Or damn, maybe it was just natural causes. Weezy abused her body and was living a pretty unhealthy lifestyle."

"How did you meet her?" Tyler could tell I needed to process Weezy's death and was encouraging me to talk about it.

Probably not a bad idea.

"Well, it all started about two months ago when I was out on the boat with Ben and his class, and we pulled up a dead body."

Tyler's mouth fell open in surprise, which lifted my spirits a little. Tyler was hard to surprise. I continued with the rest of the story and brought him up to date.

We were walking back to the hotel when Gina called me back.

"This is Gina. Do you mind if I take it?" I asked Tyler.

"Please, I insist! At this point I want to know what happened to Weezy too!"

I answered, "Hey, Gina! Are you okay?"

"Yeah, geez, I'm sorry, I didn't mean to ruin your trip."

"Don't be ridiculous. You're my friend."

"It's just so weird. I haven't talked to her in ten years, then twice in two weeks and now she winds up dead. This is Hilo. Sleepy Hilo…people don't die off that fast here."

"I know, I was thinking the same thing. Has Kawika figured out what caused her death?"

"It's not his case. They actually found her body at daybreak this morning, some guys out at Pohoiki, surfing at dawn, pulled her to shore and called the cops. Kawika didn't find out about it until he went in this afternoon, and by then someone had ID'd her. He knew I grew up with her, so he called me. After I got your message, I asked him what killed her. I was thinking it could have been that asshole she was hanging with. I'd love to see that bastard go to jail. But he says it looks like natural causes. I guess someone told the investigating officer that when she was young, she and her brother used to climb out on those rocks near Mackenzie State Park to pick opihi. They think maybe she was high and thought she could do it again, at night."

I knew Mackenzie State Park, just a couple of miles south of Pohoiki. It had beautiful cliffs and jagged lava formations. The ocean waves crashed against those rocks like rebellious teens fighting authority.

Gina talked a little more, but after a few minutes, she grew quiet. We said our goodbyes and promised to paddle out and offer a lei for Weezy to the ocean when I returned.

Tyler looked at me expectantly. Impatient, he tried to hold his silence. But that was not in his skill set.

"Well? Do they know who killed Weezy?"

"They didn't do an autopsy, but it looks like it wasn't a who, but a what."

"What?"

"An accident - it doesn't look like her abuser killed her. It looks like she was on a dangerous section of the coastline, probably picking opihi, and got dragged out to sea. They are a local delicacy, and every couple of years someone gets killed trying to harvest the sea snail. If they don't eat them themselves, they can sell them for a lot of money."

"They risk life and limb for a sea snail?" Tyler scrunched his nose and lifted a corner of his top lip.

I shrugged. "I've never had it. But you eat mussels and oysters. They are ugly, slimy things, too."

Tyler rolled his eyes at me.

"People in Hawaii love it. And local lore is that the tastiest opihi grows on the most treacherous rocks. And poor Weezy, a mind impaired by narcotics was more susceptible to becoming fixated on an enticement like opihi." It made me sad that Weezy had risked her life for the local delicacy that she prized so highly she would scramble out on untenable, slippery rocks, risking the quixotic mood of a poltergeist-like ocean.

"I don't buy it," Tyler said. His eyebrow lifted and mouth twisted.

I stopped walking. "What?"

Tyler stopped too and turned to face me. "Well, you know Ali was killed. And you said Weezy told you she knew something. I bet somebody lured Weezy out to that park and pushed her off a cliff."

It made sense. But I've seen Tyler go down the rabbit hole before. He has always loved a good conspiracy. I'm not sure I wanted to get sucked into seeing malevolence around every corner. I started walking again and gently tried to talk him down from his murder scenarios. Back at the hotel we said good night, and I went to my room and fell into a troubled sleep.

Chapter 24

The conference begins

Our conference was at La Posada, and I loved the location. It was close to the plaza and Canyon Road and set up more like a spa resort than a conference center. But because our conference was small, they could accommodate us. My talk was the first session after the keynote. I enjoyed the keynote speaker, which helped keep my nerves at bay.

My talk went well, no misspelled slides or questions I couldn't answer. Tyler sat in the back row. He didn't ask any questions, but he had smiled, nodded, and exuded encouragement. The crowd had lots of queries, and they were the good kind of questions, of someone curious or inspired, rather than aggressive or belittling, "gotcha" comments. With a mixture of relief and jubilation, I entered the next talk in the neighboring room and slipped into an empty seat next to Tyler on the back row. When he realized it was me sitting down, he winked and gave me a thumbs-up.

When the second session ended, we started making our way to the next talk we had picked out the night before. Tyler put a hand on my elbow to stop me.

"Cleo, I think I'm going to duck out of this session. I just saw an old flame, and he is giving me signals to go meet him. I think we'll probably go grab a coffee or something. Is it okay if I meet up with you sometime later?"

"Of course. Is it anybody I know?"

"I don't think so. He's the guy over there in the red shirt and khaki pants."

I smiled at the handsome young man who was watching us with interest. He smiled back.

"Nope, I don't know him, but why don't you introduce me later? After you guys have had a chance to catch up."

"Sure thing!" Tyler said, already on his way across the room before the words were out of his mouth.

When the conference paused for an extended lunch break, I was ready to get outside and walk. I hadn't seen Tyler since he left to catch up with his friend, so I snuck away from the crowd as they were discussing where to eat, and walked toward the Railyard district. I needed to stretch my legs with a brisk walk, and group decisions always involved lots of standing around and slow walking.

I strolled along the river to Guadalupe Street and found a fun-looking café called Cowgirls. It had a sunny patio out front, which was full by the time I got there, so I was seated inside. Historical pictures of cowgirls covered the wall, and an old west theme enveloped me. I ordered the harvest salad and devoured my heaping plate, as I savored the roasted beets, fennel, and goat cheese.

The sky was a cornflower blue, with a few puffy cotton clouds when I emerged to head back toward the conference. I walked past an old church with day laborers waiting for work on one side of the road and on the other, skateboarders flaunting their skills. I crossed over the Santa Fe River to follow a trickling stream in the direction of the conference. I walked on old cobblestone roads edged in low-slung adobe buildings with a foot and a half thick walls. I loved the sassy purple doors and blood-red trim around the windows and stopped to take a picture. It somehow worked with the cantaloupe-colored adobe walls.

And much like Rome, all roads in Santa Fe led to the plaza, a square in the heart of this capital city filled with shady trees and benches. Tourists loaded with cameras, maps, and shopping bags filed along a sidewalk on the edge of the square, underneath the overhang of boot shops, galleries, and restaurants. Locals filled the benches and spread out on the grass in the middle of the plaza, enjoying the weather and catching up with friends.

I followed the tourists on the north side, along Palace Avenue, where Native American artists spread blankets and displayed their art. I was tempted to buy a pair of satiny-silver earrings, but I wasn't sure whether or not it was appropriate to bargain. I loved to travel, but I hated looking like a tourist. I flowed with the slow-moving crowds past the blankets but peeled off at the corner and headed for a recently vacated bench on the square to people watch while my luncheon feast digested.

A guitar-carrying street musician played a western song I hadn't heard before as I watched people enjoying the afternoon, many with their dogs. Evidently, Santa Feans loved their dogs, because the hounds were out in force. I watched a woman in red jeans and white T-shirt laughing as two beagles dragged her across the square as she waved goodbye to another woman in a lemon-yellow sundress. A stately Great Dane sat calmly next to his elderly gray-haired companion, who was smoking a pipe. A high-strung silky terrier and a playful doodle with a crowd of kids fawning over her were scattered around on other benches with their owners.

I wished I could have brought Suki. Maybe I would come here on sabbatical and bring her with me. It would be fun to have her in such a dog-friendly city.

A grizzled looking guy about sixty with long stringy gray hair and an acoustic guitar started belting out "Suzy- Q" just as the other musician finished. There was a slight coolness in the autumn air, and I had chosen a seat in the sun. I reveled in mellowing out before I had to return to the conference. Some young people were playing hacky sack, and a couple of dog owners, one the beagle lady, stopped to talk, while their companions on the other end of the leash sniffed each other.

A third person stopped to pet the beagles. In my relaxed, almost drowsy state, I experienced a jolt of alertness when I realized that the person had finished petting the dog and was looking directly at me. Grinning, he waved goodbye to his friends and headed to my bench. A split second after the surprise of being observed, I realized the face was familiar. By the time he reached the bench, I'd blinked the drowsy out of my eyes and had a smile on my face to welcome him.

"I guess I'm not the only one who needed peace from the maddening crowds," Luc said, as he approached my bench.

Luc, the main organizer of the conference and the person who had invited me to give my talk. I had forgotten how glorious he was. Lucas Alessandro Bastien. Years ago I heard his friends tease him with the nick-name LA. Someone had told me his mother was

Italian, his father, French, and Luc had gotten the best bits of both nationalities. From what I've heard from conference gossip, Luc was in the fast lane. After growing up in Europe, he graduated with a BS from Harvard, gone on to get a PhD at Berkeley, and afterward landed a tenured position at Stanford. Faced with his dazzling smile, movie-star good looks, and graceful elegance, as he grinned down at me, I couldn't remember, for the life of me, why I hadn't followed him to his room like a little puppy dog, at that conference a couple of years ago.

I realized it was my turn to talk.

"It's such a beautiful day, I needed a few minutes outside to enjoy it." I tried to put a sheepish look on my face.

"A perfectly sensible way to spend a lunch break." Luc sat down next to me on the bench far enough away to stretch out, laid both arms along the back of the bench at shoulder height, and fully extended his legs out in front of him. He lifted his gaze to the branches of a nearby tree, watching a bird.

"So how are you enjoying the conference so far?" But before I could answer he continued, "Your talk was fantastic by the way, there was a great discussion afterward. That was my goal for this conference. To get people talking." He turned to look at me. "But I interrupted. Are you enjoying yourself at the talks?"

I wasn't sure I could bear going back inside for the afternoon talks when the weather was this perfect, but since he was one of the organizers and looked at me with those soft, playful eyes... I tried to be diplomatic.

"The talks are really interesting. It's just hard to sit inside all day when it's so beautiful out here. I wish the presenters could move out onto that patio at the hotel."

His eyes crinkled as he smiled at me. "I hear you. I asked, but the hotel said no."

We sat there for a minute. It had been awhile since I had seen him. He looked even better than I remembered.

"I saw you petting the beagle over there. Are you a dog lover or just being friendly?" I asked.

"I'm a dog lover. I think this is the first time in my life I haven't had a dog." Luc paused. "My fourteen-year-old Weimaraner died last year. I can't quite bring myself to replace him." Luc's smile faded.

My stomach knotted. *Dear God, let Suki be all right.* "I'm sorry. It's hard to lose a dog. And Weimaraners are beautiful. I haven't seen one in a long time. It's hard to import dogs to Hawaii. We don't have many different breeds there."

"That's right, it's rabies free, like England and Australia, isn't it?"

"Right. But to keep it rabies free, there is a crazy extensive process of shots, titer tests, and paperwork to bring in a dog. And puppies can't complete the process before they are about nine months old, unless you are going to fly it in from Australia, but then that adds thousands of dollars onto a dog that is probably already pretty expensive." Something tickled my brain. I wasn't sure why, but I had the feeling I said something important, but I didn't know what.

"I have a Bouvier de Flanders," I said. "Best dog I've ever had, but if I lost her…" I swallowed the lump in my throat. "I don't know how I would replace her."

We were both quiet a minute, watching people walking their dogs on the square.

"When you have a good dog, I'm not sure they are

replaceable." He cleared his throat and smiled. "Besides, in my case, I travel so much now, it would be unfair to the dog, especially a puppy. I thought about getting a rescue dog, that's what everybody here tells me, maybe an older one. But just because they are a rescue dog, doesn't mean they don't deserve a home where they get the attention any dog needs."

I blinked in surprise. I'd never seen this side of Luc. I knew he had an amazing career, was stunningly attractive, and I've heard he was kind of a player. Oh yeah, that's why I didn't follow him to his room at the last conference. I have learned to avoid players.

But I never pictured him as the type to get his heart broken by a dog.

I had a soft spot for men who had a soft spot for dogs.

But I was also monogamous I reminded myself, so this must be a friendly soft spot I was feeling. Not romantic... more like the soft spot I have for Tyler. Although that was more about his sense of humor than dogs, and he was gay. Luc was not. I shifted in my seat.

"I hate to say it, but we better get back to your conference." Yes, a nice, safe, unromantic conference.

"If you say so," Luc said and stood up, another big grin on his face and eyebrows raised. "But before we go back to artificial lighting and stackable chairs, I want to invite you to my house for dinner tomorrow night."

Uh-oh, was my soft spot showing? Had I sent off I'm-interested signals?

"I'm having some people over that you might find interesting. I live five minutes outside of town, so if you are getting tired of restaurants and conference food - I'd love to have you join us."

"Uh, sure." *Did I just say that?* "Well, I mean, I have to check my schedule…" *Oh God, how stupid am I, he is on the committee that made the schedule.* "Well, I guess, you probably already know the schedule. Yeah, um, yeah. I guess. Sure, that would be nice."

I sounded like an idiot. *Just shut up, Cleo!*

But by this time Luc was guiding me back to the conference room, not the way I had come, but a more direct route. We walked on covered sidewalks of wood and stone, past a gallery where a twelve-foot dragon, looking freshly hatched, appeared to be crawling out of the top of a building. Luc sauntered alongside me, comfortable and relaxed, telling me a little about the other people who would be at his house for dinner. A couple of those that he mentioned, I knew, the others I had heard of, but not met. Professionally, it was an impressive group, well, except for me. But before I could get insecure, he was pointing out landmarks and explaining some of the history of Santa Fe, until, way too soon, we were back at the conference.

Chapter 25

Dinner with Luc

I yawned. It was time for a coffee break. It was milling-around-looking-for-the-next-talk time. I saw Tyler and tried to catch his eye. He had turned up back at the meetings after lunch, looking flushed and happy. He had a rental car and was always looking for an excuse to skip out of a meeting. When he finally noticed me across the hall, I raised my eyebrows in question. He grinned and pulled his keys out and jangled them in my direction. I grinned, and he started toward me.

"You look like a woman who needs a coffee," he said. "Shall we go look for a coffee shop?"

"I think they had coffee at the registration table," a person standing nearby commented.

"Not what I consider coffee," Tyler said.

"That's my boy!" I could always count on Tyler to insist on good coffee.

We ducked out of the conference hall but, instead of driving, walked to a nearby coffee shop. Once there we saw a colleague we knew, Fara. The three of us had shared an office in grad school, but now our jobs were spread out across the country. After getting our lattes, Tyler and I went to her booth and slid in across from her.

"Now, catch me up on what has been happening with you. I haven't seen you since... God, when was that

191

conference in Vancouver?" Fara asked.

"Too long," I answered. I caught them up with the big changes in my life, some of them Tyler had heard the night before, some of them not, moving in with Ben, tenure, and my latest research ideas. We, in turn, heard about the latest on Fara's family, a job offer from Ohio State that she was struggling over whether or not to accept, and her dog, a young Newfy mix that had just chewed up her best pair of shoes.

There's that tickle again. What was it about talking about puppies that made me think there was something I was missing? Was I worried about Suki? Was I worried about Ben taking care of her and Bella? Wait! Bella! Bella was a borzoi puppy. I didn't know of any borzoi breeders on the island, and I knew Bella was younger than three months when Ali got her. The puppy was only four months now. Bella couldn't have come from the mainland. Ali didn't have that kind of money to fly a dog from England or Australia, it was even more expensive than from the mainland. I guess maybe she could have scraped together the price of an unusual purebred puppy like that. Maybe. But I didn't see how she could afford to import one. And I haven't seen any other borzoi puppies around, so I'm sure that puppy didn't come from Hawaii. So where did Bella come from? And how did she land in Ali and Kai's house? When I got back, I needed to check into this. Or better yet, I picked up my phone and texted Ben to ask Kai.

Tyler laughed at something Fara had said, and snapped me back to the present. Evidently, she had a two-year-old boy who had flushed a flash drive with four years' worth of data down the toilet. Tyler claimed that the boy's talent for destruction could reach back to in utero. Fara had a rough experience with morning sickness through much of her pregnancy. Tyler ran into Fara several times a year at professional meetings and local conferences. A couple of years back, they had all gotten together when another lab mate had gotten married. I had just moved to Hawaii and couldn't afford to fly back for a weekend in the middle of the semester. It was one of the challenges of living in Hawaii, my friends and family were a couple thousand miles away. There were no quick weekend getaways for a reunion or a chance running into each other at the local conferences. This was what Ben put into the category of the high price of living in paradise.

We finished our coffee and begrudgingly headed back to the conference. I missed my old coffee buddies. Many a time we'd broken the tedium of data collection or analysis with a coffee run to Tyler's latest and greatest coffee shop. We had been a good research team, shared lots of laughs, and genuinely liked each other.

As we walked back to the conference, Tyler teased me about how he had seen me coming back from lunch with Luc, implying we had snuck away for a tryst.

I chuckled and raised an eyebrow. "We just ran into each other on the way back to the conference. But I think *you* must be projecting… what exactly did you and your friend do for lunch?"

Tyler burst out laughing and lifted his hand to cross his heart. "I'll never tell!"

We made it back for the last talk, in much better spirits than when we had left.

****

The next evening I arrived at Luc's house. He had arranged for a van to bring eight of us, up into the northwest hills on Tano Road, just outside downtown Santa Fe. Luc's house was a work of art, if you like funky, hippy art. The adobe structure had been planned and designed by a '70s guru, and there was not a ninety-degree angle anywhere in the house. A large living area ran the length of the house, with floor-to-ceiling windows on both sides of the room.

As the sun set, the mountains to the east were a velvety lavender with a baby pink and dusky blue sky. Through the window on the west side of the room, I watched the robin's egg blue sky flame into oranges and hot pinks slashed with a sultry purple, an explosion of colors. Edged along the sides of the view were feather outlines of pine needles extending from young juniper trees, black against the vibrant hues.

"No Instagram tinting needed," a young woman murmured. We admired the view, some with rapt longing in their eyes, others pulling out their phones to take pictures. I fell into the rapt longing category. What was it about a flamboyant sunset that seized the heart? An ephemeral beauty of something so sumptuous, that we couldn't keep, touch, or own? Or was the arousal a drive instilled in us by our ancestors, a warning flare that night was approaching and predators would soon be on the prowl?

Despite the staggeringly incredible sunset, people were easily distracted, and soon our little group shifted attention from the wild, breathtaking nature outside the tall windows, and were commenting on the unusual objects cradled within the room.

There were masks from Africa, ancient pots from China, and a carved paddle from a Northwest Native American tribe. Adobe houses, like Luc's, came in all shapes, with shelves and alcoves that appeared randomly in a structure. The result was objects that looked as if they floated at different levels along the creamy white wall that stretched the length of the room.

The other guests laughed and talked as they examined the oddities among Luc's collection. But my gaze slipped out the window. My back would turn to the group without my noticing, until I'd recognize the antisocial nature of my behavior, and I would turn back to listen to the conversation. But an inner voice wished they would be quiet so I could meditate on the drama transforming the sky outside. I forced myself to turn my back once again to the sunset and attempted to engage in the conversation. My gaze traveled the unusual and fascinating room. As my eyes roamed, I caught Luc observing me. Our eyes locked for a minute before he approached me.

He extended his hand and said, "Come with me."

I took his hand as he led me to an alcove in the back corner of the room. As I approached, I realized a tiny, circular, copper staircase was concealed by a curve of the adobe wall.

He released my hand and waved me up the narrow, spiraled steps.

"Be sure to hold the rail," he said. "The steps are narrow."

I did as I was told, and after negotiating the precarious spiral staircase, I stepped out of the cave of the stairwell into a curved room surrounded by windows on three sides– which looked out on a 250 degree view of the most amazing sky I had ever witnessed.

The strident purple, pinks, reds, and fiery orange had exhausted themselves, and what remained was the softest, richest heavens I had ever seen. I wanted to throw myself into the sky and roll around in its velvety beauty. The first stars appeared like diamonds sprinkled on a midnight-blue silk scarf. The mountains were barely visible, with a soft gray-lavender outline, edged in a thin line of glowing burnt-chili orange. A buffer of sage green faded between the last warm color and the lowering shade of star-sprinkled, indigo blue.

It took my breath away, and I realized my eyes were welling up with the beauty of the moment. I blinked the tears away, glad for the dim light, and turned to Luc. A strand of hair was slipping in front of my eyes, but before I could push it out of the way, Luc extended a finger to lift it behind my ear.

"This is why I bought the house," he said quietly. "It's why I am setting up a new branch of the institute here, and why, when I'm in Santa Fe, I almost never leave home at this hour."

"I can understand that," I said.

"I thought you might." His eyes watched the incremental lowering of the velvet blue curtain being slowly lowered on the day.

I stood in the almost dark with the passion of nature melting into an afterglow. My pulse quickened as the intimacy of the moment struck me. I noticed a king-sized bed under the western window. I was standing here, alone, with this intense, wildly attractive man, in his bedroom. As if he heard my heart beating faster, he turned his gaze to me.

We looked at other for a moment, and an overpowering wave of 'oh-my-God-I-want-to-jump-him-here-and-now' smacked up against an equal current of 'don't-be-ridiculous-this-is-impossible,' and we stared at each other, floating in a sea of tension.

Good sense won out.

"I should return to my guests, stay up here and enjoy the view. But, please remember to be careful on the steps."

I watched the last dying spasms of the day before I followed Luc back down.

Dinner was good and the conversation interesting. Luc, who kept this vacation home here, currently runs a think tank in Berkeley, and they had started some new initiatives. Several of the people invited tonight specialized in those areas, so most of the conversation involved them and their projects. After dinner, Luc and those most closely involved with his foundation's projects moved to a sitting area at one end of the long room, notepads spread out on the table, with several people jotting notes about budgets and updating Luc on their progress. The rest of us, four junior faculty, took our coffee and sat in front of a roaring fire at the other end of the room. We chatted quietly about what we were working on and the talks that had impressed us the most thus far at the conference.

After the large meal and good wine, I was not the only one feeling a little drowsy, and our discussion comfortably dissipated as we stared into the flames. A fire was a beautiful thing. Not a gas fire, but a real fire that left ashes and soot and warmed the heart. No wonder people spoke of 'home and hearth' and 'keeping the home fires burning' as sacred things. A burning fire was mesmerizing to watch. Red pops swirled around like fireflies, violet heat hugged the black, brown, and cream of the inner wood, with roasted pumpkin flames. It mimicked the extravagant sunset we had seen earlier.

Except this orange was not dying, but alive and vitriolic. In a real fire the tongues of the blaze danced and changed constantly. And as I stared at them, I began to perceive faces. Devilish faces that leered and laughed at me … daring me to move the fire screen that protected me from them.

"Are you ready to go?"

My head popped up. I had begun to nod off. I looked up, and people were beginning to move toward the coat rack near the door to get their light jackets.

"Sure," I said, jumping up to hide the fact that I had started to doze off.

One of the guests who had been sitting around the fire with me grinned and winked.

"Don't worry," he said. "I was falling asleep too, I won't tell anyone."

I smiled back, and we grabbed our coats, thanked Luc, and loaded up in the van for a trip back to the hotel.

Chapter 26

Patio chat

I sat on the patio of our hotel two days later, talking with Tyler and a couple of other colleagues that I often ran into at conferences. One was Bert Apatschik, one of the grandfathers of the field. He has worked to bring about peace in the Middle East. Indefatigably optimistic, every time he was asked how things were going over there, he responded, "Peace is just about to break out!" as if he truly believed it. I liked the guy. Bert told wonderful, humorous, self-deprecating anecdotes, and despite his international renown, never took himself too seriously.

The other two, Rick and Cammy, were newer on the scene. Younger than me, they had gotten their PhD's with power players in the field. Rick, who had been at the dinner at Luc's the night before, had been one of Bert's students. Both of these young researchers had their dissertations published in top journals and, lest they be classified as one-hit wonders, had followed up with equally strong studies that were making an impact on our field. To say I felt humbled in this grouping was like saying the high desert of Santa Fe wasn't too humid.

Tyler had given his talk this morning and was also on the patio with us. It was our last day of the conference, when people relaxed and let their hair down. Bert was his usual, gentle, inclusive self, and I enjoyed the late afternoon sun, light breeze, and listening to the banter about who had the worst dean. The margaritas we were sipping weren't too bad either.

"On world travels, I don't think you measure up to me and Cammy," Rick said, leaning toward Bert. "I give you the fact that you've spent more days abroad. But how many continents have you been to? Or countries? Granted, you've covered the Middle East, but anywhere else?" Rick had downed one too many margaritas, and his testosterone was spilling.

I watched a hummingbird that was visiting each and every flower on an agastache bush, enjoying the hum of beating wings and the intensity of his food quest.

Bert smiled. "I'm sure you are right, Rick, my boy. I've been stuck in a rut for the last forty-five years. Back and forth between D.C. and the Middle East. The only other place I ever go is Florida. The wife and I head down there every year to see her family."

"How about you, Rick? How many continents have you visited?" Cammy asked.

I was only half-listening, still watching the hummingbird, which had alighted on a low pinon tree, hunkered down as if ready to defend his top branch. With his long needle-like beak, he surveyed the world self-assuredly from his elevated perch. He looked a bit like Rick.

"Every continent except Africa and Antarctica," said Rick. "I went to a conference in Tokyo last year and stopped off in Sydney to give a talk, a conference in Brussels the summer before. And this summer I gave a talk in Chile."

"Me too, but I did a safari in South Africa, so I'm

one continent ahead of you. Ha!" Cammy thrust a fist into the air.

I glanced at Tyler who was looking at me, grinning. We exchanged a look that recognized we were too old for this kind of discussion and glad of it. Tyler dipped his chin and raised one eyebrow as a devilish grin appeared.

"How about *you,* Cleo?" he drawled. "You've traveled quite a bit, haven't you?" His grin widened.

I was halfway to sticking my tongue out at him for dragging me into this childish competition, when out of the corner of my eye, I saw Luc walk through a wrought iron gate onto the patio. I quickly pulled my tongue back in and shifted straighter in my seat. I had a feeling I was also blushing. Tyler looked over his shoulder to see what I was looking at, and when he turned back to look at me again, his eyebrows were so high they almost bumped into his hairline. By then I had gotten control over... whatever that blush was about and shrugged back at him. The others in the group greeted Luc and invited him to join us. I added my "Hello" with the rest of them. Back to my calm, cool, collected self.

Tyler, with that glint in his eye and, if possible, an even more mischievous grin, said, "So, Cleo, you were getting ready to tell us about your travels before Luc joined us." All eyes turned to me, including Luc whose gaze appeared more focused than the rest. Or was that just my imagination?

"I don't know, Tyler. I've traveled a lot, but the world is big. There are loads of places I still want to see."

Luc smiled but didn't comment.

"Well, I remember you were with the group that Peace Today invited for a conference that started in Ramallah and continued to Tel Aviv and Egypt," said

Bert.

"And I remember eating mussels with you at the Brussels conference. And didn't you go on to Tiblisi?" The corners of Tyler's mouth turned up impishly.

"And I think I saw you at a meeting in Hong Kong," Luc said. "If I remember correctly, your talk included data you had collected in Shanghai."

Damn, I was blushing again. What was wrong with me? "Yes."

"How about Africa?" Cammy asked. "I was in South Africa, how about you?"

"Egypt is in Northern Africa," Bert said.

"Yeah, on that trip I went to see some of the border towns of Morocco, Tangiers, and Casablanca, but I didn't get to the interior. I wanted to go to Fez but ran out of time."

"Fez is great, you'd like it," Luc said. "Much closer to old Morocco, and beautiful sunsets."

"You've been?" I asked.

"Yes, I hate to be all new-agey, but in Fez there is a strong sense of magic or spirituality. It's got some kind of mojo going." He smiled at me.

And wow! Fez wasn't the only thing that had some mojo going on.

As Tyler looked meaningfully my way, he stretched and said he had scheduled a massage and was leaving. Bert, encircled by his two young colleagues, began an earnest discussion about a new theory that one of them was developing. I should have been interested and paid attention. But for some reason, I wasn't. And I didn't.

Luc moved to Tyler's seat, next to me. He wasn't listening to the other discussion either but watching me. I smiled at him, trying to think of something to say.

Before the pause could continue to an uncomfortable length, Luc spoke. "There was something I wanted to talk to you about the other evening at my house, but I missed my opportunity." A rueful twist of his lips. "Do you have time now?"

I nodded, my mind raced. I tried to read his face.

"I've been talking to some people about starting a new project. I've almost got the private money lined up to support the study, but I could use someone with your expertise on it."

"What kind of project?" I asked, my pulse fluttering again. Luc had earned a reputation for organizing and leading big-time projects. No way this would work out, I was small potatoes, but it would be fun to play along and pretend for a little while.

"That's the thing… I've got a deep-pocket funder who is interested in my work and wants to start an institute here. I've got to figure the logistics and what the focus will be. Not a university, but something that will foster both research and practical applications for the community. I think your ideas on immigration and acculturation are something we should target."

Professionally, this would be a dream come true… or a disaster. I'd probably have to leave Hawaii, and I'm pretty sure Ben wouldn't follow me here. The high desert was a tough place for a marine scientist to find work.

But pretending was fun.

"Sounds interesting. What did you have in mind?"

He grinned. "First, let me buy you a drink. These types of discussions are always more creative with a drink. What will you have?"

"Hmm." A giddy, reckless feeling came over me. "What do you suggest?"

"How about a market gimlet?"

"What's that?"

"Vodka, grapefruit juice, tarragon agave, and cuke, over ice."

I love grapefruit juice. I smiled. "Sounds perfect."

He ordered two and pulled out a moleskin notebook.

"Ok, this is what I've got so far..." And Luc launched into his ideas, occasionally referring to the notebook and asking my impressions. He seemed to like my ideas, and by the end of the discussion, I think I had a little glow, and not only from the gimlet. He ordered a second, and I was tempted, the cold, tangy flavor was energizing, but if I was at all interested in doing this, I should keep a level head. I declined a second drink, at least until we finished talking business.

Chapter 27

Air travel

"It's not even reading that it's plugged in," the pilot said.

"You just have to wiggle the thing-a-ma-jiggy," came a voice through the open cockpit door.

"OK, now it's working. Shoot! No it's not."

This was the upside and downside of flying on tiny airplanes. When a plane only seats twelve people, there was no separation between the cockpit and cabin. I could hear every problem they were having.

"Anything?" came the voice through the door again.

Evidently, there wasn't 'anything' because the pilot unsnapped his seat belt and climbed out of the cockpit, a tight, forced smile on this face.

"It's going to be a couple of minutes, folks," he said as he hopped out the door and down the short stairway.

"That's not good," the man next to me mumbled to himself. The lady in front of me told her seatmate how screwed up her trip was going to be if they canceled this flight.

Me? I would rather they make sure everything was working peachy-keen before we took off. There were *no* plans I cared enough about to go up in a plane that needed a thing-a-ma-jiggy wiggled.

Ten minutes later the copilot shouted, "Hey, it's

good!"

The pilot climbed back onto the plane.

"It was a problem with the ground equipment, but it's working now. Sorry about the delay, we will be taking off shortly."

Everyone else cheered. I hoped it was a permanent fix, not just the result of a little wiggling. I liked a nice, safe, little airplane.

Minutes later, we started off down the runway, building speed. Until the engine noise changed and momentum stopped. We slowed and turned back toward the small terminal. As we pulled in front of it, the pilot came on the intercom.

"Folks, sorry about the delay again. We had a warning light go on. But we have already corrected the problem. It was nothing. We just have to inform our dispatch, and then we can take off."

I saw relieved expressions on the passengers around me. That was not the expression they would find on my face.

I wanted off this plane. So what if it screwed up my travel arrangements and I left a day later. I wanted a safe airplane with no warning lights going off. Was that too much to ask?

Yeah, that's not unreasonable. I would tell them I wanted to get off. This was the only flight out today, so I would have to leave tomorrow, but that was not a big deal. I could get someone to cover the class I would miss, and Ben was watching the dogs. But could I get a hotel? There was some big festival this weekend in Santa Fe, and I heard all the hotels in town were booked up. But surely I could find something. Or Luc had a house here. I'm sure he'd offer to let me crash at his place if he knew my situation. Our planning session yesterday ran late. We'd both gotten caught up in talking about ideas for the project, and we'd lost track of time. Luc's assistant tracked him down, or we both would have missed the last event, a banquet with our final speaker. The speaker was entertaining. I'm glad I didn't miss it. And the project Luc and I sketched out was intriguing. He'd probably end up hiring someone with more prestige than me to run it, but it was fun to plan. If I stayed tonight, we could get a lot more done. Email and zoom were fine, but there was nothing like face-to-face meetings for making plans. Of course, staying at his house might not be a great idea. I was focused through most of our discussion... really engaged with the ideas, but there were times that my eyes wandered to his finely chiseled cheekbones and his dark hair falling over those George Clooney eyes.

Maybe it wouldn't be such a good idea to stay here again tonight.

I remembered the touch of his hand on my arm when he wanted to emphasize a point he was making. My gaze shifted out the window. Damn, we were in the air. While I daydreamed about Luc, we had taken off. Sheez, if I got this carried away just thinking about him, it was a very good thing I didn't stay an extra night.

****

I huddled around the outlets at gate 74 of LAX, with other technology-dependent travelers. It was bad enough to sit shoulder to shoulder on the airplane for the six-hour flight over the Pacific Ocean to the tiny archipelago I currently called home. But the five-hour layover between flights, and the crowds around the power outlets, added another layer of aggravation to the trip. A good thing Ben hadn't come with me or I couldn't have resisted raising the issue of our self-imposed isolation, caused by our continued residence in Hawaii. And that would have started another argument. I could hear him now. "If you didn't have your self-imposed *need* for technology or *need* to travel, this would not be a problem."

I took a deep breath, rolled my shoulders, almost dislodging the iPad my neighbor had delicately balanced on the armrest between us, which was plugged in to her son's computer, which was plugged into my neighboring outlet. If I wasn't living this headache, I would laugh. I would rather laugh.

I unplugged. I would use my laptop until it stopped working, and then so would I. Whatever was left undone could wait until tomorrow. Feeling a hundred percent better with this decision, I packed up my computer bag and decided to stretch my legs. While unzipping my laptop sleeve, I looked around for the first time since I'd sat down two hours ago to charge up and work. I noticed a familiar face, Mason was standing nearby, scoping out the outlet situation.

It was a strange phenomenon running into somebody I knew in a major airport like LAX. For years, I traveled the world and never ran into anyone I knew unexpectedly. Until United Airlines started a direct flight from Hilo to LAX and that changed. It was the only flight out of Hilo that left the state, so anybody in Hilo going anywhere out of the state usually took this flight. Hilo was such a small town that on every flight there was at least a couple of people I knew, and on almost every flight there would be a random encounter at LAX thousands of miles from home. I waved to Mason that my spot was opening up. He smiled with relief and maneuvered around the luggage carts and cords to the seat I had emptied.

"Thanks," he said, "my iPad is completely dead, and I rented some movies to watch for the trip home. I was going to be pissed if I couldn't charge up."

"No problem. I've done all the sitting I can handle, before I have to get on that plane." I stood up and stretched. "Where are you coming from? Somewhere fun I hope."

"I wish." Mason grimaced. "I had to meet with my father. He had a meeting in Denver and required my presence." Mason bent over to plug in his iPad cord. "Dad is still twisting my arm to go into his business, and if I want his help with the dive shop, I have to show up for these mandatory business experiences."

I heard disgust in his voice.

"Hell, I'm twenty-seven years old, you'd think he'd give it up and quit trying to run my life. I mean the dive shop is doing great, it's a success. He should get off my back already."

I nodded. I sympathized with Mason's dad, but it wouldn't be polite to verbalize it at this moment. From what I've heard, the dive shop was doing well before Kai got arrested, but only because of Kai. The coconut telegraph said that the only thing Mason had contributed to the shop were decorating ideas. And start-up money, which he got from his father.

"Have you heard anything else about Kai's case?" Mason asked.

I shook my head. "I've been out of town for the last five days, how about you?"

He shrugged. "I've only been gone three, but I didn't hear anything before I left either."

"So, where were you?" Mason smiled. "Somewhere

fun?"

"I was in Santa Fe, for a conference, but yeah, I had a good time." A memory of Luc standing behind me in his bedroom looking at the sunset flashed in my mind. Was I blushing? "I mean Santa Fe is such a great little city, isn't it?" I rushed on, trying to get the image of Luc out of my mind. "I mean the art galleries, the great restaurants, the plaza…"

"Yeah, I was there a couple of months ago with a chickie," Mason said, checking to see that his iPad was charging after plugging it in. "It's a fun town."

"On vacation?" I asked.

Mason shook his head. "Another one of my father's errands. He collects art, and he's trying to get me to take an interest in that too. There was a painting there by Lynden St. Victor at a gallery he was thinking of buying and wanted me to stop by and look at it in person."

Mason smiled. "For once I actually liked something he'd picked out. It had a weird but erotic woman with a dog in it. And the dog in the painting was a cool dog. The chickie I was with was really jonesing for the dog. It had some kind of inspirational name like Love or Joy or something, but the woman in the painting had an up-to-no-good look about her I thought was pretty sexy… a better name would have been 'Evil Alice and the—' " Mason stopped cold and looked shocked at what he'd said.

"I mean no disrespect for the dead, I'd feel awful if Kai heard that, he loved her so much. It's just, you know how Ali could be… she had that sex-kitten look one minute, then was a bitch and a half the next."

"Ali had her moments." And to move the conversation along, I asked, "So, do I know this 'chickie' of yours?"

An indecipherable look passed over Mason's face. Then a devilish grin replaced it so fast I thought maybe I imagined it.

"Why, Cleo, I'm a gentleman! You don't think I'd kiss and tell, do you?" He laughed.

I'm sure Rikki would be glad to know that.

I wanted to walk and stretch my legs before climbing back on another plane for the last flight, across half the Pacific Ocean. I made my exit as soon as it was polite. Mason was glad to get my seat as well as the outlet. I made a couple of laps from gates in the 60s, 70s, and 80s, and it was time to head back to my assigned gate and wait for the cattle call of my boarding group.

Chapter 28

A Hilo Welcome

The downside to traveling as much as I did was jetlag, tensions with Ben, and environmental guilt. But the upside to so much flying was an airline upgrade. I relished the early boarding so I could stow my bag overhead, and the bigger seat. Today there was entertainment. A young soldier was on this flight. I'd seen him in the waiting area, reddish-gold hair, freckles on his face, and looking like one of the freshman in my class, except for the army fatigues and phantoms in his eyes. But there was a shy smile on his face when he walked past the first class and 'elite' flyers to board early. I was bumped up to the last row of the first-class section, Mason was also flying first class, but several rows ahead of me. I noticed the young soldier was sitting right behind me on the first row of the economy section. A mother and her two young boys boarded and filled the row next to him. I planned to grade papers on the flight, but the kids, fascinated by the soldier, began questioning him in strident voices.

"Are you a Navy seal?" one of the little boys asked.

"No, I'm in the Army, but my sister is in special ops."

"They let girls in?"

"Only if they are super smart and super fit, and my

sister is.

"We're from Vancouver," one of the little boys said. "Have you ever been to Vancouver?"

"I went to Vancouver one time, but it's not a tale for little ears," the soldier answered solemnly.

I smiled. I'm sure the mom must be wracking her brain on how to divert this conversation. She said something in a soft voice I couldn't hear over the sound of the engine. Whatever it was, it worked.

"I play hockey," one of the little boys said. "Do you play any games?"

"You'll lose teeth if you keep playing hockey," the soldier said. "I lost a tooth doing that when I was a kid."

"But now they have faceguards," said the mom.

"I had a faceguard," said the soldier, "but I'd crashed and was on the ice and another player's skate crashed into my face. The blade must have slid under the guard somehow because I lost a tooth and got this little scar."

"Whoaaa," the kids said.

"I like soccer," said the soldier. "And rugby. And probably American football third."

"How about baseball?" asked one boy. "Baseball's my second-favorite sport."

"Not crazy about baseball, it's a little slow. I like faster games that don't stop, like rugby and soccer. Actually, rugby may be my favorite sport, and soccer is second."

"What's rugby? Is it that game people play with a long stick?" one of the boys asked.

"No, you're thinking of cricket," said the soldier. "I hate cricket. It's worse than baseball. But everybody in the Middle East loves cricket. They all play it."

The little boys thought about that for a minute, then asked him to explain rugby. The sports discussion continued and moved on to favorite video games. If that soldier hasn't earned a medal for combat, I bet the mom was ready to give him one for entertaining her two small, obviously active boys on a five-hour flight. I don't know why I found their conversation so riveting. Maybe it was the childlike delight I heard in the soldier's voice talking about his favorite games. A soldier who has probably seen more than his fair share of tragedy. Or was it the innocent awe in the boys' voices—a mixture of fascination and hero worship? Eavesdropping on their conversation was a pleasant way to pass the flight. At some point, I drifted off and woke just as we landed.

I made my way off the plane, stretching to wake up, and walked along the open-air hallway to the steps which lead down to baggage claim. It was a warm, humid night. It would probably start raining soon. The smell of ginger floated in the air. Yep, we'd landed at Hilo Airport. As I walked down the steps, I saw people, laden with leis of plumeria, puakenikeni, and twisted ti leaves, waiting for their friends and relatives.

As I scanned the colorful, sweet-smelling crowds, I finally saw Ben. No lei in his hand, but he had shown up. He smiled and stepped toward me as I reached the bottom. We hugged and moved out of the way so other passengers could receive their two-cheek kisses from their welcome crews, and stepped toward the baggage carousel. While we were waiting for my checked bag, I told Ben that Mason was on the plane, and we decided to offer him a ride home if he didn't have someone picking him up.

By the time my bag arrived, a light rain had started,

and the bags glistened with their dampness as they glided around the luggage conveyer belt. I pulled my suitcase off and unzipped the outside pocket to pull out the umbrella I kept there. It rained almost every time I needed to walk to the car with my bag from this airport. Mason hadn't shown up in the baggage claim area. He must have carried on his bag, so we walked by the taxi area to look for him. We passed the crowds of people who were drive-by-picking-up arriving passengers. As we wound our way around a large group with about ten pieces of luggage, a dark-haired, laughing young man turned away from hugging an older woman, stepped back, turned, and crashed straight into me.

"Oh my God, I so sorry! I didn't take one look. You okay?" The young man caught my arm as I was halfway from falling over my suitcase and helped me catch my balance.

"Yeah, I'm OK," I said. I was a little shaken and looked up into the friendly, worried eyes of Kevin.

"Cleo. Oh my God, I did not know it was you! How you been?"

I laughed. "I'm good, Kevin, except for people almost knocking me over... I'm good!"

"Yea, yea," he said. "But I saved you from hitting the ground. So no shame." Smiling, he gave me the traditional two-cheek-kiss greeting.

Ben, who was behind me when this happened, made his way up next to me.

"Kevin, you know Ben, don't you?" I turned to Ben. "And you remember Kevin, right? He paddles at the club. I'm pretty sure you guys met at one of the races last summer."

They nodded and shook hands.

"Were you traveling, Kevin?" I asked.

"No, we heah, picking up my auntie from Oahu. She heah fo' my mother's birthday next week, we will have one big family luau wid a pig and everting. She came over dis week to get the cookin' started. How 'bout you? Looks like you were away on one trip."

"Yeah, a conference. Hey, we were looking for Mason. I know he was on my flight, and I wanted to see if he needed a ride home."

"I saw him, and I know he needs a ride. I told him we take him if der was room after Auntie's bags are in da truck. He can ride in da back if he want. But she got a lotta bags." Kevin pointed to a large white pickup truck that had just pulled to the curb. "He's over der, talking to Mele."

I looked in the direction he pointed, and saw Mason talking nonchalantly to Mele. She was giving me the Stink Eye.

I thanked Kevin and wished his mother a Happy Birthday. I gathered up my courage, and Ben and I walked in the direction of Mason and Mele, dragging my roller bag behind me. In the crowd, I had to concentrate to avoid catching my bag on anybody else. I also avoided looking at Mele but could feel her staring at me in a bone-chilling way that made my skin crawl. When we got within an arm's length, Mason noticed us.

"There you are, Cleo! Hi, Ben!" He stuck his hand out for Ben to shake.

I said hello to both Mason and Mele. Mason grinned back at me. Mele stared stonily without responding. We offered Mason a ride, and he accepted. I think feeling the tension, he rushed his goodbyes to Mele and Kevin. The three of us walked toward the parking lot. The rain that had greeted the luggage had stopped.

As we walked from the brightly lit airport into the inky darkness of the parking lot, Mason pulled even to me and said in a low voice, "Boy, Mele doesn't like you."

I shot him a sideways look. "Yeah, I've kinda noticed that. I don't know why, I've never done anything to her."

Ben, who was a few steps ahead since he was the only one who knew where he had parked, spoke up. "Kevin is her boyfriend, right? And he looked awful glad to see you, Cleo."

"But Kevin's like that with everybody!" I sputtered. "He's not into me like that at all."

"It doesn't matter," Mason said. "You know how those local girls can be."

My back stiffened. I hated when people used stereotypes. I struggled with whether I should correct him and point out the high rate of inaccuracies in stereotypes, but I didn't want to sound like I was lecturing him. I mean, I was a professor, but I didn't want to sound like one outside of class with my friends. Before I could make up my mind how to respond to Mason's comment, he started speaking again.

"And Mele is the worst. I mean you're right. Kevin's like that with everybody, but she only gets that way when he talks to women. She was furious, ready to kill Ali at a party one time when she caught Ali and Kevin talking, before Ali was with Kai. She doesn't like Kevin interacting with other women *at all*. I don't know how Kevin stands it. No chickie is going to boss me around like that and get away with it."

We reached the car and started loading our bags. I

pushed Mason to take the front passenger seat for his longer legs. He accepted and climbed in. I slid into the back seat and closed my eyes, resting my head on the head rest while I listened to Mason chattering away. He peppered Ben with questions about updates on Kai and what had happened in Hilo while he was gone. I could tell Ben was tired, but he answered all of Mason's questions. Kai was still depressed, maybe even more so. He missed Ali, felt like he had let her down, and was crushed that she had been pregnant and hadn't told him. The lawyer was trying to build a defense, but Kai had given up.

As we turned into Mason's neighborhood, he twisted around, left arm propping him off the seatback, and looked at me.

"I've been thinking, Cleo, I really think Mele is a suspect we should look at more closely for Ali's murder."

I roused myself from my drowsy state. "Yeah, Rikki mentioned that too. I just didn't get a chance to follow up on that before I left." Remembering that walk in the park with Rikki and Gina, I realized that was the last time any of us had seen Weezy alive.

"By the way, Mason, do you remember when we ran into each other at Liliuokalani? You were running, and Rikki, Gina, and I had stopped to talk with Weezy, Gina's friend?"

"Sure," Mason said. "Rikki was looking hot in that spandex." He grinned and wiggled his eyebrows in a fake-debonair manner.

I didn't smile back. "I got a call from Gina while I was gone, Weezy died."

"Really? You're kidding."

"You didn't tell me about that." Ben glanced back in the rearview mirror, his voice worried. "Who died?"

"I just heard about it when I got to Santa Fe. You didn't know her, Ben. She and Gina grew up together but hadn't stayed in touch. Gina just reconnected with her again in the last couple weeks when we ran into her at Liliuokalani Park a couple of times."

"How did she die?" Mason asked.

"The police think that she was picking opihi off the rocks and got knocked out by a wave and drowned."

"Wow," said Mason. "That's sad. Poor Weezy."

"Yeah, if that's what really happened."

"What? You think it was something else?"

"Well, I don't know. But I was telling a friend about it, and he thought it was strange. First Ali dies, then Weezy tells us she knows something about Ali's death, and then, before she can tell us what that is, Weezy winds up dead. The more I think about it, the more I think he might be right."

Ben turned a corner, and I realized we were on Mason's street. As we pulled up to Mason's driveway, he turned to me. "This could be getting dangerous for you, Cleo. I know some people who knew Weezy, I'll ask around and see if you're right. But you and Gina should stay out of that area of the investigation. Ben, don't you agree?"

Ben sighed. It was dark in the car, but I could see the profile of his face outlined by the streetlight. "Yes, I think all of us should stay out of it and hire professionals to look into this." He turned to look back at me, right arm resting on the seat back. "I'll tell the lawyer your ideas and check into a private investigator. You should leave it alone for now, Cleo."

I didn't answer Ben, but as Mason got out and retrieved his bag from the trunk, I moved into the front seat next to Ben.

We drove home in a tired silence, while I thought over what he had said. I understood that he was worried, but I hated it when men got all "leave it to us, little lady," and then didn't do anything. Was a private investigator going to believe in Kai like we did? Could we afford to pay a lawyer *and* a private investigator? Mason probably could, but he was pretty quiet about hiring a P.I. when Ben suggested it. These thoughts bounced around in my brain as we pulled into our driveway and walked up the steps into the house, but when I kneeled down to greet the dogs, my worries were washed away under a shower of puppy kisses from Suki and Bella.

Chapter 29

Suki!

A few days later, I took Suki in for her follow-up appointment at the veterinarian.

"I think we need to schedule that surgery," I said. "The meds haven't worked. Her leg is worse, and we haven't let her run off leash at all."

"Hmm, yes, I can see the limp is worse," the vet said. He kneeled on the floor next to the dog and ran his hand up the leg that was giving her problems. "Let me see what that feels like, baby."

I watched his face, and his expression changed. Something was different.

"I'm going to give her a sedative," he said and murmured something to his assistant who left the room immediately. "I think we should X-ray this to make sure it's the ACL before we do the surgery."

"Did you feel something?" I asked.

"Maybe, but let's look at the X-ray before we drive ourselves crazy guessing." He smiled as the assistant returned to the room with a big needle. He looked at Suki's chart.

"Eighty-five pounds, a big girl, but I can manage that." He scooped her up to put her on the metal examining table. His assistant, a young woman smaller than me, handed the vet a needle and held Suki while he gave her the injection. I watched Suki fight against the lethargy, looking at me, as if feeling guilty for being lazy. I petted her and told her it was okay and not to worry. Tears welled in my eyes. I blinked them away, angry with myself. No reason to stress out yet, this was just an X-ray. But Suki's struggle to stay awake upset me. I took deep, calming, three-part yoga breaths so my anxiety wouldn't transmit itself to her, and continued to murmur soothing things and stroke her belly. After a few minutes, she appeared to relax and fall asleep.

Meanwhile the vet had left to tend to another patient, and the assistant found someone to help her put Suki on a stretcher to carry her to the X-ray room. Suki appeared to be fully asleep when they put her on the stretcher and lifted her up, but as they left me in the room, Suki struggled to sit up. Even completely drugged and out of it, she didn't want to leave me unprotected. The techs set the stretcher back down on the table while I soothed Suki back asleep. They strapped her in so she couldn't jump off the stretcher, and carried her out. Suki struggled feebly and lifted her head to look at me until she was out of sight. I broke down and full-out ugly-cried for a minute before talking myself back. I kept repeating, "We don't know anything yet. It can be fixed. She's young, she will heal quickly," over and over like a mantra. I got control of myself and stared at a magazine with red-rimmed, unseeing eyes until the vet stuck his head back in the room.

"Let's go look at those X-rays together."

I tried to smile back and followed him through a warren of hallways with small rooms on each side. At the last room before the back exit, he waved for me to step in ahead of him. Suki was lying on a table and lifted her head to greet me, lethargic but aware of my presence. I petted her, running my fingers through soft black curls on the top of her head, while I watched the vet put the X-ray against the light screen and stare at it perplexed. I looked at the X-ray too but realized I didn't have a clue what it meant. So I watched the vet. His brow furrowed, and never taking his eyes off the screen, he shifted position on his stool and wiped his hand from his forehead down his face.

"This is bad," he said, "very, very bad."

My eyes welled up with tears, and I leaned over to kiss Suki on the head, blinking them away. I lifted my head. "OK, so what is it?" I tried to keep my voice as level as I could.

For the first time since we entered the room, the vet looked at me, and the sadness on his face was like a blow to my belly.

"I'm afraid it's bone cancer," he said. "A very aggressive type of cancer in dogs." At that point, my brain kind of switched off as he pointed to the X-ray and talked about star-burst patterns and delineation of an outer lining of the bone. All I could think of was that I had to hold it together. Dogs in general, and Suki in particular, feed off an owner's energy, and my panic and grief were spiking into the atmosphere. Suki was coming out of the anesthesia, and I needed to keep it together for her. As the vet had finished his explanation, I managed to force myself back into some semblance of calmness. I asked the vet about treatment options, surprised at how normal my voice sounded.

"I'm afraid there aren't any good ones," he said. "The first step would be to amputate the leg and keep our fingers crossed it hasn't spread. If she was a small dog, I might recommend that, but with a dog her size…" He shrugged his shoulders. "It's your decision, but I have seen a dog this size manage well on three legs." He quietly went on to explain a couple of other "second step" treatments but that all of them would be expensive and very uncomfortable for her, in some cases painful. And even with all that, there was only a twenty percent probability of extending her life significantly. And none of them were available in Hawaii. If we chose to do radiation or chemo, we'd have to move to California for her treatments.

I stood in stunned silence for a minute while the vet and his assistant looked at me with sympathy.

I needed to say something.

"I hear what you are saying. And it makes sense." I said. "It's just… I really love this dog—"

Except when I got to the word dog, it came out as a sob, as my breath caught in my throat and the tears streamed down my face. Suki struggled to try and see what was hurting me. I leaned down and let her lick the tears off my face, then buried my face in her silky curls and once again got myself under control.

The vet assured me he understood and suggested we give her pain meds and some antibiotics on the slim chance it was a deep bone infection instead of cancer. We would make another appointment in two weeks to check her progress and give me some time to think about the options.

****

Ben looked as shell-shocked as I felt. I had returned home with Suki, and she was lying at my feet. Bella kept trying to entice her to play, but Suki ignored her. Ben scooped Bella up and absently stroked her belly, still processing the news I'd brought from the vet.

"Wow," he said. "I didn't see that coming."

"I know. She's so young. I can't believe this is happening. What a crappy month this has been. First Ali's death, Kai's arrest, and now Suki…" I just wanted to crawl under the covers and not get up till it all went away.

I reached down and let the black curls on top of Suki's head slide through my fingers. I struggled to empty my mind of the overwhelming sadness that lurked in all corners of my thoughts. I watched two green, day geckos face-off, ready for battle on the windowsill next to Ben. When we first moved here a couple of years ago, the only geckos we ever saw were the ghostly pale grayish-pink 'night' geckos. I would only see them at night if I turned a light on and unexpectedly picked up something like dish soap or watered the plant in the window. When I moved the object, the sweet, shy, ethereal gecko would be sitting there, eyes blinking, toes splayed, and ready for action should any bug dare to approach. But then the day geckos moved over from the Kona side. Those bad boys were another kettle of fish. Everyone thought they were cute at first, brash, bellicose, and garishly bright. Day geckos were brilliantly colored- a parrot green fading to aqua blue with jaunty dark salmon dashes. They were not shy and would stare you down if you entered their territory. If you stood up to their challenge, they might eventually back off, but day geckos were not afraid to bluff someone a thousand times their size. It was fun to watch at first. But they were fertile little fellows. I guess, like humans, female geckos were drawn to beauty and bluster. Soon we had not just one day gecko on our porch, but another one had taken over our living room, then another in the bedroom, and on and on, until each room had its day gecko. And the night geckos? I'm not sure where they went. I'm worried about them. The last time I saw one, I was sitting on the back porch one evening, just as it was getting dark. I was writing my lecture notes for the next day when... *flappp*. Something dropped from the ceiling onto an open book. When I looked closer, I saw it was a green day gecko and my ghostly night gecko locked in a roiling, writhing battle. I liked my night geckos and didn't want him hurt, so I intervened, using my pencil eraser to try and dislodge the green gecko, which seemed to be winning. When I did that, the gray gecko used the distraction to make a run for it, and the green gecko slowly sauntered off. I think I even saw his chest swell in cockiness. Now, there are too many day geckos for even the day geckos. At least once a week, two males battled for territory. I couldn't remember how many gecko battles have been fought in that particular window behind Ben. It must be primo gecko country.

It was going to be interesting when Bella realized they were there. Right now she was relishing Ben's cuddles. But as soon as she saw the geckos, she would make like Wile E. Coyote, paws running in the air trying to get to them faster than the speed of light. She loved to hunt geckos. I was getting ready to warn Ben so he could move the beer he had sitting on the end table under the window when he spoke first.

"I guess you realize with Suki being sick, it's another reason not to leave for sabbatical."

I felt sick to my stomach. My heart was breaking, and Ben wanted to use Suki's cancer to win our argument over sabbatical. It didn't matter that he might be right. That he would even bring up our sabbatical argument at a time like this left me cold.

"Let's deal with one catastrophe at a time," I said and stood up. "I'm not hungry, I think I'll go sit on the porch with Suk. How about you figure out dinner on your own tonight."

I walked out of the room with Suki on my heels. I'd give my old friend Anna a call. There was something about a childhood friend who knew you, before you became who you are, that was precious. Yes, I'd call Anna, and she would commiserate with me, without an agenda.

****

Friday, I had a meeting with the assistant vice chancellor. There was a large international grant that Luc had encouraged me to apply for during our discussion on the patio in Santa Fe. It would be good for my career, and Luc thought I had a shot at getting it. But the grant would require buy-in of my time from the university, so I needed to start lining up support from the administration. If successful, the grant would bring international recognition and money to the university; but because it would take me away from some of my teaching, it was going to be a hard sell. But I'd done my preparation, organized my research, and planned arguments.

As I made my way across campus, I saw Walker Wolf standing in front of the library, a bevy of pretty young coeds laughing at something he had said. As I approached them, he poured something on first the back of his own hand, and then on the back of a young woman's hands. Suggestively, he gave the world's slowest lick to his own hand while staring into the eyes of the young woman to whom he had just applied the cream. She blushed and appeared lost in his gaze. He nodded at her and gave her a crooked smile. She giggled and pulled her own hand up to her mouth and licked. The other women in the group watched for her reaction, jealousy shooting from their eyes. My curiosity was piqued, and I slowed my steps to observe. I wanted to figure out what the hell Walker Wolf was doing. But Walker must have seen me out of the corner of his eye, because his sexy smile thinned to an angry line, and he shoved his hands into his pockets, one of them holding something.

"I have to get to class now," he said. I assume he was talking to the young women surrounding him, but he glared at me as he spoke. He turned abruptly and stalked off. The students startled at the sudden departure, quickly recovered, grabbing the hand of their friend for a close look at the licked area. Giggling and chattering commenced. It was an octave higher than my comfort zone, and since I didn't know any of them, and they didn't look distressed, I decided not to hassle them with questions and continued to my meeting. When I got to the administration office, the receptionist told me the administrator was sorry, but a student emergency had come up, and we would have to reschedule.

Sighing, I rescheduled for a month in the future and made the cross-campus trek back to my office. As I passed in front of the library, I replayed the episode with Walker and those female students. *What creepiness was Walker Wolf up to?*

Before plunging into data analysis, I checked my email, I have been nagging Ben to ask Kai where Ali got her borzoi puppy. Nothing from Ben. But an email from Luc popped up, and my pulse quickened. *Oh, grow up, it's probably just a form email he sent to everyone who participated.*

But it wasn't. Luc was following up to see how Suki was doing. He said he had been thinking about me and hoped her limp had improved. I think he must have suspected it hadn't. Come to think of it, in our discussion, the dog he recently lost had died of bone cancer. He must have recognized Suki's symptoms. Luc's email was a gentle offer of support if I needed it. I blinked away the tears as I responded, updating him on Suki's diagnosis. I thanked him. Perhaps he was a player. But he was a kind player. I also mentioned that I was following up on the grant he had mentioned before sending the email off and opening up my SPSS program to start wrestling with my latest data set.

Chapter 30

A decision and confrontation

We made it to the covered deck before the cloud opened up. It had been a beautiful Saturday morning, and we'd piled the dogs into the car and come up to the farm. Now that we knew Suki's injury wasn't a torn ACL, the vet said we could let her run again. In case we decided to amputate, we were bringing her up here a lot so she could run as much as she wanted while she had all four legs. She limped a little, but Bouviers were famous for not showing pain. It was hard to tell how much it hurt her. We didn't push it but let her choose her activity level, until a little rain cloud drifted over us and started releasing baby butterfly raindrops.

Ben, the dogs, and I sat in dryness, well, dampness, on the covered deck, as the rain pounded down around us. A high-pitched hum emanated from the tin roof overhead as it was assaulted by a million bullet raindrops. And the musty smell of our small herd, five black angus and one red angus, rose as they come to cluster around us. Our deck was raised, so the floor came to the head height of the cows and was surrounded by a railing. The overhang of the tin roof allowed the cows to shelter their heads out of the rain, if not their bodies. Or maybe they just liked our company. They followed us up and gathered at the rail, staring as us, with dry heads and wet backs. Soon the black cows got bored and put their heads down, munching. But the red one kept angling her head up to see what we were doing. Her big brown eyes and thick peach-colored lips had a patient smile on them. She reminded me of my old kindergarten teacher, kindly and observant, if not too energetic.

"It looks like we may be here for a while unless we want to get soaked hiking it down to the car," Ben said, breaking my reverie.

I looked up and realized that while I had been watching the cows, the small rain cloud had expanded, and a thick gray mist now extended in every direction.

"I say wait it out a bit more, we might just be in the middle of this raincloud right now," I said. We stared out at the silvery haze surrounding us.

Ben cleared his throat. "I've been doing some research on Suki's condition. On the internet, and with people I know at a vet school in California. They all say amputation is the way to go."

I watched the red cow reach her head around to chase some flies off her back. I'd been reading up on it too. I knew most of the sources said it was the best thing, but… how happy could she be on three legs? Dogs were not people. They couldn't rationalize that three legs were better than dead. Would she understand that?

"You think I should get an appointment for them to take her leg off?" I asked.

"I know it's hard. But she's in pain, Cleo. Everything I hear is that she is in substantial pain with bone cancer. The pain goes away when they amputate. If it hasn't spread, it extends her life, maybe a little, maybe a lot, but it extends it. And it takes the pain away for a little while."

"Will she be able to manage it here at the farm with three legs?" Tears filled my eyes. I blinked them away.

Ben put a hand on my shoulder. "We'll help her if she can't. I'll drive her up here to the deck if she can't make it up the hill. She can sit with you here on the deck and watch the cows."

A tear escaped and slid down my cheek. Ben reached a finger up to catch it.

I nodded. "OK, I'll call the vet when we get back to the house. You're right."

We sat there, watching the rain let up before Ben's phone rang. It was Mason. Ben answered, and grimaced as he listened. I tried to figure out why Mason had called but wasn't getting much from Ben's grunts and noncommittal comments. It was good to know I wasn't the only person Ben treated that way on the phone.

When he hung up, I asked. "What did Mason have to say? Does he have any news?"

Ben gave a heavy sigh. "He tried to call Kai today. Kai wouldn't talk to him. The auntie that Kai is staying with said Kai is depressed and doesn't talk to anyone that calls except his lawyer. He's not eating and not sleeping well. And from what I hear from his lawyer, Kai doesn't really say anything to him even when he *does* answer the phone. The poor kid seems to be sinking deeper and deeper into a pit." Ben shook his head. "The lawyer is doing his best, but it doesn't look good, Cleo."

Ben heaved a frustrated sigh and ran the fingers of his right hand through his hair, releasing angry energy. "And that uncle calls too. According to the person Mason talked to, Ali's uncle calls just about every day, trying to talk to Kai."

The uncle. Tino. We hadn't thought about him for a

while. "Did the lawyer ever track down what day the uncle arrived in town?" I asked. That was on one of our early lists, and I'd never followed up on that.

Ben shrugged. "I don't know. I can ask the lawyer on Monday. I hope Ali's uncle isn't harassing Kai, making him feel worse."

I agreed, but part of me was feeling a little hopeful that we might have another suspect to divert police interest from Kai. I promised myself I would follow up on Monday. Having an action plan improved my mood. And scheduling Suki's surgery was an action plan too. It was a traumatic step to take, but if it removed her pain and extended her life... Who knows, maybe if we did it quickly we could catch the cancer before it spread. Yes, an action plan always made me feel more optimistic. And look, a ray of sun was breaking through the clouds.

"Come on, puppies," I called. And while Ben headed back to the fence he had been working on, I took the two dogs out for another romp to the stream, maybe Suki's last as a four-legged dog.

****

Monday I nagged Ben into calling the lawyer first thing. He was in a meeting but would call us back. Next, I called the vet and got an appointment for Suki's amputation. They would get me in the next day. Ben and I then left for the university.

About an hour later, I had just hung up the phone in my office after talking with a student, when Ben called. The lawyer had followed up, and the uncle had flown to the Big Island two days before Ali had been killed. *Score! The action plan was working!*

The rest of the day was a blur of students, emails, and lecture preparation. I stopped at the grocery store on my way home, I had rice and veggies at home that I'd picked up at the farmer's market, but I thought I'd run in and grab a piece of fish. Big mistake. Once I got inside, I realized the store was packed. Instead of waiting in the long line to get a piece of fresh opakapaka, I grabbed a tub of poke, a not-too-spicy variety that Ben liked. As I turned to go, I was boxed in by some aunties who had run into each other unexpectedly and were using the opportunity to catch up. I was tired and ready to be home, so I tried to squeeze the other direction and go the long way around the line of people waiting at the seafood counter. I saw the end of the line and got ready to cut across to the other side just as Ali's uncle Tino stepped into line. I almost ran into him. I stepped back just in time. He was so large, and so used to people displacing themselves around him, I don't think he even noticed me. I thought about slinking past and hoping he wouldn't see me, but decided that was the coward's way out.

I took a deep breath, straightened my shoulders and said, "Hello again."

His eyes focused on me, hardening as he realized who I was.

"Oh, it's you."

"Yeah." I should ask him if he had an alibi for the night Ali was killed. I should ask him if he knew David was out of jail. I should ask him —

"I heah you try get Kai boy outta trouble. You got that mutha fucka who kill Ali outta jail."

"Yeah, but Kai didn't—"

He raised a tree trunk of an arm from his side into a V shape and leaned toward me, with one finger extending into a point that rested no more than an inch from my chin. He blocked out the fluorescent light above me.

"You listen heah, you niele haole. If you get dat bastard dat killed Ali off da hook, and nobody pays fo' her death... I'm comin' afta you."

I didn't pee my pants. Almost. But I managed not to. I swallowed, hoping sound would come out when I spoke.

"Kai didn't kill Ali. I'm trying to find out who did. But it wasn't Kai."

And with as much dignity as I could, when one has shaking knees, I walked past him and toward the door. I left the poke in the milk section. It would stay cold that way for someone else, but no way I was going to risk running into him again in the checkout line. Ben and I could eat vegetarian tonight.

Ben wasn't home when I got there anyway. As I walked through the door, he sent me a text he wouldn't be home for dinner. I heated up a frozen lasagna. My mother would cringe if she knew I ate these. She was a big believer in cooking from scratch, probably the reason that the restaurant she and my father ran was so popular. There was no more word from Ben about why he wouldn't be home. He was probably working late. I decided to take the dogs for a walk. After putting the leash on Bella, Suki uncharacteristically didn't want to get up. She just lay there, looking at me with her big soft eyes. She must be in pain, or she would never pass up a walk. I guess it was good she was getting the amputation tomorrow. After stroking Suki's head for a minute and telling her she would feel better tomorrow, I gathered up the puppy and headed out the door. Bella was getting better on a leash, so we walked down the hill to the Bayfront downtown area. Bella was a pretty dog and an unusual breed, and she received lots of petting from strangers, which was good for her socialization. We walked under the covered walkway in front of the art galleries, Dragon Mama futons, and the health food store along the north end of Kam Ave and were just about to walk past Cronies Bar, a 1920s structure that was a favorite hangout, and turn up Waianuenue to head back toward our house, when out of Cronies Bar stumbled Mason.

"Cleo… and the bella Belllla!" From the way he dragged out Bella's name, I could tell he'd been drinking. A substantial amount. He swayed as he ran a clumsy hand along Bella's back. Bella didn't seem to mind. She wiggled delightedly, licking his hand whenever she got the chance. Watching her, so happy to see Mason, reminded me of my visit to his house that day, when he wasn't home, but Bella and I got chased by his neighbor. I guess now was as good a time as any to ask him about it.

I described the incident to him. My words pierced his drunken fuzziness. He stopped playing with Bella and looked at me with narrowed eyes.

"So… it got me to thinking… did Ali spend much time at your place?"

"What are you asking me, Cleo?" Mason's face was dead serious now. His tipsy playfulness washed away like sand on a paddle after a first stroke.

"Well, I mean, your neighbor, she really didn't like Bella. And she talked about Ali. She didn't like her either. She, your neighbor I mean, acted like Bella had spent a lot of time there … caused problems. I was wondering… I don't know. You have a reputation as a guy who gets around…"

I shifted and could feel myself blushing under his penetrating stare.

"I mean… you *have* gone out with a lot of women. Right? I'm just trying to make sense of it." I had sputtered all I could sputter. He knew what I meant. Would he answer me or dodge the question? He was friends with Kai, sure, but for some guys that didn't matter when it came to beautiful women. And Ali Bacunawa had been a beautiful woman.

We stood there in silence, Mason stony faced with a withering glare, me, fidgeting under it. Bella quit her happy dance and sat on her haunches, looking back and forth between Mason and me as if trying to figure out why we didn't want to play.

Finally, Mason spoke. "Yeah, Ali and I had a fling. But it didn't last long, and it was over way before she got with Kai, when I first got to the island. Ali didn't tell Kai, and neither did I. It didn't mean anything, and it would only hurt him to know. The only reason my neighbor knows Bella is one time Kai asked me to puppy sit while he took Ali for a weekend on Kona side. And yeah, Bella pissed off my neighbor."

A small sigh of relief escaped from me. I didn't really believe Mason could be Ali's killer, but I had to ask, right? I smiled at Mason. "I figured it was something like that. I won't violate your confidence. Kai won't hear it from me," I said.

Mason's face was etched with anger. "If I were you, Cleo, instead of worrying about Ali's old escapades, I'd focus on Ben's current ones." He lifted his chin and his eyes in the direction of the door to Cronies. A bitter smile appeared on his lips, and he walked away.

What the hell did he mean by that? Was Ben in

Cronies? Was Ben *with* someone in Cronies? I had assumed he was working late.

I couldn't take Bella inside, and in case Mason looked back, I didn't want him to see that his words had bothered me by catching me trying to look through the open door. Bella and I continued in the opposite direction from Mason around the corner. Cronies had windows on that side of the building too. As soon as we got around the corner and I was out of view of Mason, I stuck my face right to the glass. With an arm through Bella's leash and both hands blocking out any glare from a street lamp that had just come on, I took a good long look inside. Cronies was hopping tonight, every seat was taken. I don't know where Mason had been sitting, but somebody had already claimed his spot. There was not one empty chair. Eventually, I found Ben, his back was to me but he sat at a table with some of the staff and students that work with him on the boat. There were women as well as men at the gathering, but from my mini spy surveillance, I didn't see Ben cozying up to any woman in particular. Mason was just trying to stir up trouble. That was a side of him I haven't seen before. What a jerk.

Feeling silly, I stepped back from the window and almost into a young Japanese couple walking up the street.

"Anything interesting going on in there?" the young man asked. The woman with him giggled. Luckily, the light was fading quickly, and it was dark enough they couldn't see my blush.

"Uh, just looking for my friends, see if they are there tonight. Nope!" I gripped Bella's leash and gave the couple an embarrassed smile before I walked quickly up the street with Bella at my heels.

I was going to wait up for Ben and ask him about his evening. Not because I was worried. Just to reconnect. But it had been a long day, and soon my eyes were drooping. There was no sign of Ben, and I crawled into bed to read while I waited for him. Surely, he'd be home soon. And of course I trusted that he was having a perfectly innocent evening with friends, so I wasn't worried. I must have fallen asleep and woke just as Ben crawled into bed next to me. I didn't know what time it was, I wasn't awake enough to check my phone. But I was awake enough to roll over and cuddle him, burying my nose into his neck and took a big sniff. No smell of perfume or hairspray, just a mix of stale beer and toothpaste. I smiled to myself, of course that's all I smelled. I wasn't worried.

Chapter 31

Ho'olau'lea

Suki was recovering from her surgery. The doctor had her on heavy pain meds so she wouldn't feel like running or playing and tearing the stitches out, and this left her semi-zoned out. The puppy didn't understand why Suki was unresponsive and became more and more energetic in her attempts to tempt Suki to play. I could tell poor Suki's patience would not be endless, so I scooped up the playful troublemaker and drove down to Bayfront. I couldn't let the puppy off leash because the highway was too close at one end, but I had a flexi leash so she could run in large circles around me as I walked along the edge of the shore. The waves were larger than usual, and I let her get her legs wet but no deeper. Bella had no interest in swimming anyway, she would run out until the water got to her shoulders, then backed up, unsure. But she seemed happy charging the waves as they came in. And it was hilarious how proud she looked after they washed back out. She chased them away and then would look over at me to make sure I had seen her conquest. She didn't bark much, not like Suki. As a pup Suki barked at the waves like she now does with the cows. Damn, I hoped she was okay. I didn't know what I was going to do without that dog if the cancer has spread. My eyes filled, no sense crying yet. She would be fine.

As I blinked my tears away, I recognized one of the pickups that had pulled up to the beach. Rather, I noticed it after its owner got out and stood at the shore surveying the waves. It was Kevin, and what a relief, Mele wasn't with him. I waved and walked over, the puppy raced ahead on her flexi-lead to greet him. He stooped down to pet Bella, and when I reached him, Kevin straightened up and kissed me on both cheeks. "You get one new dog? I taut you had one big black one."

"Yeah, I do. This was Ali's puppy. I'm taking care of her until Kai clears his name and comes home."

"Hmm, I woulda taut Ali would have one little dog, you know, da kine dey stick in one purse and carry 'round? But dat wild, yuh? About Kai being arrested, I mean. I wudda taut by now dey figure out, he too nice a guy fo' dat."

"Yeah… I thought so too. But that reminds me, coconut wireless has it that you were messing with somebody the weekend that Mele was gone. Any chance that was Ali?"

"Ha! No… I learned my lesson wid dat one."

"What lesson?"

"You knew Ali. It's like she didn't know how to stay happy." The smile slipped from Kevin's face. "You know life wid Ali was wild fun! Dat girl was crazy, in a good way, when I was wid her I wuz nevah bored." Kevin's brow creased. "But den alluva sudden, no ting enough. I cannot do anyting right, and she got mean. One day she cleaned out some money I been saving, and took all her stuff and was gone. She no answer da phone or text. I wen run into her at one party, and she laughed at me. She made fun of me in front of all our friends, 'cause

I asked her to come back."

Kevin's eyes refocused from the faraway look that had entered them. He shook his head and ran his fingers through his thick black hair.

"I may not be so smart as you professors, but somebody hurt me like dat, and I don't touch it again."

I smiled at Kevin. "I don't know, Kev, you sound smarter than a lot of people I know, professors included."

Kevin shrugged, and his smile magically returned to his face as he leaned down to pet Bella. He stood back up to his full height and pulled his phone out of his back pocket.

"Yeah, well, I don't know 'bout dat. But what I *do* know is ders rocks on da road! I gotta call da guys and tell 'em to get down here wid der boards!"

I laughed and waved goodbye to leave him to make his calls. 'Rocks on da road' referred to conditions where the waves in Hilo Bay grew in intensity and crashed in such a way that it threw rocks onto the highway. When that happened, surfing conditions on Hilo Bay were at their finest. Because of the breaker wall, Hilo Bay didn't usually get a surfable wave, but when they came in, just the right direction and intensity, it produced a long, clean wave. Surfers said it was one of the longest waves on the island. And there was a special surfer-coconut wireless that spread the word when that happened. The police would put up blockades and direct traffic around that small stretch of highway, but before they could do that, the place would be jammed with surfers parked on every square inch of roadside. The surfers always, always beat the police to the waves. I better move along before the surf crowd took over the beach.

I walked away and thought about Kevin. He didn't

go to college, but he knew how to live a happy life. Ali hurt him, and he walked away. Mele acted mean and tough to everybody else, but she must be nice to Kevin. She must make him happy. I wish Kai had walked away before Ali got killed. He wouldn't be under investigation now. Damn, what was I thinking? That's victim-blaming. I lectured on that in class, I won't do that. Kai didn't do anything wrong, he loved Ali and tried to make her happy. He shouldn't have to worry about being convicted. I had to figure out who could have done this. I've got to give his lawyer a plausible alternative suspect. I had Kevin on my list, but now I wasn't so sure. And not just because he was a perpetually happy-go-lucky guy. But when he walked up, he didn't know Bella was Ali's dog. Ali and this puppy stuck together like glue while Ali had her. If Kevin had been sneaking around with Ali at that time, he would have recognized Bella as Ali's dog. But maybe Mele didn't know Kevin hadn't messed with Ali… that was somebody who deserved a closer look. Maybe I'd get my Scooby-Doo crew, as Gina called us, to start checking into Mele's whereabouts on the night that Ali died.

****

Work was chaotic. The department was re-evaluating the requirements for graduation for Psychology. The emails had been flying fast and furious, and there was still no consensus. When emails weren't gathering in my inbox, I got cornered in the hall, with colleagues asking which direction I thought the department should go. I also had lines of students at my door. The class average on the test in my Cross-Cultural Psych class had been low. Some were coming in to figure out what they got wrong and why, but some were angry and wanted to know how it would affect their final grade.

Gina and Rikki had called and texted me all week with their efforts at tracking down news on Ali's uncle Tino, Mele, and Kevin's whereabouts and motives for Ali's murder. It was hard for all of us to believe that Kevin was a murderer, but we decided it was important to follow up, even the longshots. My money was on Mele, though. Her alibi didn't hold up. She said she'd had to work late, she was a guard at the Kulani prison, but Gina knew someone who worked there and asked them to check on it. Mele hadn't been on the schedule. Yesterday I'd called Kai's lawyer. He promised he would follow up on it, but he had wanted to know what her motive would be. When I said that she was mean as a snake and hated anybody that talked to her boyfriend, he seemed less than excited. He gently suggested we'd have to find a stronger motive or more evidence that Mele hated Alice more than anybody else who talked to Kevin. Otherwise, the prosecution could point out that if that was all the motive it took, there would be a lot more dead women in Hilo. I saw his point. But I still thought it was Mele. Gina, Rikki, and I continued searching for a stronger motive. We had also been looking into the uncle. After my run-in with him in the grocery store, I was thinking it could be him. But I was afraid that he would find out we were looking at him as a suspect. He scared me.

Suki was recovering from her surgery. The first week, we had to use a sling just behind her belly, to help her get up and go outside to the bathroom. I said "we," but Ben was working as hard as ever, so most of the time it was me. The vet said it was important to have her get up and move while she was healing, but not too strenuously, because it might rip out her stitches. My arms were in great shape now. Lifting the hind end of an eighty-five-pound dog as she hopped around the yard, five or six times a day, does that.

After a week of struggling to keep my head above water, it was music to my ears when on Friday afternoon, my colleague, Crystal, reminded me that it was Hilo's Ho'olau'lea this weekend. A ho'olau'lea, was a big community party. And most communities have one every year. In Hilo, this happens in September, and it was a huge block party. They closed off a stretch of Kam Ave and Haili Street, brought in a bands from around the state, and set up rows of food, arts, and crafts booths. It was free, and absolutely everyone showed up. I appreciated my little house close to downtown. We could walk down without worrying about parking or dealing with traffic.

Ben took off work, and Saturday evening we made our way to Ho'olau'lea. The streets were blocked off, and the bands were playing their first set. We left both dogs at home. The walk was too far for Suki, and the loud music and crowds of people might spook Bella. Her socialization was coming along well, and I didn't want to have a setback.

Ben and I walked downhill along Haili Street with other small groups of families, young people, and laughing women. We could feel the vibration of the drums of the closest band and stepped around the chairs of people already settled in for a good view of the main band. One person had rolled an old recliner into the middle of Haili Street. Someone shouted our names, and I saw Gina and her husband Kawika in line at a booth selling kalua pig plates, roasted pig with two-scoops of rice. Ben and I walked over. It was too loud for the four of us to hear each other with normal voices, so Kawika and Ben leaned in to talk. Who knows what about. Kawika never said more than two words to me.

"Good to see you and Ben here," Gina yelled as I turned my ear toward her. "We got Kawika's nephews with us, and I could use a break from kid craziness."

I looked around but didn't see any kids not hanging off a parent, nearby.

"Where are they?" I yelled back to her.

Gina shrugged. "Don't know. Don't care. It was Kawika's idea to bring them. We were down visiting his auntie in Puna, and his sister's kids were driving Auntie crazy. Kawika volunteered to bring them up here and spend the night with us."

Gina shot a glare at an oblivious Kawika who must have said something funny because he and Ben burst into laughter. About that time two adorable shaggy-haired, caramel-skinned, chocolate-eyed boys ran up to Gina, funnel cakes in hand. The smallest one opened his arms, half a funnel cake flailing in one hand, and looked as if he was going to grab Gina like she was home base in a game of tag. Gina extended one arm with her palm facing them.

"Freeze!" she shouted loud enough to be heard over the music. Both boys stopped in mid-step. The smaller boy windmilled his arms so the momentum wouldn't move him a step, hair and funnel cake flopping with the sudden cessation of forward movement.

"I don't want your sticky hands on my clothes," she said. "Go hang on Uncle." Then after a half beat, she added, "Unfreeze."

And the boys rushed to Kawika.

I laughed. "You've trained them well."

Gina shrugged again. "They completely ignored me until I told them it was a game. I would yell stop, and it was like they were hearing impaired … didn't even slow down. But one day I taught them freeze tag, and I realized they would break their necks to stop whatever they are doing if I yell 'freeze.' " Gina gave an impish grin. "I just have to be sure to tell them unfreeze."

It was Gina and Kawika's turn to order food. I got a water, but I didn't feel like pork, I wanted to see what was available at the other booths. We waited while they got their food, then moved over to a curb under a palm tree. Gina passed out the food, and they ate while we listened to the band. When she finished her food, Gina stood up and yelled to Kawika and Ben.

"You guys can finish eating with the boys, Cleo and I gonna cruise." Kawika nodded and probably gave his usual grunt of agreement, but I couldn't hear it above the band.

Ben smiled, waved us off and mouthed to me, "Meet you back here in an hour." I nodded, and Gina and I took off. We walked another block away from the band, and she pulled me around the corner of a building so the noise from the band wasn't quite so loud.

"There's somebody here you might be interested in seeing," Gina said.

"Who?"

Gina nodded her head in the direction of the booths we hadn't passed yet. "I'll show you." She led me to the next to the last booth.

I was checking out the food booths as we walked past, to see what looked good, when Gina stopped and elbowed me. I looked up. Two booths ahead, across the street from where we were standing, Walker Wolf was behind a counter working a booth. From where I stood, I could see him deliver his dazzling smile to a young woman who was at the front of a line of young women. There were so many giggling, fawning, sycophantic sweeties crushed in around the front of the booth I couldn't read the sign strung across the front of the counter. There was a banner overhead too, but it was twisting in the wind and also unreadable. Most of the booths were either local nonprofits earning money for their organization, or local businesses who set up a booth at Hilo's biggest party to get some name recognition. I couldn't figure out what Walker was doing there, until I realized maybe it was a booth set up for the university. I couldn't see him as the volunteer type, unless he thought it would help him get promoted.

"Like bees to honey," Gina said. And we both smiled at the sea of women in front of his booth. One blonde in a skin-tight, white T-shirt and short flowered sarong separated herself from the pack and sauntered toward us.

My smile widened when I recognized Rikki.

"Hey, kiddo!" Gina called, and she kissed both Rikki's cheeks when she approached.

"Ladies, while you stand back at a distance, I've been up close investigating our suspect business professor."

I laughed. "And what did you find out in that sea of females?"

"That half of them are hoping to sleep with him, and the other half are claiming they already have." Rikki raised her eyebrows, proud of her find. "Not that I necessarily believe them. There were a lot of insinuations and bragging going on over there."

"Could you see what he was selling?"

Rikki shrugged. "I didn't get close enough to the front, but I think it was suntan lotion. That's what it looked like people were carrying when they walked away."

"That's bizarre. Why would Walker be working a suntan lotion booth?" I asked.

"I dunno," said Gina, "but it's starting to get really crowded, let's move behind the booths."

We agreed and navigated through the crowd to the closed highway that ran behind the booths and the bandstand. There weren't as many lights, and we could see Hilo Bay thirty yards away, unimpeded except for the black silhouettes of coconut palms as they wafted in the breeze, backlit by moonlight against the sky. The three of us walked along slowly, enjoying the breeze and the ocean and the not-quite-so-loud band. A cluster of policeman stood talking and watching the crowds. Gina called "howzit" to them as we walked past. They smiled and waved back ... must be friends of Kawika. A few steps past them, Gina spoke again.

"You know, seeing Joey over there," Gina tilted her head to indicate the policemen we had just passed, "reminds me of something I wanted to tell you."

We reached the end of the closed off street and stood there, leaning against the barricade, waiting for Gina to continue. "You know how we decided to find out what we could about Mele?"

Rikki and I nodded. It was dark, and we were far from the bright lights of the street party in full swing, but the moon was almost full, so we could still see each other.

"Well, one of the people I talked to was Joey, because somebody told me that he dated Mele in high school."

Rikki perked up. "He is kind of cute. The tall one, right? The one on the left with his back to us? If that's Joey, I get to ask the follow-up questions!"

Gina shook her head, dark curls bouncing in the moonlight. "No need. I got our answers."

"What answers?" I asked.

"Mele. He dated her all right. He was crazy about her for a while. Crazy being the key. She got real possessive, and he was young, like seventeen, you know, still a kid. Anyway, he got restless and messed around with some other girl in their class." Gina's voice dropped, and Rikki and I leaned in to hear.

"She was some girl from Maui. I guess she was super cute and really nice. Since she was new, all the guys at Pahoa High School were chasing after her, so Joey figured when she flirted with him, he'd have a go. I mean he was seventeen, you know how guys were at that age."

"At that age? Other than Kawika and Ben, all the guys I know are *still* like that." Rikki gave a pretty little pout.

I smirked. "Rikki, you don't know what you would do if a nice sweet guy, looking to settle down, asked you out. You are still looking for adventure, girl, and anybody who knows you can see that."

"*Anyway*, if you'd like me to finish…"

"Yeah, yeah, please, go on," I said.

"Yeah, I'm sure Cleo's finished giving me crap." Rikki laughed. "Seriously, go on, Gina."

Gina gave an exaggerated sigh. "You guys are going

to quit laughing when you hear what I'm trying to tell you. So Joey messed around with this new girl, and Mele found out."

"I bet that wasn't pretty."

"No, the girl ended up in the hospital, Mele busted her up and good. She knocked her so hard the girl lost one of her eyes. She had to get a glass eye after that. Her parents wanted to go after whoever had hit her, but the girl would never tell. She was too scared. The whole family moved back to Maui as soon as she got out of the hospital."

"Did she tell the police then?" I asked. "I mean Mele couldn't get her on Maui, right? She was in high school, so she wouldn't have the money to fly over and back."

"Mele has tons of family over there. Her grandfather is an old Puna family, but her grandmother is from an old Maui family. I guess Mele told Joey that if the girl ever ratted her out, she'd send her cousins over to finish the job. Joey believed her. He broke up with Mele after that. He said she gave him the creeps, knowing what she had done."

"He's a policeman now, though. Can't he go after her for that now? Or if not for that, has he told Kawika about that, so maybe Kawika will take a closer look at Mele as a suspect?" I asked.

Gina shrugged. "As much as she creeps him out, he feels some loyalty toward her. He feels guilty that he cheated on Mele and blames himself for what she did to that Maui girl. And now… he says Kawika's got his guy, he doesn't want to stir the pot."

Aaargh, I could just scream. Two steps forward and two steps back.

"Did you tell Kawika what Joey said? Kawika wants

to get the guilty person, right?"

"Yeah, of course I told Kawika, and yeah, he wants to get the guilty person, but he thinks he has him. He said if everybody who beat someone up in high school was on the suspect list, then the list would run off the paper. He told me to keep my nose out of it and let him do his job."

Uh-oh, I didn't want to cause problems between Gina and Kawika.

"If you want to cool it on working with us on this, I understand, Gina."

"Cool it? Cool it? I'm all in now, girlfriends." Gina smacked her hand so hard on the railing it vibrated. "I'm just getting started!"

Crack! A bottle shattered about twenty feet away from us, and we jumped. It came from the dark side of the street, away from the Ho'olau'lea lights.

"Fucker!" We heard a male voice scream from the other side of the closed-off street.

We were standing against the barricade on the makai, or ocean side of the street, whoever was yelling was standing on the other side of the barricade on the mauka, mountain side of the street. He was drunk. We could see him sway. I think he threw the bottle in a fit of rage, directed at the universe, not us. He didn't appear to be aware that we were here.

Luckily, the bottle landed on the other side of a barricade, which shielded us from any splintered glass.

"Keep it cool, brah, da cops are jus' ova der. You don' wan no trouble, brah." Another male voice calmed the bottle launcher.

"*My fuckin' sista's dead!*" the drunken, agitated, man screamed. "*An she nevah know!* She nevah know, brah." I heard anguish in his voice.

The other, calmer voice said something I couldn't hear.

"I'm goin' *kill* da fucka!" the bottle-launcher argued, but he wasn't yelling anymore, and I couldn't make out what he said after that.

"I think that's Ali's brother, David," Gina said quietly. It was too difficult for me to tell in the dark, but the size and shape was about right. I'd only met him once. I trusted Gina's island roots on this one.

We watched as the calm-voiced friend convinced David to move off away from Ho'o'lau'lea, I looked down at my watch and realized we'd been gone from the guys for almost an hour. The three of us walked back to where we had agreed to meet the menfolk. It was more crowded than when we left, and we had a hard time finding Ben and Kawika. One of Gina's nephews ran up and grabbed Gina.

"This way, Auntie Gina, Uncle got us a spot unda da cova in case it rains. Pili and I wanted to get close to da band, but Uncle said it probly rain and better to be under da cova." Pili's big brother dragged Gina, with Rikki and I following her, back to the covered walkway in front of the shops.

Ben and Kawika were leaning against the wall talking when we get there. The band was coming back from a break and just getting started. Conversation became difficult again. Positive Motion was playing, and we leaned against the wall enjoying the music. Rikki was dancing with the little boys. I smiled watching them. Despite the happiness around me, my mind wandered back to the scene we had witnessed of David. It didn't match up with my first interaction with him. The first

David seethed anger toward his sister, a cold anger. Tonight ... he sounded like a man in pain. He was drunk. Was it just the alcohol? Or was there a side of him that still loved his little sister ... his almost twin ... even if she sent him to prison?

Ben leaned in and put his mouth next to my ear. "I'm ready to walk back whenever you are."

I nodded and turned to my friends, Gina was leaning back against Kawika. He had one arm across her chest. I watched as he kissed the top of her head, and Gina's face took on a slow lazy smile. I caught her eye and gave a small wave goodbye to her, she blew me a kiss with her free hand. I turned the other direction and saw Rikki talking to one of her surfer friends, laughing at something. As Ben and I walked past her, I tapped her shoulder and gave her the little goodbye wave too. She leaned into me, and we kissed cheeks before I walked past her, leaving Rikki to dance the night away.

Chapter 32

A phone call

I was thankful for the results of the amputation. Suki appeared to be completely without pain. It had taken a week or two for her to get used to being on three legs, but now it barely slowed her down. She appeared to relish rounding up the cows and playing chase with Bella. Now they were conked out at my feet. Ben was working on the other side of the farm, and I was relaxed. The clouds rolled toward us on the horizon, making their way across the Pacific Ocean to gently release their moisture as they slowly made their way up the slope of Mauna Kea. The sleeping dogs and cool breeze had a soporific effect on me. My phone rang, and even as I slowly reached for it, I wasn't sure if I was in the mood to talk with anybody and disturb the tranquility of the moment.

"Hello?"

"The bitch deserved to die. Leave it alone!"

Stunned by the harsh but muffled voice, I blurted, "Excuse me?"

The person hung up, and I stared at a 'blocked call' message on my phone. Self-disgust at my ridiculous response blossomed in me. 'Excuse me'? Why in the world would I need to excuse myself to someone who said something so horrible? Damn my southern upbringing… politeness at all costs. Would I ever get past that? I shook my head.

Focus, Cleo, who was the caller? He was male. The muffling disguised the voice. I thought of all the people who had a grudge against Ali. Walker Wolfe, maybe? He didn't seem fond of her, but did he hate her that much? Although something weird was going on with him. I forgot to follow up on his booth at Ho'olau'lea and figure out what he was up to with that suntan lotion. And his hand-licking behavior with the two female students on campus the other day was just creepy and really inappropriate. I needed to find out what was going on with him.

Another possibility for the source of the call might have been Ali's brother, David. If I hadn't heard his drunken, anguish at Ho'olau'lea, I would have thought it was him. She helped send him to jail, and when we spoke at the beach he seemed angry. But he also appeared torn up about her death that night he was drunk. 'Deserved to die' were strong words. Although maybe he killed her, and that is what he regrets. He wouldn't be the first person to kill in the heat of a moment and regret it later.

Woah…there was another person we hadn't looked at closely. Maka, the drug dealer that Ali sent to jail at the same time as her brother. Kai's lawyer had tracked him down to being released on Oahu before Ali died. There was no record of him missing parole. But did we ever look to see if he had taken any inter-island flight in between parole visits? Hmm, we should follow up on him. Could he have been on-island when Ali was killed? I should definitely track that down - but how? I don't want anyone in the Scooby-Doo crew getting hurt by asking too many questions about such a dangerous guy.

The dogs jumped up in a scramble of claws on wood and broke my train of thought. Bella ran as Suki did her awkward-looking, but effective, hop down the steps of the deck to Ben as he walked up the hill to us.

"Did you call the police?" Ben asked after I'd told him about the phone call.

"And say what?"

"That you were threatened!"

"But I wasn't threatened. Whoever it was told me to leave it alone, but there was no threat." I'd replayed the call in my head a thousand times, and although the tone of voice was menacing, the words did not contain an "or else" or anything that could be interpreted as a direct threat.

Ben disagreed. It was sweet that he worried about me, but I didn't want to look like an idiot in front of the police. Not when I was trying to convince them Kai was innocent, and Kawika wasn't taking us seriously.

"So, who could it have been that was *not* threatening you?"

"I don't know. I told you I couldn't recognize the voice, it was muffled like he had something over the phone. I'd think it was Mele since I was asking questions about her and Kevin the other day. But it was a male voice."

"Does she have any brothers? Or could it be the boyfriend?"

"I hadn't thought of that, I don't know if Mele has any brothers." I thought for a minute. "But I'm pretty sure it wasn't Kevin. I would have recognized his voice. Although with the muffling, I guess... maybe not."

Suki dragged herself over to put her head in my lap. The puppy had plopped down and instantly fallen asleep again. I ran my fingers through the silky black curls on the top of Suki's head, thinking.

"I guess it could also be Ali's uncle. He hasn't been wild about me trying to help Kai."

"How about Ali's brother?" Ben asked.

"Maybe. It was so fast, and I was so surprised I didn't really concentrate on the voice. I'm kind of thinking it might have been Walker Wolfe or maybe that drug dealer, Maka, that the lawyer is trying to track down as a possible alternative suspect."

"That's a lot of people who might be ready to hurt you." Ben moved closer so he could reach out and push a lock of hair that had fallen into my eyes behind my ear. He gave me an intense, unreadable look, then shook his head and stood up.

"Let's head home, it looks like the rain is comin', and I'm dirty and starving. But from now on, please be careful. No more evening walks without me or Suki. Okay? I can't make you tell the police about this, but you and I both know this was a threat to get you to back off. And while I'd love it if you stopped this investigation... I know, I know." He held up his hands in surrender. "I realize you aren't going to stop looking into this. But at least take some precautions and let me and Suki protect you. Even three-legged, I bet she'd fiercely defend you."

It was hard to argue with that, and when he leaned over and kissed the top of my head, I could smell the salty tang of recent sweat produced from hard work. I'd always liked that smell on Ben. I smiled and stood up to kiss him back on the mouth. The sky opened up, and the rain fell all around us. I leaned into Ben and wrapped my arms around his waist. One thing led to another, and soon we were lying naked on the wooden slats of the deck, listening to the rain gently fall on the tin roof and the wind rustle in the bamboo, as Suki and Bella curled up next to our bare bodies.

****

Ben and I both had a busy week planned, but my Scooby-Doo crew continued the investigation. The three of us met for coffee on Tuesday. I told Gina and Rikki about the ugly phone call I'd received, and they were more determined than ever to help me get to the bottom of this and get Kai out of this mess. I had tried to follow up on Walker Wolf and see if he had an alibi, but he wasn't answering my calls and was never in his office when I went looking for him. Gina, Rikki, and I had ruled out Kevin as a suspect. We decided that the fact that he hadn't recognized Bella could have been faked. But there was nothing linking him to Ali, and he had been on the other side of the island, camping and surfing with friends of Rikki the weekend Ali was killed. So, he had an alibi.

Mele was an open question. But we hadn't found anything more concrete for a motive than her jealousy. No progress on finding any more information on Uncle Tino, but Gina did find out that Maka, the drug dealer, had come back to the Big Island last week. He still had parole visits on Oahu, but he had permission to come back for the funeral of an auntie who died about two weeks ago. There had been no approved visits from his parole officer around the time of Ali's death, though. It doesn't mean Maka didn't fly here and kill Ali, but, we had no information that suggests he did.

We also decided that David's drunken heartbreak over his sister's death that we witnessed at Ho'olau'lea didn't necessarily preclude his killing her. Gina pointed out that he could have killed her in drunken fit of rage and now regretted it. And after a week of internal struggle, I also floated the idea of adding Mason's name to our list of suspects. Gina and Rikki looked at me like I was crazy. But after making them swear to keep it secret, I told them about Ali and Mason's fling before Kai. I watched Rikki's face in particular, knowing that she had 'a thing' for him. I knew she wouldn't tell Mason, I trusted her. But was she more into him than I thought? Would this hurt her?

Rikki's eyebrows flew up in surprise when she heard the revelation. But then she laughed when she saw Gina and I watching her intently.

"I always knew he was a bad boy... so no heartbreak here." And a mischievous look came over her face as she wiggled her eyebrows. "But how about I take the lead on investigating this bad boy?"

I smiled at her. "Sure, girl, you got it. Just remember to keep his affair quiet. We don't want to hurt Kai or damage their friendship. Mason is a long shot. He and Kai are close, and I can't imagine he would do anything to hurt him. It's just, like Kevin, we've got to follow up all possibilities, no matter how unlikely until we can cross them off." We finished our coffee and rushed to our work lives, promising to touch base on the weekend.

Back at the office, I worked on my grant proposal, and after meeting with some of students from Cross-Cultural Psychology, I offered to hold an extra review session for the class on Friday. It would not be required, but since there were so many unhappy students from the last test, I would give them an extra opportunity to ask questions before the next one. The department meeting on graduation requirements was also on Friday, and the hectic pace continued through the week. I was relieved to lock my office Friday evening, knowing I had nothing to grade and a weekend to catch up on sleep.

Chapter 33

David at the Park

Suki was not looking good. She had no energy and has been grouchy toward the puppy. I was starting to feel sorry for baby Bella, despite the fact that she had chewed up my favorite pair of slippers. I slid on my second-best pair of slippers and grabbed some treats and Bella's leash, and we went to Liliuokalani Park to give Suki some peace and quiet. It was Sunday, so there should be lots of people in the park and another good chance to socialize the young dog.

We crossed the flat, zig-zag bridge and scrambled over the steep, high bridge and were making a loop on the sidewalk that led to the short pier. There were people fishing, and I got that prickly feeling that someone was looking at me. As I scrutinized the faces on the pier, a hand grabbed my shoulder, and my heart thudded as adrenaline surged through my body. Before I could turn and try some learned-long-ago self-defense moves, the grab was followed up with a...

"Boo!"

I couldn't stop myself from the spin around that I'd started, but I could hold up on the punch my arm had prepared to throw at my attacker... who was Rikki.

"You idiot, you scared me to death!"

"Ha! I know! You should have seen how you

jumped." She laughed.

Rikki pulled the earbuds out of her ears. She was wearing her barely-there running outfit, and her body gleamed with sweat. Rikki had a big smile on her face, looking much happier than I would during a run.

"Howzit? Where's Ben? On a beautiful Sunday afternoon in the park, I'd expect such a happy couple to be strolling along hand in hand. No trouble in paradise I hope." She smiled a goofy smile, so she wasn't really worried about me and Ben, just teasing me. I guess she had been running long enough for the endorphins to kick in.

"Ben is working. He has to cover Kai's labs during the week, so he spends the weekends catching up on grading. Bella and I needed to get out of the house, though. The weather is too nice to sit inside."

She reached down and petted Bella while I was talking. Her smile had faded when she stood back up. "Poor Kai. Has the lawyer heard any good news on his case? Has anything we found been able to help his lawyer or the police?"

"Not yet."

Rikki sighed. Endorphins or not, a sad look came over her face as she absently turned her eyes toward the ocean.

Rikki stiffened, and her eyes narrowed. "Don't turn your head and look, but guess who is fishing on the pier."

"I have no idea. And why can't I turn my head?"

"It's Ali's brother, David… and he was watching us pretty intently until he caught me looking at him, then he turned away."

I couldn't help it. I turned and looked in the direction Rikki had indicated. Sure enough, he was there packing up his fishing gear.

"You should talk to him again," Rikki said.

She was right. But I'm not the pushy type, and trying to talk to someone who didn't want to talk to me…was outside my comfort zone. It was hard enough the first time.

"He told me he didn't have anything to say to me," I said.

"Yeah, but times change, and he was staring at you. And we heard him at Ho'olau'lea. We know he's sad about Ali's death. What can it hurt?"

Rikki made a strong case. The only thing at risk was my self-esteem, and maybe now that he regretted her death, he would confess. Or maybe he knew something about Ali's life that could help Kai. I sighed.

"Okay, here goes," I said. A surprised puppy who had just settled into a nap jumped up to follow me.

David was packing up his fishing gear, wasting no time getting out of there. But when he glanced up and saw me heading his way, he sighed and stopped. He stood and waited for me to approach. His eyes settled on the puppy who kept getting her leash tangled in her legs and tripping. A shadow of a smile tugged at his mouth.

"Is that Ali's dog?" he asked, pointing at Bella, who, now that we had stopped, was biting at the leash and shaking her head.

"Yeah."

"She say she had one puppy, but I thought she was goin' get one fru-fru dog. You know, a little kine, white dog," he said.

"Well, she's mostly white, but she's going to be a big girl." While David smiled and watched the puppy's antics, I rushed on. "So you talked to Ali then, I mean,

264

since she got the puppy, not too long before she died."

The smile disappeared. But he kept looking at the puppy, who continued to fight the leash, even though we were standing still and it wasn't pulling her anywhere anymore.

"Yeah, I wen talk to her," he said. Then slowly he raised his eyes to mine, and I saw he had made a decision.

"I was still mad at her, but she was my sista. And she didn't deserve to die."

He looked back at the puppy. "She was kina like dis dog," he said, pointing at the puppy. "All pretty and sweet looking, but always tripping over herself and fighting when no need."

He was quiet for a minute, and I held my breath, afraid to break the spell Bella seemed to cast on him.

"From what I heah, Kai is a nice guy, and he wuz good to her." He looked up at me, a question in his eyes.

"He's a great guy. He adored Ali and would have done anything for her. I know he didn't kill her." I spoke softly, desperately willing him to believe me.

He nodded his head slowly. "Yeah, dats what people say. She wuz my sista, no one should get away wid killing her and let Kai take da blame. Da cops here, dey always blame da boyfriend." He shook his head. "And dey don't like our family anyhow, I don't tink dey really care." His voice had an edge to it. "But I know someting—"

I waited, breath held, this may be the break Kai needed.

"Yeah?" I prodded when he didn't continue.

He didn't answer, but his gaze focused on something or someone behind me.

"I gotta go now, but we talk later," he said and returned to packing up.

"But wait, can't you tell me now?" He ignored me and secured the latch on his tackle box. I looked behind me and saw Rikki had inched her way over so she was about twenty feet away rather than the fifty feet away from where I'd left her. Mason had joined her. She was talking to him but watching David and me. David finished packing his gear and beat it out of there. Rikki and Mason approached.

"That looked intense. Any good news?" Mason asked.

"No, he was just about to tell me something, but then changed his mind and took off."

Rikki grimaced.

"Sorry. It was probably my fault, for walking too close to you guys. It's just at first it looked like he was softening up and smiling, then his eyes got real hard and he looked pissed, so I didn't want to be too far away from you in case you needed help."

"Thanks for having my back." I smiled at my friend. "You're right, Bella seemed to have a calming effect on him. And he said, or at least implied, that he knows Kai is innocent."

"He looked mad at the end," Rikki said. "Was he mad at you? That's what had me worried."

"It was strange, he seemed to get mad that Ali was dead. I couldn't tell who he was mad at, though, himself, the police, or someone else. And I'm pretty sure he was about to tell me something. I'm not sure if it was something about his sister, an admission of guilt, or something that could help Kai's case. It's so frustrating. Because of Bella I think he was actually ready to open up to me."

"Well, good try, Cleo!" Mason said as he started his pre-run stretch. "I've got to get my run in, but it's great that you are making progress with Ali's brother. "And, Rikki, I'll call you tonight about that drink you promised me." With a wink and a smile, Mason started on his run.

"A drink?" I asked as soon as Mason was out of earshot. "Is this for investigatory purposes or fun?"

"Maybe both," Rikki said with a little smile. "But Mason's right. It was a good effort to talk to David."

I reached down to pet Bella's head, and she licked my hand.

"At least, the last thing he said to me before he left was that we would talk soon. I guess that is progress. He's open to talking to me. Maybe the next time I talk to David, I'll be able to get something that will help Kai."

Rikki leaned down to pet Bella's back. "Yeah, just make sure you have the beguiling Bella with you when you do."

****

I was training for the rough water swim, and classes were in full swing. Ben was hardly ever around, either working late in his lab or taking students to Kona side to collect marine science samples. He had a heavy workload, but I knew he stayed away from home even more than he had to. The thing I didn't know was why. Was it because I nagged him too much about sabbatical, or was he avoiding watching Suki's decline? She got weaker and appeared in more pain every day. I would ask him, but he wasn't much of a talker about his feelings.

I had called Gina to get her take on our situation. My friend was rough and tough but big-hearted and happily married for seven years. She and Kawika argued, but they also enjoyed each other. Not all couples could say that after seven years together. She was happy to meet me for lunch on Thursday, but her only advice was 'stick with it.'

"There's a bunch of times I was almost out the door. I mean I love Kawika, but like any man, he's tough to live with sometimes. He's a good guy, but he is a guy! He gets busy with work and forgets about me, takes me for granted. I just do my own thing, until he misses me, and then I bitch him out for not being there for me, and then we make up." Gina smiled. "And the making-up part gives me, and well, us, I can see it in Kawika too, it gives us both a good feeling and keeps us happy for a long stretch."

I was delighted for Gina and Kawika. But I wasn't sure their strategy would work for me and Ben. What works in one relationship doesn't necessarily work in another. I had a strong sense that Ben and I were drifting apart, and I didn't know how to stop it. I guess I could try Gina's approach and do my own thing. I would move forward with the tough stuff, like Kai's investigation and making Suki as comfortable as possible, and also move forward on the fun stuff, like planning a sabbatical and swimming the rough water swim race.

Chapter 34

Rough Water Swim

When I raced with my crew at canoe regattas, I was a competitor. We didn't always win, but more often than not, we took home a medal. Swimming... not so much. In a rough water swim, I was more of a 'completer' than a 'competer.' As I pulled into the parking lot at six forty-five, the morning of the race, I saw Rikki already in line to check in and get her number. Rikki was a competer. She had driven over last night to give herself that extra sleep time this morning. She talked with another professional-looking swimmer, arms waving, facial expressions changing faster than you could blink an eye.

We had world-class swimmers on the Big Island. The original Ironman Triathlon has been held here since 1981. Many people who have competed in it multiple times eventually decided to settle here, after retiring from that pesky job that interfered with their triathlon training. I left the competing to them. My goal was not to come in last in the race. That was an award they gave that I did *not* want to win.

Today's race was the Kukio, 1.2 mile, blue water swim on the west side of the island. We started at Kua Bay and followed the coast as it varied in its hug to the ocean, to Uluweuweu Bay and finally up to Kukio Beach. A swimmer had options on the line she could take. I expected it to be a beautiful, uncrowded swim, going over deep water, with an abundance of coral, fish, and turtles. My favorite thing about the race was the post-race food. Not your typical beer and hamburgers, but mimosas, quiche, and sushi. Some of the more serious racers grumbled about not enough piled on their plate. For me, it was a gourmet delight that was worth the price of the entrance fee.

As I made my way down to the beach, I saw a few people I knew from work, a biology professor and one of the advisors in student services. I waved hello but didn't join them. I loved these swims, but I had butterflies beforehand. I have mostly overcome my fear of sharks, but swimming on the surface in deep water revived it. These races were one of the ways I worked to overcome my anxiety. Oddly, scuba diving didn't scare me. I felt like a shark wouldn't see me as food if I was at eye level. But on the surface, just a dark outline against the backlit surface of the water, I must look like a seal… shark comfort food. I didn't know if there was any data to back up my ideas, but fears weren't always rational. Swimming in deep water, by myself, I felt like shark bait. That's why I liked these races. There was almost always another swimmer in sight and lots of rescue boats and rescue surfers ready to paddle over if anyone got into trouble.

I signed in, stretched, and saw Rikki again, also stretching and doing a little running in place to warm up. We waved, but I knew better than to go chitchat with her. She would be trying to focus now as starting time grew near. I left her in peace and would find her after the race.

We lined up on the sand in a crowd, about six people deep and fifty feet along the beach, tense, waiting for the starting gun.

With the pop of the starting pistol, as one organism, we surged into the water.

I had placed myself in the back of the crowd at the starting line. The last thing I wanted was to get trampled and drowned in the first hundred yards as the crowd rushed into the surf. Because the race was longer, and the course followed the coastline rather than laps on a circle, it would thin out considerably after the start. The leaders distanced themselves quickly, and the rest of us spread out soon after leaving the beach.

It was a beautiful swim, and I felt good. My training paid off, and I slowly passed several people before the first turn out of the bay. The ocean had moderate swells but nothing intimidating. With a steady crawl I floated up and over as the swells passed. The course took us deep, and the ocean floor was blanketed with rock formations and fish. We swam about fifteen feet over the reef fish, which hovered close to their coral. From this distance, we didn't disturb them, and their calmness helped me relax into my stroke. At about a quarter mile through the course, I passed more people but was still way behind the main group.

At a half mile I saw more of the helper surfboards with swimmers who had given up hanging on for a rest. I was starting to tire but still felt strong and took pleasure in the view of the rocks, fish, and occasional sea turtle feeding on marine plants. I kept my shark panic in check and enjoyed the swim. Several of the surfers had towed tired swimmers into shore, and the swimmers near me thinned out. I stopped and picked my head up to look around and see the closest swimmer behind me was at least a hundred feet away, and in front of me a swimmer was about the same distance. I kicked into a faster pace to see if I could chase down the swimmer in front of me. To maintain my calm and not overdo it, I kept my eyes on the ocean floor, watching for sea turtles and pretty fish. After what I estimated was another quarter mile, I picked my head up and looked around again. I saw a surfer sitting up, waving his arms at me. Damn, I'd gone off course and headed farther from shore, I'd missed the cut back in to follow the coastline. My power swim lost me time because it took me off course.

I signaled to the surfer I was okay and had seen my mistake. I struck out back toward the course, frustrated because I couldn't see the swimmer who had been in front of me or behind me. I had lost ground, and they probably were both in front of me now. I was starting to get tired, so I would have to be careful with any sprints, but I knew I had enough left to make it to the finish.

I was almost back to the course, when out of the corner of my eye, I saw a sea turtle rising from a large cave in a rock. I kept my focus on the course, but I didn't want to take all the fun out of the swim. I glanced back to watch the turtle glide up toward me. But as the dark shape separated from the dark rock formation, I realize it wasn't a turtle. My heart stuttered as my shark fear crashed into my mind. But after the first shock, I saw it wasn't a shark either but a scuba diver. He was heading straight in my direction. I didn't know who he thought I was, maybe his lost dive buddy, but I needed to get my head back into the race. When I was tired, my mind wandered, and I couldn't afford to get off track again. I lifted my head to figure out where I was. I was heading in the right direction but still in a large gap from other swimmers. The surfboard helper that had waved me back on course was about fifty yards away with two swimmers who had abandoned the race and were resting, hanging on to his board. I would try to reach the swimmer in front of me. It would be hard to catch her before the finish, but I would try.

As I kicked out, something clamped down on my ankle. *A shark!* My adrenal surged, and I felt a burst of energy. In my blind terror I instinctively kicked with everything I had. The kick connected, and I was free. I looked down and back to see if the shark still pursued me, only it wasn't a shark, but the diver I'd seen. The diver had not only a mask and regulator but a hood on, unusual in warm Hawaiian waters. He was coming at me again - with a knife in his right hand. I knew I couldn't outswim him, with his long fins, so I lifted my head out of the water and yelled "Help!" Then I swam with everything I had toward the surfboard helper. My heart pounded in my ears, I gulped saltwater as I took the quickest breaths I could as my exhausted arms powered through the water. When the splashing of the surfboard helper was about ten feet away, without lifting my head from the water, I looked back and saw the diver melting back into the lava cave from which he had emerged.

I stopped to tread water and lifted my head up as the surfer helper approached. *Who was that, and why did he come after me?* I put my head back under to make sure the diver wasn't returning for a second try. *No sign of him. Probably hiding in the cave.*

"Are you okay? Here grab on to my board," the surfer helper said firmly.

"I'm fine now," I said. I would not grab his board. If I did, I was automatically disqualified. I didn't need to win, but I wanted to finish. "A diver grabbed my foot. I think he was trying to pull me under." I tried to catch my breath, gulping for air in between words.

The surfboarder narrowed his eyes and frowned at me. "Why don't you grab on just in case," he said. "It's easy for your mind to play tricks on you when you're overly tired." He leaned a hand out to me as if to coax me onto the board.

I ignored his extended hand. "No, really, I'm fine. I'm not imagining things, a diver was coming at me, and he had a knife in his hand."

The surfboarder sat back up and raised an eyebrow. "So if I look down there, I'm going to see a diver with a knife?" He didn't sound like he believed me.

"Probably not, the last time I looked, he was swimming back into a cave." *But could he be coming back again? Even with the surfer helper here?* I looked underwater again. No, there was still no sign of him.

I lifted my head again. There was nothing the surfboarder could do for me, even if he did believe me. He didn't have a mask or a radio, there was nothing more he could do.

"Well, if you won't take a rest, and you're sure you are okay, I should return to those I left treading water when I thought you were in trouble."

I think he was trying to be patient with me, but there was a hint of accusation in his voice. His patience was wearing thin.

"Yeah. Sure. Okay. Just keep an eye out, in case the diver comes back and tries it on someone else. And I'll tell the race officials at the finish line," I said.

"You do that." He had already turned his board around and was heading back to the two dog-paddling swimmers a hundred yards away.

I ducked my head to make one last look underwater toward the cave; no sign of the diver. But a clump of swimmers that had been behind me were catching up, and I let them. I didn't want to be out here alone. I paced myself to stay about ten feet in front of them, even though they were fading and getting slower by the minute. As soon as the finish line was in sight, I sprinted in, letting all my post-diver-attack anxiety surge into my muscles.

I staggered up the beach, past the cheerers, and God bless their indefatigable enthusiasm, I know the winning swimmers had hit the beach ages ago. I saw Rikki, who was among them, watching for me. She had made good time I'm sure and looked recovered and refreshed. When she saw me, her cheering grew louder and more exuberant. She walked over to greet me, a bottle of water extended in her hand as she pulled me into a hug.

In between gulps of water and gasps of air, I told Rikki about the diver. Her happy look plummeted to one of shock, and she led me to a race official that she knew. He was busy, issuing orders to volunteers and stacking slips of paper people handed him, but when what I was telling him sank in, he stopped what he was doing … slips of paper still in his hand. A sad look came into his eyes as he shook his head.

"Damn, I've heard of runners and bikers getting run off the road by cars and even stuff thrown at them. But never swimmers. The mean-spirited wackos have always left us alone. What's the world coming to?"

Then he took a deep breath and pulled back on his mantle of authority.

"I'm glad you weren't hurt. I'll radio the rescue boats to keep an eye out. Thanks for letting us know."

And he returned to his slips of papers and volunteers.

"You're sure you are okay?" Rikki asked me as we walked away.

I rolled my shoulders and stretched my arms. "Yeah, at least nothing is so wrong that a hot meal and hot shower won't cure."

"Well, I can't help you with a hot shower, but there is a mimosa waiting for you while we wait for the last swimmers to come in and we can start on the hot food. I hear it's a salmon and artichoke quiche!" Rikki grinned.

"That should do the trick." I laughed and followed her to get my plastic glass of orange bubbly.

It ended up that my time wasn't as bad as I was afraid it would be. Not my best, but considering my wandering off the course and the lost minutes talking to the surfboarder, not too shabby.

After a lovely, light, but protein-filled quiche, and a mimosa or two, I felt less shaky. Combined with the let-down from the adrenaline high and physical exhaustion from the distance swim, I had the energy of a jellyfish stranded on the beach. I needed to head back to Hilo, Ben was expecting me home by one. We were going to try to do 'something' together for a change this afternoon. But I had a little time to spare. And I gave myself the excuse that I should hang out on the beach another hour to drink water and give the mimosas a chance to get out of my system before the one and a half hour drive back to Hilo. Stretching like a cat, I waved goodbye to Rikki who was going into Kona with another friend of hers, and I lay down under a palm tree so that I was in partial shade and drifted off for a quick nap.

My phone woke me three hours later. It was two. The sun had shifted, and I was lying in full shade now, or I would be lobster red. I groggily stuck my hand in my bag, feeling around for my phone. It had quit ringing by the time I found it. It was Ben, and so were the three texts that had started coming in an hour ago. I sighed and hit the call-back button. As soon as he picked up, I started talking, he didn't even get a "hello" in.

"Sorry, Ben, I fell asleep on the beach. I didn't mean for you to worry." Maybe that would take the edge off his anger.

A terse "Right" came though my phone. He was still angry. "You have to admit it's ironic, though. You always get mad at me when I don't call you if I'm going to be late. And now when you go to Kona, you are an hour late, and you don't answer texts and don't call. You didn't do this on purpose, did you? Just to show me what it feels like?"

Now, I was angry.

"Believe it or not, I'm a little more mature than that." I could hear the snarkiness in my voice.

"I left the house at five a.m., swam as hard as I could for a race that is over a mile, almost got drowned by some maniac, and ate a big meal afterward -"

"What? What did you just say? Are you at a hospital?" I think there was some concern in his voice now, even if I still felt a tinge of anger across the line.

"I'm okay," I said. "I just fell asleep on the beach. I'll leave now and can explain everything when I get there."

We said a quick, stilted, goodbye. I don't think either of us knew if we were still mad or not. We kept it short so as not to say anything to make it worse.

****

Ben was distant when I returned home. He didn't

come out of his study even though I know he heard me. I took a deep breath and reminded myself that my parents liked Ben, that I had decided it was time to settle down. I went back to tell him I was home. He didn't ask anything about the race or the attack I had mentioned on the phone. If he didn't care enough to ask, well, then he didn't care. Why should I share any of that experience with him? I left him in the study, and he didn't come out until dinner. Things thawed a bit after we ate, but he still didn't ask about my day, and I decided I wouldn't tell until he asked. I hoped Gina was right and one day he would miss me. It didn't look like that was going to happen anytime soon, though.

Chapter 35

A Package Arrives

After my underwater attacker, I took a week off from lap swimming. Today was my first day back. And it felt good. Whoever that diver was, I wasn't going to let him take my swimming away from me, especially on a beautiful sunny day like today. The water was the perfect temperature, and the stretching that came with each stroke, combined with regular, steady deep breaths that swimming required, revitalized me. Instead of heading back to the office, I picked up a grilled eggplant sandwich from Short 'n' Sweet Cafe and went to Liliuokalani Park. I sat at a picnic table, watching the small waves of Hilo Bay wash over the lava rocks, and savouring my sandwich when my phone croaked. Rikki.

"Hey, girl, how are you?" I asked.

"Great, how about you? Have you been back in the water since the race?"

"Just finished my laps and eating lunch now."

"Good for you! Hey, I've been meaning to tell you who I saw at the Kukio race. With that diver going after you, it slipped my mind."

"Who?" I asked.

"Well, you know I hit the beach a little earlier than you, well, I was walking around looking at a couple of booths... and guess who had a booth there?"

"Who?" I asked again.

"Walker Wolf was selling suntan lotion. Or more precisely, the booth was there, but no one was manning it, which was weird. After you left, I was back at the beach to meet up with a friend, and that's when I saw Walker Wolf. He was packing up his suntan lotion."

"Hmmm, interesting."

"Yeah, I thought so too. Do you think he could have been the diver that attacked you?"

I thought back to the dark shape. I had no idea. The diver was all in black and wearing a hood.

"I don't know, maybe. I couldn't tell. But I think he just moved up my suspect list," I said.

"Yep, me too... gotta run now. I've been meaning to call you all week and pass that on."

We hung up. My tranquility broken, I might as well run an errand in the time I had left before class. I needed to pick up a package at the post office. The postwoman had left a notification in our mailbox a couple of days ago. It wasn't my birthday, and I hadn't ordered anything from Amazon lately. I had no idea what was in the package. The post office wasn't far from campus. If the line was short, I could get it and be back in plenty of time for my next class.

There was no line, and I soon had my package. As I stood in front of the post office, I gave in to the temptation to open it. I started to work on the tape across the top of the box. Just as it started to give, I heard, "Cleo, is that you?"

I looked up. Mason walked toward me. Or maybe he was walking to the post office, since I was standing in front, blocking the entrance.

"Hey, Mason! Sorry, am I in your way?" I stepped

to the side.

"What ya got there?"

"That's what I'm about to find out," I said. I got the last of the tape off and opened the top. It was an art book that Luc had told me about when he was trying to convince me to return to Santa Fe. I opened the cover and recognized Luc's handwriting.

Cleo, A few of the beautiful things I want to show you in Santa Fe. Please consider my offer to take your sabbatical here. I will do my best to make it worth your while. Ciao!

Luc

I flashed back to our conversation in Luc's bedroom watching the sunset, and the trail of fire he left on my cheek as he slid the strand of hair off of my face. The impulse to step closer to him, and the question in his eyes.

Then, bam, I was back in Hilo, in front of the post office, the scent of ginger wafting on the humid breeze and Mason looking at me with a quizzical smile on his face.

"Oh, it's from a friend in Santa Fe." *I hope I'm not blushing.* Feeling tongue-tied, I rushed on. "You know, I went to that conference there a couple of weeks ago. Well, a friend there said he was going to send me a book of art from their local galleries."

Oh geez- I'm talking way too fast now, babbling, but maybe if I just keep talking, I can get back to normal again. And he won't realize there are a herd of butterflies in my stomach just thinking of Luc.

"So, you said you got a painting there for your father, right? Maybe it's in this book." I held the book up to show him the cover. "What was the name of the artist?

Or the gallery?"

Mason's face tightened. Damn, was he hypersensitive to his dad issues, or was I acting super weird? I wonder if he would say anything to Ben. I'll tell Ben about the book, of course. I mean, there's nothing wrong with someone sending me a book, right? It's just a book, and he's just a friend. I've done nothing wrong.

But I felt guilty, and by the strange look on Mason's face, I could tell he sensed my guilt. I suddenly remembered my next class.

"Gosh, I've got a class. I'm going to have to run, Mason."

A wave of relief at escaping the situation washed over me. Later, I'd explore the awkward feelings this book, and its inscription, aroused in me.

Mason, who had been silent since he noticed my weirdness, finally spoke.

"When will you and Ben be home? I wanted to talk about something with you guys, and I'd rather do it at your place where there's privacy. As soon as possible."

I stopped to think. "Ben's on Kona side collecting data this evening and tomorrow, but I think he's back tomorrow evening."

"How about you?" Mason asked, an intense look on his face. "When will you be home?"

"I'll go home briefly around four, then Suki has a vet appointment at four thirty, then I should be home by six. And tomorrow I'll be in the office most of the day, so tomorrow evening is probably best."

Mason nodded and started toward the post office door again. "OK, I'll give you guys a call and see if Ben can get together when he gets back."

I agreed and headed to my car and back to campus.

Class went well, and a few students followed me back to the office to ask questions about their projects. By the time they left, I had to rush to pick up Suki and make it to the vet.

"She's really adapted to three legs," I said. But I heard pleading notes in my voice.

The lines in the vet's face deepened as he ran his fingers, gently prodding, over Suki's abdomen. I felt her low rumbling growl vibrate briefly, then stop just as suddenly as his hand dropped away. Tears filled my eyes, and I hugged my arms tightly across my chest, waiting to hear Dr. Rei's assessment.

"I'm sorry. I was hoping we'd taken the leg off before it had spread. I knew it would spread eventually, amputation doesn't cure it, but it can prolong life sometimes." That hand that precipitated Suki's rumble now reached to tousle the black curls on her head. She tilted her head up to lick his fingers. "But I'm really sorry. It looks like it has already spread to some major organs. I can feel several lumps in her abdomen."

An invisible hand sucker-punched me in the stomach. I sucked in a big mouthful of air to stave off a sob. I nodded, unable to speak, tears streamed down my face.

Dr. Rei looked from Suki to me. "I really am very sorry. She is a special one, your girl. I see a lot of dogs in here, but Suki is one of my favorites."

Does he say that to all of his clients? But I read sadness in his eyes. I guess it didn't matter if he said that to everyone, if he meant it every time he said it.

I managed to hold it together. Yes, I had red eyes and a wet face, but no sobbing, and I forced myself to pay attention to what we should expect. He gave me pain meds for when she was uncomfortable and warned me that she would go downhill fast.

When I arrived home, I was a train wreck. No matter how much you prepare yourself for pain, it still hurt. In a wallop-you-upside-the-head and then push-you-down-the-stairs kind of way. I called Ben and updated him on Suki. He expressed his regret over the prognosis but seemed distracted. I felt like he wanted to get off the phone and back to work.

I was pissed by his lack of sensitivity and decided to call my childhood friend, Anna. She cried with me as I told her about Suki. During our commiseration, Anna decided to come visit me next month. She had been promising ever since I moved here, but it was a long trip. I was delighted to hear her commit to the visit. I felt a weight lift off my shoulders. Having my lifelong friend here would give me solace, even if it was just for a long weekend.

"I am so glad you are coming," I said. "Ben has not been very supportive. I know having his student accused of murder is sapping his emotional energy, but geez—I know he cares about this dog, and he knows how much I love her. Anyway, with all that's been going on, it will be great to have you here, I can't wait! Book those tickets! I won't believe you are coming until I know your reservations are made."

"I'll do it tomorrow and text you the itinerary," she promised. We said good night and hung up.

It would be good to have Anna here. In addition to grieving over Suki, I wanted to tell her about Luc, and how much I have been thinking about him. I couldn't decide if it was a symptom of my problems with Ben, or something in and of its own right that I needed to process. And I wasn't quite ready to tell Gina or Rikki about it. Whatever *it* was. There were no secrets on an island. Anna was clear-headed and unbiased, and she has known me forever. She would help me untangle it.

It was too early to go to bed, and I didn't feel like working. I could look through the book that Luc sent me. But after emptying my book bag and checking the car, I realized I must have left it at the office. I gave up on that idea and took Bella on a last walk, followed by a hot bath and bed.

The next morning dawned sunny and bright, and after a good night's sleep, I was looking forward to Ben coming home and trying to reconnect with him. Work was busy, so the day passed quickly, and before I knew it, my watch showed five thirty, and I knew Ben would be home. I brought the book that Luc had sent. I was determined to show it to Ben, and maybe we would look through it together. Yeah, that would be good. That would stop this quiver of guilt that ran through me every time I thought of the book, or Luc.

As I walked to the car, I remembered that Mason wanted to tell us something, and I wondered what he'd found. I knew he was talking with some of Ali's friends, maybe he had heard something. I hadn't made any progress with Walker Wolf. I think he was avoiding me. I emailed him, but he never responded. I hoped Mason had made more progress than me.

I walked through the front door and was greeted with dog kisses from an energetic puppy and a subdued Suki. I called out to Ben but heard no response. I set my book bag down in its chair, noticed a note on the table. Ben had been home but had run to the office to check and see that his lab was running smoothly, and would be back soon. I sighed. I was all ready for makeup sex, even if he probably didn't even know I was peeved at him last night. I told myself this was just a small delay, we would make up when he got home. I opened my laptop to check my email while I waited for him. Nothing of interest except an email from Anna. I opened it, excited to see her travel plans and how I could work my schedule out to accommodate her.

"Sorry, but I'm not going to be able to come. I'm going to be busy the next week or so, but let's talk soon. Sorry I can't be there to help you, I know you are going through a lot, but maybe Ben can stand in for me. I chatted with him, and I got the feeling he wanted time to work things out with you. Better if I'm not there right now I think. Love, Anna"

My good mood evaporated, like mist in a desert sun. I couldn't be upset with her, she had her own full life and was respecting my relationship. But I had counted on Anna to help me cope with everything. A tear rolled down my cheek. How ridiculous, I was a grown woman with a grown-up relationship, dealing with grown-up problems. I could manage this without a girlfriend to share secrets. I wiped the tear away, straightened my shoulders, and shook my head to swing the hair out of my face. I closed the laptop and heard Ben at the door. As he walked in the door, my first thought was how tired he looked. I got up to greet him, and his eyes fell on me.

"What's wrong?"

The fact that he could tell I was upset softened me. I stepped to him and wrapped my arms around his waist, burying my head in his neck.

"I'm sad about Suki. I've missed you. And Anna's not coming."

His warm strong arms wrapped around me, and he spoke into my hair. "I'm sorry. I know you were looking forward to seeing her. But I'm home now, and I'm going to try not to be gone so much. We should spend as much time with Suki as we can while we still have her. And I've missed you too."

When I pulled back to look up into his face, the weariness was gone, and only concern remained.

"Well, you're back now, that's what's important."

My movements transitioned from comfort-seeking to something else, as my hands played with the hair at the nape of his neck.

"Shall we make up for some lost time?" I asked with one raised eyebrow. Ben's smile widened as he grabbed one of my hands and led me into the bedroom.

****

Later, as we ate leftover spaghetti, I asked Ben if he had heard from Mason.

"No." He slurped a noodle off his fork. "Was I supposed to?"

"Well, I saw him the other day, and he said he wanted to talk to both of us. I got the feeling it was about Kai's case, but I was in a hurry to get to class and didn't get the particulars."

"Maybe he'll get in touch tomorrow. I hope it's good news. I was going to call Kai tomorrow. It would be great if I could tell him something encouraging."

I agreed between mouthfuls of spaghetti. After scarfing it down, I offered to take both the dogs on a last walk for the night, since Ben was tired. He took me up on the offer and was asleep when we got back. I put the dogs to bed and locked up, happily anticipating sliding back into the sheets with Ben's sleeping body.

Chapter 36

An Accident

It wasn't until the next morning as I ate a quick breakfast across from Ben, that I realized the art book Luc had sent me was untouched in my book bag. And I had not mentioned it to Ben. A pulse of guilt flitted through my stomach, but I pushed the feeling aside. I peeked at Ben out of the corner of my eye. Last night we had connected, and it was great, but it felt more like a Band-Aid than a problem solved. I needed to get to the office and prepare for my first class of the day—this was not the time to start a conversation that could get complicated. I returned to gobbling cheese toast and slugging down coffee. And of course, just when I'm in a rush, my phone rings. It was Gina.

"You won't believe what Kawika just got home from doing."

And why would I care? My mood had turned grumpy with guilt weighing on my shoulders. Fortunately, the snarky comment didn't make it past my lips. This was Gina, and she was my friend.

"What?"

"David, Ali's brother, is dead, and Kawika was at the scene investigating."

I sat up in my chair so fast Suki lifted her head to look at me and the puppy jumped up on the alert for my chair to move back. Ben never looked up from the newspaper he was holding.

"What happened?"

"I don't know yet. Kawika got called onto duty about five this morning. It looks like David was drag racing on one of the horseshoes and went over the edge. Somebody saw his car and called it in as they drove out of the valley going to work early this morning. You know what that road is like, Kawika had to climb down through the mud and jungle to get to the car and wait until they got David's body out of there. It was muddy, slippery, and wet. He came home for a quick shower and change clothes, then he's going back to the station. He told me it was David before jumping in the shower. Oh wait, I just heard the shower turn off. I'm gonna make him a hot breakfast before he goes back. Call you back when he's gone!"

Beep-beep-beep was the next sound I heard... Gina had ended the call.

Stunned, I laid my phone on the countertop and sat back in my chair. Ali's brother, dead from drag racing. The bodies were piling up here in little Hilo town. I looked over at Ben. He was still engrossed in the newspaper, slowly, mindlessly spooning his cereal into his mouth. He turned the newspaper over to read another page, then back to spooning his milk-sopped cheerios.

A sense of surreal dislocation overtook me. How could my life be so grotesquely violent and simultaneously humdrum boring? Ben slurping his cereal with eyes glued to a newspaper while corpses accumulated. Whether by accident or malice, three people were dead ... and the rest of us went on with our daily lives untouched. I guess this happened all the time, but such existential thoughts didn't usually occur to me, especially before I've finished my first cup of coffee.

I glanced at the kitchen clock. Damn, I was not going to be able to finish my coffee, I'd be late for my first class if I didn't run. I stood up and headed for the door to snatch my book bag and keys, saying a quick goodbye to Ben over my shoulder. Suki and Bella followed me to the door to see me off. Ben didn't look up.

The morning went by in a blur. I had back-to-back classes with students waiting at my door in between. There was no time to catch my breath or think about anything except work, until lunch. Before grabbing lunch at the on-campus café, I went by the office to pick up exams the secretary was going to copy for me, only to find that she was out sick and there were no copies waiting for me. I raced back to my computer, printed out the test, and returned to stand in line for the copy machine.

I wasn't the only one who had sent her things to copy at the last minute. By the time I'd reached the front of the line, I'd caught up on all the university gossip but had barely enough time to make my copies and run to class. Okay, I managed to make a short detour and grab a coffee to go. Lunch could wait, coffee could not.

The grades were pretty low on the last test in this class, and I hoped to see improvements on this one. I passed out the tests and sat down for the first quiet moment of the day. I had brought papers to grade, but first, I wanted to enjoy my coffee and a quiet moment observing my students.

I enjoyed watching them at work. There was such variety in their facial expressions and body language.

Some stretching and rolling their heads, others sitting on the front edge of their seats, hunched over the test. One young woman smiled at some of the questions as she slowly and methodically moved down the page, twisting a lock of hair with her thumb and third finger of her left hand. The person next to her had a pained look on his face and kept flipping back and forth between the pages without making a mark.

As my students worked in silence, my mind wandered. I was not getting anywhere in my attempt to find something that demonstrated Kai's innocence. Walker Wolf had moved to the top of my list. He suddenly had a new business start-up right after he turned Ali down on her idea, and then she winds up dead. And he was at the swim race and missing from his booth at roughly the same time I was attacked by a diver. It was all circumstantial, but I was beginning to think his dazzling smile hid a sinister interior. Mele was also still high on my list. From what Gina's cop friend told her, Mele's jealousy has led to violence before, and she clearly felt possessive of Kevin. I know the research, and people who are violent once are at increased risk of future violence. And there was the fact that her alibi didn't check out. It was possible that she could have felt threatened by Ali and lost her temper again. I just couldn't seem to find the pieces of the puzzle that put her in the right place, right time, and right circumstances. It didn't mean they won't fit, I just haven't been able to make them fit yet.

Ali's uncle Tino was also a person with violence in his past. Although he was farther down my list because there didn't seem to be a triggering event. He has maybe been angry at her for years for putting her brother in jail, but why kill her now? Especially now that David was out of jail? Maka, the drug dealer, was a little higher than the uncle. We didn't know for sure he was on the Big Island, but apparently it was possible he had slipped over here. And the timing worked, because he hasn't been out of jail that long and may have been nursing his anger for years. I just didn't have anything concrete to tie him to being on this island at the time of Ali's death.

They were all possible suspects. I just haven't been able to find any real evidence to dissuade the police from Kai. I chewed my lower lip, if only Ali's brother hadn't crashed, or Weezy hadn't gotten caught in that wave. They might have been able to tell me something that would throw suspicion on someone else. David seemed to have doubts that Kai was the killer. And he wanted to tell me something. And Weezy sounded pretty smug when she said she knew something. The more I thought about it, the more I realized that it was just a little too convenient that both David and Weezy had died, right before they were going to tell me something.

"Heah, Miss, I finish da test."

I looked up into big brown eyes and a soft smile. I smiled back at my student as I took the test from his hand. With his fists now shoved in the pockets of baggy, knee-length shorts and a backpack over his shoulder, the student walked out of the classroom door, starting to whistle even before the door had closed behind him. Several students shot jealous looks at his back as he sauntered out, and I knew tests would come in fast and furious for the next ten minutes. My best students usually turn in their papers very early or very late. My worst tests usually came in not long after that first person. My theory was that unprepared students knew quickly that they didn't know how to answer, but they waited to see what was a reasonable time before they turned in their tests.

I was busy accepting tests, and when the rush passed, the last couple of students often use this time after most people have left to ask a question. While they struggled with their last questions, I might as well struggle with my paper grading.

Halfway through my second paper, a soft voice said, "Here's my test, Professor."

I looked up and smiled at the young woman. I took her test and was about to tell her, "Have a nice weekend," but something in her manner made me hesitate. Was she working up the courage to say something? She automatically returned my smile, but then the brows on her young face drew together, and the smile disappeared.

"I work in Dr. Rei's office. I heard about your dog. I'm so sorry."

My stomach clenched. I was so distraught when the vet told me about Suki's inoperable cancer I didn't notice my student worked there. I blinked away the tears that began to form.

"Thank you. It's hard, but…" *But what? My heart was breaking over this dog*.

"But… at least you have a cute puppy around to help entertain your dog," she finished for me. "In my family, we had an older dog who was dying and had stopped wanting to play with us. We got a new puppy, and that old dog started playing first with the puppy, then us. She lived another year, and it was a good year for her."

She smiled encouragingly at me.

"And it was a nice thing you did, taking in Bella. I think it will help your dog too." The young woman shifted her book bag from one shoulder to the other and looked like she was ready to bolt out of the room. This woman hadn't said a word in class this semester, and now she appeared nervous having said so much.

Before she could turn to go, I asked her if she knew where Bella came from.

She nodded. "I knew Ali growing up. We weren't exactly friends, but we went to school together." Her eyes filled with tears. "David too."

Had word of David's death gotten around already?

A tear spilled out. We heard paper rustling and the sounds of the last test-taker packing up. The young woman wiped her eyes with a sleeve and turned to look at the wall with her back to the last young man as he brought his test to me. To my surprise, she didn't rush out the door with him. After he left, I put my hand on her shoulder.

"Are you okay?" I asked her.

She turned back to me and nodded.

"You knew David?" I asked. I spoke softly even though all the other students had left and we were alone in the cavernous lecture hall.

She nodded. "I know he got into trouble, messed up with the drugs. But when we went to Keonepoko Elementary, he was a good guy. I was small for my age and shy, and sometimes the older kids picked on me. But David always stood up for me."

She sniffed.

"Ali too. She could be a real tita, even then, but David would make her stop. He didn't fight with her, he just had to ask, and she'd stop for him. I guess I kinda had a crush on him when I was little."

"I heard David and Ali were close growing up," I

said, hoping she would tell me more about the backstory on the tragic siblings.

"Yeah, until high school. Then David got really messed up with the drugs."

Her eyebrows drew together, and her mouth puckered as if she'd been sucking on an especially sour li hing mui candy.

"He stopped being nice, to me or Ali. That's the only time I ever saw them fight was when he was on the drugs." Her eyes began to fill with tears again. "But I heard he was getting his life back together after he got outta jail. He was doing better. I saw him at a party a couple of weeks ago, before Ali died, and he was drunk-but nice drunk, you know?" A tear slipped from her eye, and she wiped her nose on her sleeve. "You know he's dead too?"

I nodded. "Yes, I heard. I'm sorry, I didn't know he was a friend of yours."

"He wasn't really my friend anymore." She straightened up and readjusted her book bag on her shoulder again.

"It's just not right. He was getting his life back together again. It's just not right that he dies now."

My grieving student left, and I gathered up the papers I'd started grading and the tests that now also needed grading and walked back to my office. My mind returned to stress, whether from a test or grief. People developed different strategies to manage anxiety. Ben shut down and put walls up. I, like my student, cried. Ali and David got angry when stressed. What made one person react so differently from another?

People argued about whether it was caused by nature or nurture, but science has demonstrated it was a combination of the two. Early experiences, such as prolonged exposure to severe stress while we were young, caused hormonal and structural changes to our brains. Experiments with rats suggested that young rats that grew up in stressful, overcrowded environments had more stress hormones running through their bodies, which affected receptor cells in their brains. When they were grown and were removed from that setting, they still acted overly aggressively, even when moved to a non-stressful setting. Initially it was a 'nurture' influence, but it caused biological changes and became a 'nature' influence later in a lifespan.

Ali and David grew up in a troubled family and had anger issues as they grew up. Their parents were addicted to drugs. The uncle who was supposed to care for them viewed beating as an appropriate punishment. They also had Maka to handle. A childhood friend who grew into a controlling bully dealing the same addictive drugs that had destroyed Ali and David's parents. Was it any wonder they had residual anger?

Ben had an abusive father who favored him but abused his sister and mother. He was just a little boy and couldn't challenge his father or have any control over the situation. He learned to tune out aggressive responses, but not to problem solve. That's why he puts his head in the sand when a problem comes up that he doesn't think he can control.

I thought back to my childhood. My parents ran a restaurant in Ruckersville, Virginia. My childhood memories were mostly of watching them work at the café. Dad in the kitchen, Mom working the tables and talking to customers at the counter. I don't remember much conflict, just gentle chiding or teasing. They had lots of 'discussions,' but mostly those ended with a hug or a heavy sigh and a head shake, indicating the discussion was not over, but not important enough to disrupt whatever they were doing. My family was not much on histrionics, but there was a lot of love. I knew that, even as a kid. Which reminded me, I haven't talked to my folks this week. I better call them tomorrow morning.

Chapter 37

Horseshoes

"Sweet!" I said, although no one but the dogs were around to hear. I walked toward the thin guava tree bursting with small yellow and green balls, hanging like Christmas ornaments from every branch of the juvenile tree. With guava, the small ones were the sweetest. The larger fruit could be found for sale, but the little ones were prized and never made it to market. This little guava tree was in the middle of our bamboo patch up by the deck. I hadn't seen the fruit before because the bamboo blocked it from sight. But today as I weeded, I rounded a corner and found it in all of its sweet, yellow, delicious glory. I grabbed as many ripe ones as I could and carried them in the front of my T-shirt. I'd lifted up the bottom to form a fold that held dozens of the sweet little fruit.

Ben would be happy with my find. Maybe this would make up for the nagging I dropped on him at breakfast this morning about his lack of response to my sabbatical ideas. The deadline for sabbatical applications was less than a week away. I've presented options. He didn't argue with me, he just never responded to any of my ideas. "I'll think about it" or "I guess that is a possibility" was as much of response as I ever received. Usually, he ignored my ideas completely and picked up his phone to check email or something. It reminded me of a TED talk I had watched by Sherry Turkle on being connected but alone. Her idea was that email and texting allowed us to skip out of a conversation if we were bored, or as in Ben's case, wanted to avoid.

I didn't know how that behavior became acceptable. I couldn't get away with that growing up at my home in Ruckersville, but Ben seemed to think I was overreacting when his texting or emailing at the table bothered me. His argument was that he was so busy out on the boat, he had to catch up on his emails when he had an opportunity onshore. Oddly, his emails were most critically important when I wanted to talk about possible sabbatical plans. Oh well, maybe I would start bringing my iPad with me everywhere. When everyone else was checking their text/emails, I could pull out my tablet and read an ebook but pretend to be emailing. That idea made me smile. I picked a few more little guavas before heading back to the barn to share my juicy wealth with Ben.

As we were driving back to the house, I got a call from Gina. We hadn't talked since her early morning call about David's death. We'd been playing phone tag, between my heavy teaching days and Gina babysitting her nephews for the week. She didn't want to talk about the death in front of them.

"Hey, chica!" I said. "Any keiki ears around, or can you talk about you-know-what?"

Ben turned his head to glance at me out of the corner of his eye. We hadn't talked about David's death. We hadn't really been talking about anything lately. He was probably wondering what "you-know-what" meant.

"Oh my God, my sister finally came and got the

kids. They are adorable but a handful. Kawika told me a little about what happened after the kids were in bed last night. He thinks David was drunk and driving his car too fast, maybe drag racing up the Hamakua coast. His car slid off one of the horseshoes."

The Hamakua coast stretches from Hilo north to Honokaa and Waipio at the northern part of the Big Island. The 'horseshoes,' and there were three of them, were north of Ben's farm on Highway 19. Twenty-two miles north of Hilo, there were three gulches that reached from the slopes of the mighty Mauna Kea to the ocean cliffs. When the highway hit the valleys, the large horseshoes were created. The highway curved sharply to hug the valley walls, then curved back out to continue its northern trek, clinging to Mauna Kea's slope. Rocky cliffs, with occasional falling rocks attempting to reclaim the edge of the mountain that had been scraped away to create the highway, were on one side, sheer hundred foot drops to the rocky ocean were on the other.

I shuddered, thinking about what would happen to a person in a car that went over the edge.

"He was pretty messed up according to Kawika," Gina said. "But nothing suspicious. Kawika checked, since Ali just died. He wanted to be sure there wasn't a connection. But it looks like his blood alcohol level was very high. He thinks it might be suicide, in case he's the one who killed Ali. But there isn't any way to prove that. You know, he is considering evidence that might help Kai. He wants to be sure they get the right guy."

"I know."

Poor Gina. I had been so worried about getting Kai out of trouble for this murder, I forgot that I was putting her in an awkward position with Kawika.

"Tell him thanks for checking," I said. "And is it okay if I pass the suicide-because-of-guilt idea on to the lawyer?" I asked.

"Sure, I already talked to Kawika about that, but according to him without any evidence to support that theory, it probably won't carry much weight. But go ahead and let the lawyer worry about that."

"Thanks, and tell Kawika thanks from us."

I ended the call.

Ben was driving but glanced over with eyebrows raised. "What was that about? Any news on Kai's case?"

I explained what Gina had told me. Ben suggested I use his phone to call Kai's lawyer. I noticed that in addition to the lawyer, Ben had a ton of other people's numbers saved. A lot of his contacts were people I didn't know. I filed that information away and would think about it later.

The lawyer didn't answer, and it went straight to an answering machine. It was Sunday, so that was understandable. I summarized the situation for him in a message, but got cut off. At least I think the message gave him the basics, and Ben could explain the rest when they talked. I looked over at Ben, thinking he would want to discuss Kai's case some more, but his face was set with jaw locked and eyebrows drawn together, eyes staring straight at the road.

He looked as if he was thinking dark thoughts. And I left him alone with his somber musings.

Chapter 38

Sabbatical Finale

I entered my house and dropped my purse and book bag just to the side of the front door. I didn't even make it to the chair. I was every which way of tired—physically, emotionally, and mentally wiped out.

In Methods lab today students analyzed data for their projects. I had rotated from one student to another, for three hours, helping each of them on their data sets and analyses. By the end I was so mentally exhausted, I don't think I could figure change if I went for a coffee. I used the ninety-minute break to go swim laps and eat a fistful of nuts and an apple in my office. My friend Anna sent a confusing email about why she had canceled her trip. She felt really bad about it, but after she had talked to Ben, she could tell he didn't want her there, that he really wanted the space to work things out with me. *Well, that's a joke. He tells my best friend not to come and then ignores me.* But I shrugged. I had too much to do today to think about that.

The afternoon classes went fine, but sabbatical applications were due by five p.m. today, and I had waited until the last minute to submit mine. Expecting -- scratch that -- hoping Ben would call or send an email agreeing to one of the plans for both of us to go somewhere together. Weeks ago, I'd written up three proposals for myself, two of them for places with good opportunities for Ben, on projects for which he had expressed at least grudging interest. I even wrote a proposal for him for those places. I sent those two proposals to Ben telling him I wouldn't push, but if he wanted to come with me on sabbatical, he needed to submit one of those and I needed to know which one to submit. I waited for a call or an email from Ben until four forty-five, to submit by the five o'clock deadline.

The message never came.

I was angry. I had waited all day to hear from him and then nothing. Not even a 'do what makes you happy, maybe I'll visit' email. Nothing. *Screw it.* I uploaded my third proposal option, my Santa Fe plan. Santa Fe… a high desert town, no 'marine' anything for a thousand miles in any direction.

I pushed send and packed up for the day. A heaviness settled in my chest.

Watching Suki struggle to get up so she could greet me brought tears to my eyes. It was getting dark earlier now, and the neighborhood lights were beginning to come on. I saw a shaft of light appear in the hall. Ben must be in his office and had just turned it on. If he heard me enter the house, he didn't acknowledge it.

I didn't want to see him right now. I sank down to the floor, still in the entryway, and gathered the top half of my big, black, three-legged dog in my arms and quietly cried with my face buried in her neck. I wasn't completely sure why the tears flowed.

I suppose I cried because of Suki and how fast the cancer was taking her, and because I was hurt that Ben didn't want to come with me next year. But mostly I felt like everything was coming to an end. Ben, Suki, and me, our happy family, was dying from attrition. And any hopes I might have had for a baby in our future were evaporating.

****

Hilo earned her reputation for queen of Hawaiian rains. The sun was in hibernation, and medium-to-hard rain has persisted the entire week. At the university, class sizes were shrunken and faculty sullen. Waiting to hear on my sabbatical, watching Suki weaken every day, somehow, I muddled through the week. I trudged through my courses, graded my assignments, and tried to keep my head down. After my last class there was a break in the rain, and I ducked out early for home. Lucky I did. As I pulled into our driveway, the sky opened up, and a downpour replaced the light rain.

There was no sign of Ben, and the dogs seemed content to sit on the porch and watch it rain. I toweled off and opened my laptop. There was an email from the dean. Although there were statements in which the dean claimed to agree with me and my reasons for not accepting the late paper from the student, she ultimately said she didn't want trouble with the student. She asked me to accept the paper late without a penalty to avoid a headache for the university. Angry, I went into the kitchen and looked for Ben's stash of junk food.

Oreos. Bingo! Emotional eating was not a good idea, but I figured it was better than breaking things.

I had made a serious dent in the package when my phone buzzed. Rikki wanted me to meet her and Mason at Cronies, the Bayfront bar, to touch base on Kai's case.

Rikki and Mason? I guess they were a thing now. I agreed and jumped into my car to drive the five blocks. The rain continued to pour. They had a table by a window and stood when I joined them. I air-kissed cheeks with both of them and then sat.

"Hey, guys. What's up?"

Mason put one elbow on the table and leaned across it toward me.

"Well, my girl here." And he nodded toward Rikki who was sitting next to him, his other arm on the back of her chair. "We were talking about the whole Ali and Kai thing, and I thought it would be good if you could join us. And we could all catch each other up at the same time." He paused, then raised one eyebrow. "I guess Ben is working again?"

I shrugged. "Yeah."

Rikki looked from me to Mason and back to me.

"Ok-a-a-y, so, I managed to find a way to follow up on Maka, the drug dealer that Ali helped put in jail."

Mason and I both turned to look at Rikki.

"Really?" I asked. "That's great!"

"Well, yes and no. I have this client who takes private yoga lessons from me, and I just found out this week she works in the prosecutor's office. So-o-o... I asked her if she could track down someone who had been in jail, whether they have been flying off-island during parole."

"And she just gave you that information?" Mason raised an eyebrow at Rikki.

Rikki gave an impish smile.

"I might have made it sound like it was an old boyfriend, who might still be mad at me and maybe stalking me. She's cool. Anyway, she called me today to say he has been on Oahu since his release this summer. He had to stay on that island for parole for six months after his release. She also said he had permission once to go to his auntie's funeral, but he could probably sneak over here if he wanted. There should be airline records, and she is going to see if she can get ahold of those to see if he was over here near the time of Ali's death without telling his parole officer. I told her I thought I'd seen him following me but couldn't be sure." Rikki winced. "I feel bad lying to her, but I didn't know how else to get the information. And if the airline records don't show that he was here, I'll drop it. I don't want to get him in trouble if he is innocent."

"Thanks, Rik," I said. "That's a huge help."

"How is that a help?" Mason asked.

"Well, it's not a smoking gun, but he is still a plausible alternative explanation to Kai if airline records show he was over here when Ali was killed. Motive and opportunity."

"Sounds good," Mason said. "How about you, Cleo, what have you been up to?"

"Walker Wolf still avoids me, if he is there during his office hours, he doesn't open up when I knock. But I saw an advertisement for his suntan lotion. The flyers claim it is edible and comes in three flavors, lilikoi, papaya, and rambutan."

Mason perked up. "Lilikoi-flavored, edible suntan oil?"

"Right."

"But that was Ali's idea."

Rikki and I turned to stare at Mason.

"What?" I asked.

Mason's face turned red. "Well, at least… Ali came to me with that idea. She wanted me to fund her business idea of edible Hawaiian flavored suntan oil. She specifically mentioned lilikoi."

"Wow."

"Yeah, wow," Rikki echoed. "What did you say to her?"

"I told her I was all tapped out. The dive shop had cost a lot to get started, and no way my old man would front another business venture. She was pissed, but she got over it and didn't mention it again."

"Well that's another good lead!" We all three clinked glasses. "I'll pass that on to the lawyer."

Maybe something good might come out of this wretched week.

Chapter 39

Goodbye

Suki's story ended today, much too early. She was only four and half years old. The vet said the cancer had spread to her spleen, and from there she went downhill fast. In about a week, her stomach was swollen to the extent I would have thought she was pregnant.

If I didn't know better.

She was in so much pain at the end it took both Ben and I lifting, me with a sling under her hind end and him trying to lift up her front, to get her up and out to the bathroom. The last day she growled at Ben and feebly snapped at him. She had never done that.

Never. Ever.

Her pain must have been unbearable for her to snap. I couldn't let her continue to suffer. I made an appointment with the vet for the next day. They got me in quickly because they knew why I was coming. The vet looked almost as heartbroken as me. Ben went with me but couldn't watch, or be in the same room, while I said goodbye and waited for her to go to sleep for the last time. I just kept telling her what a good girl she was... the best ever. Whenever she had her last moment, I wanted that to be the last thing she heard.

I had a dog die before I was with Ben. That dog was old, almost fifteen years. I was on my own at the time, but I remember somehow managing to get the body of that seventy-pound dog into a friend's borrowed truck. I drove to a wooded field out of town, where I used to take her to run. And I dug her grave. I buried her myself in that field, and as hard as it was, I felt some closure at the end of that experience. I told Ben about that, and how I wanted to bury Suki at the farm. We drove straight up there from the vet's office with Suki's body.

I thought Ben would want to take part. She was my dog, but I knew he loved her. I thought Ben would want to help me dig the hole. But when we got there, he asked me if I could manage by myself, that he needed to mow.

I was surprised, but I guess everybody deals with grief differently. Ben dealt with it by distraction. That was why on this gorgeous sunny day with a balmy breeze rustling the leaves in a spreading guava tree, I stood alone, sweating, sobbing, and covered with dirt.

An eighty-five-pound dog needed a big hole, and I wanted it deep enough that the feral pigs couldn't dig her up. Ben decided he needed to mow right around the area I was digging. Instead of the peaceful, respectful, contemplative experience I had with the last dog burial, I had the roar of the tractor engine rumbling first close to me, then reverberating farther away as Ben made his loops on the tractor, pulling the mower behind it. Bits of dirt and grass flying in the air. It turned the sweat rolling down my face and body into mud and gave me a chalky, gritty taste in my mouth. I felt my sadness morph into a growing bitterness at Ben and his noisy, flying dirt.

Chapter 40

Halloween

It was Halloween night. Ben was on the Kona side with students. Again. Dusk was arriving, and I was left to man the candy bowl by myself. The first of the trick-or-treaters, a couple of little munchkins, had come by and wrapped their tiny fists around a piece of candy and put it in their plastic orange pumpkins.

I missed Suki. She had loved kids. She was so big and black, she was the perfect Halloween decoration, scary, until she started wiggling with delight at each little urchin who came to the door. They would creep up with trepidation when they saw her, but most were happy to run their fingers through her hair before they grabbed their piece of candy. Puppy Bella wasn't quite there yet. It was good socialization for Bella to see and smell all the little kids, but she could get a little crazy with excitement, and I didn't want her knocking over the candy bowl or darting through the screen door when I opened it to give out candy. I kept her on a leash, and when I heard kids coming, I tied it to the heavy chair that was home to my book bag. We got trick-or-treaters, but not a steady stream, and I didn't want her tied up all evening.

I had just handed an adorable little devil a junior pack of Skittles, when the aggressive wail of tsunami sirens burst through the night. The little devil's father standing just behind him said, "Holy crap! We gotta go!"

He swooped up the surprised youngster before he could even open his mouth to complain, and they dashed down my steps and into the night.

"Holy crap is right!" I said to Bella and turned on the TV to hear why the emergency alert had sounded. There had been a severe earthquake, in the Aleutian Islands of Alaska, and their first buoys recorded a large tsunami heading our way. That meant we had four to five hours to prepare. It could die down before it reached us, or it could hit us full force. We wouldn't get another reading on its size until just before it made landfall, which would be too late to make preparations. Now we had time to prepare, and people in the tsunami zone had time to evacuate. And Hilo would prepare. If the tsunami hits full force, it could wipe out downtown, our port, and possibly damage our airport. We would be an island without access to the rest of the world if a large tsunami arrived.

Our house was a block above the tsunami zone, so I didn't need to evacuate. Instead I ran to the bathtub to start filling it with water. Then into the kitchen to take stock. When you live on an island in the middle of the Pacific Ocean that is susceptible to hurricanes, earthquakes, volcanoes, and tsunamis, you store a lot of staples in case of an emergency. If there was damage to the harbor, the barges couldn't make it in, we could be on our own for a while. I double-checked that we had plenty of canned food to make it through at least a week or two. We wouldn't be eating well, but we would be eating. Then I checked for toilet paper and paper goods. We were good there, too. Dog food, check. I filled up every water bottle I had so I'd have drinking water in case we had major damage to infrastructure and the water lines were damaged. By now my bathtub was full, and I turned it off. That was just in case the water lines were down for a couple of days. We wouldn't have to use our drinking water for washing.

I tried to call Ben and make sure he would be out of the water, but all the lines were busy. I sent a text making sure he knew about the tsunami warning, and that I had prepped everything here. Pleased with myself I checked the candy reserves. There were not going to be any more trick-or-treaters, so I had hit the bonanza on leftover candy.

I popped a tootsie roll in my mouth, then remembered... *gasoline!* My car was on empty, and in a rush to get home before the trick-or-treaters, I hadn't filled up. I jumped into my car and headed to the closest gas station a couple of blocks down the hill in the tsunami zone. The line wound down the street and around a corner. I got into line and crawled along with everyone else. The cars were full of a mix of families with costumed kids, evacuating and getting gas on the way up the hill, and college students, in Halloween costumes, piled into trucks with coolers in the back, taking their Halloween party with them. There was an energy to the caravan of gas-seekers. The excitement of potential disaster, mixed with the Halloween party exuberance that had started before the tsunami alarms went off. People were taking it seriously and preparing, but no one was panicked, and most seemed to be having fun. I was amused people-watching, as a guy in a Captain Hook costume climbed out of a passenger car and walked a couple cars back to lean in a window. A young blonde in a sexy nurse costume climbed out of that car and walked back up to the first car. Sexy witches and zombies soon joined that group, and then a vampire from another car strolled over. I felt sorry for the drivers. A new 'walking party' had erupted where a growing group clustered, laughing and talking as they walked along next to the cars, empty except for the poor drivers and the coolers, that inched forward. Costumed partiers made occasional runs back to their own cars for refills from their coolers, chatting with drivers along the way. I guess with the tsunami, cops won't be checking for open-beverage violations.

I was almost to the pumps, just four cars ahead of me, where the line turned into the gas station property. I was leaving a gap, so that a car that had finished pumping and was waiting to exit could get out, when a little red Toyota Corolla, coming from the other direction on the street, zipped in front of me to cut in line, blocking the exiting car from leaving.

"I can't f-ing believe this! He cut in front of me, that SOB!" I shouted to my empty car and banged my steering wheel.

I'm not prone to violence, but I started looking around the car for something to go slam into that car's windshield. It didn't take long for me to realize I didn't have a baseball bat, and slamming one into a windshield would be a very bad idea. I took a deep breath to calm myself, and caught a glance in my rearview mirror of two very large Hawaiian guys climbing out of the lawn chairs they had been sitting in, on the back of the pickup truck behind me. They walked past my car, one on each side, toward the offending Corolla. They walked slowly, with their arms out to the side because the bulging muscles in their forearms wouldn't let them lie flat against their sides. They weren't in costume. They just *were* big and scary on this dark chaotic night. I couldn't see the driver or hear what he said, but I heard the deep rumbling vibration of the Hawaiian voice as he leaned down and said, "Der's a line. You just cut in da line. Dat's not polite. You need to go to da end a da line."

"Yeah," seconded the Hawaiian standing on the other side of the car, leaning in the passenger side window.

If it had been me, and those two outrageously big guys had leaned in and stared at me on both sides… I think I'd have peed my pants. These men were mountains. I think they could have lifted the car up and carried it if the driver didn't decide to do it himself.

The driver of the Corolla must have realized this too, because the Corolla turned back out onto the street and headed toward where the end of the line must be. I assumed he went to the end of the line because I couldn't see the end anymore. Without another word, the Hawaiian guys headed back to their lawn chairs in the back of the pickup behind me.

As the one on my side of the car passed my car, I stuck my head out, and said, "Thanks."

He nodded in acknowledgment and kept on going.

Shortly after that episode, I pumped my gas and was back home breathing a sigh of relief. Whatever the tsunami did, I was prepared. I switched on the TV to check the news for an update on evacuation efforts. We wouldn't know any more on the tsunami until it hit the next buoy in a couple of hours. But the news had a split screen showing Waikiki with people in costume partying on one side, and on the other a long line of cars stuck in traffic trying to head mauka, up the mountain. It was surreal.

Then I noticed the red light blinking on the answering machine, and my iPhone sitting next to it showed I had a missed call and voicemail. When I ran out for gas, I'd left in such a hurry I forgot to take my phone. Both messages were from Ben. He was driving back over Saddle Road. He was safe from the tsunami but checking that I was prepared. The second message was also from him, it must be after he had gotten my text, he was worried about Kai's shop. He was afraid Mason wouldn't think to check it, and the shop was in the tsunami flood zone. In his message Ben told me where the key to Kai's shop was and asked me to try and load some of the most expensive equipment from the shop and store it in our garage. The last thing Ben said in the message was to make sure I was out of there in plenty of time before the tsunami was expected to hit.

I checked the news, and it looked like we had a little over three hours before it was due. Kai and Mason's shop was five minutes away. I could work for two hours, loading and unloading, and be out more than an hour before the tsunami hit. The predictions were good, but not perfect. I didn't want to take any risks. And maybe Mason was already there, and we'd get it done twice as fast. For the second time since the tsunami siren first went off, I jumped in my car, this time headed to Kai's dive shop.

Chapter 41

Saving the Dive Shop

All the lights were off. Mason must be at a Halloween party and not thinking about the store. I noticed activity at all of the old storefronts around me. A fairy princess and a gorilla lugged a stack of two surfboards stretched between them from the neighboring surf shop to a nearby van. On the other side, at Dragon Mama's futon store, appropriately enough a dragon was hauling out bolts of jewel-colored fabric and throwing them in the back of a station wagon. This night just got stranger and stranger.

I parked my little car in a no-parking zone, just like the gorilla and dragon had done, and using the key Kai had given Ben, I opened the door to the dive shop. It was eerily quiet. The street lights shone through the large windows, but because of the green and aqua-blue paintings of sea turtles, seaweed, and fish on the windows, it entered the dive shop as murky, muted underwater light. Although I'd been to the dive shop before, I wasn't a regular visitor and never alone with the lights out. I looked around for a light switch, but it was too dim and too much stuff on the walls to tell anything from any distance. The light from the street lamps pooled in the middle of the room, and the walls were in deep shadow. I started near the door, where I expected to find a light switch. When I didn't, I continued to feel my way around the perimeter of the room, checking the walls for anything that looked or felt remotely like a light switch in the dim light. It was slow going, running my hands behind hanging merchandise in case they had hidden the switch from a customer's view. About halfway around I thought to dig in my pocket for my phone. Damn, I'd thrown it in the car this time but left it on the front seat. I should find a light switch soon, anyway.

I tried to make a note in my head of what I was finding and whether I should move it out in a first trip or was lower priority. As I navigated closer to the cash register at the back, I came upon spear guns. I didn't realize Kai and Mason sold spear guns, but I guess it made sense. A lot of skin divers here in Hilo used them to catch their family dinner. As I tried to oh-so-carefully feel the wall behind the spear guns without accidently setting one off in the dark, I accidently tripped over a big bowl of something. I jumped out of the way of the spillage, not sure what was falling out. As my hand flung back to catch myself from knocking into something else, it came up hard onto the wall and, thank God, something that felt like a light switch. I flipped on the lights and saw the mess I had made. Little round silver balls were everywhere.

I dropped to my hands and knees to try and collect them, and saw that they had rolled way under the cabinet under the cash register. I couldn't see under there, but I stretched my arm under to try and sweep as many out as I could. As I was lying full out on the floor, I realized I was an idiot. A tsunami was powering toward us, and I was worried about leaving a mess. There were expensive items in the store that I should try to rescue, rather than worrying about these stupid silver balls. As that thought crossed my mind, my hand, extended under the counter, hit something soft and rubbery. I grabbed it, hoping it was merchandise and not something truly disgusting that the two bachelor owners had shoved under there long ago and forgotten. Against my better judgment I pulled it out. And breathed a sigh of relief at seeing it was a mask. A used mask that someone had painted on and personalized.

I started to throw it aside so I could finally start loading equipment, the regulators, I think. Just as my fingers were letting go, they tightened again. The personalized painting said 'Ali.' I sucked in a gust of air. *My God! Ali's mask.* Whenever Kai came home, he would want it, as a keepsake. To remember how she tried to learn how to enter his world. Maybe it would offer him some solace. Instead of throwing it aside, I grabbed a shopping bag that was hanging from a hook next to the register and gently put the mask inside. That's when it hit me. I felt like I'd been kicked in the stomach, all the air I'd sucked it came out in shocked rush. Ali's mask! The mask that was missing from her body when she was found! Oh, my God! I had been so sure that Kai was innocent. But whoever was with her when she died, whoever killed her, pulled her mask off and cut her regulator mouthpiece. And here was her mask… in Kai's shop.

"Hello! Are you here, Cleo?"

Mason, it is Kai and Mason's shop. And Mason is here. Now!

"Yeah, I'm here, I just knocked over your bowl of loose shot weights and was trying to clean it up. Stupid, huh. I should be loading regulators, right?"

I dropped the bag with the mask and pulled myself up off my knees by hanging on to the cash register cabinet. Kicking the bag with the mask back under the cabinet where I had found it. I needed to think this through. I couldn't believe that Kai was a killer, somebody else could have put this mask here to frame him. We were lucky the police hadn't found it. I should talk to Ben before I tell anyone about it, even Mason.

"Thanks for coming." Mason smiled back at me. "I got a text from Ben, he said you were on your way. I never even thought about the shop until I got his text. I was at a crazy Halloween party in Volcano Village. It was getting really wild as the Hilo parties moved up the mountain."

Mason looked flushed, with a happy grin on his face. Forever a party boy. I could see why everyone said Kai had kept the shop profitable, Mason clearly didn't worry his pretty little head about the business. My mind was still whirling over finding Ali's mask, so I had no patience for the party boy.

"Where should we start?" I asked.

"How about we start here." He nodded toward the regulators. For the next twenty minutes, we loaded first his pickup truck, then my little VW until they were bursting at the seams, or at least had wetsuit legs sticking out the windows.

"I'll meet you at my house, and we'll get this stuff unloaded, okay?" Mason called, heading toward his car.

"Wait," I called out. "Our place is much closer, we can make twice as many loads to our house as we can running out to yours. And it will be easier to bring it back tomorrow if there isn't any damage to the store."

Mason stopped and turned to look at me coldly. Was

that suspicion on his face? Probably just my imagination.

"No. Let's take it to my place. One thing my father taught me about business is that an owner should keep track of his merchandise. I can do that at my place."

It seemed crazy to me. Did he think I was going to steal it? Mason's house was fifteen minutes away versus five minutes to our house. But it wasn't my stuff, and I was going to quit an hour before the tsunami was due whether he had all his stock or not.

I nodded and followed him to his house. Once there, we unloaded. I checked my watch. Only two hours had passed since the tsunami alarm had first gone off and the little devil had been whisked off my porch in the arms of his father. It felt more like days. We made trip after trip, Mason with his car, and me with mine. As we carried carloads of dive equipment into Mason's back bedroom, the room gradually became a disorganized mess. When I had finished unloading my car for the third time, my back ached, and Mason still had several more loads to make since his truck was bigger and held more. He didn't seem to perceive the rush. I guess he still had a little buzz on from the party.

"How about I try to stack some of this stuff up so we can make room to fit more merchandise in here," I said, starting to pile boxes of masks into a tall stack in the back corner of the room.

"Sure, I've just got a couple more loads to get out of the truck, then we can head back down. We may need to put some of it at your and Ben's house after all." He gave a rueful grin and returned to his truck.

I stacked the masks. It took longer than expected because I kept tripping over rebellious wetsuits that insinuated themselves into my path. We had thrown dozens of them into an unruly pile on the double guest bed, and they kept sliding off onto the floor. I noticed a closet along the back wall. I could hang the wetsuits up in there to get them out of the way. I grabbed a few from the floor and opened the closet door. Bingo… an empty rack and even a few hangers for the wetsuits that had lost theirs when I dragged them out of the shop. I shoved an armload into the closet, but there were some random boxes in the bottom of the closet. If I put them on a shelf above the wetsuit rack, I could slide some of the dive computers underneath the wetsuits. As I lifted the shoeboxes and empty computer boxes to the shelf above, a long tube was exposed, I pulled it up and saw that it was part of a regulator. The mouthpiece with part of the tubing that should connect it to the tank in back. I didn't realize those parts came separately. As I picked it up, I saw little pink hearts, hand-painted on it, matching the mask I had found earlier. In tiny script… the painting on the tube read 'Ali's lifeline to Mason' followed by three hearts. I stared at this thing in my hand. Finally, I had a piece of evidence that Kai was not the killer! Thank God! I have to admit finding the mask in the dive shop had shaken my faith. *But Mason? Really?*

A cold chill ran down my spine. This evidence pointed to the killer here in the house with me! My hands shook, and fear-inspired adrenaline surged through me. *I can't let him know I found Ali's mouthpiece! Where to hide it?* The room around me was chaos, there had to be some place. But my mind was numb with shock as I tried to game plan out how I was going to get out of here with the incriminating mouthpiece. I moved away from the closet to search through all the dive equipment we'd just dragged from the shop. What could I put this in that would make sense for me to turn around and carry out? He was going to be back any minute! *Damn it, think!* Then I heard Mason in the hall as whatever he was carrying bumped the wall. *Get a grip! He's coming!*

I shoved the mouthpiece under the few remaining wetsuits that were on the bed, piling them on top of it, praying they wouldn't slide off to reveal what I'd found. I had just barely gotten the mouthpiece hidden and was gently holding the wetsuits in place, afraid to let go in case they slid, when Mason entered the room.

I tried for a natural smile. But I wasn't sure I pulled it off. As soon as Mason entered the room, his eyes flew to the open closet door.

He scowled. "What the hell are you doing in my closet? I didn't tell you that you could go in there."

Any doubts that Mason had hidden that mouthpiece vanished.

"I thought if I hung up the wetsuits it would give us more room to stack stuff on the bed." I straightened up and tried for an innocent smile, as if I was ready to carry another load of wetsuits, praying like a priest that he wouldn't encourage me to continue to hang these last wetsuits in the closet.

Mason's eyes narrowed as he watched me. Sweat poured out of places I didn't know could sweat. I tried to continue the smile and added a questioning look so he wouldn't think I knew why he didn't want me in the closet.

After a lifetime, Mason must have decided I didn't know about the mouthpiece, because he put down the flippers that he had carried in. His eyes were hard, but he gave me a stiff smile. "Sorry, I didn't mean to snap, but I've got some expensive family heirlooms in there I don't want mixed into the shop stuff." He firmly, but without slamming, closed the closet doors. I stepped back from the bed and the wetsuit hiding place and picked up some boxes of dive lights.

"Okay, sorry, then I'll just pile stuff in front of the closet, okay?" To demonstrate my innocent intentions, I piled the dive lights in front of the closed doors.

"I've only got a couple more loads," Mason said. "You should head back down to the shop and start loading your car up again. I'll be following in a few minutes." He waited for me to leave ahead of him. It was obvious he did not want to leave me alone in the room again.

"Sure," I said, frantic to get the mouthpiece out of there. As suspicious as he looked, he would check if I had disturbed it. And when he found I had moved it, he would destroy it.

After I had passed through the front door, with Mason following close behind, I feigned distress.

"Oh damn, I left my phone on the bed, I'll just go grab it and then meet you at the shop."

"I'll get it," Mason offered, clearly loath to let me alone in the room again.

I didn't slow down. "No, you go ahead and finish your unloading. I know right where it is in that mess," I said, trying for breezy and unconcerned.

I rushed back to the bedroom before he could react. I was sure he could hear my heart pounding but he hesitated before he followed me. I grabbed the mouthpiece and stuck it under my shirt in the back, then tucked the T-shirt into my jeans. If I could make it outside before he came back in, it would be dark, and I fervently hoped he wouldn't notice the bulge in my back.

I couldn't turn my back to him.

"Got it," I said. I pulled my phone out of my pocket as I sprinted past him in the living room, I waved it at him as I sidestepped out the front door and continued toward my car.

Desperate for the safety of my car, I lied, "I'll head to the shop and start loading." *No way in hell I was going to put myself in a room alone with him again*. This man had killed Ali and was capable of how much more? The adrenaline rush triggered some memory flashbacks. I remembered Weezy at the park, about to tell me something about Ali's death, when Mason had walked up. She had shut down and wound up dead before she could tell me anything.

I jumped in the car, locked my doors, and tried not to peel out as relief flooded my system. My hands shook, and the mouthpiece dug into my back as I sat awkwardly in the car seat, but I didn't want to remove it until I got around the corner. It was dark but with a street light. I wasn't sure what he could or could not see.

Mason lived on a dead-end street, so I turned around and had to drive past him again on the way out. He had watched me since I exited the house, and just before I was ready to drive past, he stepped in front of my car to stop me and raised a hand as if he wanted to tell me something.

I cranked on the air conditioner, to have an excuse for keeping the windows up, and rolled the driver's side window down just two inches to hear what he had to say. He stared at me through the narrow opening of the window.

"I just wanted to say thanks, Cleo, you are really helping a lot, and I know you don't have to. It's not your shop. I really appreciate it."

"Sure," I said. "And I might grab a cold drink on the way, so if I'm not there before you, I'll be there shortly." I lied again. I didn't want him coming to look for me right away, when he got back to the shop and I wasn't there. With the tsunami watch on, I wasn't sure how quickly I would be able to get through to the police. And Mason knew where I lived.

I pulled away and drove two blocks the other direction so Mason wouldn't happen upon me before I had pulled the mouthpiece out of the back of my shirt. If there was any DNA evidence on there, it was probably ruined now. But what the hell else could I have done? I texted Gina so she would tell Kawika that I had evidence that it was Mason who killed Ali. With the emergency situation that the tsunami warning triggered, he was much more likely to answer her text than mine. Besides, I doubted they would do anything about this until the tsunami had passed.

Next, I texted Ben and told him the same thing. After that I didn't know what to do. I didn't want to go home. That would be the first place that Mason would look for me if he went back into his closet and saw that Ali's mouthpiece was gone. I drove slowly and aimlessly, but out of habit in the general direction of downtown and my house. My mind started to piece things together. If Mason killed Ali, he probably also killed her brother. He was there the day David was going to talk to me. Just like Weezy. Mason was present when both of them told me that they knew something and were willing to talk. The pieces were beginning to come together. Thank goodness, I'd found the mouthpiece and mask.

The mask!

I left it in the shop. Damn, damn, damn… I didn't want to go back there. I looked at my watch. It had only been a couple of minutes since I drove away. It would take Mason at least ten minutes to finish unloading the equipment from his car. If I was quick, I could get in there and out with the mask before he got back. I sped, way over the speed limit, back to the shop and parked around the corner so Mason wouldn't see my car if he was looking for it. And the only thing I was going to load up was a mask, so no need to be close. I looked around, there were a lot fewer cars or costumed characters loading stock. People had either finished, or figured it was too close to the ETA of the tsunami to stay down here. Mason and I had worked a lot longer than I realized. The occupants of the shops on either side were locked up and dark with no one around. About a hundred yards away, there was still a shop with a light on and a couple of cars that I hoped would blend in with mine.

My hands shook as I tried to insert the key. I couldn't get it in. Tears of frustration welled up before it finally slipped in and the door opened. I stepped through the door, and my phone rang. It was Ben. I answered without slowing my steps to the back of the shop and the cash register cabinet under which I'd kicked the mask. Luckily, I'd navigated the shop last time in the dark, so I had a mental map of the place and didn't bump into too many things.

"Cleo! I got your text. Are you sure? Really? Mason?"

"Yeah, I don't see any other explanation…" *Was that a noise I heard outside the door?*

"Look, Ben, I'll call you back, I'm picking up

something here at the shop and as soon as I get out --"

"You're at the shop?" Ben cut me off. "What the hell are you thinking? Get out of there!"

"I just have to get one thi—" *I'm sure that sound was just outside the door.* I hung up on Ben. I could explain to him later. I put my phone on silent mode. If Mason was coming, I didn't want to alert him I was here. I'd hide and sneak out after he left.

I made it to the cash register and stooped down to grab the bag with the mask in it, when the lights blazed on. *Damn. There must have been a light switch by the door that I missed my first time here.*

"Why didn't you turn the lights on, Cleo?" Mason asked.

I tried not to breathe and stayed crouched down so he couldn't see me.

"I know you're here, Cleo, I saw your car down the street." He paused, and I could hear a smile in his voice. "You must not be planning to load up merchandise if you parked way down there." Another pause.

"Are you." An accusation, not a question.

I remained silent and texted Ben.

—Mason is here—

I pushed send and hoped that Mason wouldn't hear the swoosh of the text being sent. I listened for sounds of movement. The store was in disarray but still crowded with racks and cases of dive gear. I could ease myself away from him if I could tell where he was going.

There! I heard a noise to my right. He was taking the path along the wall that I'd taken my first time here, and it sounded like he had bumped into a box. I stayed low and as quietly as possible eased to my left behind a cardboard cutout of an underwater Sea Doo Sea Scooter.

"I know you found Ali's regulator. You must also know her mask is here. That's what you came back for, isn't it? To get the mask." He spoke soothingly, as if to a child.

He was making a lot of noise opening a case or something as he spoke. I figured while he was distracted I'd move farther left, away from him and the cash register, since he knew I'd come for the mask. Now I was behind the dive watch display case. I stayed low and peeked to the side to see if I could see what he was doing. My blood froze. Mason was holding a spear gun and moving toward the cash register cabinet like a hunter stalking his prey.

I looked farther to my left at the door. It was about twenty feet away. If I made a run for it, he had plenty of time to turn and shoot me with a spear before I could get the door open. I'd have to take it slowly and carefully until I could get closer and have a shorter distance to dash. I'm not a fast sprinter on land.

I inched left behind a rack of rash guards but in the process accidently kicked an electric cord, which shifted something eight feet behind me. From underneath the rack, I saw Mason orient toward the sound. Predator-like, Mason glided toward the spot he had heard the noise.

"I didn't want to kill her. You have to know that, right? But she left me no choice. She was going to ruin everything." His voice was preternaturally calm. "Just like I don't want to kill you. But you see, I can't let you get away now, can I?"

While he was looking so intently at the spot eight feet behind me, I inched another couple of feet closer to the door, behind a stack of boxed, underwater lights.

God, if I ever made it out of this shop alive, I will buy one of each of these things I am hiding behind. Thank heavens for diving toys.

I was close - so close now.

Pffhhht.

A spear flew past my head. My ear felt the breeze, and it might even have cut some hairs.

The jig was up, he knew my location. I used every ounce of energy I had to race to the door, willing my feet to move faster, faster, my heart in my throat. Expecting a spear through my back at any minute. I got to the door and yanked it open... and a startled policeman blocked my path... mouth open in an 'O' of surprise and right arm extended as he reached for the door.

"Ah, ah, ahh... you don't think I'm going to let you get away, do you?" Mason said from behind me.

"No!" I yelled as I threw myself to the ground. Another spear came flying, over my head and into the shoulder of the cop, standing just in front of me.

"Aiye!" he howled in pain. "Officer down, need backup," he called into his radio.

Another cop appeared, magically, just as Mason reached me at the door. A shocked look came over Mason's face as he saw it wasn't me he had hit but a cop. The second cop looked at his partner on the ground with a spear through his shoulder and then up at Mason with the spear gun in his hand, and quickly pulled his gun out and, from just a few feet away, pointed it directly at Mason's chest.

"Put the spear gun down. *Now!*"

I felt arms grab me and pull me over. I looked up into Ben's stricken face.

"Cleo, are you okay?" His voice was stressed, worry

etched on his face.

"I'm fine. Mason hit the cop, not me." And before the last words were out of my mouth, I found myself crushed in his arms. A crushing had never felt so good.

Chapter 42

New beginnings

Paul Simon's "50 Ways to Leave Your Lover" was playing on the radio as I packed my bag.

I should have been excited. Things had worked out fine.

After Mason tried to shoot me and hit the cop instead, he had been arrested. Not for Ali's murder, but for an attempted murder of me and shooting the cop with the spear gun. Come to find out, the cops hadn't been responding to my text to Gina, but had been knocking on doors in the tsunami zone to make sure everyone was evacuated. Ironic, wasn't it?

Even though I'd found the incriminating evidence of Ali's regulator mouthpiece that had been sliced off her tank, there were no prints, and Mason's lawyer was trying to argue I'd planted it at Mason's house and shop. Mason's dad had come through with a well-paid criminal defense lawyer flown in from Chicago, who argued that I could have planted the mouthpiece because I wanted to clear Kai's name. But the local judge said it was good enough to release Kai, even if the prosecutor didn't think it was enough to charge Mason. I think the prosecutor wasn't prepared to go up against the Chicago lawyer without an airtight case. The attempted murder on me was airtight, what with it happening in front of two cops, and the texts I'd sent before he shot me, telling two different people, including a cop's wife, that I had evidence incriminating Mason. The prosecution had motive and credible eyewitnesses.

Mason's lawyer tried to say that it was an accident. He claimed Mason didn't know I was coming to help load, and he thought I was an intruder, trying to loot the place during the tsunami warning. Fortunately, the fairy princess and gorilla who had been loading up the shop next door remembered seeing me help Mason load up before the incident. And without their costumes, they appeared as credible witnesses. Made me glad I hadn't been wearing a Halloween costume. They might not have recognized me.

Mason was in jail without bail, awaiting trial. And Kai was free. Auntie Charmaine was happy, and I was a frequent recipient of her warm and wonderful hugs and island-famous banana bread.

And the tsunami? Well, after a tense hour, trying to get Mason arrested, the cop who had been shot to the hospital, and all with an active evacuation in progress … when it came, the tsunami was a pussy cat. A couple of fishing boats tore loose from their moorings and sustained damage, but that was about it. That's the way it happens. Sometimes the tsunami starts out as a giant and comes in like a lamb. And sometimes they start out as giants and come in like really, really pissed-off giants, angry about crossing an ocean and ready to make someone pay for their frustrations. The Pacific Tsunami Museum on Kam Ave tells those stories. Hilo and East Hawaii have seen more than their fair share of lives lost to tsunamis. We took the warnings seriously, and there were not too many grumbles if the tsunami was smaller than expected. No, Hilo doesn't mind non-tsunami events, not one little bit.

We wrapped up a couple of other mysteries that night, before Mason's lawyer got ahold of him. In all the chaos, Ben and I were told to wait with the cop who had Mason in custody, while the one cop got his partner in an ambulance to the hospital, and all the other cops were helping with the evacuation. We had to wait there awhile. Their primary concern was to be sure everyone had evacuated, before they could question us and take Mason to the police department. As long as Mason was under control, the police were more concerned about protecting life and limb from the tsunami. And I was okay with that priority. Mason was handcuffed, and Ben and I sat nearby, asking him why. And he talked. I think it was a relief to get it off his chest, and maybe he was a little proud of all his machinations.

As I suspected, Mason had been sleeping with Ali, even after she was with Kai. Mason saw the affair as fun. For Ali it was career advancement. Ali saw him as her ticket off this island and into the lap of luxury in California. When she got pregnant, she figured her investment had literally borne fruit, and she could extort, at the least, a juicy monthly child support payment for the next eighteen years, and at most, a jackpot of a well-heeled marriage and permanent wifely income. Mason tried to buy her off with a trip to Santa Fe, when he had to go there for his dad, and then after she saw the painting, he illegally smuggled in a borzoi puppy for her. But Ali stuck to her plan. When Mason balked, she announced that she was going to tell Kai. Mason panicked. If his dive shop failed, he would have to go back and work in his father's company. That was the agreement he'd made with his parents to get them to front him the money for this endeavor. Mason may not know much about business, but he knew Kai was critical for the dive shop's success. The shop would fail, and fail spectacularly, without Kai. That's why Mason had tried to make Ali's death look accidental, and even though it diverted suspicious from him when Kai was arrested, it's why he really did work to find a way to get Kai off the hook. Short of incriminating himself, that is.

That's why he had hung on to the mask, if he had to incriminate a credible suspect other than himself, he was going to plant it somewhere. That's why he had also brought the mouthpiece back after cutting it off her tank and ripping it out of her mouth. But when he got it home, he saw she'd pointed the finger at him with her personalized pink paint, so he panicked and just stuck it in his closet until he figured out what to do with it.

Mason had approached David to find out what he knew. Ali had told David about her pregnancy and that she was using it to get Mason to marry her and take her to California. She wanted David to come with them. Mason told David that he had planned to marry Ali. He brought a lot of alcohol with him to the meeting and feigned grieving with David over Ali. He pretended to be drunk until he was convinced David was thoroughly intoxicated, then dared him to a race. He'd killed David by getting him drunk and challenging him to a drag race on one of the curviest, dangerous stretches of the highway.

Mason had also killed Weezy. She was trying to blackmail him. She had seen Ali and Mason leaving the dive shop late one night when she was drinking in the park across the street. The night Ali was killed. That's why she told me she knew something in front of Mason and then walked off before she would tell us. Mason had agreed to meet her at MacKenzie Park, late one night to give her money. Instead, on those deserted cliffs, he had knocked her on the head and thrown her off the thirty-foot cliff onto the rocky coastline, where the Pacific Ocean crashes into the precipice.

I could even lay some of the problems that Ben and I were having at Mason's door. When 'Ben' had talked Anna into not coming for a visit, it was actually Mason on the phone. He had broken into our house to find the art book that Luc had sent me. The painting his father had wanted him to buy was in that book. Mason had seen the cover when we stood in front of the post office, and it was the same book his father had given him with the painting circled so he could recognize it. Mason was afraid I'd see the picture of the painting of a beautiful doppelganger for Ali, or "Evil Alice" as Mason had nicknamed it, and see that the other focal point in the painting was a borzoi. He assumed if I saw that painting, I'd be able to figure out that he had taken Ali to Santa Fe and given her Bella.

After seeing the photo of the painting, I understood why Ali, who had never been a dog lover, wanted a borzoi puppy. She wanted to become the woman in the painting. The painting was eerily similar to an elegantly dressed Ali and a borzoi, with almost the exact coloring of Bella. I have to admit, if I had seen that painting, even I might have been able to make the connection. Luckily, I'd left the book at the office when he had searched the house. But while he was looking, he heard the phone ring and the answering machine pick up. Anna left a message that she was on her way to Hilo to help me solve my mystery. As she was leaving her flight details, Mason picked up and, pretending to be Ben, told her we were having problems, and it would just make it more difficult if she came for a visit now. Which is why she canceled and was vague about why.

When Mason explained that, I felt awful about the suspicions I'd had of Ben. He gave me a funny look but evidently didn't want to talk about it in front of Mason. Or maybe he was still in the glow of saving my life and didn't want to look too closely at what had happened between us over the last couple of weeks.

Unfortunately, he still didn't want to look.

Paul Simon listing the many ways to leave a lover floated from the radio.

Even with Kai back, Ben was still putting major hours into being away from home, or more specifically, away from me. But that was Ben. If there was a relationship problem, he stuck his head in the sand and hoped it would go away.

Which is why I was packing.

And Ben was not.

My eyes filled with tears. I wasn't making Ben happy, any more than he was making me happy. I hadn't seen him smile since he realized I wasn't the person who was shot with the spear gun. In many ways, he was a great guy, and I loved him. But we had some major differences about how we wanted to live our lives, and how to deal with problems. We decided maybe a break would be good for us. I'd received approval for my sabbatical in Santa Fe, and I was leaving tonight. I guess it made sense. With Suki gone, and Bella back with Kai. Our little family has officially dissolved.

The doorbell rang. I blinked tears away, leaving the

bedroom to walk toward the living area. My steps slowed as I saw who was on the other side of my screen door.

"I don't want to disturb. I just came by to say thank you."

On the other side of the thin screen, Ali's uncle Tino stood, looking like a mountain lion, alert, but not on the hunt.

I wasn't sure how to answer that. To say you're welcome seemed like I agreed I had earned the thanks. I just stumbled into finding the mask. As I struggled to find the appropriate words, he saved me the trouble.

"I know you probably don't understand, but my connection with Ali and David was a strong one. They were my *hanai keiki* after their parents were gone. My boy too, he was gone about the same time. I wasn't close with Ali like I was with David, but that didn't make one difference. They were my *kuleana*, I was supposed to take care of them, and I did not. I appreciate you finding out who did it, who killed them. It would be a bad, bad thing if he had gotten away with it. And not just for Kai-boy.

Anyway, that's all I came to say. *Mahalo.* I thought you just some *niele, malahini, hoale* girl. But you are not." The devastating grin glinted across his arresting face. "Well, maybe you are all those things, but you okay anyway."

And he turned and walked off my front porch back to his normal life of leaving weak-kneed women in his wake, without me ever saying a word. I shrugged at that man's ability to leave me speechless, and went back to finish packing.

The exchange reminded me of another man with a dazzling smile that I had suspected, Walker Wolf. I heard through the coconut wireless that he would be leaving the island the same time as me. But he wasn't coming back. My colleague, Crystal, informed me that one of Walker's undergraduate girlfriends had filed an ethics violation with student services when he dumped her. Walker, whose edible sunscreen business was taking off like wildfire, agreed to resign to pursue his business interest, on the mainland.

This was a good thing. I remembered the creepy scene of him licking his sunscreen hand and gazing into the eyes of those undergrads. That was not appropriate behavior for a professor.

I shook my head to dismiss that image as I folded a shirt and placed it in my suitcase.

Tino had reminded me that there was a bright spot in all this. Kai. After the threat of jail was lifted, and with his name cleared, his friends threw him a huge "get out of jail free" party, lots of grilled fish, Kalua pig, taro leaf wrapped laulau, lilikoi cheesecake, and mochi.

Sitting in jail, and working on the remote farm, had given Kai time to think, and grieve, over his relationship with Ali. Despite her affair with Mason, and the fact that she had been ready to dump him, part of Kai still loved her. And that part wanted to keep Bella. He said Ali had loved the puppy, and to honor Ali, he would too. He'd never had a dog, but he took the responsibility seriously. I've seen him walking Bella all over town. She was at the party and held court as if she was his queen presiding. I think she may have channeled a little bit of Ali during the event. And of course, you get a handsome guy walking a beautiful, eye-catching puppy, and presto-chango: a chick-magnet is born. I'm sure Kai still has dark moments, but most of his moments seemed to be filled with puppy licks, slow, warm smiles, and a whole lotta love flowing his way. I was glad. It helped sustain my belief in happy endings.

Book Club Questions for *Evil Alice and the Borzoi*

1. Did reading this book change your ideas about Hawaii? If yes, how so?

2. Cleo was a lover of travel. Ben never wanted to leave home. Do you identify with one lifestyle more than the other?

3. What did you think of Cleo and Ben's relationship? Was Cleo right to walk away from it, or do you think she made a mistake?

4. When Gina and Cleo run into Weezy at the park, Gina says, "There, but for the grace of God, go I. Remind me to give my parents a call and say thanks." If you ran into an old childhood friend after many years and found them on the road to ruin, what would be your thoughts? Your actions?

5. Ali came from a troubled family and had a painful upbringing. Do you think she would have overcome her background to become successful if she hadn't been murdered? Or do you think she was making poor choices and would probably end up unhappy and dissatisfied?

6. Other than Cleo, are there any characters you especially liked? Disliked?

7. If you lived in Hawaii, would you want to have a farm? Or would you spend all your free time at the beach?

8. Is there a scene that stuck with you?

9. How does the book's title work in relation to the book's contents? If you could give the book a new title, what would it be?

10. Are there lingering questions from the book you still think about?

A word about the author...

After graduating from Davidson College with a Psychology degree, DK Coutant applied her behavioral training to animals and took a job at Sea World, training dolphins and whales. Realizing that scrubbing fish buckets might get old, she went back to graduate school and received a Ph.D. in Psychology, specializing in Social and Cross-Cultural Issues. Starting her academic career at the University of Southern Maine, DK made the jump to Hawaii and worked at the University of Hawaii at Hilo, rising to Department Chair of the Psychology Department. After many happy years in Hawaii, DK made the move out of academics to geopolitical forecasting. She is now a Superforecaster with Good Judgement, Inc. and INFER (ARLIS). The new career allows her time to write and travel freely as she forecasts for intelligence agencies and think tanks. DK splits her time between Santa Fe, NM, Olympia, WA, Switzerland, and France.

@dkcanddog on Instagram
@dkcoutant on twitter
https://dkcoutant.com/

Thank you for purchasing
this publication of The Wild Rose Press, Inc.

For questions or more information
contact us at
info@thewildrosepress.com.

The Wild Rose Press, Inc.
www.thewildrosepress.com